Hope at the End of the Road

HOPE AT THE END OF THE ROAD

DL GRINNELL

XULON PRESS

Mill City Press, Inc.
2301 Lucien Way #415
Maitland, FL 32751
407.339.4217
www.millcitypress.net

Printed in the United States of America

Paperback ISBN-13: 978-1-66284-098-2
Ebook ISBN-13: 978-1-66284-099-9

Dedicated to my wife, Maree, who has stood
faithfully by my
side since the day we met. She is the love of my life.

Also dedicated to my children, their spouses, and my
grandchildren—the ones who are already here and the
ones yet to come.

Heather and John

(Bailee, Braelyn, and Brynn)

Spencer and Kayla

(Tali and Oaklen)

ACKNOWLEDGEMENTS

SINCE THE AGE OF TWELVE I HAVE DREAMED of someday publishing a novel. The book you hold in your hand represents the fulfillment of that lifelong dream. I wish to express my deepest thanks to those who helped make this dream a reality. Special thanks to Hannah Wingert for the many hours she spent editing. Special thanks to the very talented Kristin O'Connor for the cover design. Special thanks to my test readers who provided valuable feedback: Heather, Terri, Vonda, Jeff, Jodi, and Brittany. Also, special thanks to my friend Kevin for sharing his knowledge of automobiles and to my brother Steve for sharing his law enforcement expertise. I love all of you and I am so grateful for the help you each provided. Most importantly, I thank God for placing this story in my heart and mind and for guiding me through the writing process.

1

JAKE LEDGER SLOWED HIS LINCOLN BLACK
Label Navigator down to about five miles per hour. As he
approached his destination, his heart began to rapidly pul-
sate. He had not been here in forty-two years and still wasn't
sure why he needed to come back. Too many ghosts lived
here, ghosts he had spent the last forty-two years trying to
forget. His eyes widened with nervous anticipation as he
brought the Navigator to a complete stop. After putting the
Navigator in Park and shutting the big V8 down, he sat for
a moment, staring straight ahead, breathing as heavily as if
he had just completed one of his marathon runs back home
in New York. The cold air blasting from the air conditioner
could not prevent tiny beads of sweat from forming on his
forehead. He struggled for another breath as his mind
became flooded with tormented memories of a distant past.

Suddenly, he found himself confronted by an old
familiar pain, a pain he thought he had left behind when
he moved away. But there it was, like an old enemy lying in
ambush, ready to thrust a dagger deep into the very core of
his soul. His gut told him to turn around and drive away

1

fast, but he couldn't. Though he did not want to be here, he knew he was here for a reason. A force greater than his fears had compelled him to return. It was an unrelenting force that first came to him in his dreams in the form of a voice, a woman's voice that spoke only two words to him. Simple though these words were, they haunted him, stirring up dark memories that he had managed to keep buried for more than four decades. Night after night, the voice pierced through the darkness, shaking him from his sleep and sometimes causing him to sit straight up in bed, drenched in a cold sweat.

The dreams started exactly one month to the day after his wife's accident. At first, Jake thought his grief was causing him to experience delusions. The couple had enjoyed an amazing life together. Since the day they met, they had practically been inseparable, but now he was forced to face each day without her, a task that he found excruciatingly painful. They had never spent a night apart throughout their entire marriage. Even when she gave birth to their children, he'd remained by her side, never leaving the hospital. Though they had accomplished many things together over the years, they would both tell you that their greatest accomplishments were their children: Maddie, Mason, and Alexander, all three of whom were now part of the thriving family business.

For forty-two years, the blissful couple had done everything together, and you rarely saw one without the other. They made it a habit to devote at least one hour at the start of each day to just sitting together and talking. Jake loved to hear her voice. Even to this day, he still remembered the first time he ever heard her voice, the sound of which always soothed him. Before he'd met her, Jake's life was anything but peaceful. There was no consistency, no stability; only pain and disappointment. But it wasn't long after they met, he discovered that her presence alone was somehow able to ease the pain of his past. The longer they were together, the more he forgot the ghosts (or maybe we should call them demons) that once haunted every aspect of his life.

Then came the accident, and Jake found himself alone. His children tried their best to comfort him, but nothing they did or said could dispel the immense grief that now dominated his heart. For forty-two years, she had been the center of his life, the anchor that kept him grounded. And now, due to a violent act for which he blamed God, Jake's life was forever changed. Every night he went to sleep alone, every morning he woke up alone, and after dressing for work, he would sit for an hour just staring at the chair where she used to sit during their morning talks. All the peace and joy that her presence had provided for him had been violently ripped away. Being the polite gentleman that he was, Jake would always muster a smile when someone tried to comfort him by saying, "I know how you feel." He would offer an appreciative nod, but secretly he hated them for what they were saying because no one truly knew the pain he now suffered every waking moment of the day.

No one knew what a struggle it was just to do the little day-to-day things that most people accomplish without even thinking. So many little things reminded him of her which, in turn, reminded him that he was now alone. No one understood the treasure that had been stolen from him. And absolutely no one understood the loneliness that haunted him every single moment. He hated going to bed. He hated waking up. He hated going into the office. He hated meeting with clients. He hated going through the motions of a day-to-day life that now seemed grey and meaningless.

Then he started hearing the voice. At first it was only in his dreams. It would start as a whisper and slowly become louder until it was so loud that it jolted him from his sleep. It was always a woman's voice, and it was the same voice each time, but it was not the voice of his wife. The voice spoke only two words: "Come home." At first, he thought nothing of it, assuming that his dreams were either due to his grief or were a side effect of the medication the doctor had prescribed to help him cope. But then he started hearing the voice at other times. He would hear it in the shower; he would hear it when he was out for a run; he would hear it in the car on his way to the office; he would hear it at work: "Come home." Always the same voice. Always the same two words, nothing more.

Jake did all he could to ignore the voice because the last place he knew as home before going away to college had been a place of great pain and disappointment. Going back was the last thing he ever wanted to do. But as he ignored the voice, it became louder and more insistent. He knew there was only one way to stop the voice: he was going to have to go home.

Still hesitating behind the wheel of the Navigator, Jake thought about the looks on the faces of his children when he'd told them he was taking a road trip. Without warning, he had called his children and all of his staff into the conference room and announced that he would be taking a road trip for a few days, maybe a week. "Maddie will be in charge while I'm away," he'd told them.

No one in the room could remember the last time Jake had decided to take off without warning and without extensive planning. He was too committed to the business, to his family, to his employees, and to his clients to do something this spontaneous. No one knew what to say at first. The room was filled with an awkward silence for what seemed like minutes. Though he attempted to project a calm demeanor, everyone was concerned. They wanted to help this man who had been such a rock to them over the years, but no one knew what to do or what to say. The accident had taken something out of him; it had changed him and made him a different person. This man who had been so strong for so many now appeared to be crumbling right before their eyes.

They were worried, especially his daughter Maddie. His children loved him. Jake had been a wonderful father to them over the years. He'd never missed a ball game or a recital or a school play. He always had time to talk with them and, no matter what issues they faced, he was always patient and full of wise counsel. He was a great father and a doting husband, a very strong presence in the lives of those he loved. But, since the accident, he just wasn't the same man. He wasn't the same Jake Ledger.

As great as their dad was, Jake's kids had noted over the years that there was always an underlying sadness in their father. He seemed haunted, but they also could see very clearly that their mother was able to soothe him. The moment she walked into the room, a visible change would come over him: his eyes would brighten and a smile always came across his face. She was his rock. But, since the accident, the sadness had taken over and nothing they'd said or did seemed to help. An overwhelming hopelessness now consumed their father. To make matters worse, Maddie was the spitting image of her mother, which only seemed to cause Jake more pain when he looked at her.

After he announced that he would be away for a while, they all returned to the business of the day, each of them secretly hoping this road trip would somehow bring back the man they loved and missed. At 4:30 PM, Jake emerged from his office. Normally, when he headed home at the end of the day, he carried a briefcase full of papers, but as he stepped out of his office this time his hands were empty. He took just a few steps before stopping in front of the door of the office next to his. It was her office. The door was closed. No one had been allowed to occupy that space since the accident; the desk and the furniture were still in place. He stood silently for a moment, staring tearfully at her name, which was still on the door. Gently, he slid his thumb across the nameplate and then, in complete silence, walked out the door.

Sleep seemed to elude Jake that night, but finally, he drifted off after a couple of hours of tossing and turning. Then, at 4:00 AM, he was startled from his sleep by the voice, but this time something was different. It was louder and more insistent. And this time the voice addressed him directly and loudly, "JAKE! COME HOME!" Jake knew it was useless to try and go back to sleep, so by 5:00 AM, he had loaded the Navigator with a small suitcase and a box full of travel snacks and hit the interstate. Stopping only for gas, he drove continuously for the next ten hours all the way to Kernersville, North Carolina. This was the last place he had called home before leaving for college. He had not been back since 1978, but now here he was. In obedience to the mysterious voice that had invaded his nights, he now found himself sitting in front of the very place to which he had vowed never to return.

Exhausted from the long drive, Jake closed his eyes and leaned his weary head back against the seat. His eyes felt heavy and tired. He wanted to sleep, but he knew he had to push forward if he was going to understand why the mysterious, haunting voice had called him back to this place of horrible memories. In New York, Jake had been a regular marathoner, and he'd run a pretty good time for a man of sixty, but at the moment, he was struggling to find the strength to push open the car door that now seemed to weigh a thousand pounds. Planting his feet on the ground, he placed both hands on the top of the door and pulled himself out of the vehicle. His stomach began to churn and for a moment he thought he was going to vomit. It felt as though his shoes were made of cement, but slowly, he made his way to the front of the Navigator. Like a tsunami, nightmarish images began flooding his mind. Jake suddenly felt weak and leaned heavily on the vehicle to keep himself standing. Closing his eyes, he uttered a prayer for strength; then, taking a deep breath, he slowly turned to face the dark past that was now before him.

"Okay, lady, whoever you are," he whispered, "I'm here. What do you want with me?"

2

It was early June and a warm breeze blew across Jake's face, slightly displacing his salt and pepper hair. Pushing the wayward strands back into place, he took a step toward the entrance of what was once the mobile home park where he and his mother had lived during his last year of high school. He couldn't believe it, but all of the mobile homes from his youth were still there, although they had been abandoned and were now in a state of decay, covered in rust and mold. Grass and shrubs had all but swallowed many of them. Glancing to his left, he noticed that the sign for the property was still standing at the entrance. The letters on the aged sign were almost completely faded but you could still make them out: Hope Park.

Jake had no idea why the voice had called him back here, but he felt that he would somehow find the answer inside the trailer park. A rusted old gate blocked the entrance, although it did not appear to be locked. As he looked beyond the gate, he could still make out what used to be the dirt road that divided the park. There were ten mobile homes on each side of the narrow passageway that led to a gazebo at the opposite end. Jake was surprised that the old gazebo was still there and, from where he stood, that it looked as if it was actually still in decent shape. A faint smile slowly spread across his face as he remembered some of the events that had taken place under that gazebo.

The neighbors who had once lived in the trailer park were as close as family, often gathering at the gazebo for a cookout, an ice cream supper, or any other summer activity someone might dream up. He remembered how the adults would sit and talk late into the night while the kids played games in the surrounding grassy field. Sometimes they played Red Rover or Kick Ball and sometimes they just tossed a Frisbee back and forth. When it got dark out, they'd caught fireflies and put them in the empty soda bottles left over from the cookout. Closing his eyes, Jake could still see the kids running about waving bottles that were filled with the glowing lights of fireflies like it was the Fourth of July.

He remembered how they'd decorated the gazebo at Christmas time that year when he lived here. The trailer park was located at the end of a dead-end road, and every year, on the Saturday after Thanksgiving, some of the men from the park would go into the woods adjacent to the property and cut down a tree. They would place it in the center of the gazebo and then all the neighbors would come out to decorate it. They would sing Christmas songs, eat homemade baked goodies, and drink hot cider. It was a tradition that began long before Jake and his mother moved in and was one of the few good things he remembered from that time in his life.

Not everything that happened in the trailer park was bad, but not all of it was good either. Slowly, Jake's expression changed as he began to remember the darker episodes of his life that had transpired behind the rusted gate before him. As memories of that year started to erupt like a volcano, a discomfort began to stir deep within Jake's soul, memories that brought much pain, memories that he had buried deep within, and memories he hadn't given thought to for many years. Once again, fear began to overwhelm him, so he closed his eyes and prayed for strength.

"*Just do it, Jake,*" he said to himself. "*Just push open the gate and get this over with so you can get back to New York.*"

Drawing in another deep breath, he placed his hand on the old gate and began to push when he was startled by a female voice calling out to him from the other side of the road.

"Don't nobody live there no more, Mister."

Chills covered his entire body at the sound of the voice behind him. *"Could this be the voice I've been hearing?"* he asked himself under his breath. He was hesitant to turn around, half sure he would see a ghostly, translucent spirit standing behind him.

"Did you hear me, Mister? I said don't nobody live there no more. Ain't nobody lived there for years. I don't even know why it's still there. When the owner of that property died, he left it to his kids, and they pretty much abandoned it. There's likely snakes and rats livin' all up in there. You couldn't pay me to go in there, and believe me, I could use the money."

"Doesn't sound like a spirit. A spirit would likely use better grammar," Jake thought to himself.

Slowly, he turned his head to see who was speaking to him. What he saw brought a smile of relief to his face. Walking across the parking lot of an old run-down restaurant across the road was a young, attractive waitress carrying

a bag of trash to the dumpster and chewing quite aggres-
sively on what appeared to be a huge wad of blue bubble
gum. When Jake had first pulled up, he had been so focused
on the trailer park that he hadn't even noticed the restaurant, which was a little place referred to by the locals as the
Tavern at the End of the Road. He couldn't believe it was
still there after all these years. They used to serve breakfast and lunch during the week and hosted live country
music bands on weekend nights, an event that always drew
big crowds.

Tossing the bag of trash into the dumpster, the waitress
gave Jake a charming smile that immediately set him at ease
and said, "Mister, it's after 2:00 PM so we're closed now, but
the grill is still hot. Not all the food's been put away yet, and
you look like you could use somethin' to eat. You want me
to fix you a bite?"

With a measure of apprehension, Jake began walking
towards her. "I greatly appreciate the offer, but I don't
want to put you to any trouble, Miss. I'm sure you want to
get home."

The waitress placed her hands on her hips and fixed Jake
with a hard glare. "I'm gonna be straight with you, Mister.
I was just bein' nice when I said you looked like you could
use somethin' to eat. To be honest, you look like death on a
dried-up cracker, and I feel obliged to put some food in you
before you fall over right here in this parking lot. I would
hate to have to throw your lifeless corpse in this dumpster."

Jake let out an involuntary laugh. He couldn't remember
the last time he had laughed like that. "Okay, young lady, I'll
take you up on your offer. But I insist on paying you extra
for your services."

The waitress smiled and motioned for Jake to follow her into the diner. Once inside, she pointed to a booth and then headed behind the counter. Jake obeyed the silent command to be seated and looked over the menu while she prepared a tall glass of sweet iced tea and brought it to him.

"What'll you have, Sweetie?" she asked.

Jake hadn't heard a waitress call someone Sweetie since he'd left North Carolina, and he could not remember the last time he had sweet tea. Glancing at her name tag, he said, "I'll make it easy on you, uh, CJ, is it? I just want a house salad, no cheese with light Italian dressing."

CJ dropped her notepad on the table, placed her hands on her hips and looked at Jake in disbelief. "Either you ain't from around here or you been gone a long time. There ain't nothin' light in this restaurant, Mister, except the bulbs in the ceiling; we put cheese on everything; and if you want anything Italian, you're gonna have to go to Italy to get it. 'Round here we are known for ketchup, mustard, mayonnaise...and we don't have dressin's 'cause we don't serve salad. That stuff's for rabbits, not people. We serve real food here, Mister!"

CJ smiled and gave him a playful punch on the arm. "You just sit there and enjoy your tea. I'll fix you up with one of my specials."

As CJ stepped into the kitchen, Jake couldn't help but notice how drastically his mood had improved since he came into the diner. His new friend had an infectious smile, and the way she spoke to him set him strangely at ease. Within minutes, Jake smelled a wonderful aroma from the kitchen. Soon, CJ came out and presented him with a delicious entrée that he would never have ordered for himself: a hamburger with all the fixings and a pile of hot crispy golden fries. She also had a plate for herself with a mountain of fries and what appeared to be a pimento cheese and bologna sandwich.

"You care if I join you?" CJ asked. "We were so busy today I didn't even get a break."

"Absolutely," Jake replied, excited for the chance to get to know more about this very colorful young lady who now sat before him. Placing her blue bubble gum on the edge of her plate, CJ dove into her fries without concern for good etiquette. He had become accustomed over the years to the refined behavior of his upper-class New York friends and colleagues, but today CJ's free-spirited, uninhibited nature was quite refreshing to him.

"My name is Jake, by the way."

"Nice to meet you, Mr. Jake," CJ responded as she stuffed a fork load of crunchy fries into her mouth. As the next few minutes passed, the subjects of their conversation were quite general: they talked about how delicious the food was, but how bad it was for their health; they talked about how long the Tavern had been there; he explained to her that he had just driven in from New York City where he had lived and worked for many years. CJ seemed genuinely interested in everything Jake had to say and, in turn, shared bits and pieces about her own life.

After a brief pause in the conversation, CJ's demeanor became more serious, "Can I ask you a question, Mr. Jake?"

"Certainly," he replied.

Leaning slightly forward over the table, she said, "When I was in the kitchen cookin', I looked out here a couple times and saw you starin' over at the old trailer park. You seemed troubled in your thoughts. Would it be too personal for me to ask you what that place has to do with you and why it seems to bother you so much just to be lookin' at it?"

Jake popped the last two fries from his plate into his mouth and washed them down with the last bit of his sweet tea. He could feel his body tensing up in response to the question. He felt his face grow hot, and his breathing became somewhat shallow. Realizing that her question had stirred something up in her new friend, CJ reached forward and, placing her hand on his, she gently said, "If you can't talk about it, that's fine. I didn't mean to pry."

"No, no," Jake assured her. "You've been very kind to me and I feel very...well, I feel oddly at ease with you. So I think I can talk about it. I just have one request before I start."

"What's that?" she asked.

Jake smiled and timidly slid his empty tea glass in her direction. Returning his smile, CJ grabbed the glass and bounded toward the kitchen, "I knew you couldn't drink just one glass of my sweet tea," she boasted.

While she was in the kitchen, Jake began to formulate his thoughts. Here he was about to unfold his most painful memories to a complete stranger, a young waitress who likely had no more than a high school education, yet he was as nervous as he might be standing before a royal dignitary. Jake had not spoken about this part of his life to anyone since he had left North Carolina so many years ago, but maybe, opening up to a complete stranger was exactly what he needed. He struggled to understand what it was about CJ that made him feel safe opening himself up to her as he was about to do. *She's barely thirty years old*, he thought to himself. *Will she be able to even understand? Can I really do this?*

CJ returned to their table with a full pitcher of sweet tea and a whole apple pie that had not yet been sliced. "I'm ready if you are," she said with anticipation.

"How much time do you have, young lady?" he asked.

Taking a seat across from him, she said, "Well, my boss left me here to close up the place, so I've got all afternoon. There's plenty of tea and pie, and the bathroom is 'round the corner if the tea starts talkin' to ya."

"Okay," he replied nervously. Reaching for the pitcher of tea, Jake slowly re-filled his glass. He paused to collect his thoughts as he stared soberly out the window. "My mother and I moved into that trailer park with her aunt Hazel in the summer of 1977. We lived there until I graduated from East Forsyth High in '78. I had turned seventeen a couple weeks before we moved in, and my mother let me drive all the way from Charlotte to Kernersville, the place that would be our home for the next year."

Jake paused for a moment with his gaze fixed on the neglected property across the street, squinting his eyes as if trying to get a better look at the details of a photograph that had faded with the passing years. "Some of the most painful experiences of my life took place in that trailer park," he said grimly. "But oddly, I also found something there that brought me a measure of happiness that I never dreamed possible. That little trailer park represents some of the darkest and the brightest experiences of my life, both good and evil, all in one place. When I left, I took the best with me and, until recently, I've managed to keep the worst part of it buried. To be honest, I have been able to forget most of it. But sitting here and looking out this window, it's now starting to seem as if it happened yesterday."

3

"Slow down, Jake! As I recall, the police in this town don't have much patience with speeders!"

"Would you please quit telling me how to drive, Mom! I know what I'm doing," Jake boasted with typical adolescent arrogance.

"You ain't been drivin' for hardly a year yet, son, so you actually have NO IDEA what you're doin'! And you're forgettin' that I grew up here, so you would be wise to listen to me. And turn that radio down. It's givin' me a headache." It had been years since she had been to Kernersville, so Jake's mom began looking for something familiar to help her navigate. "Take this next right. I'm pretty sure it takes you into downtown Kernersville. We can pull over and ask somebody how to get to the trailer park." He took the turn and slowed the car to a speed that seemed to satisfy his mom. It wasn't long before they spotted a man on the sidewalk walking his dog.

"Pull over here," Jake's mom said excitedly. She quickly fumbled through the glove compartment until she found the little mirror that she used to check her hair and lipstick before reaching the stranger and his dog. As Jake brought the car to a complete stop, his mother winked at him, fluffed her hair up with her fingers, and then leaned her head out of the window. Speaking loud enough to draw the attention of the stranger, she called out, "There's just somethin' about a man and his dog that makes my heart flutter."

The man stopped and turned toward her. Intrigued by this beautiful, flirtatious stranger, he returned the smile and proceeded with curiosity toward the car.

"Well, hey there, Darlin'," he said as he swaggered up to the car door. "What's your name, Baby Doll?"

"My friends call me Jo," she replied, "but my closest friends usually call me after dark." As Jo spoke those words, she let loose with a lecherous smile followed by a wink to ensure that the stranger got the hint. "Do you have a minute to help us?" she asked with a certain damsel-in-distress tone.

The man leaned in to get a closer look, but was startled when he saw Jake and took a step back.

"Oh, you don't have to worry about him, Baby; that's just my son."

This seemed to ease his nerves a bit so, once again, he leaned in with his hands just inside the open window. "Sweetheart, I would thoroughly enjoy helpin' you with anything you need."

"Aw, you're so sweet," Jo said, running her index finger gently across the back of his hand. "What's your name, Honey?"

"I'm Garrett; so, what can I do to help you?" he asked, not attempting to hide his lustful interest.

"We are looking for Hope Trailer Park," Jo replied. "Me and my boy are movin' in with my aunt today."

"Oh, that's great!" Garrett said with a tone of aroused anticipation. "Where y'all movin' from?"

"Well, we've kinda lived all over the place," Jo answered, still stroking his hand. "But for the last year, we've been livin' in Charlotte. So, can you point us in the right direction, Baby?"

"Glad to," Garrett said. He took a step back from the car and pointed down the road. "You just keep goin' in the direction you're headed now. Go for about two miles and turn right onto Apple Grove. Go another mile and turn right again onto Macy Grove Lane. That's a gravel road, and they just put down new rock, so you be careful. Hope Park is at the end of the road on your right, just across from the Tavern. You can't miss it," Placing his hand gently on Jo's bare arm, Garrett winked and added, "By the way, I'm at the Tavern every Saturday night."

"Is that an invitation, Baby? Jo asked, returning his wink with a seductive one of her own.

Garrett grinned as if he had just discovered a valuable hidden treasure. "There's plenty of room at the bar, Angel. I'll be lookin' for ya."

Before Jo could respond, Jake pressed the accelerator and sped off, leaving Garrett stumbling backwards away from the car.

"Jake, that was very rude," Jo said with disapproval. "There's no tellin' how long we will live here, and we have to make a good impression on people."

"You call that a good impression, MOTHER? You just threw yourself at a guy who looks to be twice your age."

With a sigh, she explained, "Those are the ones that's got money, Baby."

—

As Jake continued to unfold his story to CJ, he could feel the muscles in his jaw growing tense. His hands trembled slightly as he lifted the glass to his lips for another sip of sweet tea. "I was so angry at her. I hated that part of her personality. I had hoped that returning to her hometown to live with Aunt Hazel might change the way she lived, but watching her with that complete stranger made me doubt her sincerity about changing."

CJ reached across the table placing her hand on Jake's forearm. The expression on his face and the tension in his muscles had exposed the anxiety of his heart. "I'm so sorry, Mr. Jake," she said tenderly. "It had to be hard watchin' your mama act that way."

Jake glared out the window, focusing his gaze once again on the trailer park. "Oh, it gets worse, much worse."

"Are you able to keep talkin' about it?" CJ asked. "You know, you don't have to." Her concern seemed genuine to him. The tone of her voice was both compassionate and empathetic, setting him greatly at ease.

"Yes," he responded, nodding his head in affirmation. "I would like to tell you more."

"What was it that brought y'all to Kernersville?" she inquired.

Jake's eyes were still fastened on the trailer park. His quivering chin thwarted his attempt to hide his emotions. All the pain of his past was rising to the surface and he couldn't stop it. He turned to CJ and tried to smile, but when he did, tears began trickling from his eyes. In an attempt to divert the swelling emotions, he grabbed a fork from the table and plunged it into the yet uncut pie that sat before him. He stuffed a large piece into his mouth and washed it down with another swallow of sweet tea.

"A near death experience brought us here," he explained. "A few months earlier we had been staying with some acquaintances of hers in Charlotte. One night, they started getting high, so I decided to take a walk. When I returned, I discovered that she had been rushed to the emergency room from an overdose. It had nearly killed her and, if the house we were staying in had not been right next to a fire department, she may well have died that night. When they finally let me back to see her in the emergency room, she vowed that her life of drugs was over. She promised me she was going to get clean and that we were going to get out of that town and go back to where she grew up. She told me that, over the years, her Aunt Hazel in Kernersville had often invited us to come live with her. She told me that Kernersville was a nice little town full of good people who really cared about each other. She said I would love it. I'll never forget the look of sincerity and hope in her eyes as she spoke about Aunt Hazel and Kernersville. I believed her. She seemed so genuine that, once again, I had great hopes that a new chapter in our lives was about to be written. But watching her interact with that guy the way she did brought back doubt...and fear. For a moment, she sounded like the same old Mom trying to find a new Sugar Daddy to help support her. So, I sped away from that man as fast as my car would go, and we headed for Hope Trailer Park. I still remember the rage I felt that day..."

Jo knew her son very well and could tell he was angry with her. "Jake, Honey, slow down. This is the first turn we're supposed to make," she said softly, hoping to curb his anger towards her.

"Mom, before we get to the trailer park, I have a question," Jake stated with trepidation. "Are you going to be okay? I mean, are you going to make it this time? I just don't know if I could handle another relapse. We have a chance to start over here, and I want you to be careful about the choices you make, but the way you were just talking to that guy..."

"Baby Boy, stop talkin' for a second and listen," Jo reached over and began rubbing his shoulder, "Baby, I'm gonna be fine. You know how I flirt. That didn't mean nothin', so don't you worry. We *are* gonna start a new life today, right here in Kernersville, North Carolina. I know you don't know Aunt Hazel very well, but you're gonna love her—and let me tell you, the woman can cook!

Her words seemed truthful and comforting. "I believe you, Mom. Just promise you will talk to me if you start feeling weak."

"I will, Baby. Here's Macy Grove Lane. Now, remember, the man said they just put new gravel down, so go slow."

Just as she spoke those words, one of Jake's favorite rock songs came on the radio, inspiring Jake to have a little payback fun with his mom. "Let's see what this thing'll do," he said. Cranking up the radio to full blast, he pressed the accelerator to the floor, thrusting the car violently forward causing the old yellow Nova to fishtail a bit, kicking up a rooster's tail of dust in the process.

Bracing herself against the dashboard, Jo cried out, "Jake, you idiot! Slow down! You're gonna get us both killed!"

A devilish grin came over Jake's face as he ignored her pleas and pressed the pedal to the carpet.

"JAKE, I'M 'BOUT TO WET MYSELF! STOP THIS CAR RIGHT NOW! YOU'RE FIXIN' TO PASS THE ENTRANCE TO THE PARK!" Jo screamed.

There was a thick grove of trees just beyond the entrance to the trailer park. Realizing he may have taken his little game too far, Jake slammed his foot on the brakes and tried to make the turn into the park. However, his effort to stop the speeding car on the new gravel road just sent the vehicle into a full spin, creating a small tornado of dust and pebbles. As the car finally came to a stop, Jake looked over at his mom and realized she had forgotten to roll the window up after talking with the stranger. He knew he was in big trouble.

Her hands were still pressed against the dashboard and her long, jet black hair was disheveled; her entire upper body was now covered in dust. Her clean white shirt was now a yellowish-tan color. Turning her angry face to Jake, she blew a piece of hair out from in front of her fiery dark brown eyes. Clenching her teeth together, she spoke to him in a tone that let him know he now needed to keep his mouth shut.

"Boy...my Aunt Hazel ain't laid eyes on me in years. What's she gonna think when she sees me walkin' up to her door lookin' like this?" Jake glanced down and noticed that a little wet spot had formed on the front of Jo's jeans. He'd tried not to laugh at the ridiculous sight before him, but he couldn't help it. He quickly thrust his hand over his mouth in an effort to hide his delight. Realizing that she had indeed lost control of her bodily functions, Jo back-handed her son's shoulder as hard as she could. "If you're still alive at the end of this day, it'll be by the sheer grace of God. Now, put this car in gear and find lot number nine." Quietly and quickly, Jake obeyed his mother and slowly steered the car into the trailer park. He tried to appear apologetic about his mother's current state of disarray, but inside he found himself quite amused.

As they proceeded into the trailer park, the first thing that caught their attention was a beautiful two-story country house on the right side of the road with a huge wrap-around porch. Large white columns held up the roof that covered the porch which appeared to be made from California redwood. Though the house was old, maybe late nineteenth century or early twentieth century architecture, it was spotless white and the yard looked as though it was professionally maintained.

As Jake proceeded cautiously down the narrow drive, he noted that the entire mobile home village was buzzing with activity. Many of the residents were out working in their yards filling the air with the scent of freshly cut grass. Each lot was immaculate and every trailer was well maintained, unlike some of the mobile home communities he had seen back in Charlotte. Jake was careful to maintain a slow speed as he moved forward because the neighborhood was also crawling with children who were not wasting a moment of this warm summer day but were out in full force. Some were riding their bikes while others were playing hopscotch or jumping rope. In one yard, a handful of kids were playing touch football.

A smile came to Jake's face when he noticed that the quarterback was a bossy but cute little girl in pigtails. She could not have been more than eight years old but the boys under her command seemed to have no trouble following her lead. In another yard it appeared that a game of hide-and-seek was underway. The entire place was filled with joy and laughter, two qualities of life that had not been a normal part of the Ledger family's existence. As they drove on Jake couldn't help but notice the strange stares his mother was getting from some of the children. A few were even pointing at their car which, caused Jo to become very self-conscious.

"I'm gonna kill you," he heard her utter under her breath as they searched for lot number nine.

"There it is," Jake said, pointing to a quaint, double-wide mobile home on the left side of the road. "Second one from the end."

Aunt Hazel's lot was warm and inviting. A welcome sign stood at the end of the short gravel driveway which led up to the steps of a screened-in porch attached to the side of her white mobile home, which was adorned with red trim. Fastened under the windows on the end of the trailer were two flower boxes placed evenly side-by-side, both of which were overflowing with red geraniums. The little bit of lawn she had was neatly cut and manicured. It was clear that Aunt Hazel took great pride in her humble home and treated it with immaculate care. Jake and his mom were barely out of the car before Aunt Hazel came bounding down the steps of the porch, nearly taking the screen door off its hinges in the process.

"Land sakes alive! My babies are finally here! I've been watchin' for y'all all day!" Hazel could not contain her delight. She ran first to Jo, throwing her arms around her niece and covering her face in kisses without making a single comment about her unkempt appearance. Spotting Jake out of the corner of her eye, Aunt Hazel hurried around to the other side of the car making certain he felt equally welcomed.

"Who is this MAN standin' here in front of me?" she exclaimed as she threw her arms around Jake. "The last time I laid eyes on you, you were just a little thang. I've finally got somebody in the house who can reach the top shelf." Aunt Hazel was just under five feet tall and had never weighed over a hundred pounds in her entire life. Though she was approaching her mid-60s, she still worked full time at the Kernersville Savings & Loan and had the energy of a gazelle. Known for her quick wit and humor, Hazel kept things lively wherever she went. Nudging Jake toward the porch, she spoke with an authoritative tone, "Y'all come on in and get settled. The neighbors are grillin' burgers and hot-dogs later to welcome you to the neighborhood. They're all excited to meet y'all. I've been tellin' them about you for weeks. Did you see the sign on the gazebo when you pulled up?"

"No, we didn't," Jake replied. Stepping to the back of the car, he looked at the gazebo at the end of the gravel drive. There were colorful streamers and balloons tied all around it and hanging over the entrance was a huge hand-painted sign that read "WELCOME HOME!" For some reason, the sign seemed to warm Jake's heart and, for almost a full minute, he couldn't take his eyes off of it. Maybe it was the word *Home*, which was something he felt he'd never had before. He desperately wanted to believe he was finally home, finally in a place where he could have peace of mind and some semblance of a normal life. But there was still a cloud of doubt in his mind. A peaceful life, a normal life would depend much upon his mother and whether or not she could turn her life around and leave her tainted past behind.

"Jake, Honey," his mother said, interrupting his thoughts. "I'm gonna go on in and freshen up. Can you get our stuff out of the trunk?" Trusting her son to follow her instructions, Jo went inside to change her freshly stained clothes and remove the dust that still clung to her face and hair.

As Jake opened the trunk, his attention was suddenly captured by the sound of music coming from somewhere nearby. It was a very familiar song to him and he immediately recognized it. It was a song about the rambling existence of a man whose father died when he was young. He laughed to himself as he thought what a fitting reception this song was for his first day at Hope Park. Ramblin' was exactly what he and his mother had been doing since his father's death. He slowly turned full circle, trying to discern the location of the music, but to no avail. Shrugging off his curiosity, he reached into the trunk and grabbed two faded suitcases that contained the meager sum of his and his mother's entire net worth. Everything that they owned fit comfortably inside these two pieces of tattered luggage. Before Jake reached the front door, he was startled by the unexpected interruption of a voice he had never heard before.

"Did ya lose 'em?" Jake spun around to see who was speaking to him, but saw no one. He turned to the left.

"You're cold," declared the mysterious voice. He looked to his right.

"Even colder,"

Bewildered, Jake finally called out, "Where are you?"

"Look up, Einstein!"

4

Following the sound of the voice, Jake lifted his eyes upward to the rooftop of the trailer that sat in lot number ten and found the answer, not only to the question concerning the mysterious voice that had been calling to him, but also the answer to the source of the music he had heard just seconds earlier. A girl who looked to be about his age sat cross-legged on the edge of the roof next to a record player. The moment he laid eyes on her, he was completely captivated, stunned to the point of utter silence. He could find no words and, for a second, he wondered if this was how it felt when mere flesh and blood stepped unexpectedly into the presence of the divine.

Not wanting to forget a single detail of this celestial encounter, Jake quickly began to lock away in his memory the details of the vision that was before him. Cascading down upon her soft white shoulders was the most beautiful strawberry blonde hair he had ever seen. Although he couldn't see her eyes clearly from that distance, they appeared to be blue which made her a rare treasure.

Looking down on him from her lofty perch, she smiled at him the way a kind princess would smile from her chariot upon the admiring subjects of her kingdom, bringing them great joy as she passed by while out for an afternoon ride. She was wearing a yellow tube top with cut-off blue jean shorts, and was leaning slightly forward with her forearms resting on her thighs as if to get a better look at Jake. To complete the heavenly portrait, the afternoon sun, shining brightly from behind her, cast its light in such a way as to create an angelic glow all around her. Jake was done for.

He found himself bombarded with a host of unanticipated thoughts and emotions he had never experienced before. He felt excited and sick all at the same time. He was too nervous to speak lest he make himself look like a fool, yet he felt compelled to say something, anything that would prove him to be a confident, potential suitor worthy of her affection. *Will she like me?* he wondered to himself. *If I ask her out, will she accept or will she think I'm just another stupid boy who can't control his impulses? She's so beautiful. I mean, she probably has a boyfriend already, and I have no chance of ever being anything more than a friend.* As Jake pondered these questions, panic began to wash over him. His body temperature seemed to have increased by at least ten degrees and the palms of his hands became so sweaty that the suitcases he was holding escaped his grip and fell to the ground unnoticed by the now smitten Jake.

"So, did you lose 'em?" She asked again.

About twenty seconds went by before he realized she had asked him a question. He also realized that, for those entire twenty seconds, he had not taken his eyes off of her, and there was a pretty good chance that his mouth had been wide open the entire time. Here was his opportunity to impress the most beautiful girl he had ever seen, and he was certain he was coming off like a big dumb oaf. Clearing his throat, Jake prepared himself to respond to her question. He knew that the next words out of his mouth could either secure his chances of someday winning this beauty's heart or could forever consign him to the pitiful role of loser-friend who would have to sit and painfully listen to her talk about the boys she really liked. Seconds were ticking away and she was still waiting, so he mustered up the wittiest and most self-confident response he could.

"Uh...uh...wha...what...I'm sorry...what was the question again?" As he stammered, Jake could feel his IQ plummeting into the single digits, like a boulder falling off a cliff. He was certain that he had just earned her pity and would forever be the sad little neighbor boy she felt sorry for. He would be the village idiot that she might hang out with when she didn't have a real date.

"I asked if you lost whoever it was who was chasing you," she said. "The way you came flyin' into the park, I figured you had just robbed a bank or somethin.'"

Jake literally could not think of a clever response, but instead stood dumbfounded before her in absolute silence.

"It was a joke," she explained. "But I guess if I have to explain it, it must not be funny. Oh well. So what's your name, Boy?

Finally, a question he knew how to answer. "Jake. My name is Jake. What's yours?"

She couldn't help but smile at her new neighbor's awkwardness. "I'm Sammi, Sammi Sullivan," she answered.

"Good to meet you, Sammi. I'm Jake." His face turned bright red as he realized he had just told her his name twice. Hoping to regain some measure of dignity, he attempted to redirect the conversation. "So, what exactly are you doing up there on the roof?" he asked.

Sammi pointed to the small record player sitting next to her. "I come up here just about every day to listen to my records. My folks and I don't exactly have the same taste in music. You wanna come up here and sit with me for a bit?" Jake glanced nervously toward his Aunt Hazel's trailer. He knew his mom would soon be looking for him, but this was an invitation he absolutely could not turn down.

"Yes," he answered, trying to muster a cool, nonchalant composure. "I can come up for a minute or two."

"Just climb on up," Sammi said, pointing to a ladder propped against the trailer next to a window. Not wanting to appear overeager, he resisted the temptation to scurry up the ladder like a squirrel after the last nut on the tree. Suddenly very self-conscious, he moved cautiously toward the ladder, trying very hard not to stare at Sammi. As he stepped onto the roof, she stood to welcome him. Looking around, he noticed right away that she had quite a layout.

Toward the center of this rooftop oasis he saw a lawn chair with an open, red and white striped umbrella strapped to the back. Beside the chair was a cooler filled with assorted beverages and snacks. Under the chair, protected by the shade, was a cardboard box that appeared to be full of records. Stretched out in front of the chair was a long, pink beach towel held down on each corner by small stacks of Teen Magazine; and in the center of the towel was an assortment of sun-tan lotions. Sitting a few inches from the rooftop's edge was a small record player attached to an extension cord that disappeared into the window right below.

"So, do you actually live up here?" Jake inquired with a smile.

Smiling back, Sammi slipped her hands into the back pockets of her jeans, shrugged her shoulders and answered, "I'd say I'm up more than I'm down. Unless it's rainin', this is where you'll likely find me."

A moment of silence passed between them as Jake's expression went from a smile to a gaze of wonder. "They're blue," he said out loud, looking directly into her eyes.

Sammi was visibly flattered by his attention to detail. "Well, thank you," she replied, "they've been blue my whole life."

Another few seconds of awkward silence passed before Jake spoke. He couldn't seem to turn his eyes away from her. "You know," he said with a nervous quiver in his voice, "it seems like I read an article a while back that said it was very rare for people with your hair color to have blue eyes. I think it's like less than a one percent chance."

"Wow," Sammi replied, slightly impressed with his knowledge of eye color as it related to the hue of one's hair, "I guess that makes me some kind of a weirdo."

"No," Jake said with sincerity, "it just makes you very... extraordinary."

Sammi gave no reply, but the soft smile on her face spoke volumes. It was becoming clear that a mutual admiration had already begun to develop between them. In the movies, a moment like this might be followed by some grand romantic gesture, but in this instance, the potentially intimate scene was interrupted by a loud and irritatingly intrusive voice from below.

"JAKE, WHERE YOU AT?"

"Oh my gosh," Jake said as he dropped his head in utter embarrassment. "Sammi, I would like to go ahead and apologize to you for the train wreck that you will occasionally hear me refer to as my mother."

Jo had stepped out of the trailer looking for her missing son. "WHERE YOU AT, BOY?"

"I'm up here, Mom, talking to Sammi," Jake shouted with a tone of agitation.

"Sammi who?" Jo asked. "You done made a new friend?"

When Jo glanced up and saw her son's new acquaintance, she stopped suddenly in her tracks. "Whoa! That's some hot little new friend you got there, Son."

Turning to his mother, he silently mouthed the words, "Shut up! Shut up!"

Ignoring her son's desperate pleas, Jo looked at his beautiful new friend and, in a crude attempt to compliment her, said, "Girl, you are one foxy little mama, ain't ya!"

With his face as red as a tomato, Jake turned to Sammi and whispered, "I am so sorry. Please don't judge me by her. I haven't found the paperwork to prove it yet, but I'm pretty sure I'm adopted."

Sammi laughed, "Don't worry about it. Just wait till you meet my folks."

Jake began to awkwardly back toward the ladder. "I guess I better go help get us unpacked. Will I see you at the cookout tonight?"

"Absolutely," she said with an assuring nod, "I'll meet you at the gazebo."

Unable to take his eyes off of Sammi, he continued backing toward the ladder. "Okay then," he said, giving her a thumbs up, "the gazebo it is."

Never underestimate a beautiful girl's ability to make a young man forget where he is. As Jake took what he thought was the last step backwards before reaching the ladder, he suddenly realized that he had run out of roof and now watched the expression on Sammi's face turn to horror as he clumsily tumbled backwards off the roof onto a clump of bushes below, ripping a storm shutter off the window on his way to the ground.

5

"JAKE, BABY!" JO RUSHED TO THE AID OF her thoroughly humiliated son who was now lying prone in what, a few moments earlier, had been a beautifully man-icured hedge of boxwood bushes. Sammi hurried down the ladder in hopes of finding her new friend unharmed by the fall.

"Jake, are you okay?" Sammi asked with much concern. "Are you hurt?"

Jo leaned over the bushes to examine the situation. "Hon', you scared me to death. Is anything broken? Are you bleedin'?"

"Uh, no. I think I'm fine. Maybe a few scratches, that's all," Jake said as he tried to free himself from the bushes with as little struggle as possible, but to no avail. He was wedged in pretty deep. Overwhelmed with embarrassment, he asked his peering audience of two, "Could you ladies just turn around while I try to climb out of here?"

"Sure, Baby, we can do that," his mother assured him as they both turned away.

With the ladies' backs to him now, Jake fought ferociously, but awkwardly, to free himself from his mortifying predicament, all the while thinking to himself, *Yep, village idiot. This is how she will always remember me. I'll always be the dang fool who fell off her roof.* It took about thirty seconds, but finally he was able to work himself free of the boxwood tangle.

"Alright, I'm out," he announced with humiliation. Not wanting to look either of them in the eye, Jake rushed past the ladies before they could get turned around, picked up the suitcases, and sprinted toward Aunt Hazel's trailer.

"Jake, I'm glad you're okay," Sammi said in hopes of lessening the damage to his ego. "I'll still see you at supper tonight, right?" Jake was still too humiliated to turn around, but gave an affirmative nod to her question before disappearing behind the screen door of Aunt Hazel's porch. Jo followed him inside, deciding that it was best not to bring up what had just happened; instead she asked her son to go back out to the car to make sure they had brought everything in. Once outside, he made a beeline from the porch to the car without so much as glancing in the direction of Sammi's house. He just didn't think he could tolerate a look of pity from her at this particular moment.

He didn't see any other bags or items of importance in the car, so he started to close the trunk. But as he did, he noticed something sticking out from under a pile of old newspapers. It was his baseball bat, the one his mother used to hit him with when she was high. It had been a while since she had taken a swing at him, but the memories were still very fresh and very real. Instinctively, Jake began rubbing his left shoulder which had been the target of his mother's last fit of rage with the bat.

Suddenly, a sense of dread fell over him. Not dread of the past, but of the future. He was big enough now to disarm his mom if she came after him, but the thought of seeing her relapse again made him break out in a cold sweat. His whole life had been controlled by her addiction, and he'd truly hoped for new beginnings in this quaint little mobile home park. He pulled the bat from the trunk and headed inside but paused as he reached the porch. Looking down at the bat in his hands, he remembered how excited he had been when his mother had given it to him on his eighth birthday, one of the few she actually remembered. But this bat did not stir up the fond memories of a normal childhood. There were no memories of little league baseball games or home run hits. There was not even a single memory of batting a ball in the front yard with his mom.

The only memories attached to this bat were those of broken lamps, smashed dishes, holes in the wall, and bruises. She never hit him hard enough to break a bone, but she'd left lots of bruises. All of them had healed except the ones that were permanently etched on his heart and still deeply embedded in his soul. The bat represented a very painful past, and Jake did not want it in the house. Instead, he threw it several feet under Hazel's porch, far enough into the shadows that his mom would not be able to see it.

"Get in here, Boy!" Aunt Hazel called as she poked her head out the porch door. "Let's get y'all settled." Following her orders, Jake went inside where he and Jo received a grand tour of the entire double-wide mobile home. The gleam in Aunt Hazel's eyes as she walked them through was evidence of the great pride she took in her snug but inviting home. As they moved down a narrow hallway, Hazel stopped and pointed to a small bedroom on the right. "Jake, this will be your room across from mine. And Jo, your bedroom is there at the end of the hall. Unfortunately, we will all have to share one bathroom, but as long as we stick to a schedule, we should be fine."

Leading them back into the kitchen, Hazel opened all the cabinets and drawers so her new residents could see where everything was. As the tour ended, her eyes began to moisten with tears. "I can't begin to explain how happy I am that y'all are here. Ever since Charlie died two years ago, it's been way too quiet and lonely. I want both of you to feel at home here. What's mine is yours."

"Thank you, Aunt Hazel," they both replied simultaneously.

"Alright now," Hazel said, composing herself. "We've got a couple hours before the cookout so whatever you need to do between now and then, just help yourself: take a nap, take a shower, just whatever you want."

Jake went into his new room and closed the door behind him. Aunt Hazel's generosity and hospitality made him feel quite at home. He just hoped his mother understood that a chance to turn her life around was right in front of her, and he prayed that she would do nothing to blow it. Opening the window to let in some fresh air, he began putting away his belongings and arranging the bedroom furniture to his liking. The room was small, but he loved the fact that it was *his* room, a quiet place that he could call his own. He even had his own closet and a chest of drawers for the few clothes that he owned.

After putting all his clothes away, Jake reached into his suitcase for his most prized possessions, seven books that he greatly treasured: *The Art of War* by Sun Tzu; *The Republic* by Plato; *The Iliad* and *The Odyssey* by Homer; *The Tempest* by William Shakespeare; *A Tale of Two Cities* by Charles Dickens, and *The Metamorphosis* by Franz Kafka. Jake carefully dusted off all seven books with the same care one would employ to dust priceless silver and proudly placed them upright on top of the chest of drawers.

Glancing out of the window, he discovered the added bonus of being able to see Sammi's house just across the yard. After getting everything in order, he stretched across the bed on his back with his hands behind his head. He began to daydream about what his future might hold. Because of his mother's lifestyle, Jake was often bombarded with dark thoughts when he was alone, but there were times when he would allow himself to dream, and this was one of those times.

He desperately wanted to have a better life in his adult years than the life he'd experienced throughout his childhood and adolescence. Lying on the bed staring at the ceiling, he began to envision the many potential paths that lay before him. Coming to Kernersville represented a new beginning that he hoped would lead to a better future. An unusual sense of calm came over him as he lay there, and it wasn't long before he drifted off into a peaceful sleep.

The nap was short-lived, however. As supper time drew near, he was awakened by the appetizing aroma of hamburgers and hotdogs cooking on the grill. He continued to lie in bed for a few moments longer as his room became redolent with the scent of a summer-time barbeque. He found himself amused by the chatter of voices just outside his window as the neighbors began to gather at the gazebo which was located practically right next to Aunt Hazel's trailer. He could hear children laughing, which brought a smile to his own face. He heard the sound of ice being poured into plastic cups and of ceramic dishes clinking together as they were being lined up buffet-style on a table to be served.

"Where do you want me to put the trash can?" a voice queried.

"Same place as always," snapped another voice with a slight tone of impatience.

"Which part of the table do you want the desserts on?" inquired another.

The same impatient voice answered the second question, "Desserts always go at the end of the table, Fanny, you know that. What's wrong with you? Did you get your pills mixed up again this mornin'? The green one is for the mornin' and the red one for the night. You'd think we've never had a cookout before!" The impatient voice obviously belonged to someone who was either in charge or thought she was in charge. As the crowd grew, several other questions were asked, each of which were answered by the same person who seemed to grow more irritated by each one. As he lay there honing his eavesdropping skills, someone knocked on his bedroom door.

"I'll be out in a minute! Don't open the door!" Jake snapped, assuming his mother was the one who dared disrupt his quiet thoughts.

"Oh, I'm sorry," came a soft feminine voice from the other side of the door. "I didn't mean to bother you. I just came to see if you wanted to walk out to the gazebo with me."

Jake shot straight up on the side of the bed. His heart raced out of control, and he could feel his face getting hot. It was her! It was Sammi! *I am* not *prepared for this*, he thought to himself. Moving quickly to the door he suddenly became aware that he might have nap-breath. Cupping his hands over his mouth, he took a whiff which confirmed his fears; his breath was horrible.

"Gum! I need gum," he muttered to himself under his poisonous breath. He remembered pulling a pack of gum out of his suitcase earlier, but wasn't sure where he had put it. Frantically rummaging through his chest of drawers, he finally found the gum and stuffed a piece in his mouth. Hoping that his breath was now tolerable, he reached to open the door.

"Sorry it took me so long. I fell asleep after unpacking," Jake explained.

"I'm sorry," Sammi said with a sheepish grin. "I guess I should have gotten Hazel's permission before just walkin' in here, but she's outside givin' orders to everyone, and I didn't want to interrupt her. Is it okay that I knocked on your door?"

He wanted to say, "You can knock on my door anytime," but he didn't want to sound cliché and risk embarrassing himself in front of her again, so he kept the comment to himself. "It's okay that you knocked on my door. The food out there smells great and I'm starving. You wanna walk out now?" he asked, motioning toward the front door.

"Sure. I thought I would stick close and help you navigate through this crazy bunch of neighbors you have now. I'm sure you're gonna grow to love 'em. They're quite an interestin' lot;" Sammi explained proudly, "we're all family here."

As they stepped out onto the porch, they had a clear view of the gazebo and could see that a large number of adults and children were already gathered and preparing to eat.

"I didn't realize so many people lived here," Jake said, pushing open the screen door.

"Hold on a minute," Sammi said, pulling Jake back from the screen door. "I wanna tell you about some of your neighbors, but I don't want 'em to see we're talkin' about 'em."

Pointing toward the gazebo, Sammi said, "You see that tall distinguished lookin' black gentleman standing in front of the entrance to the gazebo? That's Mayor."

"The Mayor of Kernersville?" Jake asked.

Sammi laughed, "No, he's not *the* Mayor. His name is Mayor. He actually owns the land and all the mobile homes here at Hope Park. He's a very nice man. He's got enough money to live in a big house in town if he wanted to, but he chooses to stay here with us. He and his wife live in the big white house on the right when you first come in. He opened this mobile home park back in the early fifties and he wanted it to be a place where anyone from any background could come and be treated fairly and equally. He wanted it to be a place where people who were down on their luck could come and find hope. That's why he named it Hope Park. He's always sayin' 'no matter how bad your circumstances, you can always find hope.' He really cares about all of us. He never judges a tenant's outside appearance, like skin color or the kind of clothes they wear, or how much money they make. He's always more concerned about what kind of hearts they have, and because of that we can always be sure that we have good neighbors. That's why you will notice that the folks who live here are not all the same color, and there are a few who barely speak English. Everybody is accepted here, just as they are, and without judgment. You should really try to get to know Mayor. Now, do you see that little short woman over by the food table givin' everybody orders?"

Jake laughed. "You mean my Aunt Hazel?"

"Yes," Sami answered. "There's somethin' you need to know about her. Mayor owns the place, but your Aunt Hazel is the law around here. Mayor relies on her a lot and nobody gives her much backtalk. What she says pretty much goes with little or no argument. She might as well be wearin' a badge. This mobile home park would be a mess without those two, but they keep things runnin' smooth so nobody argues with 'em."

After pointing out a few other key members of the neighborhood, Sammi led Jake out to the gazebo and began introducing him. He was overwhelmed with how nice and welcoming everyone was. After everyone was present and accounted for, Mayor offered a prayer of thanksgiving over the meal and as soon as he said *Amen*, everyone rushed the food table like a pack of starving dogs. The sight made Jake laugh.

"Hold on, hold on, everybody!" Mayor interrupted. "I believe you've all forgotten your manners. In case you haven't noticed, the Welcome Home sign is up because we have two new members of our little family joining us today. It's our custom that when someone new joins the family, they get to go first; so y'all step aside and let the Ledgers go to the front of the line."

No one seemed to begrudge the honor that Mayor had bestowed on the newcomers, so Jake and his mom graciously moved to the front of the line. After loading his plate, Jake sat down under the gazebo. Whoever had built this grand structure had attached a wooden bench along the inside perimeter of the rails, making it possible to seat a large crowd under the roof. Jake had only taken three bites when Sammi came and sat down right next to him.

He couldn't help but smile at the man-sized portions this petite little beauty had managed to pile onto her plate.

The next hour and a half proved to be one of the most enjoyable times Jake had ever had. The food was delicious and just about everyone seemed to want to get to know him and his mother. A couple of men in the neighborhood had brought their guitars and set up a little bandstand, drawing a crowd of country music fans under the gazebo. No one seemed in a hurry to go home and it was obvious that they enjoyed being together. But what pleased Jake the most about the evening was the attention he had received from Sammi. She seemed quite content to stay by his side. He was beginning to think he had a very special new friend.

All was going well until the festive occasion was suddenly interrupted by a warning from one of the neighbors, "Heads up everybody! Here comes the devil!" The music stopped as all the voices fell silent and every head turned with nervous dread toward the entrance of the park. Sitting ominously just inside the gate was a shiny red Ford F150 with what appeared to be three men inside staring straight ahead at everyone gathered at the gazebo. The whole scene felt menacing. Every few seconds, the driver revved the engine as if to announce his presence.

Jake stepped off of the gazebo and slowly approached Mayor. "Who is that?" he asked.

The small town of Kernersville was a quaint southern paradise filled with residents who cared about each other genuinely. The folks here lived life together. It was one of those towns where all the people knew each other. Children could run and play in picturesque tree-lined streets without fear of harm. Residents could leave their doors unlocked at night without worry of intruders. There was an abundance of churches where people gathered every Sunday to worship together, pray together, cry together, and help carry one another's burdens. When someone died, everyone grieved. When someone got married or when a baby was born, everyone celebrated. If you lived in this town, one thing you could be sure of was that you always had friends. Kernersville was a little piece of heaven. But every garden of Eden has at least one serpent; Kernersville had Scott Robertson.

Mayor responded to Jake's question, "That there is the meanest boy, probably in the whole state of North Carolina. He is good for absolutely nothin'. His daddy got rich in the hosiery business, and the boy has never had to do anything for himself. He's a spoiled and entitled brat. He dropped out of school when he turned sixteen and he's been nothin' but trouble since. He'll likely end up dead or in prison for doin' somethin' stupid. The local police can't do nothin' about him because his daddy always shows up with enough money to get him out of whatever trouble he gets himself into, so he just runs around with his two shiftless friends doin' whatever pleases him."

"What does he want from us?" Jake asked hesitantly.

Mayor paused for a moment before answering. "He wants her, Jake. He wants Sammi. He comes 'round here a few times a month lookin' for 'er."

Jake was suddenly overwhelmed with apprehension. He turned to look for Sammi, but she was not sitting where she had been a few moments earlier. Frantically, he looked around for her, but he couldn't see her anywhere. Seeing the troubled expression on Jake's face, one of the men who had been playing the guitar pointed toward the center of the gazebo and then placed his index finger over his lips as if to hush Jake. The neighbors had instinctively pulled her to the middle of the gazebo and then surrounded her to hide her from Scott Robertson's view.

Feeling a slight sense of relief, Jake turned back toward the truck, which was now moving very slowly toward the gazebo. The tension increased among the neighbors as Scott and his friends drew closer. Finally, after what seemed like hours, the truck stopped right in front of the food table. Another minute or two passed before Scott opened the door. As he stepped out from the driver's side, his two friends slithered out of the passenger side.

Standing tall at six feet, three inches, Scott was an intimidating figure. He had on cowboy boots, dark jeans, and a tight-fitting black t-shirt that highlighted his sculpted biceps and chest muscles. He walked around to the front of his vehicle and leaned back against it with his arms folded. The smug expression on his face hinted at the pride he took in his ability to intimidate others.

"Well, well, well," Scott said as if to scold. "Looks like somebody planned a party, but I don't remember gettin' an invitation." The arrogance that Scott exuded immediately reminded Jake of some of his mother's suitors from the past.

With his fists resting on his hips, Mayor boldly spoke up. "Scott, you know you are not welcome here, and you also know why you are not welcome here. You need to turn around and go home."

"Well, howdy there, Mr. Mayor. Look, Boys, it's the lord of the land in all his glory and splendor," Scott said mockingly.

"There's nothin' here for you, Scott," Hazel said with a tone of authority. "So you need to just go on, right now."

Scott sneered, "Oh, I beg to differ, Miss Hazel. There *is* something here for me, or should I say, someone. Y'all know who I'm lookin' for, so where is she? I came to see if she wanted to take a little ride with me tonight."

"She don't want you, Scott, so just leave her alone," a voice cried out from the back of the gazebo.

"Oh, she wants me. She just don't know it yet. Once she gets a taste of me, she won't be lookin' nowhere else," Scott declared brashly. Jake had heard all he wanted to hear. Every muscle in his body was tense. Sammi's honor needed to be defended. He started to step forward to confront Scott, but his mother, who was now standing next to him, grabbed his arm.

"No, Baby," his mother whispered. "I'm beggin' you to just stand still. Don't say a word. Mayor and Aunt Hazel are handlin' this." Anger was rising up in Jake like hot lava, but he decided to grant his mother's wish and, going against every inclination of his heart, he remained silent.

"It's time for you to go, Scott," Mayor reiterated.

"As you wish, big man," Scott replied with a smirk, "but tell my little sweetheart, I'll be back." As he started to walk back toward the truck, Scott eyed the food table again. Turning to his buddies, he said, "Boys, it would be rude of us to not help our friends clear the table. Grab the rest of the hot dogs and hamburgers and anything else you want and let's go." After stealing just about every remaining morsel off the table, the three miscreants climbed back into the truck and slowly began to back out. As they reached the gate, everyone breathed a sigh of relief, but instead of pulling out of the park, Scott brought the truck to a stop and sat there for a moment. Concerned, Jake stepped forward to get a closer look at what he might be up to. Scott began revving the engine again. Then, without warning, he threw the gearshift into drive and, like a rocket, the truck took off, speeding quickly toward the gazebo.

"O, LORDY!" someone shouted. "He's headin' straight for us." Panic struck each heart and everyone began to scatter as Scott's truck raced forward toward his helpless victims.

6

As he drew closer, Scott laid on the horn with one long continuous blast in an effort to further intimidate the frightened onlookers. Jake's thoughts suddenly turned to Sammi. Looking back toward the gazebo, he was horrified to see that her human wall of protection had wholly dissipated in the face of the threat that was now just seconds away.

"SAMMI, GET OUT OF THE WAY!" he shouted as he ran towards her.

But, fixated on the speeding truck that was headed straight for her, Sammi stood paralyzed with fear. Reaching her with barely a moment to spare, Jake lifted her off her feet and quickly rushed her down the back steps of the gazebo. Losing his footing on the bottom step, they both fell into the grass. A split second after hitting the ground, they heard a loud crash as Scott's truck smashed into the tables that had been set up for the evening festivities. He had slammed on the brakes bringing the F150 to a stop before reaching the gazebo, but not before hitting the tables, which were shattered by the impact and destroyed beyond repair.

Scott leapt from his truck and angrily slammed the door behind him, "I knew y'all were hidin' her! You can't fool Scott Robertson! SAMMI! Sammi, I know you're back there! Me and you need to have a little talk, Girl!"

Infuriated by the spiteful actions he had just witnessed, Jake jumped to his feet and, with clenched fists, stormed back across the gazebo toward Scott. Because of his mother's past, he had seen more than his share of abusive men and had no tolerance for them whatsoever. Stepping over the shattered pieces of the broken tables, he lunged forward, giving Scott a violent shove with all the power he could muster. But with Scott's size and strength, Jake was only able to back him up a couple of feet.

Then, before he knew what was happening, he found himself overcome by Scott's two mindless cronies who seemed to have no ambitions in life other than to be at the beck and call of Scott Robertson. One of them, Eric, had slipped up behind Jake and put him in a choke hold. The other one, Jonathan, stood next to Jake, restraining his right arm. Scott was shocked, though somewhat impressed, with the audacity of this stranger who had dared to put his hands on him.

"Who is this runt?" he asked the crowd of folks who had begun to regather.

Jake was no runt though, not really. With a moderately athletic build, he stood just a little over six feet and weighed around 160 pounds. Nonetheless, he was simply no match for the 220-pound hooligan who, at that moment, towered over him like a fire-breathing dragon. No one answered Scott's question.

Seeking to intimidate the newcomer, Scott grabbed a clump of hair on the top of Jake's head, leaned in to within an inch of his face, and asked, "So, what's your name, Boy?"

Determined not to show fear, Jake glared directly into the face of his antagonist, but didn't speak a word.

Still clutching Jake's hair, Scott took his other hand and planted a weak, but humiliating slap across his cheek. "I expect an answer to my question," he snarled.

Jake remained silent, but continued to maintain eye contact. Scott had never encountered anyone quite like this before. He usually had no trouble intimidating others and wasn't sure how to respond to this stranger's apparent defiance.

"The next one's gonna hurt," he threatened, balling up his fist.

"His name is Jake," Sammi answered anxiously as she stepped from behind the gazebo. "And I want you to leave him alone. He's new here. Today's his first day."

Releasing Jake's hair, Scott stepped back and for a few uncomfortable moments leered at Sammi with a predatory grin. His roaming eyes clearly exposed the lustful intent of his heart.

"Scott, can I talk to you over here for a minute?" she asked. "Alone, please?"

Sammi's request to speak to Scott privately unnerved Jake. Lunging forward, he tried to break free, but Eric tightened his grip.

"Let him go," Scott instructed. "He ain't gonna do nothin' now, but hold him right there against the truck. I'll be right back."

The private conversation between Sammi and Scott lasted for all of forty-five seconds, but to Jake it seemed like much longer. He tried unsuccessfully to make out what they were saying, but they were barely speaking above a whisper. Her body language, however, indicated that she was very uneasy standing that close to her stalker, and as soon as the conversation was over, she wasted no time dashing back to her trailer while Scott headed back toward the truck. No one heard what she had said to him, but whatever it was, it seemed to abate his rage.

Before leaving, Scott made one more attempt to intimidate Jake who was still pinned against the front of the truck. Pressing his fist against Jake's chest, he leaned in close, and with a tone of condescension said, "Alright, Rat. I'm gonna show you some grace today, because you're new here and too stupid to know what you were doin' when you put your hands on me. But I promise you that if you ever lay a hand on me like that again, it'll be the last thing you do on this earth, and my smilin' face will be the last thing you ever see."

Content that he had made his point, Scott motioned to Eric and Jonathan to get back in the truck, and the three of them sped out of the park, kicking up dust and gravel as they left. As soon as they were gone, the crowd rushed over to Jake, some showing concern for possible injuries he may have incurred and others applauding his bravery.

"Son, that was a bold move you made there," Mayor said proudly, as he patted Jake on the back. "I don't think I've ever seen anybody stand up to that devil."

"I've never seen anybody stand up to him either. I just hope it doesn't come back to bite you," Aunt Hazel said soberly. "That boy's got a lot of pride. You better watch your back from now on, Jake."

As Jake soaked up all the accolades, he caught a glimpse of his distraught mother in the crowd. She offered no praise for her son's actions, but instead shook her head in disappointment, then turned and went back inside Aunt Hazel's mobile home. He knew there would be an intense conversation before bedtime. Interrupting the outpouring of praise and admiration that Jake was enjoying, Hazel clapped her hands to get everyone's attention. "Enough with the flattery, we have church in the mornin' so we need to get this mess cleaned up."

At Aunt Hazel's authoritative word, everyone jumped right to it, cleaning up the pieces of the broken tables and all of the shattered dishes that had met their untimely and violent demise. Jake pitched in to help, all the while hoping Sammi would come back out, but to his dismay there was no sign of her.

When he went back to the trailer, he didn't see his mom. It appeared that she may have gone to bed, so he quietly tried to slip into his room unnoticed. But his efforts at a stealthy retreat were futile. As he crossed the threshold into his room, he heard his mother call to him with a very solemn tone. "Jake, Honey. Can you come in here a minute?" Jake pushed open the door to Jo's bedroom and poked his head in. She was already in her sleeping clothes, but was sitting up in bed.

"Come sit with me here, Baby Boy," she said, almost in a whisper. "I want to talk to you about what happened earlier." Jake stepped into the room, sauntered over to the bed, and sat down next to his mother. Taking his hand in hers, Jo began to speak quietly so Aunt Hazel wouldn't hear, "What I saw today scared me really bad, Baby Boy. Don't get me wrong. A big part of me was proud of you for takin' up for that sweet little girl. It didn't seem like nobody else was gonna do it. I noticed that even her daddy got up and went inside when things started to get out of control. So, like I said, a part of me was proud. But another part was scared. You and me both know that I've got some things in my past that I ain't too proud of. I've known dozens of men like that Scott and I'm tellin' you there ain't nothin' good in any of 'em. As soon as that boy opened his big mouth, I saw it and I know you did too. He's just like all those men I used to know. And I think that's why you got so angry. But don't forget what you said to me just before we got here today. You reminded me that we have a new start in life here with Aunt Hazel. I want us to be happy here, so I am beggin' you, Jake, please don't tangle with that boy. I heard somebody say he was only twenty-two years old, but he's got a hundred years of evil in his heart. I looked in his eyes today, Jake, and I saw the devil. So will you please just promise me that you will do whatever it takes to stay clear of that boy? Please, Son?"

"Okay, Momma," he replied, attempting to set her at ease. "I won't go messin' with the devil."

Jo smiled and placed her hand on Jake's face. "I know your heart, Son. You're a protector. You like to rescue people, and while that is a wonderful part of who you are, it's also the part that can get you in trouble. I don't want you to have to learn things the hard way like I did; and I really don't want you to get hurt. When those boys grabbed you today, I just about had a heart attack. I know you're bigger than me now, but you're still my baby. So, if you see those boys again, you just turn around and walk away. Okay?"

"I promise," he assured her.

"You're a good boy. I love you, Baby," she said as she gently kissed his forehead. "Now go on to bed. It's been a long day for both of us."

"I love you too. See you in the morning," Jake said, closing the door behind him as he left.

After a quick shower, he locked himself in his bedroom looking forward to a good night's sleep. However, his mind refused to stop replaying the events of the day so, unable to sleep, he decided to sit up and read for a while. He loved his books and would sometimes read for hours at a time. Genre didn't matter. He loved reading just for the sake of reading and he was able to retain every word he read. Around midnight, he was just about to fall asleep when he heard something outside tapping against his window.

A few seconds passed and he heard it again. Another couple of seconds went by and he heard it a third time. It sounded like someone throwing small pebbles against his window. Getting out of bed, Jake walked over and peeked through the curtain. By the light of the bright summer moon, he could see Sammi sitting on top of her roof motioning him to come over. Yet another invitation he knew he could not refuse.

7

Groping his way through the darkness, Jake was sneak-thief-quiet as he moved warily toward the front door. While crossing the yard, he glanced up and saw Sammi standing on the rooftop waiting for him. His throbbing heart could barely take in the beauty of her silhouette against the light of the moon. *Can you fall in love in one day?* he wondered to himself as he paused to drink in the vision.

"Whatcha waitin' for, Boy? Get up here," she whispered.

As Jake reached the top of the ladder, he noticed that the décor was slightly different from earlier. The chair, the beach towel, and umbrella were missing, but spread out in the middle of the roof was a soft handmade quilt with a butterfly print. Scattered about the quilt was another assortment of snacks and drinks, enough to keep a couple of teens occupied for a good while. The record player was in the same place as it had been earlier and at low volume it was already emitting some tunes that were very familiar to Jake.

"Come sit with me," Sammi said softly as she plopped down cross-legged on one end of the quilt.

Remembering his embarrassing fall from earlier, Jake stepped carefully from the top rung of the ladder onto the roof and tiptoed over to Sammi. "Won't the music and the talking wake your folks?" he enquired, as he sat down across from her.

"Not a chance," she answered with confidence. "They both take medicine at night to help them sleep. If a plane crashed in the field over there, they wouldn't as much as roll over. Besides, their room is on the far end of the trailer opposite the side where I play my records."

Eased by her certainty, Jake shifted his legs to make himself more comfortable on the quilt and reached for a bag of potato chips. Tearing open the bag, he popped one in his mouth and then, pointing toward the print on the quilt, he said "You like butterflies?"

"I love 'em," she responded with an innocent smile. "They're my favorite. I have butterfly rings and bracelets, butterfly wallpaper, butterfly sheets and pillow cases, and I even have a few books about butterflies in my room. I've loved 'em for as long as I can remember."

"That's nice," he replied, noisily grabbing a handful of chips from the bag. Sammi sat silent for a moment and just smiled at him, causing him to become very self-conscious of the loud noise he now realized he was making as he munched voraciously on the oversized portion of food he had just stuffed into his mouth. In an effort to direct attention away from himself, he extended the bag toward her hoping she would accept the offer.

"Thank you," she said, reaching in and helping herself to a couple of chips. Instead of eating however, she lowered her head and fastened her eyes on the butterflies adorning the quilt. Several seconds of silence passed before she spoke.

"I invited you up here so I could thank you for what you did today," she said, "and to apologize for runnin' off the way I did. It's just that I knew I was the reason Scott showed up today, and I felt responsible and embarrassed."

Jake sensed from her despondent posture and tone what he believed to be a bit of undeserved contrition. He paused for a moment, searching his heart for words that would comfort her. "Sammi, look at me," he said. When she lifted her head, he could see by the light of the moon that her eyes were beginning to moisten with tears.

"Sammi," he continued, "there is not one reason for you to be embarrassed or to blame yourself for what happened today. You did nothing wrong. Nothing! After Scott left, no one pointed a finger at you. They just all kept talking about how crazy and evil he was."

"I guess maybe you're right," she reluctantly acquiesced. "I just hate that your first day here had to end by having a run-in with the absolute worst person in the whole town, maybe even in the whole state. But what you did was real brave, Jake. You were a hero today. You were my hero."

"No, you were the hero," he argued. "What did you say to him to make him leave?"

Sammi seemed uncomfortable with the question. "I'd rather not say if you don't mind. I just knew I had to get him out of here because if he stayed, someone was gonna get hurt and I didn't want that someone to be you," she explained.

Jake wanted to press Sammi further, but he could sense her uneasiness and decided to drop it. Besides, he wasn't sure he wanted to know what she had said to Scott Robertson.

"There is one more question I have about this after-noon," he hesitantly said. "My mom noticed that during the excitement, your dad went inside. If you don't mind me asking, I was just wondering why he didn't stick around to defend you, or least stay long enough to make sure you were safe."

"Well, there's no simple answer to that question," Sammi sighed. "The truth is that neither of them are my actual parents. They're my grandparents on my mom's side."

"Where are your parents?" he asked.

"We have no idea," she replied with resignation. "In fact, I've never even met my mother. I've only seen pictures from when she was younger. I know that my daddy's name was Ricky and my mother's name was Blythe; that's all I really know about 'em."

Jake's curiosity was piqued. "What happened?"

Sammi didn't seem to mind revealing this part of her life to her new friend. She had already come to the conclusion that he could be trusted. "When my mother was sixteen, she became pregnant with me. Ricky, my father, obviously wanted nothin' to do with the situation and disappeared. After I was born, she continued livin' right here with my grandparents, but when I was around two months old, she took off. My grandparents woke up one mornin' and heard me cryin'. When they came in the room to check on us, all of my mother's clothes were gone. They found a note from her on the dresser sayin' that she was sorry, but that she just wasn't ready to be a mother. No one around here has seen her since, and that was seventeen years ago. I'm not even sure she's alive."

"Wow. I'm so sorry," Jake said tenderly.

Sammi continued, "This might sound cold, but I find some comfort in the thought that she might be dead, because if she's dead then I can understand why she has never contacted me. But if she is alive out there somewhere, and I've not heard from her after all this time, that means she doesn't care that she has a daughter. So it makes me feel better to assume she's dead. Does that make me sound evil?"

"Of course not," Jake assured her. "I can understand why you would feel that way."

"When I was a little girl, I used to imagine that she had been kidnapped by pirates or that she was stranded on a deserted island in the middle of the ocean and simply couldn't make her way back to me. In my head, I created lots of situations that could explain why she never came back. And any one of them was better than acceptin' the fact that I had been rejected and abandoned by the very person who brought me into this world."

Jake was speechless and deeply touched by the sadness of what he had just heard. Moved by her vulnerability, all he wanted to do at that moment was hold Sammi in his arms, but he knew they were still strangers and such an attempt would seem forward.

Sammi continued to explain the unusual relationship she had with her grandparents. "I know they love me in their own way, but one night when I was a little girl, I got up to get some water and I overheard 'em talkin' about me. I don't remember every word that was said, but, after hearin' that conversation, I realized that they saw me as an intrusion on their lives. I heard my grandfather say that he had already raised one daughter and he didn't want to raise another, 'especially if this one turns out like her mother.' They take care of me, but they don't show me a lot of attention. So I guess when my grandfather walked away from the commotion this afternoon, he did so because he just didn't want to be bothered by the drama. He probably blames me for the situation with Scott anyways. When I walked in the house, he was sittin' in his chair and didn't say a word to me as I passed by him on the way to my room."

Realizing they had something in common, Jake felt sympathy towards Sammi. He understood what it was like to wonder if you were really loved by your parents.

"What's the story with Scott anyway?" he asked.

Sammi's facial expression changed to one of disgust. "He's just pure meanness is all. His rich daddy has always given him whatever he wants and whenever he gets in trouble with the law, his daddy bails him out. He respects no one and thinks he's better than everybody else. He dropped out of school when he was sixteen and now all he does is roam the streets with his two idiot friends gettin' into all sorts of trouble. If anything gets torn up or defaced in town, everybody assumes it was Scott who did it."

"He called you *his* girl. Any truth to that?" Jake asked nervously, not sure he wanted an answer.

"Absolutely not!" Sammi answered, raising her voice for emphasis. "He thinks every girl should just swoon, flutter her eyes, and buckle at the knees when he goes by, but this girl will never swoon, flutter, or buckle. Not for him."

Jake was unable to hide his delight at her response as a smile came across his face.

"Enough about all that," she said, attempting to change the topic. "So what's your story, Einstein?"

A lump quickly formed in Jake's throat. He very much wanted her to like him and wasn't sure how she would respond if he told her the truth about his mom and the difficult, poverty-stricken life they had lived because of her careless actions and poor choices. But he also did not want to appear evasive. Jake struggled for words. "Uh, well. Not much to tell here. My dad died when I was very young and my mom and I have tried to make ends meet ever since. We've had to move a lot...for various reasons. But I think we are finally home now. I hope we at least stay here until I finish school."

Sammi could see that Jake was not ready to open up just yet so, lying back on the quilt, she shifted the conversation upward. "I love lookin' at the moon and the stars. I come up here a lot on warm summer nights and if I stare up at the sky long enough, it starts to feel like I'm floatin' through space. It makes me feel peaceful."

Jake followed Sammi's lead and stretched out on the other side of the quilt. Looking up at the moon and stars, he could see what Sammi was talking about. A sense of peace began to wash over him as he gazed upward. He had never been able to see the stars where they'd lived before because of the city lights. Looking to create an opportunity to impress her, he asked, "Did you ever sing 'Twinkle, Twinkle, Little Star' when you were little?"

His question made her laugh. "Of course I did. Didn't you?"

"Yes," he responded, "it was one of the first songs I ever learned."

After a brief silence, Jake spoke up again and said, "It's not true, ya know."

"What's not true?" Sammi asked, wondering where he was about to take the conversation.

"Stars don't twinkle," Jake boasted with an academic air. "They never have. It only looks like they do. Ya see, as the light from the star passes through the various layers of the earth's atmosphere, it gives the appearance of twinkling. But if you were up in space looking at them, I'd say you'd never see them twinkle."

Quite amused, Sammi propped herself up on her elbows. Looking at Jake with a wide grin, she asked, "Why on God's good earth would I *ever* need to know that? What could I possibly do with that information?"

Realizing he had not impressed her with his knowledge of astronomy, Jake answered facetiously, "All I'm saying is that maybe that shouldn't be the first song we teach children. It's like we're building their whole lives on a lie."

"Well," Sammi said, continuing in the spirit of joviality, "I was always partial to 'Rock-A-Bye Baby'."

"Oh, now there's a song," Jake said with a tone of feigned solemnity. "Babies falling out of trees! I mean, what kind of parents put their baby in the top of a tree anyway, especially when the forecast calls for high winds."

His comments made Sammi cackle out loud. "Jake," she said, shaking her head and lying back down on the quilt, "you are a funny guy."

Another few moments of silence passed as they continued their star-gazing.

"How did you know that about the stars?" Sammi finally asked.

"I read a lot," he replied.

"Wow," she said, finally appearing somewhat impressed. "You really are an Einstein."

"Well, not really," he started, "Einstein actually had an IQ of..."

"JAKE," Sammi interrupted with a loud whisper.

"What?" he asked, stopping mid-sentence.

"I don't care what Einstein's IQ was," she said, laughing softly to assure him that she was teasing.

Changing the subject, Jake asked, "So, why butterflies? Why do you love them so much?"

Sammi answered, "When I was a little girl, I just thought they were pretty. But as I got older, I learned how butterflies come to be. They start out as little caterpillars just crawlin' around. There's not much to 'em at that point. But then they wrap themselves in a cocoon, which is kind of like death. In fact, I read that the caterpillar's body actually dies inside the cocoon and turns to mush. But then, after a while, it reshapes itself and emerges as a beautiful butterfly. Because it now has wings, it's no longer limited in what it can do. So to me, butterflies came to represent hope. I think we all start out like caterpillars, but inside of each of us, there's a beautiful butterfly just waitin' to break free."

Jake was impressed with her analogy. For the next several hours, they talked about various subjects, occasionally dozing off until roused by an owl's hoot or some other sound from nature, at which point, the conversation would pick up again. As the night wore on, Sammi finally tired out and, drawing the quilt over her chilled body, she drifted off to sleep.

Jake found it difficult to take his eyes off of the sleeping beauty. He was intrigued by her ability to appear strong and vulnerable at the same time. From time to time, a gentle breeze blew across the rooftop, tousling her strawberry blonde strands and carrying the delicate scent of her hair across the butterfly quilt into the nostrils of the enchanted hero who was now fully captivated by her many charms.

As he lay next to her, a profound realization began to unfold in Jake's mind. Even though he had only known Sammi for a day, there was something very soothing about her presence. The sound of her voice seemed to calm the storm within him. Her laughter made him smile, and as he listened to the soft words that fell from her lips, the pain of his past somehow seemed irrelevant. He had no clue as to where this new friendship would go, but one thing he felt certain of already was that, if she were a part of his life, he would be a stronger man—a better man.

A seed of hope was planted in Jake's heart that night, a hope that his future could be very different from his past. But he also knew that the hope he sensed rising up in his heart was, in some way, tethered to the girl who was sleeping ever so peacefully on the other side of the quilt. As he lay there analyzing the many thoughts in his mind, exhaustion finally overcame him. Gazing into Sammi's face one last time, he yawned, closed his eyes, and went to sleep.

8

Just before dawn, Sammi awoke to find Jake still sound asleep. Unable to resist the opportunity to have a little fun, she pulled a ribbon from her hair, crawled quietly over the pile of snacks that were still in the middle of the blanket, and began lightly tickling Jake's nose. Thinking that a small winged creature of the night was about to make a home out of his nasal passages, Jake sat up quickly, swatting away at the ribbon.

Sammi burst out with laughter, but quickly covered her mouth for fear that she might wake the neighbors. If Jake's mother had been the one to pull this prank, he would have become agitated, but seeing Sammi's delight at his reaction only made him smile.

"What are you doing?" he asked, rubbing his eyes.

"Sun's about to come up," she replied. "We better get back in our beds or there'll be a scandal. And today is Sunday, so folks will be up soon gettin' ready for church."

"Church?" Jake asked disapprovingly. "No one said a thing about church."

Because of Jo's lifestyle, attending church was not a common activity that she and her son practiced. He had occasionally visited churches in the various towns where they had lived, but he was never very committed to the idea. Religion was something he was still trying to figure out. He primarily viewed church-going as a cultural phenomenon practiced by people who, for reasons he couldn't understand, needed a mysterious deity to rely on rather than relying on themselves.

Of the church members he had encountered throughout his life, he found most of them to be critical and judgmental, especially when they found out about his mother's lifestyle. And, since he was her child, he also found himself the target of their self-righteous judgment. Because Jake was such an avid reader, he'd once read the Gospel of John and did not find the attitudes and actions of many "church people" compatible with what he'd read in the Scriptures. Due to these negative experiences, he wasn't ready to buy into religion just yet, if ever.

"Yes, Jake," Sammi stated with conviction, "church is a big deal around here. And knowin' your Aunt Hazel as I do, I'd say you don't have a choice. Besides, almost everyone in the trailer park goes to the same church. You can sit with me."

The thought of sitting beside Sammi for an hour suddenly made church seem a bit more bearable to Jake. Shooing him off the quilt, she began gathering the four corners of it together like a hobo's bindle, leaving all the leftover chips and cookies in the middle of it.

"Grab the record player and records if you don't mind," she instructed. Jake quickly complied. It was obvious that she had done this so often that she had perfected the routine and he wasn't about to question her directives. She started down the ladder first, but as he began to climb after her, she could not resist a little more fun.

"Careful now, Einstein," she said mischievously. "Step easy. I don't think the bushes can handle another Jake bomb."

"Ha ha," he sarcastically replied. "That's the funniest thing I've heard so far today."

"I'm sorry but I can't help it," she explained. "I laugh whenever I see someone fall. I always have. One evenin' my grandpa was in the tub, and he called out to my grandma to bring him a new bar of soap. She tripped over the bathroom rug and fell in the tub right on top of him. It took her five minutes to crawl out, screamin' and thrashin' about like a dying fish the whole time. Grandpa kept gruntin' and groanin' every time her elbow or knee jabbed into some tender spot. I heard the whole thing from my room and couldn't come out for nearly twenty minutes. I didn't think I would ever stop laughin'."

Jake shook his head with a smile. "You're a very disturbed person. And you should never work at a nursing home."

"Oh, I wouldn't laugh if someone actually got hurt," she said, trying to redeem herself.

Once off the ladder, Jake helped her climb back into her room, carefully handing her the quilt, the record player, and records through her bedroom window. As he turned to walk away, he felt a hand on his shoulder.

"Here ya go," Sammi said, extending a closed hand through the window.

"What's this?" he asked.

She opened her hand revealing the ribbon she had taken from her hair earlier. She didn't say a word, but only smiled. Returning the smile, he took the ribbon, slipped it into his pocket, and headed back to Aunt Hazel's. Sneaking quietly back into his room, he fell across the bed and went back to sleep. He enjoyed another couple hours of slumber before being startled out of his sleep by an aggressive knock on his bedroom door.

"Time to get up! CHURCH!" Aunt Hazel ordered in the tone of a drill sergeant.

At first, Jake was tempted to ignore his aunt's call to reveille but was soon drawn out from under the covers by the tantalizing smell of bacon sizzling in the pan. Emerging from his room like a foraging bear coming out of hibernation, he made his way to the kitchen where he found his mother's promise about Aunt Hazel's cooking to be true. He was mesmerized by the feast before him.

One pan on the stove was full of bacon while another one was filled with what appeared to be sausage patties cooking in their own grease. A big bowl full of scrambled eggs was already sitting in the middle of the table alongside a plate full of biscuits, and another bowl was filled with sausage gravy almost to the point of running over. Also on the table were three place settings, complete with forks, spoons, knives, and coffee cups. Jake was impressed. Walking over to the stove, he spotted another pot full of what appeared to be mashed potatoes.

Raising an eyebrow, he asked, "Why are you serving mashed potatoes for breakfast?"

Hazel laughed and shook her head. "Those ain't mashed potatoes, Boy, they're grits."

"Oh yeah, grits," he acknowledged, nodding his head. "Heard of 'em. Just never ate any of 'em."

Hazel picked up a wooden spoon from the counter and began stirring up the contents of the pot. "What do you mean you've never eaten grits? Grits are a southern delicacy," she said, sounding as if she had just been insulted.

"It just never made sense to me to put something in my mouth that went by the same name as the stuff I dig out from between my toes after I've been walking in sand," Jake said. He did not realize that his attempt at humor was coming across as facetious to his aunt. He would eventually learn that there were three things you should never joke about with his Aunt Hazel: church, his late uncle Charlie, and her cooking.

"Not the same thing at all," she said sternly. "Now take hold of this handle and stir the grits until they're ready to come off the burner."

"Yes, ma'am," he dutifully replied. The last thing he wanted to do was anger his new landlord.

While he stirred the grits, Hazel began removing the bacon and sausage patties from the pans. A brief period of silence passed before she asked, "So, did you enjoy your little party on the roof last night?"

Jake dropped the spoon into the grits and his eyes grew to the size of baseballs. "Uh! Wha! What...what party?" he stammered.

"I'm referrin' to the rooftop rendezvous you had with Sammi last night," she declared with the accusative tone of a prosecuting attorney.

"Shh, quiet," Jake whispered. He looked toward his mother's room to make certain she hadn't come out yet. "How did you know?" he asked.

"Nothin' much gets past ole Aunt Hazel," she replied. Then, tilting her head forward she glared at him over the top of her glasses and demanded, "At any point last night was one or both of you naked?"

Jake gasped with shock. Red-faced and thinking that his honor was at stake with Aunt Hazel, he placed his left hand on her shoulder, raised his right hand to God and nervously swore, "I didn't lay a hand on her. That's the truth whole and, and nothing but. God, so help me, I swear!"

Aunt Hazel suddenly burst out with laughter so loud it made Jake jump. Slapping him on the shoulder, she said, "I wish you could see the look on your face right now." She continued laughing so hard she had to lean on him to keep from falling. Gaining control of herself, she said, "Boy, I am just teasin' you. First of all, I've known Sammi since she was a baby and I trust her judgment. She's a good girl and it will do you good to remember that. Second of all, I think you're a pretty good fella so I'm gonna trust you unless you give me a reason not to. And third of all, you are both practically adults so you're gonna do what you're gonna do. But I expect you to treat her with respect. Be her friend before anything else. Boys around here seem to lose their senses when she's around and they try to take advantage of her sweet nature. There's a lot to that girl, but most boys are interested in what's on the outside, not what's on the inside. You be different from all the others! You hear me? She needs a friend more than she needs a boyfriend."

"Yes, ma'am," Jake said. While he appreciated her speech on Sammi's behalf, he truly had no intentions of taking advantage of her. Besides, he wasn't really sure what Sammi thought of him just yet. It may be that she was only interested in being friends, and he did not want to lose that opportunity by being presumptuous.

A few moments later, Jo came out of her room and the three of them sat down together at the table. After Hazel said a prayer, they all dug in without restraint.

After taking three or four bites, Jake asked, "Do you always cook like this?"

"No," Hazel answered. "I used to though. When Charlie was alive, we always ate big on the Lord's Day. We would have a big breakfast, a big lunch, and then leftovers for supper. The first Sunday after his funeral, I got up early like I had done for years. I had been cookin' for nearly an hour before I realized he wasn't here anymore. I went to the bedroom and cried the whole day. Since then I don't cook much anymore except when we have a church event or a neighborhood gatherin'. But after your mama agreed to come live with me, I decided to bring back the Sunday tradition."

Stuffing his mouth with a gravy-covered bite of biscuit, Jake gave Aunt Hazel an approving nod and said, "You won't get any arguments from me."

Jo glanced up from her plate and said, "Jake, Sweetie, don't talk with food in your mouth. I keep tellin' you, nobody wants to see that."

"Oh, that's fine," Aunt Hazel interrupted. "Let him enjoy it."

Jo laughed and said, "I was hopin' when we moved here it would be me and Aunt Hazel teamin' up on Jake, but it looks like it's gonna to be the two of you against me."

"By the way," Aunt Hazel said. "I always leave for church about 8:30 for Sunday school, but I figured the two of you might want to start out just comin' to the 11:00 o'clock worship service. I asked Betty and Gerald if they would let Sammi skip Sunday school today so she can ride with you and show you where the church is. They said she could do that."

Aunt Hazel leaned over, nudged Jake with her elbow and, with an impish grin, asked, "Is it okay if Sammi rides to church with you?"

Jake decided not to commit to the direction Aunt Hazel was trying to steer the conversation. Instead, he just nodded and continued chewing his biscuit without saying a word. Jo didn't say anything either but, already aware of his budding interest in the beautiful girl next door, she smiled approvingly at her son from across the table.

When 10:30 AM rolled around, Sammi was already waiting outside, leaning against the Nova and looking like she had just stepped out of a fashion magazine. Every hair on her head was perfectly in place. She had on just enough make-up to highlight her natural beauty and she wore a cute yellow sundress with straps that hung just off of her shoulders. When Jake came out of the trailer, he was immediately enthralled by her appearance and had to remind himself of Aunt Hazel's words at breakfast: *"Be a friend first." Easier said than done, Aunt Hazel,* he thought to himself.

When Jo came out to get in the car, Sammi hopped in the back seat and closed the door. As Jo was about to get in the front passenger seat, Jake cleared his throat to get her attention. When he caught her eye, he tilted his head toward Sammi, who was already settled in the back of the car, and whispered to his mom, "You ride in the back."

"You want me to ride in the back?" she said loudly with a smile. She was amused by her son's romantic awkwardness.

"Yes," he replied quietly so that Sammi couldn't hear.

Continuing to speak at full volume, Jo asked, "You want me to sit in the back with Sammi?"

Now frustrated with his mother's feigned cluelessness, Jake rolled his eyes and speaking slightly louder said, "No. I want her to sit up here and you to sit in the back, ALONE!"

Jo laughed at Jake. "You're so easy to mess with," she said. "I knew exactly what you meant."

Jake rolled his eyes again.

"Sammi, Baby," Jo called. "Since you know where the church is, why don't you ride up front with Jake and I'll ride in the back?" Jo winked at Jake over the top of the car and mouthed the words, "You happy now?"

Jake nodded his head and mouthed back, "Thank you."

Sammi obliged and sat in the front. The ride to church was surreal for Jake. When she said to turn right, he turned right. When she said to turn left, he turned left. When they arrived at the church, he realized he had no idea where he was, how he'd got there or how to get home. As they entered the sanctuary, both he and his mother found the congregation unexpectedly welcoming. They were immediately greeted by an elderly, white-haired gentleman who led them down the aisle to help them find a seat. He was a tall man with hunched shoulders, but his face was kind and his demeanor very warm.

"Thank you, Mr. Wade," Sammi said with a smile.

"You're so welcome, Young Lady," Mr. Wade said as he returned the smile. "You look lovely today."

"Thank you," Sammi replied. "And you look dapper as always."

Mr. Wade smiled like a flattered school-boy then returned faithfully to his post to assist others in finding seats. As the three of them sat down, everyone around them took the time to welcome them and ask their names. The entire room buzzed with conversations among the members who seemed genuinely happy to see each other. At the stroke of 11:00, a hush fell over the congregation as the choir, dressed in white robes, entered the sanctuary followed by Pastor James. The pastor took his seat on the platform, but the choir remained standing to sing the opening hymn. As the choir director stood to lead the choir, Jake's mouth fell open.

Leaning over to Sammi, he whispered, "So, my Aunt Hazel is the church choir director? Is there anything she's not in charge of?"

Sammi replied with a smile, "I told you, that lady is the boss. The quicker you learn that, the happier your life will be."

As the choir began to sing, Jake leaned over to Sammi again and whispered, "I forgot to thank you for the ribbon you gave me this morning. That was sweet. Why did you give it to me?" He was hoping for an answer that might fuel his romantic hopes.

"Oh, you're welcome," she whispered back. "I gave it to you because it had been up your nose. It's yours now. Consider it a welcome-to-the-neighborhood gift." She couldn't help but giggle as she answered his question.

"Thank you. It's the most thoughtful gift I've ever received," Jake said quietly as he shook his head. "Disturbed. That's what you are. Disturbed."

"Shhh, we'll get in trouble if we keep talkin'," she said. "Keep the bulletin open so you will know what to do next."

Jake examined the bulletin that Mr. Wade had given him when they first entered the building. "Play by play instructions," he said with a tone of sarcasm. "Very helpful."

After a few more songs and an offering, the pastor stepped up to the pulpit with his Bible in hand. He stood in silence for a few moments, looking upon his congregation as a father would look lovingly upon his children. The congregation sat attentively as if waiting for words of wisdom to pour out from this man's mouth into their hearts, words that might provide direction or comfort.

The silent moment was truly sacred and Jake felt it to the core of his heart. In fact, he was caught off guard by it. In the few churches he had attended in his life, he usually found the pastors to be boisterous and condemning. But before this pastor even spoke his first words, Jake sensed that this was a man who truly cared about his people.

Pastor James opened his Bible and placed it reverently on the pulpit before him. He cleared his throat to speak. The air seemed to be filled with quiet anticipation, the kind of anticipation one might have waiting to see the sun rise over the ocean. "I want to begin the sermon today with a question," he said. The tone of his voice seemed both authoritative and compassionate at the same time, "Do you have hope? When you are alone and quiet, and when you search deep within your heart, do you find hope or do you find despair?" He paused for a moment before continuing, "Turn with me to Proverbs 13:12."

The pastor's question pierced Jake's soul, and he quite surprisingly found himself wanting to hear what this man had to say. He could hear the rustling of pages throughout the congregation as everyone paged through their Bibles for the text. He wanted to follow along in the reading, but was somewhat embarrassed because he did not have a Bible and had no clue as to where Proverbs might be.

Sammi immediately picked up on his discomfort, reached into the rack that held the hymnals, and pulled out an old worn-out Bible that someone had accidently left behind. She flipped quickly through the sacred book and found the passage for Jake just before the pastor began to read.

Pastor James invited the congregation to stand and when all were on their feet, he read the text from Proverbs 13:12, "Hope deferred makes the heart sick; but when dreams come true at last, there is life and joy." After he finished reading, he motioned for the people to be seated and for the next thirty minutes or so he expounded upon the scriptural text, speaking much on the importance of hope—the importance of holding on to one's dreams in order to find life and joy.

As the pastor continued, Jake's mind began to recall all of the pain and disappointment that had characterized his life. He'd had dreams, but he wasn't sure if they were even attainable—his mother's addiction and lifestyle had brought much darkness into his life. The threat of death loomed large ever since his father was murdered and, as far back as he could remember, he had suffered from nightmares about his mother dying or being taken away from him.

Despair, Jake thought to himself. *When I'm alone, when I'm in the dark, I feel despair, not hope.* Whenever hope did rear its head, Jake was afraid to take hold of it because it had been snatched from him so often. He thought about all the times he had prayed to God for help, but no answer had ever come. The pastor's message helped him understand why he had such sadness in his heart, but the message fell short in that it did not tell him how to find hope. The sermon plunged him into such deep introspection that he forgot about Sammi sitting next to him.

"Jake," she said as she nudged his shoulder. "The service is over. Time to go home."

As he came back to reality, he saw that the people were pouring into the aisles. The pastor had stepped to the back of the church to greet everyone on their way out.

"You ready to go, Mom?" Jake asked. Turning towards Jo, he noted that her eyes were red and there were light-colored streaks down her face where her tears had left trails in her make-up. He pretended not to notice as the three of them stood up and edged sideways toward the aisle. The line moved slowly because everyone seemed intent on speaking to the pastor. Surprisingly, Jake also found that he wanted a moment to speak with Pastor James. They had been standing in line for about three minutes when he noticed something unusual in the balcony just over the exit door.

The lights were off up there and he had noticed that it wasn't used during the service. There was no window on that end of the church so it was quite dark; but, as Jake continued to watch, he was able to make out what appeared to be three shadowy figures sitting on the front pew of the balcony. As the crowd advanced toward the door, Jake remained still with his eyes fixed upward.

"Jake, pay attention," Sammi said. "The crowd is movin' forward."

But he didn't budge. She looked up at him and saw that his gaze was fixed on the balcony. The expression on his face made her very ill at ease. Slowly she turned her head upward toward the front row of the balcony. What she saw struck fear in her heart. Three dark, demonic figures appeared to be looking down upon the congregation. They sat motionless on the front pew until the larger one in the middle slowly leaned forward so that his face could be seen in the light.

It was Scott Robertson, and his devilish eyes were fastened on Sammi. His menacing glare and wolfish grin made her blood run cold. Instinctively, she reached for Jake's arm and pulled herself close to him, partly to protect herself but also to protect him. When she did that, Scott cut his eyes toward Jake, looking down at him with a threatening scowl. After a moment, he leaned back into the darkness and sat completely still. The entire scene was sinister to say the least, yet Scott's attempt to instill fear in Jake was not effective. Jake's blood did not run cold but instead began to boil with hatred.

"Why is *he* here?" Jake asked under his breath.

9

JO WAS STANDING ON THE OTHER SIDE OF
Jake, and she'd witnessed everything that had just happened.
Jerking on her son's elbow, she said, "Jake!"

He did not respond, but continued to eye the devil in
the balcony as a shepherd would eye a wolf that was stalking
his sheep.

"Jake!" his mother again called, but this time with
greater firmness in her voice and a sharper tug on his elbow.
Jake and Sammi both turned to look at Jo. "I am beggin' you
not to tangle with that boy. Something is really bad wrong
with him. He thinks you're cuttin' in on what's his and that
makes him dangerous to both of you. Evil never plays fair,
Jake, and I just have a bad feelin' about him. I've asked you
once, but I'm gonna ask one more time, will you please just
stay as far away from him as you can?"

Jake knew he could not make and keep such a promise
to his mother. He didn't want to have a confrontation with
Scott and his cohorts, but it was at this very moment that
he knew a clash of some sort was inevitable and it would be
by Scott's own making, not his. He would have to remain

vigilant. Jake did not speak a word in response to his mother's concern. He glanced back toward the balcony, but no one was there. The three devils had slipped out as mysteriously as they had slipped in.

Sammi released her hold on Jake's arm, seemingly relieved by the fact that Scott was gone. Jake had no doubt that Scott was evil, but he was not afraid for himself. His concern was for her. He knew that Scott wanted her for himself, but how far would he go to get her and who was he willing to hurt in the process? Would he hurt her? Two days prior, Jake did not even know this girl existed. But now, he overwhelmingly sensed a responsibility to protect her even if the two of them were destined to be no more than friends.

Sammi smiled at Jake, grabbed him by the wrist, and said, "Let's go home. My family and I have been invited to have dinner with you today." As they pulled up to the trailer, Aunt Hazel was just driving up as well. Jumping out of the car and darting toward the door, she informed them that lunch would be ready by 2:00 o'clock and they better not be late.

"Go put on some shorts and meet me in a few minutes at the gazebo," Sammi instructed. "I'm gonna change clothes and then I want to show you somethin.'"

Intrigued by her excitement, Jake complied. Moments later she emerged in jean shorts, a turquoise tank top, and tennis shoes. She had tucked her hair under a tan floppy-brimmed hat for protection from the sun. "Come with me," she said with an adventurous tone.

Like a puppy, Jake followed behind her without question. She lead him out behind the gazebo, and they walked through a lush green field that was about the size of two football fields set side by side. It was bordered on the far end by a thick patch of woods which seemed to be the direction she was leading him.

"You're not afraid of snakes, are you?" she asked, as they entered the wooded area.

"Only the ones I can see," Jake replied with a bit of trepidation. He wasn't sure if she was serious or not. Grabbing him by the hand, she continued to lead him deeper into the forest. About twenty yards in, she suddenly stopped and, taking both of his hands in hers, she instructed him to close his eyes.

"Listen," she said. "What do you hear?"

He tried his best to honor her request to listen for the sounds of nature, but from the moment she took his hands in hers, the loud, rapid pounding of his heart silenced all other sounds. All of his senses were alive and operating beyond full capacity, but it was because of Sammi, not the environment. He was entranced by the touch of her hands, the scent of her hair, the sound of her voice, and the beauty of her face which, even though his eyes were closed, he could still see in his mind.

The only sense yet to be satisfied was the sense of taste which could only be fulfilled by taking her in his arms and pressing his lips passionately against hers. All of these forces were coming together at once with the power of a rogue wave crashing over the bow of a ship. His will to resist his passions was slipping away. His ability to hold the course and be Sammi's friend first was now in question. But what if he kissed her and she rejected him? It would bring a swift and sudden end to this budding new relationship.

Jake knew that he must decide now if he wanted to know the temporary thrill that would come with only one kiss or if he wanted the joy that could come with a lifelong relationship. He opted for the latter and chose to restrain the fire that burned within him. Bringing himself back into the moment, he was ready to answer her question.

"I hear birds chirping," he said. After pausing for a few seconds, he continued, "I hear the leaves rustling in the breeze...and I think I hear either squirrels or rabbits running around doing whatever squirrels and rabbits do."

"That's good," Sammi said, "but you're missin' one thing. Listen some more."

Jake kept his eyes closed and listened once more. "Is that running water I hear off in the distance? Is that a creek?"

"YES!" Sammi shouted with excitement as if he had discovered a valuable treasure that she had buried just for him. "Let's go! I can't wait for you to see it." She grabbed him by the hand, dragging him swiftly behind her. After another fifty yards or so, they came into a beautiful clearing next to a rocky creek bed that emptied into the river. You could see the river from the clearing but, because of the thick woods along the river bank, you could only get to the river by walking through the creek.

Stepping up to the edge of the creek, Sammi looked at Jake and asked, "You wanna get in?"

"Sure," Jake replied, always ready for an adventure. "But these aren't swimming clothes."

"Neither are these," she said, referencing her outfit. "But we can walk out to where the creek empties into the river. It's only knee deep."

He agreed, so they removed their shoes, placed them on a tree stump, and stepped carefully into the creek bed. The bank was steep, so Jake went in first and then turned to help Sammi into the water. He placed his hands on her slender waist and she rested her hands on his shoulders.

Lifting her off the bank, he drew her body close to his so he wouldn't lose his balance. When he did that, she placed her arms around his neck until he lowered her carefully into the creek.

As he set her down, their eyes locked onto one another and, though no words were spoken, it seemed that a bond of some sort was birthed between them in that very moment. But how that bond would be defined was still a mystery to him. So, once again he denied the burning passion within, released his grip on her, and hand in hand, they made their way down the creek bed toward the river.

"Wow! This is beautiful," he said as they came to the river's edge. "Very peaceful."

"It really is," she agreed. "I come down here a lot. Be careful if you ever come down here alone, though. One more step from this point and you're in eight feet of water."

"That's okay," he assured her. "I'm a fairly decent swimmer. Can you swim?"

"Absolutely," she answered. "I've been swimmin' in this river since I was about six years old, but my grandma never lets me come alone if I'm gonna swim. Even now she insists I bring somebody with me."

Noticing some loose stones on the creek bank, Jake suggested a throwing contest to see which one could hit the bank on the other side of the river first. Sammi agreed and handed him her hat. Cautiously, he made his way to the bank and loaded up the hat with small stones. For the next several minutes they took turns seeing which one could out-throw the other. He was impressed by her strength and accuracy, but was certain he could win this contest. After all, he was bigger and stronger. Being the gentleman that he was, when they got down to the last stone, he gave it to her.

"Last shot," he said.

Sammi took the stone, tossed it in the air a couple times and said, "Prepare to lose." Assuming the position of a professional baseball pitcher, she turned her body, lifted her left leg out of the water and threw her right arm back behind her. Then twisting back toward the river bank, she let loose with the prettiest toss Jake had ever seen. At high speed, the stone jetted from her hand, arched high above the river bed, and landed firmly on the other side.

"I DID IT, I DID IT!" she shouted with great delight. "I won and *you* lose," she bragged, laughing and poking Jake's chest. As she spoke these words of triumph, she gave him a playful shove, but with greater force than she realized, causing him to lose his footing and slide off of the edge of the creek into the river. He began thrashing about and struggling to stay afloat. As he bobbed up and down out the water, he frantically reached out for Sammi.

"I was lying. I can't swim at all! HELP!" And then, with a look of panicked desperation on his face, he slowly sank beneath the surface.

Sammi screamed. Fearful that she had just drowned her new friend, she didn't hesitate to jump headfirst into the river. The water was dark and as she looked around underneath, she couldn't see him anywhere. Genuine panic began to set in. She swam back to the surface to get another big breath of air before diving deeper, but before going back under she heard laughter coming from behind her. Turning to see who it was, she was both relieved and angered to see Jake swimming around like a pro and laughing.

Swimming towards him, she splashed water in his face and threatened, "Oh, you are a dead man! You scared me to death, Jake Ledger. What's *wrong* with you?"

"I think we lost your hat," he said, apologetically.

"Oh no," she said. "That was my favorite hat." She turned to look for it, but when she turned back toward him, he pulled the hat out from under the water and poured the contents all over her head.

"You don't want your forehead to get sunburned," he said with feigned concern, and shoved the hat down over her head. She looked so funny that they both had to laugh.

"Well, now we have to get out so we can dry off before lunch," Sammi playfully griped. They swam back to the mouth of the creek and made their way up the bank and then back to the clearing. "If you want that shirt to dry, you should probably take it off and hang it on a tree branch," she suggested.

Jake was hesitant to remove his shirt, but he knew she was right, so he reluctantly pulled it off, wrung out the excess water, and threw it over a branch. To his unexpected surprise, she removed her tank top and jean shorts as well, but before he had a chance to get too excited, he realized she was wearing a swimsuit underneath her clothes. Swimsuit or not, however, seeing her like that had an astounding effect on him.

He wondered if she was doing these things on purpose: holding his hands earlier, putting her arms around his neck when he lifted her off the bank, and now removing her wet clothes right in front of him. *Surely, she knows how beautiful she is*, he thought to himself. *Certainly she must have some understanding of the effect she has on guys. Maybe she doesn't know she's so beautiful or maybe she's doing these things to let me know she's interested in being more than just friends or... maybe I'm just thinking too much,* he pondered. The whole thing was confusing to Jake, but he decided to follow Aunt Hazel's advice and not try anything too fast.

Sammi pointed to a fallen tree trunk nearby. "Let's sit over there and talk for a bit."

As Jake turned to walk to the tree, Sammi noticed several scars on his back. They looked like they had been there for a while. One scar, about an inch long, stretched vertically over his left shoulder blade. A second diagonal scar was located half way down his back about a half inch to the right of his spine. The third scar was the most concerning to her. It was in the shape of a half circle, just above the waistline located to the left of his spine and it was at least two inches in length. It wasn't a perfect half circle, but was jagged.

Her mind was flooded with various possibilities of how he could have gotten these scars. She wondered to herself, *was he in a car accident? Were they surgical scars? Was he attacked? If so, who did that to him? He was such a nice person. Why would anyone want to hurt him? Whatever it was that had happened to him, it certainly must have been painful.*

As Jake sat down on the tree trunk, he grabbed a stick off the ground, leaned over and began making random designs in the dirt. The angle of his back as he leaned made it easy for Sammi, who was now seated beside him, to get a clear look at the scars.

No longer able to contain her curiosity, she placed her finger gently on the scar over his shoulder blade and asked, "So what happened here?"

Jake's heart pulsated rapidly at the touch of her finger on his back but he was uncomfortable with her question and didn't even look up. Attempting to play it off lightly he said, "Oh that's a conversation for another time...not a good subject to discuss right before lunch."

His response created even greater curiosity in Sammi's mind. She respected his choice to sidestep the question, however, and pushed the matter no further. He continued dragging the stick back and forth through the dirt, and eventually her attention was drawn away by a couple of squirrels chasing each other along a tree branch.

The two sat quietly, observing the wooded landscape around them and occasionally catching a whiff of a vine of honeysuckle growing nearby. After a few minutes of silence, Jake spoke, "Maybe we can talk about that on your roof sometime." He then lifted his eyes from the ground and smiled at her. She smiled back, but remained silent for a few moments before responding. She gazed inquisitively into his eyes as one might examine the pieces of a puzzle before attempting to put it together. She was curious about the picture that the pieces would form.

"I hear it's supposed to be cloudless tonight," she finally said. "Good night for more star-gazin'. Maybe we can sneak some of your aunt's leftovers and have us a little picnic. Is midnight too late for you?"

"No," Jake replied. "Midnight is fine." His heart raced at the thought of meeting her on the roof again.

Due to a warm summer breeze blowing through the trees, it didn't take their clothes very long to dry. So the two got dressed, and headed back, taking their time as they went. Even though their friendship was barely two days old, they were becoming very comfortable with each other and had no problem finding topics to discuss. As they approached Aunt Hazel's, their noses were warmly greeted by a delectable, mouth-watering aroma escaping through the open windows of her kitchen. It was her highly-praised fried chicken and the mere smell awakened a monstrous hunger in both of them.

"I'll race ya," Sammi said mischievously to Jake as she bolted for the door. He was content to let her win the challenge. Stepping into the kitchen, he was, once again, astounded by what his aunt had prepared. The table was filled with dishes fit for royalty...southern royalty that is. There was golden fried chicken, gorgeous yellow corn on the cob dripping with butter, green beans, mashed potatoes with gravy, hand-chopped slaw mixed with a generous amount of mayonnaise, glazed carrots, homemade biscuits, and sliced cucumbers soaking in vinegar. To top it all off, Aunt Hazel announced from her place by the stove that there were a couple of homemade cherry pies warming in the oven that she would serve with ice cream for dessert.

Jake leaned over and whispered in Sammi's ear, "I am never leaving this place."

"Don't blame you," she whispered back.

Sammi's grandparents, Betty and Gerald, had already arrived and Gerald was sitting quietly in the recliner watching television. He'd not even bothered to acknowledge that the two had returned.

"Hello, sir," Jake said, throwing up a hand to Gerald.

"Uh-huh," Gerald grunted, without looking up even once from the television.

"Where's Mom?" Jake asked Aunt Hazel.

"She came in from church all quiet and emotional. Went straight to her room and shut the door. Said she'd be out when lunch was ready," Aunt Hazel answered in a preoccupied manner.

Jake knew that when his mother exhibited that kind of behavior, it was best to give her some time alone. Deciding to take another crack at Gerald, he walked over and plopped down on the couch next to the chair where Gerald sat, garbed in a faded pair of overalls. He still had on the same white shirt he had worn to church but now the sleeves were rolled up and the tie was gone. His feet, comfortably propped up on a stool in front of the chair, were shod with farmer's work boots stained in the colors of grass and dirt. Mindlessly gazing at the television, Gerald did not even notice that Jake had taken a seat next to him.

"Whatcha watchin'?" Jake asked.

Gerald slowly turned his head and looked at Jake as if he had just asked the dumbest question in the world. "TV. I'm watchin' TV," he answered with irritation in his voice.

Nodding his head in Gerald's direction, Jake smiled and said, "I think I'll go help in the kitchen."

"Uh-huh," Gerald nonchalantly replied, turning his head back toward the television.

As Jake passed the table, he couldn't resist grabbing a couple of cucumbers out of the dish and popping them in his mouth. Sammi was filling the Sunday glasses with sweet tea and Betty was regaling Aunt Hazel with all the gossip she had heard in Sunday school that morning. Jake was amused seeing that his aunt was only half listening as she busied herself with the final touches to the table. At long last, she instructed Jake to tell his mom to join them at the table. When all were seated, Aunt Hazel took the hands of those on each side of her and waited for everyone to follow suit.

Once everyone was holding hands, she bowed her head and prayed, "Heavenly Father, we thank Thee for all these and Thy many blessings. Forgive us our sins for Christ's sake. Amen...Brother Ben shot a rooster, but killed a hen."

As soon as the prayer ended, everyone started filling their plates with food, but Jake raised a curious brow toward his aunt and asked, "Excuse me, but what was the last part of that prayer, something about *Brother Ben and a rooster*?"

Aunt Hazel gave no reply other than a mischievous smile.

Sammi laughed, "Your aunt is known for turnin' a colorful phrase. We just go with it."

"But it made no sense," Jake argued. "How do you shoot a rooster, but kill a hen? Did the rooster duck? Did the hen jump in front of the rooster to try to save it? I don't understand."

Giving him a firm punch on the leg, Sammi leaned toward him and reiterated, "We just go with it, Jake." Then handing him a plate, she said, "Here, have some fried chicken."

"How do I know it's not a rooster?" he asked with a flippant grin.

As the lunch conversation continued, Jo's spirits began to pick up and she joined in. "I guess me and Jake need to find some jobs pretty soon. Do y'all know of any places 'round here that are hirin'?"

"I work part time at Newlin Grocery," Sammi said. "I think I heard someone say the other day that they're hirin' part-time stockers and baggers. I'm scheduled to work Tuesday, Jake. If you wanna take me to work, I can introduce you to the owner. I bet he'll hire you right away, especially with the Fourth of July just bein' around the corner."

"The Tavern is always hiring," Betty said to Jo. "If you worked there, you wouldn't have to drive. It's just across from the entrance to the trailer park."

Jo's eyes lit up with this news. The Tavern was a restaurant during the week, but was transformed into a bar and dance hall on weekends. This was right up her alley, and the fact that it was so close made it even more appealing. But Betty's suggestion was very unsettling to Jake who knew that the atmosphere of a tavern could send his mother back to old habits.

"Maybe you should think about that before plunging in, Mom," Jake suggested.

"What you talkin' about, Baby Boy?" Jo asked. "We need to start makin' some money and this sounds perfect. Besides, we only have one car. Workin' at a place that's within walkin' distance is perfect for me and that way you can use the car for work and school. Nope, my mind's made up. First thing tomorrow, I'm applyin' for a job at the Tavern."

A sense of dread flooded Jake's heart. He knew his mother's weaknesses, and he knew what kind of people frequented taverns, especially on weekends. Jo was only thirty-two years old and very beautiful, but had always found it difficult to deny the sexual advances of needy, flirtatious men—especially the men who liked to flash their money. But it wasn't the men Jake feared the most. It was the drugs. The men usually became the means to the drugs, and the drugs always brought hell into Jake's world.

Sensing her son's discomfort, Jo tried bravely to cast a reassuring smile toward him. "Don't worry, Son, everything'll be okay."

But Jake wasn't so certain. He knew his mother too well. He also knew that Jo was going to do what Jo wanted to do. He looked with concern across the table at her, shook his head, and grabbed another piece of chicken off the plate. Biting down on a crispy chicken leg, he looked at his aunt and said, "Best rooster I've ever put in my mouth."

10

After lunch, Jake and Sammi helped clean up by washing the dishes then spent the rest of the afternoon lounging in front of the television watching old movies. Truth be told though, Jake's mind was not so much on the movies as it was on their plans to meet at midnight. He wanted to answer her questions about the scars, but he didn't want to frighten her off with the horror stories that had characterized his life.

He kept rehearsing over and over in his mind what he would say and how much he would tell her. He had always longed for someone in his life he could talk to about the messy stuff, someone he could be real with, but you can't find a friend like that moving from town to town every year. He had never had a close relationship with anyone, not even other guys.

His whole life had been focused on taking care of his dysfunctional mother and keeping her out of trouble. To maintain his own sanity, he had poured himself into reading, devouring any piece of literature he could get his hands on. He found a means of escape by losing himself in his books, but lately it wasn't enough. He needed a friend, an actual person he could share his thoughts with. Maybe Sammi could be that person.

Jake became anxious thinking about opening up to Sammi, fearful that this thing with her, whatever it was, would end if he told her too much. She was a normal, beautiful, small-town girl who had enjoyed a simple life. His life, on the other hand, had been anything but simple, and he didn't know if she would be comfortable around him once she knew everything. But he knew he had to try opening up to her.

When the second movie ended, Sammi stretched and yawned. "I'm gonna go home for a bit, maybe take a nap," she said.

As she stood up to leave, Jake stood also and walked her out. "Are we still on for midnight?" he asked.

"Yes," she affirmed with a smile. "I'll come over and help you rob the fridge. I want more of that cherry pie. See you soon, okay?"

"Okay," he replied. He couldn't take his eyes off of her as she crossed the yard to her trailer. She had this cute habit of shoving her hands in her back pockets when she walked. It was adorable to Jake. Back inside, he decided to go to his room and try to get some rest before midnight. However, his mind wouldn't shut down long enough to let him sleep. He kept rehearsing what he was going to say to her. Even reading didn't work this time and the hours moved on slowly.

Every time he glanced at the clock, it seemed that only minutes had passed since the last time he'd looked. As midnight approached, he slipped out of bed and walked over to the window to see if anyone was stirring at Sammi's. At about 12:02, he saw her bouncing across the yard, carrying what appeared to be a small basket. Jake let her in and, operating only by the light that came from the refrigerator, they filled the basket with leftovers from lunch. Once the basket was full, they slipped quietly out the door and headed for the rooftop.

Earlier in the evening, Sammi had placed the quilt, her record player and the box of records in their usual spot on the roof.

As they spread the food out on the quilt, Jake couldn't help but notice that the stars seemed brighter than usual and there seemed to be more of them tonight. A soft warm breeze added a sense of tranquility to the atmosphere as they sat down to enjoy a late-night snack of cold fried chicken and cherry pie. There wasn't much conversation while they ate. Jake was too busy mentally preparing what he was going to say to Sammi when the conversation inevitably turned to the subject she had brought up while they were at the river.

Sammi could see that he was in deep thought so she decided to wait and let him bring up the subject of the scars on his back. She started cleaning up some of the trash from their late-night picnic and, being the helper that he was, he didn't let her clean up by herself. After everything was put away, they sat side by side in silence for several minutes, gazing intently into the starry expanse above them. The silence was interrupted when a shooting star fell across the sky prompting Jake to offer another free astronomy lecture. Sammi listened quietly, enjoying the enthusiasm her new friend exhibited when talking about things that were exciting to him. When the lecture was over, he knew it was time to open up a little about his past, knowing how much he would choose to reveal would depend on her response to what she was hearing.

"Do you still want to know about the scars on my back?" he asked.

"Yes, but only if you want to tell me," she replied. "I have a rule I want us to follow as long as we are friends, Jake. When we're gonna talk to each other about somethin' serious, I want us to face each other and sit crossed-legged, knee to knee. That way we can always be sure the other is listenin'. Deal?"

"Deal. Jake agreed.

They turned toward each other as she had requested. Once they were settled, she fixed her gaze on him and said, "I'm all ears."

Jake took one last moment to collect his thoughts and then began unfolding his story to Sammi. "In order to explain the scars, I have to go back to the time when my parents first came together. They met when they were in high school, and I've been told that before they started dating, my mom was doing well in school. She was very smart and had lots of potential, but when she met my dad, she kind of lost her way. He was a drug dealer and it wasn't long before he got her hooked on cocaine. He also got her pregnant with me when she was only fifteen, which is why she looks so young. A lot of people mistake her for my older sister. I don't remember much about the first five years of my life, other than the fact that we lived mostly in hotel rooms that I assume my dad paid for with drug money. I also remember my mom sleeping a lot because he kept her high most of the time. Occasionally, he would bring strange men to the room, hand me a coloring book and send me to the bathroom. He told me to color the pictures and not come out until he called. It was several years later before I figured out what was really going on."

Jake paused in an effort to check his emotions. Sammi sat in silence with her eyes still fastened on him. He continued, "I can remember him yelling at her a lot and slapping her around. I hated him for that. Then one day, when I was five years old, the police showed up at the hotel and took Mom out into the parking lot to talk to her. As I was watching from the window, I saw her start to cry. After a few minutes, she came back into the room and told me that my daddy was not coming back and that we wouldn't see him anymore. I actually remember feeling a sense of relief when she told me that. I didn't shed a single tear. A few years later, I learned that he had been shot to death during a drug deal. After his death, Mom got tangled up with some really bad people. She never finished high school and because she was still a cocaine addict, she made money the only way she knew how—by selling her body. She's always been pretty and because of her looks, she has never lacked for male attention. Over the next several years, this became a way of life for us. She tried to hide it from me by telling me that all these men who kept coming around were just friends who had come to help her out, but by then I knew what was going on. I knew what it meant when she asked me to leave the room for an hour or so. I can't tell you the number of times I came back and found her passed out on the floor with a needle still in her arm."

Sammi could see her new friend struggling as he unfolded his life to her and placed her hand on top of his to comfort him. This assured Jake that it was safe to continue. "She saw a lot of men, but there still never seemed to be enough money. What she earned primarily supported her addiction. Often, after she would wake up, she would see me sitting beside her on the floor crying. That made her feel bad so she would take me to McDonalds or some other place where she could buy me an ice cream to make me feel better. But her addiction left little room for any other expenses. The things that most kids take for granted eluded me throughout my childhood. There were never presents under the tree at Christmas and, more times than not, there wasn't even a tree. There were times she even forgot my birthday. Pretty soon we started moving from town to town to get away from the bad people in our lives, but it wouldn't be long after we moved to a new town that she would meet more bad people. She's always been a magnet for trouble. She kept me in school, but she never attended school functions, and it never seemed to bother her that I had to change schools every time we moved. It became so hard to make friends that I just gave up even trying."

Sammi's heart broke for Jake. She could hear the pain in his voice as he spoke of his past. As he opened up, she began to think that maybe her mother did her a favor by leaving when she was a baby. She placed her hand on his knee and asked, "Why didn't you leave or ask someone for help?"

He replied, "Because there was some good buried deep down in her that surfaced from time to time and that always gave me hope. There were times she even got clean, and I thought we might be off to a new start. When she wasn't using, I felt like I was seeing the real Jo Ledger and I enjoyed being around that person. She could be very compassionate and even doting. But, sooner or later, the old demons always came knocking, and when the drugs got her again, she went from being a caring mom to being the mistress of Satan." He paused for a moment, then added, "But, as difficult as life has been with her, I still love her. She's my mother and I have always been afraid that if I left, she might die. Our relationship has always been reversed; I'm the parent and she's the child, so I feel responsible for her."

After a few moments of reflective silence, Sammi asked, "So where did the scars come from? Did they come from some of her bad friends?"

"No," he answered. "They came from her. Mom has a dark side; a *very* dark side. My father physically and emotionally abused her from the day they got together until the day he was killed. When he died, the abuse continued through her so-called friends who would often show up drunk or high. Some of them would have sex with my mother and then beat her black and blue. She tried to fight back, but she was so small that she could never fend off her abusers. She just took all the anger, all the rage, and buried it deep inside. She became a very angry woman and since I was the only other person in her life, she took her anger out on me. I never knew when she was going to explode and it seemed that the smallest things set her off. Once she lost control, she would come at me with anything that would fit in her hand. She had a very creative and assorted arsenal. Over the years she's hit me with plates, sticks, frying pans, and more than a few times, she came after me with my own baseball bat. The scar on my shoulder-blade and the scar next to my spine are from a kitchen knife. The jagged scar above my waist is from a broken bottle. Those were all very painful, but her deadliest weapon, the one that hurt me the most, was her tongue. The horrible things she used to say to me and about me tormented me. She never had to answer to anyone for her abuse because we moved around so much. No one ever got close enough to us to see what was going on and I could not bring myself to turn her in. So it just became a part of who I was, who we were."

Jake took a deep, shaky breath, trying to calm himself as he continued. "I'll never forget the first time she drew blood. As soon as I screamed out in pain, her whole demeanor changed. She dropped the knife and immediately started telling me how sorry she was. She grabbed a wet cloth from the bathroom and made me sit down in front of the mirror while she tended to the wound. I thought about running away that night, but while she was wiping the blood off my back, I could see her crying in the mirror. I can't explain it even to this day, but when I saw her tears, I felt pity instead of hate. I could see how lost she was. I saw genuine fear in her eyes that night and all I wanted to do was put my arms around her and tell her everything would be alright."

Sammi desperately wanted to respond, but emotion choked her attempts to speak. She prided herself on being a good judge of character and she knew in her heart that Jake Ledger was a good person. *He didn't deserve this*, she thought to herself. For the next minute or so, she sat in silence before him, trying to find words that would comfort the pain she could see in his eyes, but nothing seemed adequate. After a few more moments passed, she reached up, cupped his face in both of her hands, and said, "Everything's gonna be alright, Jake." Standing to her feet, she motioned for him to stay seated. She walked over to the box of records, fumbling through them until she found what she was looking for.

"There's a song I want you to hear," she said softly. "It's one of my favorite new songs. It's about a songbird. Have you ever heard it?"

"I think so," Jake answered, though he was certain he had never heard it.

Sammi started the song, then walked over and stood in front of Jake who was still sitting cross-legged on the butterfly quilt. Locking eyes with him, she reached out her hands towards him and said softly, "I wanna dance with you, Jake Ledger."

As he took her hands and stood to his feet, she moved in close, placed her arms around his shoulders, and gently pressed her cheek against his. She was so close that he could feel her breath on his neck. Resting his hands on her waist, they began to sway slowly back and forth to the music. As he listened to the lyrics, he understood why she'd chosen this song. The words promised that there would come a day when there would be no more crying and no more darkness or pain. When the song ended, Sammi kissed Jake's cheek, then softly whispered in his ear, "Everything's gonna be alright, I promise."

Jake put his arms completely around her, tightening his hold. He didn't want to let go. He felt like a man who had just found a buoy after being adrift at sea for days. Something about her made him feel safe. The words she whispered in his ear gave him a sense of hope. She told him that everything would be alright...and he believed her.

11

JAKE HASTENED DOWN THE SIDEWALK
toward the bank where his aunt worked. In his right hand
he clutched a small wad of cash. It was only $152 but to
him it was a veritable treasure. It felt good to finally have
a little money of his own. True to her word, Sammi had
helped him get a job at the grocery store, stocking shelves
and bagging groceries. Today was Friday and every Friday
was payday at Newlin's.

Before the doors were opened to the public, the store
manager called each employee into his office and counted
out in cash the wages that were due to each. The moment
his lunch hour rolled around, Jake darted out the door
and headed for the bank which was just one block down
from the store. His excitement increased with each step. In
just a matter of minutes he would be opening his very first
bank account.

Because he was not eighteen years old yet, Aunt Hazel
had agreed to put her name on the account also, but the
account would be all his. This was his first pay from the
grocery store. The timing could not have been more perfect

because the Fourth of July was just days away, and he wanted to have his own spending money.

Sammi had informed him of all the festivities that occurred in Kernersville on July Fourth. There would be a Main Street parade in the morning followed by the annual Hope Park cookout with all the trailer park neighbors. That evening, there would be a festival in the city park that included rides, music, dancing, food, and fireworks. There would also be booths set up by local retailers selling their merchandise. Even though Jake and Sammi were still just friends, he wanted to have enough cash to spoil her a little bit. With Aunt Hazel's help, it only took a few minutes to open the account. Jake put a hundred dollars in savings, kept $52 and 75 cents for himself, and headed back to the grocery store.

Counting his money as he stepped out onto the sidewalk, Jake didn't realize that another person was approaching the bank entrance. Collision was unavoidable as the two crashed into one another with force. Jake quickly stepped back and started to offer an apology until he realized who was standing in front of him: Scott Robertson. With the instincts of a vicious, untamed beast, Scott firmly planted both of his open palms on Jake's chest and shoved him backwards.

"Look where you're goin', trailer trash." Scott barked.

Not being one to be so easily intimidated, Jake charged toward Scott and returned the shove with enough strength to push him back quite a few feet. Scott was about to retaliate when he noticed that a police officer, who had been sitting in his car outside the bank, had observed the scuffle and was getting out of his car to prevent any further trouble.

Scott put his hand up toward the policeman and said, "It's okay, Officer. Just havin' a little fun with my friend." The officer seemed satisfied and slowly returned to his vehicle, but Jake's stomach churned at the thought of being friends with anyone like Scott Robertson.

Scott sneered at Jake. "I'm surprised to see trailer trash like you comin' out of a bank. You must have just robbed the place 'cause I know you ain't got no money."

Jake just shook his head, "Between the two of us, Scott, I'd say you're the one most likely to rob a bank. Now if you don't mind, I have to get back to work." With those words Jake turned to head back to the store.

"I've got a message for you to give to your little girlfriend," Scott said. "Tell her that one way or another, she's gonna keep the promise she made to me in front of the gazebo."

Jake's blood began to boil. Spinning back around to face Scott, he asked angrily, "What promise are you talking about?"

Scott shook his head in derision. "That's not for you to worry about. You just give her the message. She'll know what I'm talkin' about."

As Scott turned to walk into the bank, Jake yelled, "She doesn't owe you a thing, Robertson!"

"We'll see," Scott replied smugly as he disappeared into the bank.

When Jake returned to the store, he saw that a long line had formed at the cash register that Sammi was manning. The store only had two other baggers, Robbie and Wendell, and both were in the back unloading a truck. Donning his bagger apron, Jake quickly jumped in to assist, even though several minutes still remained on his lunch break. The look of relief on Sammi's face was worth the time lost.

As the line dwindled, Jake noticed a little boy about ten years old patiently waiting for his turn at the register. He seemed to be alone. His clothes were dirty and tattered and his face was smudged. In one hand, he held two large candy bars and in the other he jingled a few coins with which he intended to pay for the bars. When his turn came, he placed the bars on the counter in front of Sammi and proudly threw down the coins next to them. Sammi counted the change, but it wasn't enough. Looking with compassion into the little boy's soiled face, she said, "You're about twenty-five cents short here, Sweetie. Do you have a quarter?"

The expression of embarrassment on the boy's face answered the question, but Sammi didn't have any personal change on her, and letting the boy slide would get her in trouble with the owner. Her heart went out to the little guy, but there was nothing she could do. The boy stood in front of her motionless and speechless as if he wasn't sure what to do next. Realizing the awkwardness of the moment, Jake reached into his pocket, drew out a quarter, and handed it to Sammi.

She looked at the young patron, smiled and said, "You're good to go, Sweetie. Enjoy that candy."

A large grin came across the boy's face as he grabbed the candy bars and bolted toward the door. Just before exiting, he stopped, turned to Jake and gave him a nod of appreciation. Jake nodded back and smiled as the little boy ran out the door.

"That was the sweetest thing I've ever seen," Sammi said, gazing at Jake with admiration.

"It was just a quarter," he replied humbly.

"Still, it's somethin' that little guy will never forget," she said.

The rest of the afternoon went by quickly as droves of customers flooded the store to stock up on their Fourth of July supplies. The shelves emptied out quickly even though Robbie, Wendell, and Jake made numerous runs back and forth to the stock room trying to keep up with customer demand. The next day was Saturday, and it seemed that they were even busier than the day before. All the staff was on hand to meet the demands, but it was a long, tiring day.

The store was closed on Sunday to honor the Lord's Day and Jake was glad for the opportunity to rest. This Sunday was just like all the others he had experienced from the time he and his mom first moved in with Aunt Hazel; there was always a big Sunday breakfast ready and waiting as soon as they woke up; Jake, Jo, and Sammi rode to church together; and after church, there was always a big lunch. To help her tenants get to know the neighbors, Aunt Hazel invited someone different each Sunday, but Sammi was a regular at the table every single week, which greatly delighted Jake.

After lunch that Sunday, the two teens went out to the gazebo and sat on the floor for the next several hours playing card games and talking about all their plans for the next day. Jake's anticipation increased as they continued to lay out their steps for the Fourth of July. Sammi suggested that after breakfast, they drive the Nova into town early so they could find parking.

"The parade starts at 10:30 so we can just walk around town until then," she said. "I know where the best spot is to watch the parade, but we need to be there by 10:00 o'clock, or it'll get crowded."

"I'll follow your lead," Jake said as he threw down the winning hand of Gin Rummy.

As the sun began to set, Jake realized how quickly time went by when he was with Sammi. He had never had anyone in his life that he could talk to so easily. He felt comfortable just being himself around her. There was absolutely no pretense when they were together, and he could talk about whatever was on his mind without feeling any judgment or condemnation. Regardless of where things might go with them, Jake knew he had a friend for life. But deep inside, he also knew he wanted much more than friendship.

Sammi was the last thing on his mind when he fell asleep at night and the first thing on his mind when he woke up in the morning. There were so many times when he was tempted to lean in and kiss her, but the words his aunt spoke to him about being her friend first always prevented him from acting on his desires. He knew there would be a time when he would no longer be able to hold back his true feelings for her, but he also knew if he rushed it, things might fall apart. He did not want to risk losing what they had already built between them.

Just as Sammi was about to deal another hand, Jo poked her head out from the screen door, "Time for supper, Jake!"

"Be right there," he responded. Then, smiling at Sammi, he said, "I guess I'll have to whip you again on another day. You going in now?"

"No," Sammi replied. "I think I'll stay out here for a bit longer 'n see if I can spot the first star that comes out tonight."

"Alright. I'll see you in the morning," Jake said as he stood up to head toward the trailer.

"I can't wait," she replied.

"Me either," he said as he stepped off the bottom step of the gazebo.

He was about to turn and walk away when Sammi spoke up, "I mean what I just said, Jake. I really enjoy spendin' time with you. You might just be the best friend I've ever had."

The tenderness and vulnerability in her voice touched his heart. No one had ever said anything like that to him before. He took a step towards her, wanting to reply, but all the possible responses that popped into his head seemed meager at best. In fact, he was afraid to speak for fear of ruining the sudden intimacy of this unexpected encounter between them. He didn't take another step. He knew that if he moved any closer, he may not be able to contain the passion that her words had just ignited. As he stood there for a few seconds in silence, a demure smile fell across her lips which made her appear even more sweet and vulnerable to Jake. It felt to him as if she was opening another part of her heart to him.

"Better get to the supper table," Sammi said softly as he stepped toward the lane. "Don't wanna keep Aunt Hazel waitin'."

He smiled and nodded in agreement, then walked toward the trailer without saying a word. Once he was safely behind the screen door, he turned to look back toward the gazebo. She was now sitting on the bench gazing reflectively into the evening sky. Paralyzed by her stunning beauty, Jake pondered the tender words she had just spoken to him and, with a smile on his face, stepped inside to join the ladies for supper. But his thoughts were on her throughout the entire meal.

There was no question about it. He knew that he'd fallen in love with her, but for now he felt he must keep this to himself. He thought about what she'd just said to him, that he "might just be the best friend she ever had." He asked himself: *Is that all she wants from me right now? Aren't lovers also supposed to be friends*? His heart was overcome with both delight and dismay; delight that she had given him such a place of importance in her life, but dismay at the possibility that he may never be anything more than *"the best friend she ever had."*

Jake woke up early after a sleepless night of tossing back and forth between excitement and torment. At long last, the light of dawn began to break through the bedroom window and he didn't waste any time jumping out of bed. He wanted to look his best since he would be with Sammi all day. After a quick shower, he shaved what little stubble he had on his face, splashed an overly abundant amount of English Leather on his chest and neck, wrapped the lower half of his body in a towel, and darted out of the bathroom.

Thinking he was the only one awake, he removed the towel and tossed it in the clothes basket in the hallway before returning to his room. Startled by a horrified scream coming from the kitchen, he suddenly realized that he was, in fact, not the only one awake. Poking his head out of his room to find the source of the scream, Jake was mortified to see his aunt standing in the kitchen with her red, white, and blue apron pulled up over her eyes. *I'll apologize later*, he thought to himself, and quickly disappeared into his room.

Breakfast was awkward, but Aunt Hazel was a good sport and apparently had decided not to say a word. Before Jake could swallow his last bite of bacon and eggs, Sammi was coming through the door.

"Are you ready?" she asked eagerly.

"Yes, let me get my wallet and keys," he answered, as he headed back to his room to grab them from where they lay on his dresser.

"You stayin' for the fireworks tonight?" Sammi asked Hazel and Jo.

"Wouldn't miss it," Jo stated emphatically.

"Somebody already tried to set off some fireworks this mornin'," Hazel said, grinning at Jake who had just emerged from his room with keys in hand.

"What?" Sammi asked with a look of confusion.

"Uh, never mind," he said, turning red and nudging her toward the door. "It's not important. We'll see you two in town later." Jake gave his aunt a stern look as she closed the door behind him.

Once in town, Sammi was like a four-year-old at the zoo, running from store window to store window, dragging Jake every step of the way. Her enthusiasm was contagious, especially when they came upon her favorite store, Sweet Little Things. It was just a trinket store, but he could see that she loved it. There was a gleam in her eye as she moved through the store examining one shiny treasure after another. At first, Jake didn't think there would be anything in the store that would be of interest to him. But then, something caught his eye. On one of the racks, there was a cluster of necklaces with a variety of pendants. One pendant in particular grabbed his attention. It was a beautiful silver butterfly and it was the only one of its kind on the rack.

Though it was not even five dollars, there was something refined and elegant about it. He immediately knew that he had to get it for her. He had seen some of her other butterfly jewelry, but he had never seen her wear a necklace. The trick would be making the purchase without her knowledge.

Removing the necklace from the rack, he concealed it in his hand so she couldn't see it. The store was crowded and several registers were open to accommodate the shoppers, so as soon as a register became free, Jake slipped away from Sammi, whose attention was on a counter full of hair ribbons. He managed to purchase the butterfly necklace and return to her without her even realizing he was gone; he was quite proud of himself. A busy store did not seem to be the right place to give it to her, so he stuffed the necklace in his pocket and decided to wait for the perfect time and place.

"We better go if we want to get that good spot for the parade," she said.

Jake nodded his head in agreement and the two of them headed toward the door. There were so many people out on the street that Sammi grabbed his hand so as not to get separated. It didn't take long to reach the special spot she had described. It was a slightly elevated portion of the sidewalk providing a long-range view of Main Street. As 10:30 approached, hordes of people came pouring out of the stores like an army of ants and began lining the street on both sides in anticipation of the parade. Many of them were waving small flags demonstrating their patriotism. People were laughing and talking, children were playing in the street that had been blocked off for the parade, and a vendor was walking up and down the street handing out small paper bags of popcorn at no charge.

The sights and sounds were intoxicating to Jake. He couldn't remember a time when he had felt happier than he was at that moment. It wasn't long before everyone heard the *woop-woop* blast of the sheriff's siren signaling that the parade was beginning. Behind the sheriff's car was the high school band playing a medley of patriotic songs. Following the band were clowns, some of whom were riding very small tricycles with outlandish front wheels. The clowns were followed by a team of cloggers from the local dance studio. After the cloggers passed by, there was a brief lull in activity as the next group had fallen behind slightly.

It was then that Jake saw him—she hadn't noticed him yet—but across the street, Scott Robertson with his stooges, Eric and Jonathan, were attempting to blend in with the crowd packing the other side of the street. But Scott was not watching the parade. His cold, dark eyes were focused directly on Sammi. Even when the parade picked back up again, he never turned his gaze away from her.

Jake wanted Sammi to enjoy the parade so he chose not to tell her. He couldn't help but wonder what kind of evil thoughts were coursing through Scott's mind. A moment of dread came over him as he wondered how far Scott would go to make his wicked thoughts a reality. As soon as the parade ended, he hurried her back to the car, wanting to remove her far from any potential harm. When she asked him why he was in such a rush, he told her he was hungry and wanted to get back to Hope Park for the picnic.

"I don't believe you are *that* hungry," she said with suspicion in her voice. "Why the hurry?"

"I told you," Jake replied. "You know how the neighbors pounce on the food. I just want to make sure we get something to eat."

Sammi stared at Jake with her brow furrowed. He looked straight ahead as he drove, trying to avoid eye contact. "Jake," she said. "We haven't been friends long, but I can tell when you're bothered. Don't lie to me. What's goin' on?"

Jake relented. "Okay, okay. It was Scott. He was across the street from us and he never took his eyes off of you through the whole parade. I was worried that he might try to hurt you."

"I know," Sammi confessed. "I saw him too, but I ignored him because we can't let him worry us. He can only have as much control over us as we give him. So I choose not to give him any power over me at all. I think you're startin' to obsess over him and he's just *not* worth it, Jake."

"You're right about all of that. But I still think we need to be cautious. Personally, I think he is a budding psychopath, and a psychopath can be very dangerous. I'm just looking out for you, Sammi."

"I know you are," she replied smiling. "Best friend I've ever had!"

The rest of the afternoon was like a day in heaven. The picnic lunch with the neighbors was a lot of fun and afterwards, Sammi and Jake gathered the younger children in the field behind the gazebo for a game of kickball. He was impressed with how well all the children took to her, but he was even more impressed with how well she took to them. She truly seemed to enjoy playing with each of them. She didn't even seem to mind when a couple of the little boys decided to tackle her to the ground. They remained outside playing games until it was time to leave for the festival at City Park. Hazel and Jo were tired and decided to come later for the fireworks, but Jake and Sammi didn't want to miss anything, so they left early.

City Park was decorated in varying hues of red, white, and blue. Poles bearing huge flags lined the paved path that led to the entrance of the park. As Jake and Sammi entered the front gate, they were overwhelmed by an exciting variety of sights and sounds. To their left was the carousel with a long line of children waiting to mount the brightly painted steeds. To their right was another string of children with their parents waiting to board a small red train that ran on miniature tracks circling the park. Beyond the train station was a large, open grassy area with a stage set up in the center where bands were scheduled to entertain the crowds until it was time for the fireworks.

Another section of the park had been designated for more rides and yet another section was set aside for eating. A steamy, cloud of smoke hovered over the food vendors as they cooked their meats and other delicacies over open fire pits. The whole park buzzed with unbridled celebration. Jake and Sammi decided to start with the carousel and work their way to the right around the entire park.

As the evening wore on, he began looking for an ideal time to give her the butterfly necklace. That opportunity presented itself when they came to the Ferris wheel. Just before climbing into the seat, he reached into his pocket and pulled out the necklace, keeping it hidden from her view. After five spins, the attendant stopped so that those who had been riding could get off and the new riders could get on. Jake figured there would be a moment when they would be stopped at the very top and that would be the perfect place and time to give her the gift.

His calculations were correct. Just as they reached the very top, the Ferris wheel came to a gentle stop, causing the seat to slightly sway back and forth. He knew he only had a few minutes, if that long. The setting was perfect. They were so high above the hullabaloo below that the sounds of the City Park Fourth of July festival seemed muffled. The sun had set so they were surrounded by the starry night sky. As the Ferris wheel rocked gently to a stop, Sammi looked down on the crowd below and seemed mesmerized by the view.

It took a few seconds, but finally getting up his nerve, Jake cleared his throat. "Uh, Sammi? There's something I want to say to you before we get off the Ferris wheel."

She turned toward him. "What is it, Jake?"

"Well," he continued. "Like I've already told you, I have been pulled from one town to another for most of my life which has made it difficult for me to make any close friends. I've always felt like I was alone. But from the moment we pulled into Hope Park, you have been a friend to me, a good friend. I feel like I can tell you anything and it wouldn't matter what it is; you would still be my friend. I just want you to know that, since I met you, I don't feel alone anymore. I've wanted to show you how much your friendship means to me, so today while we were at the trinket store, I got something for you when you weren't looking."

Opening his hand, he revealed the butterfly necklace. Sammi's face beamed. Tears filled her eyes as she took it from him, but it wasn't the gift that was making her cry; it was his words. She turned the pendant over and over in her hands examining every detail.

"I love this," she said. "I'll wear it forever."

She turned her back to Jake and, lifting her hair off of her shoulders, motioned for him to help fasten it around her neck. When his fingers brushed across her bare neck, it caused his hands to shake a little. This made it challenging to fasten the clasp, but he was finally able to secure it in place.

Turning back to him, she said, "Now, I want to be honest with you. I know we have only known each other for a few weeks, but you are the best friend I've ever had.

I've never been close to any boys because they all seem to want one thing from me and when they find out I'm not that kind of girl, they move on. And I've never really had any girlfriends because the girls at school always seem to be mad at me. My grandma says they're jealous. But the truth is, Jake, I didn't realize how lonely I was until we met. You make me laugh; you make me cry; when I talk to you, you look me straight in the eyes; and you never turn away. You even seem to be able to hear what I'm not sayin'. It's like you can hear my thoughts. I've never had anyone to listen to me like that, not even my grandparents. I feel safe when I'm with you."

Jake was rendered speechless by the things he had just heard Sammi say. In that moment he wanted nothing more than to kiss her, but he didn't want to seem like all the other boys whose intentions toward her were clearly rooted in lust. He now understood more than ever that he must set himself apart from them. Though it was getting harder and harder each day to pull off, he was determined to be her friend first.

After getting off the Ferris wheel, they walked over to the food vendors and enjoyed a juicy barbeque sandwich and hot crispy fries. As they talked, they could hear a country music band playing in the background, the screams from those who were still enjoying the rides, and children laughing and playing. But none of those things distracted them from each other. For the next hour, they continued opening their hearts to each other, revealing secrets they had never shared with anyone else. They would have kept talking and walking, but all the festivities came to a screeching halt as the lights began to go out. It was time for the fireworks.

The show lasted for about twenty minutes. From time to time, Jake looked over at Sammi whose eyes were fixed on the sparkling lights in the sky. He couldn't help but smile as he noticed that she held the butterfly pendant between her thumb and forefinger, never letting it go. When the fireworks ended, an announcement came over the speaker that the park would remain open until midnight, but Sammi was tired and asked Jake to take her home because she had to work the next day. So they began the long trek back to the car, which was located on the far side of the parking lot. There were a few other stragglers making their way out of the park, but most of the crowd had apparently decided to stay until midnight. They were only a few yards from the Nova when they both heard something that stopped them cold. Someone was approaching them from behind.

"How long you gonna keep draggin' that mangy mutt around, Sammi? He's startin' to smell the place up." The taunting words belonged to none other than Scott Robertson. Jake pushed Sammi toward the car, then wheeled around to face Scott. Once again, he was outnumbered three to one, but Jake refused to let Scott's remarks intimidate him.

"I've had about all I'm gonna take of your mouth, Scott," Jake boldly stated.

"Poor little fella," Scott sneered. "Have I hurt your tender little heart? Have I somehow insulted you?"

Shaking his head in derision, Jake replied, "In order for you to insult me I would first have to value your opinion, which I don't; and, since you appear to have the genetic makeup of an ape, I don't plan on wasting my time listening to another word you say." Backing towards his car, he said, "Let's go home, Sammi."

"What's genetic makeup?" Eric asked with a look of confusion on his face.

"Never mind, you stupid idiot," Scott fumed. "Let's do what we came here to do."

At Scott's command, Eric and Jonathan began to position themselves on either side of Jake. As they moved in on him, Scott threatened, "We're gonna take care of you and then little Miss Sammi over there is gonna keep a promise she made to me a few weeks ago."

As soon as he spoke those threatening words, Jonathan and Eric grabbed Jake and pinned him against a car. Before he had time to react, Scott pounced on him, throwing one punch after another into Jake's stomach. Jake tried to break the hold the other two had on him but with each punch to the stomach, he grew weaker and weaker.

"Go on and knock him out before she gets away!" Eric yelled.

"Alright," Scott said. "Hold his head up so I can get a clear shot to his face."

Scott drew his fist back, but just as he was about to land a final punch to Jake's jaw, he suddenly screamed out in pain, clutched his groin, and slowly dropped to the ground. A look of confusion came across the faces of Jonathan and Eric. Jake was also wondering what had happened. As Scott slumped to the ground, they were all surprised to see Sammi standing directly behind him. She had kicked Scott squarely and firmly in his most sensitive area and, judging by the sound he was making, he was definitely down for the count.

Realizing his opportunity, Jake jerked his arm free from Jonathan and smashed him twice in the nose with his elbow, letting loose a gushing river of blood. As he turned to face Eric, he saw that Sammi was already approaching him.

Apparently fearing that he might suffer the same fate as Scott, and realizing *he* was now outnumbered, Eric quickly covered his groin with his hands and backed up behind the car on which he'd just been helping pin Jake.

"Come on," Jake said, grabbing Sammi by the arm. "Let's get out of here before they get up."

They started for the car, but then without warning, Jake suddenly stopped, released Sammi's arm and turned back toward Scott who was still lying on the ground, clutching groin and groaning in pain. Jake grabbed him by the hair on top of his head and sat him up. Looking him right in the eyes, Jake gave Scott one last warning to stay away from Sammi before he drove his fist hard into Scott's mouth, busting his lip open.

As they sped out of the parking lot a minute later, Jake looked at Sammi in shock, "That was amazing! Where did you learn to kick like that?"

Sammi answered, "When I reached puberty, my grandma made me take karate lessons at the YMCA. She said she would sleep better at night knowin' I knew how to defend myself."

Jake started laughing and Sammi joined in. Soon they were both laughing uncontrollably.

"Did you hear Scott scream?" Sammi asked between giggles. "He sounded like a little girl!"

"Yes, he did!" Jake agreed wholeheartedly. "And did you see Eric jump behind that car covering himself...down there?"

"That *was* hilarious!" she replied.

"You are full of surprises, Girl!" Jake said with pride. "Maybe you should go into professional wrestling."

All the way home, they kept laughing and rehearsing the events that had unfolded in the parking lot. Once they arrived back at Hope Park, they sat in the car for a few minutes, still riding the adrenaline rush.

"Wow!" Jake said, scratching his head. "I still can't believe what just happened. That's the most excitement I've ever had."

Sammi just smiled and nodded. After a few moments of silence, she reached down and grabbed the butterfly pendant hanging around her neck. "Thank you so much, again," she said. "Out of everything that happened tonight, this is what meant the most."

"I'm glad you like it," Jake replied.

Another few moments of silence passed as Sammi admired the butterfly necklace that dangled from her neck. By the look in her eyes, Jake could tell that she really liked the gift he had given her. He didn't want to put a damper on the victory they had just been celebrating, but a question burned in his mind that he knew he could no longer ignore.

"I have a question I've wanted to ask you," he said. Sammi turned, giving him her full attention.

"Ask," she said, "I'm listenin'."

"What promise was Scott talking about?" he asked. "That's the second time he has mentioned that to me."

"Second time?" Sammi queried.

"Yes," Jake answered. "I ran into him when I came out of the bank on Friday, and he told me to remind you about a promise you made to him. I chose to ignore him then, but I can't do that anymore, not after what just happened. So... what was the promise?"

She turned away with an expression of shame and began fumbling with the butterfly necklace again. Gently, Jake placed his hand on her chin and turned her head back toward him.

"We face each other when we have something serious to talk about," he softly reminded her. "That was your idea."

"I didn't know what else to do," she said. "I was afraid he was gonna do more damage and I was especially afraid that he was gonna hurt you. So, when I called him over, I told him that if he would leave, I would consider goin' on one date with him. I made it clear that I would only consider it and it would only be one date. But I had no intention of going through with it and I still don't. I didn't actually make him any real promises."

Jake could not hide his look of disappointment and concern. "Sammi," he scolded, "Scott has no intention of letting you off the hook. He read a lot more into your words than you intended. But, regardless of what he expects, I do not want you going near him."

"Please don't be mad at me, Jake," Sammi pleaded. "I just didn't know what else to do to make him go away." Jake nodded his head in understanding. Being mad at her was not an option for him, and he didn't want the evening to end on a sour note. He smiled, assuring her that he was not angry. As they exited the car, Sammi walked over to Jake, wrapped her arms around him, and kissed him on the cheek before walking back to her trailer. He watched her the whole way to make sure she made it safely inside.

Suddenly overwhelmed with exhaustion, he went inside his own trailer and went straight to bed. It didn't take him long to fall into a deep sleep. Around three o'clock in the morning, however, he was awakened by screams from his aunt and his mother. There was also a loud commotion outside as the neighbors were gathering in front of Aunt Hazel's trailer.

"GET UP, JAKE!" his mother screamed. "The fire department is on their way!"

Jake jumped out of bed, threw his jeans on, and ran out the door. He couldn't believe what he was seeing: someone had set their Nova on fire!

12

LATER THAT MORNING, JAKE AND SAMMI SAT in the gazebo staring in shock at the twisted, burned-out shell of Jake's yellow Chevy Nova. It was now 8:00 AM, but the acrid, greasy smoke continued to rise from the Chevy's charred remains. A couple of firemen were still there, standing around Aunt Hazel's yard in case the blaze reignited. Sheriff Blake had also arrived with two of his deputies and they were examining the car for evidence. A hundred questions were running through Jake's mind, but there was one question he didn't even have to ask: who was responsible for this?

Considering the events of the night before, Jake and Sammi both knew who'd set the car on fire, but they also knew that Scott was crafty enough not to leave any incriminating evidence behind. The Nova wasn't exactly the coolest car for a guy Jake's age to drive, but it had only cost his mother $200 and it was all they had to drive. Suddenly, the simple task of driving back and forth to work seemed insurmountable. And how would Jake get to school each day once the school year started? East Forsyth was about thirty minutes away, just inside the Winston-Salem city limits. Sammi sat in silence next to Jake with her head resting against his shoulder.

Sensing that she was likely blaming herself, he gently reassured her, "This isn't your fault, you know."

Sammi took his hand in hers and, without lifting her head off his shoulder, replied, "Just like I told you last night... you can even hear my thoughts." She had barely gotten the words out of her mouth when Sheriff Blake approached them. He was a tall man in his late fifties, about six feet four inches, with broad shoulders like an athlete. His size was intimidating, but there was something about his face that was kind and assuring. If you were a law-abiding citizen, his presence could be very comforting. If you were a lawbreaker, his presence could strike fear in your heart. He had been with the sheriff's department since he was a young man, and he knew just about everyone in town. He was loved and trusted by the people.

Resting one hand on the grip of his pistol, Sheriff Blake looked at Jake and said, "I've got a few questions for you, Son, if you don't mind."

"I don't mind at all," Jake said.

"We don't see any evidence that would point to the perpetrators. The only thing we are certain about is that they doused the inside and the outside of your car with gasoline before putting a match to it. Do you have any idea who might have done this?" Sheriff Blake asked.

Jake was not sure how to answer. The sheriff had just said there was no evidence to point out the guilty party so it seemed pointless to bring up Scott's name. Jake shook his head and said, "We were all asleep, so I can't really say who did it."

"It was Scott Robertson," Sammi adamantly declared.

As soon as he heard that name, Sheriff Blake's countenance changed to one of concern. "How do you know it was Scott?" he asked.

"Uh, we really don't know that for sure, Sheriff," Jake said.

"Yes, we do!" Sammi argued. "I mean, we didn't see him do it, but we had a run-in with him last night at City Park and, let's be honest, Sheriff, there is nobody else in this town who does this sort of thing."

"What kind of *run-in* did you have?" Sheriff Blake asked, pulling out a pen and a little notebook.

Jake hesitatingly answered, "After the fireworks, we were walking through the parking lot to head home. Scott and his two friends came up behind us. Eric and Jonathan grabbed me and threw me up against my car and Scott lit into me."

"Wait a minute," the sheriff interrupted, now noticing the cut on Jake's knuckle from where he had hit Scott the night before, "that was you? We got a call last night that there was a fight in the parking lot. By the time the witnesses got to the site of the altercation, they found Scott and Jonathan struggling to stand up. Both of their faces were a bloody mess, but there was no one else was around. By the time my deputy arrived, Scott and his friends were gone too. Are you telling me that you took those boys down by yourself?"

Jake cut his eyes toward the petite little Sammi still sitting next to him and said, "I had a little help."

Sheriff Blake pushed his Stetson back off his brow. "Are you kidding me?" he asked, shaking his head in disbelief. Looking back toward his deputies, he said, "Steve, you and Wray get over here. I think you're gonna want to hear this."

Jake and Sammi described the events that had unfolded the night before, much to the delight of the deputies who'd both had confrontations with Scott and his buddies over the past few years. Sheriff Blake, on the other hand, became even more concerned.

"I need the two of you to listen carefully to me," he said. "I know you got the upper hand on Scott and his friends last night, but you need to understand that this boy is dangerous and he's not going to let this go. You humiliated him and he's not going to forget it. In his mind, setting your car on fire is probably just the beginning. And the thing you have to watch with him is that he may not do anything more for a month or even longer, but he will continue to seek revenge. I've been observing that boy for a while and over the past few years his criminal activity has been escalating. I don't think we've yet seen just how far he's willing to go, but I know for sure that he's on a path that is either going to land him in prison or in the graveyard. If his daddy would intervene and spend some time with that boy, he might still have a chance. But Freddy Robertson is only interested in making money, and he's already got a lot of it. Rather than hold his boy accountable, Freddy's used his wealth to clean up after Scott and keep that boy just beyond our reach. Now, we can't prove he torched your car, but you said he hit you last night, right?"

Jake nodded his head, "Yes, sir."

"I only see a cut on your right hand though. I don't see any other marks. Where did he hit you?" Sheriff Blake asked.

Jake hesitantly raised his T-shirt. When Sammi saw Jake's stomach, she gasped, so horrified by the sight that she couldn't speak.

"Oh my, Son!" Sheriff Blake said as he leaned in to get a closer look. The flesh over Jake's stomach and rib cage was black and purple with bruises.

The sheriff started writing something on his pad. "Here, Son," he said, handing him the slip of paper. "This is the number and address of my personal physician. I want you to go see him right now and let him look you over. And there's one more thing I want you to do, but only the two of you can do it. We can't prove Scott and his pals destroyed the car, but if you're both willing to testify against Scott, we can get him on battery. If you're willing to press charges, we can go pick him and his friends up right now."

"Can I talk that over with Sammi and my mom and get back to you?" Jake asked.

Sheriff Blake hesitated a moment, then said, "Sure, Son, but don't wait too long. Just call us if and when you're ready. In the meantime, I've already talked to your mama about how to file this with her insurance company. I know the car wasn't worth much, but you might receive enough to help you get another car. The tow truck is already on its way to get this one. Here's my card. Call me...anytime...and go see the doctor, immediately."

"I will, Sheriff," Jake said. "Thank you." He stood and extended his hand to the sheriff. Returning Jake's firm handshake, Sheriff Blake leaned in and whispered in Jake's ear, "Watch your back, Son...and hers."

Jake nodded his head. As Sheriff Blake walked back toward his car, Sammi and Jake heard him say to his deputies under his breath, "He's not gonna press charges."

When the sheriff and his deputies had pulled away, Sammi turned to Jake, "I want to press charges."

Jake shook his head, "I don't think that's wise. You heard the sheriff. Scott's daddy will show up flashing cash and Scott will be right out on the street again, and having him arrested may make him even angrier. No, I'm afraid if we do that he might come back and torch Aunt Hazel's house...or yours. There are too many people around here I care about. Besides, Sheriff Blake said we might not hear anything out of him for a month or more. Let's just see what happens."

Sammi didn't agree, but she decided to let him have the final decision. Her greater concern right now was with the bruises on his ribs and stomach. "You *are* going to the doctor though!" she said firmly.

"Yes," he agreed, as the pain from the beating he had taken radiated through his body with each breath. "That probably wouldn't be a bad idea." As they walked over to look at the car one last time, the neighbors began to trickle out of their homes bearing comfort food. Leading the way was Mayor. As a crowd gathered, Aunt Hazel and Jo emerged from the trailer. Jo, wiping tears from her eyes, was visibly shaken by the events of the night. Hazel was just plain mad.

"Are y'all alright?" Mayor asked, placing a supportive hand on Jake's shoulder.

"Yes," Jake assured him. "I just need to find another car as soon as I can. I don't want to lose my job at the grocery store and school will be starting not too long from now."

Mayor replied, "I've got a few thoughts about that, Jake. Give me until this afternoon to look into it and I may have a solution for you by nightfall." Turning to the crowd, Mayor cleared his throat, which was the usual indication that a speech was forthcoming. "Now folks," he said, motioning for the crowd to come closer. "We've had a bad thing happen, but I want to encourage you not to let it frighten you. We can either let this thing drive us behind locked doors or we can let it make us stronger. When one of us suffers in this neighborhood, we all suffer. When one of us is attacked, all of us are attacked. We are better and we are stronger when we stand together. So I'm calling for a Hope Park family meetin' tonight at 7:00 o'clock around the gazebo. I want all of you there, and I want you to bring some ideas of how we can make our neighborhood a safer place. Most of us have been expectin' somethin' like this ever since Jake stood up to that devil. I would say it's not over yet, so we need to rally around our young friend and not let any further harm come to him, to Sammi, or to any of us. Are we all in agreement?"

"Amen!" the crowd said in unison.

As the neighbors dispersed, many of them came up and spoke encouraging words to Jake and Sammi. A few of the women carried gifts of food into Aunt Hazel's trailer while others circled around Jo and started praying for her, which made her cry even more. As Jake watched his mother cry, his concern moved from himself to her. He was afraid that all this excitement may send her back down the dark path with which they were both familiar. He had seen the pattern all too often. Jo would get clean and then there would be some stressful event that would drive her back to the drugs. *Maybe with all this support, this time will be different,* he'd thought to himself.

"I called the bank and told them I wouldn't be in today," Hazel said, approaching Jake and Sammi.

"That's good," Sammi said. Lifting Jake's shirt, she whispered to Hazel, "The sheriff said he needs to go to the doctor right now."

Hazel was aghast at the sight of Jake's bruises. "When did that happen?" she asked with dismay.

"Scott did it last night after the fireworks," Sammi said. "But he can tell you all about it on the way to the doctor's office...if you don't mind takin' him."

"Of course I'll take him," Hazel said. "We'll go right now, but let's not tell Jo yet."

Looking at Jake apologetically, Sammi placed her hand on his arm and said, "Jake, I'm so sorry, but I have to go to work. They gave me yesterday off only if I agreed to work all day today. But I'll be back in time for Mayor's meetin'. Will you be okay?"

"Don't worry about me," he assured her. "I'm in good hands with Aunt Hazel."

Before walking back to her house, Sammi stood in silence before Jake. Tears began to moisten her eyes. "I am so sorry for all this, Jake. You didn't deserve . . ."

"Stop," Jake said. "None of this...absolutely *none* of this... is your fault."

Sammi placed one hand on Jake's cheek and the other very gently on his stomach. "Come by the store after the visit to the doctor and let me know what he says. If you come at 12:30, maybe we can all go to lunch at Winter's, I have a whole hour for lunch today."

"We'll try," Jake said, and then smiled at Sammi as she went in to get ready for work.

"Winter's?" Jake asked his aunt.

"My favorite restaurant in all of Kernersville," Hazel said. "It's a tiny, narrow little place, but stays full all the time. Mr. Winter opened it in 1947...basically built a roof over an alley and turned it into a restaurant. It's *the* place to go for ice cream and sandwiches. We'll try to get there in time to meet Sammi for lunch, but first let's get you to the doctor. We need to come up with a story for your mom though. I don't want her to know about the bruises until she's had time to get over the fire."

"We can tell her I have to go to the sheriff's office to file a report," Jake suggested.

They agreed on the story to tell Jo and within a few minutes were headed to the doctor. When they arrived, they were treated like dignitaries, which let Jake know Sheriff Blake had called ahead. Doctor Charles examined Jake thoroughly and determined that there were no broken ribs, but he sent Jake straight to the hospital in Winston-Salem for more tests to be certain there were no internal damages. They finished just in time to meet Sammi for lunch at Winter's. The inside of the quaint little restaurant was shaped like a long, narrow rectangle just like Aunt Hazel had described—an alley with a roof and a kitchen.

Mr. Winter, a short, friendly man stood behind the counter with an apron around his waist and a spatula in his hand greeting everyone who came through the door with a smile. The place was packed, but it wasn't long before a booth came available. As the three of them slipped into the corner booth, Jake was amazed at how quickly Sammi was able to bounce back from the events of the previous night. Her mood was contagiously delightful, almost as if nothing had happened. He admired her ability to stay positive in the midst of difficult circumstances and wondered if that ability would eventually rub off on him.

After lunch, Sammi went back to Newlin's for her afternoon shift. Jake and Hazel went home to let Jo in on the injuries he had received in the parking lot confrontation at the festival. But, when they got back to Hope Park, Jo was nowhere to be found. Considering her fragile state of mind, Jake and Aunt Hazel were both concerned and went door to door through the neighborhood hoping someone knew where she was or maybe where she'd gone, but no one had seen her. As they were walking back toward the trailer, they heard Jo call to them from behind. She was running toward them from the direction of the Tavern with a wide smile on her face.

"You'll never believe it," Jo said, panting for breath. "I got a job...at the Tavern! I start tomorrow."

"Mom, are you sure that's the best place for you?" Jake asked.

"I know what you're thinkin," Jo answered with agitation. "And I told you, I'm fine. And now that we don't have a car, the Tavern is the best place for me because I can walk to and from work every day. You're gonna have to start trustin' me at some point, Baby Boy."

Jake didn't respond, but continued walking toward home, mulling over the news he had just received.

"I thought you'd be proud of me," Jo said, trying to force the conversation as they walked toward Aunt Hazel's trailer.

Hazel ignored the attempt and changed the subject: "There's somethin' we want to tell you, Jo."

"I hope it's good news for a change," Jo replied, ignoring Hazel's serious tone.

Deciding to keep the news of his injuries from his mom, Jake turned to face his aunt and put his index finger over his mouth in an attempt to silence her. Turning back to Jo, he said, "Uh, yeah. It is good news, Mom. Mayor told me this morning he might be able to help us find a new car. He's supposed to let me know this evening."

"Oh, that *is* good news!" Jo said gleefully. "Maybe things are going to start movin' in our favor for a change."

When they'd got back to the trailer, Jake went straight to his room to take a nap. He was exhausted and wanted to be fresh for the 7:00 o'clock meeting. He also had to go to work the next morning. As 7:00 PM rolled around, he stepped out to the gazebo to find almost every neighbor, including Sammi, already present. Mayor was standing on the top step of the gazebo about to get everyone's attention. When he saw Jake, he motioned for him to come over and stand next to him.

"Folks, let me have your attention," Mayor began loudly. Everyone stopped talking and turned their attention to him. "As you know," Mayor continued, "we had some unexpected visitors last night who turned Jake's car into charcoal. Tonight, I want us to discuss some safety procedures for Hope Park but, before we do that, I have a surprise for Jake." Mayor motioned for everybody to move to the side so Jake could see down the road. "Keep your eye on lot number three," he said to Jake. "Mr. Jones has something for you."

After a few seconds, Jake could see a car emerging from behind the home that belonged to Thaddeus Jones. Mr. Jones slowly drove the car all the way up to the gazebo. Jake's heart was racing, but he wasn't yet sure what was going on.

As Mr. Jones struggled to step out of the car, Mayor explained, "As you all know, Mr. Jones had to stop drivin' over a year ago due to health issues. His car has been sittin' in the back of his lot ever since. I spoke with him this mornin', and he has very generously agreed to sell his car to Jake and Jo." Turing to Jake and his mom, Mayor said less publicly, "If it's alright with you, Jake, Mr. Jones said he could sell it for $800, but he'll take $50 a month until it's paid off. Will that plan work for you?"

Jake was speechless. Mr. Jones' car was a white, two-door, 1974 Pontiac LeMans GT with a horizontal black stripe on each side. It was the kind of car any high school senior would be proud to drive. Jake could hardly believe what was happening. "YES!" he said emphatically. "I can handle that."

Jumping off the gazebo step, Jake ran up to Mr. Jones overwhelming him with a bear hug. But Mr. Jones hugged him back, laughing out loud. Everyone cheered as the two embraced. "I don't know how to thank you, Sir," Jake said warmly. "I'll pay you every month until it's paid in full."

"I'm not worried about that," the kind old gentleman said. "I trust you. This car has been real good to me. I'm just glad it'll be of use again."

Overwhelmed with the generosity that had just been extended to him, Jake struggled to hold back his emotions. This was the nicest thing anyone had ever done for him.

"Jake, why don't you take Sammi out for some ice cream?" Mayor suggested.

"What about the meeting?" Jake asked.

Mayor smiled, "We'll handle the meetin', Son. You two go on now and have some fun. After what you've been through, you deserve it."

Jake looked at Sammi and motioned for her to get into the car. Without hesitation, she jumped in on the passenger side. The V8 engine roared with power when Jake started her up and, as they turned to drive out of the park, the whole crowd erupted in cheers and applause. As they were pulling away, Jake looked in the rearview mirror and saw the neighbors were still cheering him on. In the front of the crowd, Mr. Jones and Mayor stood side by side with smiles as wide as the Grand Canyon on their faces. The support he had just received gave Jake a sense of belonging.

Taking Sammi by the hand, he said to her, "I think I'm finally here."

"What do you mean?" she asked.

"Home," Jake said. "I think I'm finally home."

13

THE NEXT SEVERAL WEEKS WENT BY QUICKLY without further incidents. Jo seemed to be doing okay with her new job at the Tavern; Jake and Sammi worked the same schedule at Newlin's most days, which allowed them to ride to work together and, with weekly late-night encounters on Sammi's roof, the two seemed to be building a solid foundation to their friendship. Both of them were very enthusiastic about entering their senior year and they could hardly wait for the first day of school. Many of their rooftop conversations revolved around their plans following graduation: where they wanted to go to college, what their majors would be, and what kind of careers they hoped to have. To make things even better, Scott Robertson and his two minions were apparently laying low or at least that's how it seemed.

One Saturday evening that summer, Jo was working the late shift at the Tavern. The place was packed with a rowdy crowd that had come from all over the area to enjoy a night of drinking and dancing to a live country music band. She was exhausted by 10:30 PM, having been there since 3:00 o'clock that afternoon, but the lively patrons showed no signs of slowing down. After a long night of carrying drinks back and forth from the bar to the tables, her feet felt like they were on fire. So when an opportunity for a short break came along, she took it and stepped out behind the Tavern for a smoke.

She had barely taken her first puff when, from out of nowhere, someone rushed her from behind, lifted her off her feet, and pinned her with her face against a wall, pressing the full weight of his body against hers. She screamed, but the music inside was so loud that no one heard her. Her assailant placed one hand firmly over her mouth. Her back was still to him, so she had no idea who it was.

"I know all about you, Jo Ledger," a masculine voice whispered in her ear. "I'm gonna take my hand away from your mouth, but I swear to you, if you scream again, I'll kill you. You understand?"

Trembling with fright, Jo nodded her head. When she did, the stranger slowly removed his hand. "Now, I'm gonna turn you around, but my promise still stands. It won't go well for you if you scream," he growled in a threatening tone. Placing his hands on her shoulders, he spun her body around and pinned her back against the wall. Jo froze in fear as she looked into the face of her attacker. It was Scott Robertson, but this time, his two friends were nowhere around.

"What do you want?" she asked, as her body trembled in his powerful grip.

"You know what I want, Baby? I want the same thing you give every other man. I know all about you, and I know you'll wrap those legs around any man who's willin' to pay for it. And it just so happens that I got a pocket full of hundred-dollar bills just for you."

"I'm not that way anymore," Jo protested. "I'm tryin' to change."

"You ain't never gonna change," Scott sneered. "You've been a whore your whole life and you'll die a whore."

Though Jo still feared for her safety, his comment enraged her to the point that she managed to break her arm free enough to slap him across the face. But her resistance seemed to excite, rather than deter him. Realizing the sinister nature of his intentions toward her, Jo began to strike him as hard as she could about the face and neck, but her efforts were pointless. Wrapping his arms around her waist, Scott threw her to the ground, falling on top of her as she landed. The force of his weight knocked the breath out of Jo, rendering her helpless beneath his muscular frame.

Crushed beneath Scott's weight, Jo began praying that someone would walk out of the Tavern and interrupt what was about to happen, but her prayer went unanswered. Once he'd finished, Scott stood to his feet, fastened his jeans, then reached into his back pocket and pulled out his wallet. Then, kneeling beside Jo who was still lying on her back in shock, he counted out five hundred-dollar bills, slowly placing one bill at a time on the lower part of her stomach. As he counted out the money, he warned her, "If anybody, even one person, finds out what just happened here, I'll kill your son, I'll set fire to that nice little home of yours, and then I'll kill you. If you understand what I just said, nod that pretty little head of yours."

Jo nodded her head, trying her best to hold back the tears. Before he stood up, he leaned over and kissed her on the lips. "I enjoyed our little date, Darlin'," he'd said coldly. "Maybe we can do it again sometime."

As Scott disappeared into the darkness, Jo sat up, still reeling from the assault. Looking down at her lap, she saw the money he had left with her. After staring at it for a few minutes, she took the cash in her hand and counted it out once more. Then, standing to her feet, she folded the bills, stuffed them into her bra and went back inside to finish her shift without speaking a word to anyone about the assault.

Several weeks passed, and before Jake knew it, school was starting. Once again, he found himself in his element. He flourished in the academic setting, often impressing his teachers with his knowledge and understanding of the subject matter. In spite of the fact that his mother had never been able to offer him a consistent and safe home life, Jake always rose above his peers when it came to learning and normally held the highest GPA on campus.

As the first weeks of school went by, his level of intelligence caught the attention of all of his teachers. His English teacher in particular, Mrs. Rossman, took a special interest in him. One day after class, Mrs. Rossman called him up to her desk. "Jake, can you meet me in Principal Taylor's office after school today?" she asked. The request made him nervous, but he agreed anyway. As the day moved forward, he became more and more anxious about the meeting, wondering what it would be about.

"Have a seat, Jake," Mrs. Rossman said as she pointed to a comfortable leather chair placed in front of Principal Taylor's desk. She sat down in the chair next to him. "She'll be here in a few minutes," Mrs. Rossman said. Jake became even more nervous, but tried to occupy his mind by looking at the many degrees and certificates on the wall behind the principal's desk. Each certificate bore the same name, Pamela L. Taylor, PhD.

"Wow," Jake said in awe, after viewing the principal's many accomplishments.

Mrs. Rossman chuckled. "I assume you're talking about the wall. Principal Taylor's an academic superstar. She graduated as valedictorian of her high school *and* her college. She has two masters and two doctorate degrees. That's why I want you to meet her. I've spoken with her at length about your academic skills and we have some ideas we want to put before you."

As Jake continued to peruse the room, he noticed a large bookshelf with hundreds of books stacked from the bottom of the shelf all the way to the top. Unable to remain in his seat, he walked over and began examining the collection. Eyeing a copy of The Laws by Plato, Jake removed it from the shelf and began thumbing through the pages. "I've always wanted to read this," he said.

"I'm sure we can get you a copy," Mrs. Rossman assured him.

As Jake continued reading, Principal Taylor entered the room. He was immediately struck by the confidence and authority that she exuded. Closing the door, she smiled and walked over to Jake as he hurriedly fumbled to put the book back on the shelf.

"You must be Jake Ledger," Principal Taylor said, extending her open hand to him. "I'm Dr. Taylor, but that would be Principal Taylor to you. It's so nice to meet you."

"Yes, ma'am," Jake replied, shaking her hand. She had a firm grip. "It's nice to meet you too, ma'am."

"Have a seat," she said, pointing to the chair he had vacated to look at the bookshelf.

Once they were both seated, she continued, "Jake, Mrs. Rossman has told me quite a bit about your academic giftedness. Your other teachers speak very highly of you as well. I understand that you are new to the area?"

"Yes, ma'am," he replied respectfully.

"How do you like it here so far? Have you made any new friends?" she inquired.

Jake's thoughts immediately went to Sammi but he didn't think the principal would be interested in hearing about their relationship. Instead, he answered, "Yes, ma'am, I do like it here. We live in a very nice neighborhood, and I guess I could say that all of my neighbors are my friends."

"That's good," she said. "I'm glad you are comfortable here." Principal Taylor picked up a folder that had been lying on her desk and began flipping through the contents, glancing up at Jake every few seconds. "I see you came to us from Charlotte. It must be quite an adjustment for you, moving from Charlotte to a small town like Kernersville."

Realizing that the contents of the folder were about him, Jake hesitantly answered, "Yes, ma'am. It's an adjustment alright."

"So, how did you and your mother end up in Charlotte?" Principal Taylor asked.

Jake shifted nervously in his seat. *Where is this going?* he thought to himself. *Does she know about my mom's past?* He didn't want to lie to his new principal, but he also did not want to divulge too much about his past. "Uh...my mom... she, uh...she worked in Charlotte for a year."

Oh, CRAP! Jake immediately thought to himself. *Now she's going to ask me what my mother does for a living.* Attempting to divert a potentially uncomfortable situation, Jake answered the next question he thought Principal Taylor might ask before she had the chance to ask it, "She works in the food service industry," he said.

Aware of his embarrassment, Mrs. Rossman nodded, "That's honest work, Jake. Nothing to be ashamed of."

"Thank you," he mumbled. Sensing from Mrs. Rossman's statement that he had successfully diverted the direction of the conversation, Jake became more at ease.

Principal Taylor continued examining the contents of the folder, shaking her head in what seemed to be either amazement or disbelief. Looking up, she said, "Jake, I must say that I am impressed with your academic history. I have your records going all the way back to the first grade, and I see nothing less than A's all the way through. Your attendance record is also flawless."

"Thank you, Principal Taylor," Jake said. He feared he might be blushing. "I've always enjoyed school. I like to read."

"Yes," she replied. "I can see from your records that your teachers found it difficult to keep you challenged. Some of them made notes. Would you like to hear what your fourth-grade teacher said about you?"

Jake nodded his head, "Yes, ma'am."

Principal Taylor fumbled through the papers in the folder until she found what she was looking for. "Here it is," she said. "It's from Mrs. Pennix. She wrote, 'Jake is a bright student, one of the brightest I've seen in a long time. He absorbs knowledge like a sponge. He's the only fourth grade student I've ever taught who can read Shakespeare and actually understand it. An amazing future awaits this young man.'"

"I didn't know she wrote that," Jake said with humility.

"To be honest," Principal Taylor said, "several other teachers wrote complimentary things about you as well, but all of them are along the same lines as the note from Mrs. Pennix. It seems that you have also excelled in mathematics, science, and pretty much every other academic discipline that has been placed before you. And the miracle of that is that according to your records, you have literally moved every year since you've been in school. Many students who move frequently tend to have trouble adjusting in new schools, trouble which often reveals itself in the areas of relationships and academics. But all the moving didn't affect you. That makes you very unique."

"So, our question for you is," Mrs. Rossman interrupted, "do you plan to go to college? And if so, what are you doing in preparation?"

"Yes, ma'am!" Jake adamantly affirmed. "I have every intention of going to college."

"Do you have any thoughts about what course of study you would like to pursue?" Principal Taylor asked.

"Law," Jake answered without hesitation. "I hope to be a lawyer someday."

"Ah!" Principal Taylor said with a smile. "Now I know why you were looking through Plato's last book. If you'd like, I'll let you take it home...to borrow, not to keep."

Jake's face brightened, "That would be amazing, Principal Taylor! Yes! I would definitely like to read it and I'll take good care of it."

"I have no doubt you will," she replied.

Jake looked back toward the bookshelf like a child looking into a barrel of candy.

"You might as well get it now," Principal Taylor said, smiling.

Without hesitation, Jake leapt from the chair, removed the book from the shelf and quickly returned to his seat. Mrs. Rossman and Principal Taylor smiled at one another, both noticing the gleam in his eyes as he examined the book.

"So, tell us a little about your family, especially about your parents," Principal Taylor casually asked.

Jake felt his chest start to burn with anxiety. He was not prepared for an interview, and he wasn't sure why she wanted to know about him personally, but Jake knew he had to at least attempt to answer her questions. The subject of his parents was always difficult. Jake did not want to share with Mrs. Rossman, Principal Taylor, or anyone else at the school the cycle of drug addiction or the repeated physical abuse he'd suffered at his mother's hands; so he decided to give them bits and pieces.

"There's not really much to tell," he said. "My dad died when I was five-years-old...an accidental gunshot. My mom has tried to make ends meet, but since she never completed high school, she's had difficulty finding a good job. So, we've moved a lot over the years. We came here because my Aunt Hazel invited us to come and live with her. I'm currently employed at Newlin's grocery and my mom works as a waitress at the Tavern." Jake said no more, hoping that his brief synopsis would be enough to bring an end to the personal questions.

"I'm sorry to hear about your dad," Mrs. Rossman said, placing her hand on Jake's shoulder. "I knew he was gone, but I didn't know what had happened. Was it a hunting accident or something?"

"Uh, yeah," Jake replied. "Something like that."

"Okay," Principal Taylor said. "Enough with the third degree. Jake, we brought you in here not just to get to know you a little better, but also to let you know that we want to help you in your pursuit of a college or a university education. We see a great deal of potential in you and we want to make sure that that potential does not go to waste."

"Okay," Jake said, intrigued and encouraged. "That would be greatly appreciated."

"We have a plan," Mrs. Rossman explained. "Your combined SAT scores from your junior year were phenomenal at 1590. I've personally never taught a student who'd scored that high. The first thing we would like to do is test your IQ. We know you're intelligent, but we want to know just how intelligent you are. Have you ever been tested?"

"Not that I know of," Jake replied. "But I would like to be."

"Great," Mrs. Rossman said. "I'll set that up for you."

"We also want to help you start looking into various universities to see which ones would be a good fit for you," added Principal Taylor. "I have someone here in the office who can help you with that and that same person can help you find scholarships and other financial aid resources as well."

"That all sounds great," Jake said, feeling somewhat overwhelmed. "I knew there was a lot to do to get ready for college, but things have been kind of difficult for me and my mom the past year, with moving and everything."

"We understand," Mrs. Rossman said kindly. "We will walk with you through every step."

Standing to her feet, Principal Taylor reached across her desk to shake Jake's hand, "Enjoy the reading," she said looking down at the book. "Again, it was a pleasure meeting you, Jake."

Mrs. Rossman also stood, "I'll be in touch with you as soon we get everything lined up. Thank you for meeting with us."

"Thank you," he replied as he headed for the door. "I mean that sincerely. I appreciate the time you're taking to help me."

Both ladies nodded and smiled as Jake walked out the door. As soon as the door closed behind him, Principal Taylor looked at Mrs. Rossman, "There's more to his story than he's telling us."

"What do you mean?" Mrs. Rossman asked.

"Did you notice his reaction when I asked about his family?" Dr. Taylor asked with concern. "He clearly did not want to discuss his parents. When I brought them up, he looked as if he had swallowed a grapefruit. This stays between the two of us, but I did a little checking into his parents' background. I can't divulge what I discovered, but what I *can* say is...well, that boy needs our help."

Jake ran to the car where Sammi was waiting for him. "You better drive," he said, grinning from ear to ear. "I'm so excited, I might get a speeding ticket."

"Why?" Sammi asked. "What's going on?"

"I'll tell you about it on the road," Jake said, trying to catch his breath. "I want to stop by home before we go to work. I know it will make us a few minutes late, but I have to tell my mom what just happened. I can't wait until after work."

On the way home, Jake eagerly unfolded every detail of the conversation he'd just had in Principal Taylor's office, explaining what the events of the afternoon meant for his future. He couldn't stop talking. Sammi had never seen Jake so happy and excited. As they pulled into Hope Park, he said, "I'm just going to run in and tell my mom the good news and then I'll be right back out. You can just wait in the car if you want to."

"I think, since we're here, I'm gonna change into my clothes for work," Sammi said. "I'll meet you back at the car." As they pulled up to Aunt Hazel's trailer, Jake noticed a blue, 4-door sedan parked in the driveway. He had never seen it before.

"I wonder who that belongs to," he pondered aloud, nodding toward the mystery machine.

"I don't know," Sammi answered. "Never seen it before. You want me to come in with you?"

"No," he said, slightly concerned, "You go on and change. I'll be out in five minutes." Jake approached Aunt Hazel's porch quietly and slowly opened the door so as not to make any noise. Once inside the trailer, he didn't see anyone in the kitchen or across in the living room. Approaching the entrance to the hallway, he was overcome with a sick feeling in his gut as he noticed that his mother's bedroom door was closed. With a sense of great dread, he inched softly towards the door. For some reason, the hallway seemed longer than normal. Standing inches away, he gently placed his hand on the knob. His heart raced and his breath was short. Attempting to give the knob a gentle, slight turn, he discovered that it was locked. He stood there for a moment in absolute silence as his worst nightmare began to transform into a bitter reality. There were noises coming from the other side of the closed door, noises that were painfully familiar to him. There was no doubt about it, his mom had a man in her room; and if there was a man in her room, it meant one thing and one thing only, her demons had returned.

14

WHEN SAMMI RETURNED TO THE CAR, SHE found Jake brooding behind the steering wheel, and immediately she thought to herself, *Oh, this* can't *be good.* As soon as she was buckled in, Jake put the big car in Reverse, swung it around, and headed out of the park. Turning a compassionate gaze toward her troubled friend, Sammi asked gently, "Who was in there with your mom?"

Jake answered as he glared straight ahead at the road, "A man. That's all I know. Just, a man."

"Have you ever seen him before," she asked.

"Didn't see him," he answered. "They were behind a locked door...and I think you know what that means."

"I'm so sorry, Jake," Sammi sighed. Her eyes began to well up with tears as she thought about how excited he had been to share his good news with Jo. Seeing him so disappointed saddened her deeply. Unfastening her seatbelt, Sammi slid across the seat and sat as close to Jake as she possibly could. She kissed him on the cheek and placed her head on his shoulder without speaking a word. Her silent act of compassion brought him an indescribable measure of comfort. As they drove down the road, he was amazed at how something as simple as the touch of her hand could soothe his anger and frustration.

He leaned his head over against the top of Sammi's and drew in her fragrance. With each breath, his heart grew more and more calm. Then, Sammi did something Jake didn't expect. It was a small gesture, but nonetheless, the effect on him was monumental. She gently placed her hand on his bicep and began to stroke it lightly with her fingers. By this point, the anger in his heart had completely abated, but something else was stirring inside of him.

Sammi could not only chase away the negative thoughts and emotions that plagued Jake, but she was also able to ignite in him a blaze of passion and desire. However, she was of such an innocent and trusting nature, Jake wasn't sure if she was even aware of the effect she had on him. Once again, as he had done so many times before, he reminded himself of his commitment to be her friend first. He felt this was the right thing to do considering what his aunt had told him, but he knew that the deep yearning he felt for her would soon grow to a point where it could no longer be ignored. Holding back his desire for her seemed unnatural but it had become very important to him to win her complete trust before pursuing anything romantic.

It was clear from the things she'd shared under the gazebo that she had been the object of disrespect by many would-be suitors, and Jake just wasn't willing to fall in line behind those guys. The thought of frightening Sammi away or losing her trust because of an impulsive, selfish act on his part absolutely horrified him. He just wasn't ready to risk it. He could see that she had an amazing heart that was full of compassion. From their many conversations, he had also discovered that she had a great intellect, a feature that many of her pursuers had missed because they couldn't see beyond her unblemished beauty. There were many layers to this beautiful young woman, and Jake wanted to peel back as many of those layers as he could before he revealed his true feelings for her.

When they arrived at Newlin's store, he pulled the car around to the side and parked in the employee section. As he started to open his car door, Sammi tightened her grip on his arm to keep him from getting out. Turning towards him, she rested her chin on his shoulder and asked, "What are you gonna *do*, Jake? About your mom, I mean."

Acutely aware that her lips were only inches from his own, Jake knew that he would not be able to resist the urge to kiss her if he turned towards her. So, glancing at her out of the corner of his eye, he replied, "Well...this is Friday so she'll be working late at the Tavern. When I get home tonight, I'm going to search her room."

"Search for what?" she asked.

"Drug paraphernalia," he stated matter-of-factly. "When strange men start showing up, it's usually a sign that she is supporting her habit. She hasn't mentioned having a new boyfriend so I can only assume that the man in her room today was there to pay for sex. It's what she does, or what she used to do. I'm usually able to spot the signs, but maybe I've been too preoccupied lately to notice."

"What are the signs?" Sammi gently asked.

"When she's using, she sleeps a lot and when she's awake, she seems out of it," Jake answered. "She slurs her words and her pupils get real small like the point of a pin. I can also usually spot track marks on her arms pretty quickly.

Sometimes she breaks out in skin rashes. But the biggest sign with her is that she gets mean, real mean."

In an effort to comfort him, Sammi said, "Maybe you haven't seen the signs because she hasn't started usin' yet. There might be time to intervene. If she knows you're suspicious, maybe she'll stop before she even starts."

"Maybe," he reluctantly replied. He grew silent as his mind involuntarily began pulling up images from his past. Sammi could see little beads of sweat breaking out on his forehead as he tightened his grip on the steering wheel. He had already told her about the things his mother used to do and say to him when she was using, so there was no need to rehash former conversations. Patiently and silently, she continued to hold on to his arm while he fought to gain control over the storms that were raging in his mind and his heart.

Jake finally released the wheel. Smiling at Sammi, he said, "Thank you."

"For what?" she asked, smiling back.

"Just for being here beside me," he said. "You've helped me more than you realize. Now, let's go to work before we both get fired."

Friday nights were always busy at the store, so their shifts went by quickly. Stocking shelves and bagging groceries kept Jake's mind occupied the entire time. They both worked so hard that they were famished by the time the store closed at 10:00 PM.

"Let's stop by McDonald's," Sammi suggested as they climbed into the car to head home. "I'm cravin' French Fries."

Jake was not one to deny Sammi's wishes, and besides, he was quite hungry himself. Arriving at McDonald's, they quickly realized that half the students from the high school were there already and more would soon follow because the football game that night was a home game.

"Is it okay if we go through the drive-thru?" he asked. "Looks pretty crowded inside."

"Yeah, that's fine," Sammi said. "We can just eat in the parkin' lot. It's probably way too loud in there anyway."

After getting their food, they circled the building waiting for a parking spot to open up. Finally spotting an empty space, Jake parked the big car, rolled the windows down, and popped in an 8-track while Sammi pounced on her hot, steamy fries.

"So, are you still gonna go through your mom's room when we get home?" she asked.

Quickly swallowing a mouthful of burger, Jake replied, "Yes. I won't be able to rest until I know if she's using again. I know where all of her hiding places are too, so if there are drugs in her room, I'll find them."

"What's the plan if you find drugs?" she asked.

"I'll confront her," he said, "but probably not tonight. She works late on weekends and won't be home until 2:00 AM or later. But I will most definitely confront her tomorrow."

"Well, I really hope you don't find anything," she said sincerely. "But, in case you do, I want to be there when you find them. You okay with that?"

Jake smiled. Thus far he had not regretted letting Sammi into the darker parts of his life. She seemed to handle it well and without passing judgment. "You've come this far," he said. "Might as well keep going."

Just as he got the words out of his mouth, the car jolted suddenly as if someone had jumped on the back. Looking in his rearview mirror, he saw two individuals sitting side by side with their backs to him on the trunk of the Pontiac! At first Jake thought someone must have mistaken his car for theirs, but then he heard a voice he hadn't heard in a while. Before he could get out of the car, Scott Robertson was already at his door holding a half empty bottle of beer. Leaning down to look inside, he leered at Sammi for a moment and then asked, "What are you doin' still hangin' around this piece of trash when you..."

Jake interrupted angrily, "Watch your mouth, Scott. Show some respect for the lady."

"Boy, you still don't know who you're talkin' to, it seems," Scott snarled at Jake.

"I know *WHAT* I'm talking to," Jake retorted. "A cretin!"

"A what?" Scott asked, not sure what a cretin was.

Jake smirked at Scott, realizing for the first time that the big, mean dope before him seriously was inferior to him in intellect. "I don't have time to give you a vocabulary lesson, Scott. You need to step away from my car." Dolt that he was, Scott did have enough sense to realize he was being insulted and resorted to his usual barbaric threats.

"Yeah, I heard you had a new car," he said. Then, with a sinister smile, he leaned in closer to Jake and asked quietly, "What happened to the last one you had?"

"We both know what happened to my last car," Jake said accusingly, as he stared coldly into Scott's eyes.

"Let's see," Scott said, scratching his head. "It was a yellow Chevy Nova, right? Perfect color for a coward like you. Say, Boy, has your girl had to do any more of your fightin' for you lately?"

"I'm not your boy," Jake said angrily, reaching for the door handle. Unafraid, he was ready to take on Scott and his friends again. Scott stepped back to let him out of the car, but Sammi grabbed his arm, desperately pulling him back inside.

"No fightin' tonight. Please, Jake! Just ignore him," she pleaded.

Jake already had one foot on the blacktop, but as he looked into Sammi's eyes, he could tell that she was frightened. He hated seeing her upset. Nodding his head, he gave her an assuring smile as he slowly pulled his foot back into the car and closed the door. Putting the car into Reverse, he turned and looked at Scott through the open driver's window, "You know, Scott, if I were you, I wouldn't be doing too much talking in public about the night a 110-pound girl dropped me in the dirt with just one kick. Doesn't make you look too good."

Scott quickly looked around to make certain no one else had heard what Jake had just said. By the time he'd turned back around, Jake was slowly backing the big Pontiac out of the parking spot with Eric and Jonathan still sitting on the trunk. Putting the car into Drive, Jake glared at Scott one last time then sped off causing the two would-be toughs on the back to tumble hard onto the pavement. As Jake drove away, Scott hurled the beer bottle at the car, smashing it against the rear bumper as he yelled out, "Say hello to your mom for me!"

"Just ignore it and keep drivin'," Sammi said.

"I wonder what he meant by that last comment?" Jake asked.

"He's just tauntin' you," she said. "Don't let him get in your head."

By the time they pulled into the drive between their trailers, Jake's mind had already turned to the daunting task of going through his mom's closet and drawers to see if his suspicions were correct, but as he came in, it appeared that his aunt was still up. He didn't want her to know what was possibly going on, at least not yet. His aunt was a moral, church-going person and if she found out that Jo had had a man in her room, Jake wasn't sure what she would do. And, if there were in fact drugs hidden in the house somewhere... he felt certain that he and his mom would both have to find a new place to live.

He started to become angry thinking about the possibility that his mother was about to disrupt his life once again; this time, for the first time, there was much more at stake. He could lose his chance of getting a scholarship to college, he could lose his job at the grocery store, but most alarming to him was the thought of losing Sammi.

"You still want to go through her room with me?" he asked her.

"Yes, I do," Sammi nodded resolutely.

"I want to wait until Aunt Hazel is in bed," he said. "When it's clear, I'll turn my bedroom light on and you can come on over." Before getting out Sammi turned toward Jake, placed her palm on his cheek, and smiled. "Everything is going to be okay," she said softly. "I promise." Then, stepping out of the car, she headed toward her trailer as he looked on admiringly until she disappeared into the darkness.

Inside, Jake found Aunt Hazel stretched out in her recliner enjoying a bowl of ice cream.

"Have a bowl," she offered, as he entered the living room.

"No, thank you," he answered. "Sammi and I just ate." Taking a seat on the couch next to her chair, he thought he might pick his great aunt's brain a little about her history with his mom. After all, Hazel had known her niece for her entire life. Jo had always been somewhat tight-lipped with her son about her childhood. Thinking perhaps that Aunt Hazel could provide some background that might help him with his present concerns, Jake spoke up suddenly, "Can I ask you a question?"

Aunt Hazel put the last spoonful of ice cream in her mouth and then placed the bowl on the table next to her chair. "Ask me anything you want."

"Well," Jake began, "It's about my mom."

"I thought it might be," Hazel inserted.

"I assume you know about her addiction issues. But what I don't really understand is how it all started. I know that my father was a drug dealer and that he'd got her hooked on cocaine. But whenever I ask her about her life leading up to that point, she either gets mad and tells me to mind my own business or she changes the subject. She has told me very little about my grandparents other than the fact that they are both dead, but she has always talked about you, very positively. In fact, if she hadn't always referred to you as her Aunt Hazel, I would have assumed she was talking about her mother. There are just a lot of pieces of the puzzle missing and I thought maybe you could fill in the missing parts."

Aunt Hazel looked at Jake with sympathy. Rising from her chair, she said, "Let me get us both something to drink and then we'll talk. But I need your promise that what we talk about stays between us. There's a reason your mother has not wanted to talk about her past, but I think you're old enough to hear at least some of it."

He agreed and Hazel stepped into the kitchen emerging a minute later with two tall glasses of ice-cold milk and a plate of homemade cookies.

She snuggled back into her chair, threw a blanket over her legs, and cleared her throat as if she was preparing to make a long speech. "Your mama was a beautiful little girl, beautiful like she is right now. Her long black hair and dark brown eyes were always attention-getters. But she was also smart. When that young'un was just three years old, she could carry on conversations with adults as if she was one of them. She always made high grades in school, just like you. In fact, I have no doubt that you got your smarts from her. You sure didn't get that brain of yours from your daddy."

Hazel reached for a cookie, took a bite and then continued, "Your mama was a real crackerjack. But when she was twelve years old, somethin' changed. She became sad and acted like she didn't want to be around anybody...stayed in her room a lot. Her grades started droppin' and before long, she was failin' all of her classes. We tried to talk to her to find out what was wrong, but she would always clam up. For the next two years, she just kept gettin' worse and worse; started rebellin' and stayin' out all night. Sometimes she would disappear for several days at a time. It was a mystery to all of us until Christmas Eve of her fifteenth year. Charlie and I always stayed with them on Christmas Eve so we could spend Christmas mornin' together. I'll never forget that night. About 2:00 in the mornin', I got up to get some water and, as I passed by her room, I heard some strange noises comin' from the other side of the door. So I threw open the door, turned on the light, and saw a sight that torments me to this day."

Hazel's countenance turned dark as she sat silent. After a few moments, she continued, "Her daddy, my worthless brother-in-law, was in her bed without a stitch of clothin' on. He had her pajamas and her underwear down around her ankles and was holding her arms up over her head so she couldn't get away. He was on her like a dog in heat. I will never forget the look of torment on that baby girl's face when I walked in that room. I was so shocked that I screamed out loud and that brought Charlie runnin' into the room. By that time, your mama's daddy was trying to get his clothes back on, but Charlie could see what was goin' on and tore into him like a mama bear protectin' her cubs. I turned around to go call the police and saw her mama standin' there. I could tell by the look on her face that she was not surprised by what was going on, which angered me even more. Come to find out, he had been doin' unspeakable things to Jo since she was twelve years old."

The expression on Jake's face was one of horror, so Hazel stopped long enough to let him process what he had just heard. "Keep going," he finally said. "I need to hear all of it."

"Well," Hazel continued, "after the police came and took her daddy away, I lit in to her mama for not stoppin' him. She was my sister but I could never forgive her for that. We never spoke again after that. We took Jo back to our house that night and I slept in the bed with her all night. We both cried until mornin'. My heart still breaks for that baby. That evil man killed her spirit. The real Jo never came back to us. We tried to get her to move in with us, but she had already met your daddy and decided to move in with him and his parents instead. That was the worst decision she could've made because they were all drug addicts. A couple months later, she got pregnant with you and dropped out of school. We rarely saw her after that. I don't think she started usin' the drugs 'til after you were born and I'm thankful for that. When we came to see you at the hospital, I begged her to leave your daddy. Jake, if she had left him right then, your mama could have been a doctor, a teacher, or anything else she wanted, but she just could not tear herself away from him. And I guess you know the rest of the story after that."

Jake was horrified by what his aunt had just told him. He had never heard any of that before. Suddenly overcome with emotion, he slumped forward, buried his face in his hands, and wept bitterly for his mother. Aunt Hazel scooted up to the edge of her chair, placed her hand on his shoulder and wept with him.

After a few moments, Jake composed himself and asked, "What happened to her dad? Did he go to prison?"

"No," Aunt Hazel replied. "When they got him back to the jail house, they put him in a cell by himself because there was no judge available at that time of night, especially on Christmas Eve. When they came to get him in the mornin', he had hung himself. I guess he was too much of a coward to face what was comin.'"

"What about her mom?" Jake asked.

Hazel shook her head, "Jo hated her for lettin' him get away with it for so long. She never saw or spoke to her mama again...didn't even come to the funeral. Your grandma died from a heart attack when you were about three years old. Your mama's been runnin' ever since, Jake. She's never really tried to get help. She just kept goin' after the drugs. But there is one thing I want you to know. She loves you, Boy. She doesn't really know how to show real love because she's never received it herself. She's still lost, Son, but I have no doubt that in her eyes, the sun rises and sets on your shoulders."

Aunt Hazel's words brought the tears back to Jake's eyes. For the next several minutes, they both sat in total silence as he tried to process all he had just heard. As he sat there, he attempted to imagine what it must have been like for Jo, but even with all of his intelligence, he was unable to fathom the pain she must have endured. Though he couldn't put himself in her place, he was able to have a deeper level of compassion for her than before. He was even more worried now about what he had almost walked in on earlier and decided to bring his aunt into the situation.

"Well, there's only one thing to do," she said once he had told her what he had seen and what he feared. "You know her better than I do and if you think she might be usin' drugs or gettin' ready to start usin' 'em again, we need to know so we can try to stop her. Let's search her room now."

"Hold on a minute," Jake said. "Sammi wanted to be with me when I searched the room and I told her I would turn my bedroom light on when I was ready."

Aunt Hazel smiled at the mention of Sammi's name. "That's a very special girl. I'd hold on to her if I were you."

"I'm hoping to," he answered.

"I feel bad for her too," Hazel said. "She's smart and beautiful like your mama used to be. But she gets very little love or attention from Betty and Gerald. Has she told you her story?"

"Yes," Jake replied. "Kind of sad, but she's the most positive person I've ever met."

Jake flipped the light on in his room and, in just a minute, Sammi was walking through the door. She seemed surprised to find Aunt Hazel still up and ready to help, but after Jake told her all that he had just learned, she understood why he wanted to make Aunt Hazel aware of his suspicions. The three of them moved to Jo's bedroom and began to search for drugs, needles, or cash, any of which would confirm Jake's suspicions.

Because of his experience with his mom, he told them where to look, but they found nothing. They searched

Jo's dresser and nightstand drawers, making sure to check the folds of her clothes. They searched her closet, looking inside of her shoes and the pockets of the clothes that were hanging on the rack. They looked under the bed, under the mattress, and even behind the pictures that were hanging on the wall. Jake was starting to feel some relief. Just as they were deciding to end the search, Sammi jerked the sheets up off of Jo's bed. Though there was nothing under the sheets, she noticed a small slit in the side of the mattress.

"What's this," she asked as she started to reach inside the slit.

"NO!" Jake shouted. "Don't put your hand in there. I'll do it."

Startled, Sammi jumped back. Kneeling down by the bedside, Jake slowly reached inside the mattress and cautiously groped about to see if anything was there. When his countenance suddenly dropped, Sammi and Aunt Hazel knew he had found something. When he drew out his hand, he was clutching a small brown paper bag. All three of them held their breath as he dumped the contents of the bag out onto the mattress. As one item after another fell from the bag, Jake's heart began to pound rapidly. The bag contained several needles, five small bags containing a white powdery substance and about $300 in cash. No one spoke a word. After a few minutes, Jake broke the silence.

"I'm going to have to confront her about this when she gets home from work," he said. Aunt Hazel and Sammi tried to comfort him, but their efforts were in vain. Jake knew he had to talk to his mother that very night. After another hour passed, Sammi went home and Aunt Hazel went to bed, but not before taking Jake by the hand and praying for him.

At 2:15 AM, Jo quietly entered the house and tiptoed down the dark hallway toward her room. When she turned on the light, she was met with the unexpected image of Jake sitting in the dark on her bed.

"OH MY!" she screamed, as she clutched her heart in surprise. "Jake, what are you tryin' to do to me? Why in the world are you sittin' here in the dark?"

Looking his mother squarely in the eyes, he didn't speak a word, but paused to let her figure out what was about to happen.

"Jake, what's wrong?" she asked, growing serious. Slowly, he turned his eyes toward the bed to draw her attention to the items lying there next to his hand. When she saw that he had discovered her secret, Jo took a staggering step back. Jake quickly reached out and grabbed both of her wrists, turning her hands upward so he could look at her forearms. There they were: several little bluish-black track marks, each about an inch in length. He struggled to find words. His hope was that she would show remorse, perhaps even cry over the fact that she had relapsed, again. Instead, when he looked up into her eyes, she was glaring at him in anger. They stared at one another for what seemed like minutes to Jake. Finally, she had something to say, but it wasn't what he had hoped for.

"I HATE YOU!" she yelled. "You're no son of mine and you had no right to go through my stuff." Jerking her wrists violently out of his hands, she angrily stuffed everything back into the brown paper bag and stormed out of the bedroom and then right out the front door, slamming it behind her. Utterly stunned, Jake fell back across the bed and stared blankly toward the ceiling.

15

Two days passed with no sign of Jo at home or at work. Most people would have called the police by then, but Jake was all too familiar with his mother's pattern and knew that calling the police wouldn't help. She was very likely holed up in a hotel somewhere with a steady stream of male visitors. In another day or two, she would show up as suddenly as she had vanished with her hair and clothes disheveled, crying and begging everyone's forgiveness. She would then make promises that she would never do drugs or leave again. Jake had been down this road many times with her.

The difference this time, however, was that he now knew more about her history, which helped him feel more sympathy towards her. But showing sympathy was still not easy. Regardless of what she had been through as a child, her actions were still selfish and extremely reckless. When Jo was using, she never gave thought to how her actions affected other people, especially Jake. It was not fair to him or anyone else in her life to allow her past to dictate her future or theirs. Her son's sympathy only went so far.

There were a few other things that made her running off this time different for Jake. He had the support of Aunt Hazel, he had the support of Sammi, he had the support of Principal Taylor and Mrs. Rossman, and he had a steady job. With all of these positives working in his favor, he felt much stronger than he'd ever felt before. He decided not to let his mother's bad choices have a negative impact on his life.

He continued to wake up each morning, ride to school with Sammi, go to work after school, and get his homework done to keep up his grades. He was more determined than ever before to keep focused on what he had to do regardless of the drama and turmoil his mother might be causing. Jake had finally found solid ground to stand on, and he had no intention of losing his footing.

After having been gone for five full days, Jo finally found her way back home around 6:00 o'clock one morning. She tried to be quiet, but Aunt Hazel and Jake both heard her come in. She went straight to her room, fell over onto her bed, and was out cold in just a few minutes. But her rest was about to be short-lived. After a few minutes, she felt someone tugging at her toes.

"Wake up, Jo," Hazel said with a firm tone. "We need to have a talk. I'll give you ten minutes to pull it together and then you need to come to the kitchen table."

Jo grunted in protest, but Hazel kept jerking at her toes until she agreed. There was a chill in the fall morning, so Jo slid out of bed and bundled herself in a robe and a blanket. Stumbling into the bathroom, she tried to start putting herself together, but the sight in the mirror was not pretty. Her face was pale, her black eye shadow was smudged, and her raven black hair was a mess. Her head was pounding, and she felt sick to her stomach. All she wanted to do was go back to bed, but she knew her Aunt Hazel would not allow it. She turned on the hot water and waited for it to warm up.

While she waited, Jo examined herself in the mirror and relived the events of her days away from home. She felt filthy and disgusted with herself as she thought about all the men she had slept with in the past five days. The cycle was always the same: see a couple of johns, then get high; see another couple of johns and get high again. She hated herself for falling back into the same old pattern.

She hated herself for not being strong enough to resist the temptation. She hated herself for possibly ruining things for herself and Jake again, and she was definitely not looking forward to what she was about to hear from her aunt, and maybe even her son. After brushing her teeth and combing through her hair, Jo tightened her robe and made her way into the kitchen where Aunt Hazel and Jake were seated at the kitchen table waiting for her.

"Here," Aunt Hazel said, pushing a cup of steaming black coffee in front of Jo.

Cupping both hands around the hot mug, Jo lifted it to her lips and took a long, noisy sip. "Thank you, Aunt Hazel," she said quietly. "I guess y'all want to know where I've been."

She got no response from the two sitting across from her, and Jake would not even look at her. Instead, his hands were folded and resting on the table in front of his own cup of coffee with his eyes cast downward.

After a painful minute of awkward silence, Aunt Hazel asked, "So, what happened this time, Jo? What or who knocked you off the path?"

Jo sat for a moment, looking at her cup of coffee and trying to formulate a response. She didn't want to tell them that it had started the night she was raped by Scott

Robertson. After taking another sip of coffee, she put the mug down and slid it away from her. Resting her elbows on the table, she hid her face in her hands for a few seconds while she came up with a neatly packaged lie.

"It started several weeks ago," she said lifting her head. "This guy came into the Tavern one Friday night, a real cute guy. His friends called him Tracker, but I don't think that was his real name. Anyway, he treated me real nice; kept tellin' me how pretty I was and how he wished he had a woman like me to come home to every night. He made me feel good, ya know? Well, he stayed until I got off that night, and he asked me if I wanted to sit in his truck with him for a little while. I didn't see no harm in that so I went with him to his truck and after we talked a bit, he offered me a joint. I hadn't had one in a while, so I had a little trouble resistin' the temptation. Then, he started kissin' my neck and I couldn't resist that either. We kissed for a while and then he told me that he had somethin' at his house that I would enjoy a lot more than the joint. I knew what he was talking about, and I know that I should have jumped out right then and run home...but I didn't. When we got back to his house, he brought out a bag of cocaine and some needles. I just couldn't stop myself at that point. He brought me home the next mornin' before y'all were awake, but he never came back to the Tavern after that night. Jake understands, once you put that stuff into your system your body craves it and you'll do just about anything to get it. The only way I could get it was to make some new friends, men friends."

Hazel knew what kind of men she was talking about, "And where did you meet up with these men?" she asked.

Jo answered with great hesitation, "Sometimes in their houses, sometimes in their cars, sometimes in a motel, and sometimes..." she paused and lowered her head. She didn't want to finish the sentence.

"Sometimes where, Jo?" Aunt Hazel demanded.

Jo started to cry. "Sometimes here," she sobbed. "I'm sorry, Aunt Hazel, I didn't mean to disrespect your home, I really didn't."

"Oh, goodness," Aunt Hazel said with dread. "How many came here?"

Jo shrugged her shoulders, "Not sure, maybe five or six."

Aunt Hazel's mouth dropped open in shock, "Did the neighbors see anything?"

"I'm pretty sure Miss Fanny noticed, because she asked me who those men were. I told her they were door-to-door salesmen, but I don't know if she believed me or not," Jo said with shame coloring her voice.

Hazel shook her head in disgust, "If Fanny knows about it, then everybody does. So, where have you been these last five days?"

"At a hotel in Winston," Jo answered. "When I saw that Jake had found the drugs, I was mad and embarrassed, so I hitched a ride out of town." Jo laid her head down on the table and began crying uncontrollably, while Jake and Aunt Hazel looked on silently with a mixture of pity and anger. Suddenly, Jo raised her head and looked at Jake with tears streaming down her face.

"Jake, Baby," she said, her words choked with pain. "I just remembered what I said to you when I left that night."

Jumping up from the chair, she grabbed him in a bear hug from behind, laid her head on the back of his, and wept profusely.

Jake stiffened up like a stone the second his mother touched him, but she didn't seem to notice.

"Sweet Baby, I'm so sorry. You know I love you," she cried, continuing to hug him. "I'm not myself when I'm usin', you know that."

Jake gruffly pushed his mother's arms away. "You embarrassed me in front of Aunt Hazel and Sammi," he said. "You promised me when we first got here that if you started feeling weak, you would let me know. What happened to that promise?"

Jo hung her head in shame. She had no answer for his question.

"Sit back down, Jo," Aunt Hazel said firmly, pointing to the chair. "We've got more talkin' to do."

Jo sat down and took another sip from her cup. "Cold," she said.

Hazel got up and refilled the cup with fresh hot coffee from the pot simmering on the counter. After sitting back down, she covered Jo's hand with her own and said with sincerity, "You know I have always loved you, Jo, ever since the day you came into this world. That will never change. I love you like God loves you, unconditionally. But I'm not gonna turn a blind eye and let you go down this path again. So here's what we're gonna do: I've told Jake that he can stay with me for as long as he needs to—his days of following you from town to town are over. But you, on the other hand, have a big decision to make and you're gonna make it right now, this very minute. We found a place for you to go where you can get some help gettin' those drugs out of your system. You can either let me take you there today, or you can pack up and find another place to live today. The program lasts for three to four weeks so you can either be gone for a month or gone for good. The choice is yours."

Jo quickly realized that there was really only one choice for her. She did not want to leave Jake and, besides, she had nowhere else to go. In her heart, she truly wanted to beat the addiction and she thought maybe this would be the way to do it. Within the hour, she was packed and ready to go.

As Jake loaded Jo's suitcase in the car, he remained silent in spite of his mother's repeated attempts to get him to say something. Just before sliding into the passenger seat, she grabbed him and hugged him tight around the neck, clutching him like she would never let go. Jake finally relented and halfheartedly put his arms around her to return the hug, which seemed to give a small measure of comfort to Jo.

As Aunt Hazel backed out of the driveway, Jo rolled her window down.

"Bye, Sweetie," she called out to Jake as the car pulled away. "I love you, and I'm gonna be a brand-new Jo when I get back...a brand-new mama."

"Love you too, Mom," Jake returned as Aunt Hazel drove away, although he was not sure if Jo heard him or not.

Jake stood in the driveway and watched the car pull away until it was out of sight. As he watched the tail lights disappear into the morning fog, his resolve left him and he felt an enormous sadness come over him. He really did love his mother, but he had heard her make the same promises many times before. In the past, he had believed her many times and, every single time, he ended up disappointed and disillusioned. His troubled years had now made him wiser and more cautious.

Jake was not so quick this time to put his confidence in Jo. He now understood that if he were to have any chance for success or happiness, he would have to put some significant distance between himself and his mother. He knew it was time to think about his own life and begin to plan for his own future. As he pondered this revelation, his thoughts were interrupted by a voice with which he had become very familiar, a voice that always warmed him from the inside out.

"Good mornin'," Sammi called out, practically skipping across the yard toward Jake.

"Good morning," he replied with a smile. As he stood in front of her, gazing into her penetrating blue eyes, Jake was overwhelmed with the sudden realization that he may very well be looking into the face of his future.

16

THE NEXT THREE WEEKS PROVED TO BE VERY fruitful for Jake. With his troubled mother away, his academic life excelled in ways he had never dreamed possible. Principal Taylor and Mrs. Rossman spent numerous hours each week guiding him in making preparations for his college years. A strong mutual respect developed between the three of them as they worked together to plan Jake's future, a future for which his mentors had very high hopes. Jake also gained increasing respect and admiration from his other teachers as he continued to impress them with his maturity and intelligence. Even his peers admired his hard work and dedication to school.

At the advice of Mrs. Rossman, he signed up to run track in the spring even though he had never given much thought to running for sport. She said the extracurricular would look good on a college application. Jake and Sammi also joined the student-led committee that was in charge of the school's Fall Festival. For the first time in his life, he was finding his place. The path forward was becoming clearer to him with each passing day. His future was looking bright and it would soon be time to invite Sammi into that future. He just wasn't sure yet how to go about it, but he knew he wanted it to be special.

Jake adjusted quickly to life without his mother. He sometimes wondered if he was a bad son because he didn't even seem to miss her. With schoolwork, applications and his new extracurriculars, he was never at home when Jo called, and three full weeks went by with no communication at all between them. As the time for Jo's return drew near, a sense of dread began to fill Jake's heart, but he knew there wasn't anything he could do about it. Only time would tell if Jo had really gained anything from rehab, but Jake would not allow his hopes to rise where she was concerned—not this time.

When the Friday of Jo's homecoming finally came around, Jake's anxiety level was high. His aunt thought it might help him if they had a special breakfast together with Sammi before she left to go get Jo. An uncomfortable silence filled the air as the three sat around the table devouring one of Aunt Hazel's traditional southern-style breakfasts. No amount of anxiety ever seemed to affect Jake's ravenous appetite.

"I know you're worryin' about how your mom is gonna be when she gets home," Aunt Hazel said, interrupting the silence. "But when she gets here, she'll need to feel our trust and our support."

Sammi nodded in agreement with Aunt Hazel, but Jake remained silent and skeptical.

"I know you mean well," he said. "But I've been down this road with her many times before. I believe she really does want to stay clean, but the demons in her are too strong. They eventually get the better of her every time."

"We just have to pray hard for her," Sammi said. "And we can each take turns watchin' her."

Jake admired Sammi's good intentions, but over the years, he had come to the conclusion that prayer didn't work unless the one being prayed for actually wanted to change. He believed that even God couldn't help his mother unless she was ready to be helped. One thing he had come to learn about her was that when she wanted drugs, she was going to find a way to get them regardless of the cost. It didn't matter who she hurt as long as she got what she wanted. Not wanting to dampen Aunt Hazel and Sammi's hopes, he decided not to argue with them and instead let them see for themselves. After breakfast, Aunt Hazel left to bring Jo home while Jake and Sammi headed to school.

Throughout the day he struggled to maintain focus as many thoughts bounced around in his head, but by the time his last class ended he had regained his confidence and determination to stay the course and had decided not to allow his mother to derail him. Too many good things were in the works and he could not allow himself to be distracted. As they headed to Newlin's together that afternoon, Sammi was delighted to see the change in his disposition.

"I'm glad to see a smile on your face," she said. "I have to admit I was worried about you this mornin'."

"No need to worry," he replied. "I've learned a valuable lesson these last three weeks. My first responsibility is to myself, not to my mom. If she can stay clean for good, then no one will be happier for her than me. But if she doesn't— if she can't—there's not one thing I can do about it. I've always tried to be her savior, but I've never actually been able to stop her once she starts down that bad path. She's going to have to find her own way, and I'm going to have to find mine."

For the remainder of the ride, the conversation focused mainly on the school's Fall Festival, which was only two weeks away. Jake and Sammi were in charge of setting up games in the gym, and both were very excited about the event. It was the first time he had ever been a part of anything like this, and he couldn't wait for the day to arrive. But there was one thing he was even more excited about. He had finally come up with a plan for letting Sammi know how he really felt about her and it would soon be time to set things in motion.

"I've been wanting to run an idea by you," he ventured during a break in the conversation. "The festival is two weeks from tomorrow, and I thought since we've been working so hard on it that we should reward ourselves with a picnic lunch the day after."

"Oh, that sounds amazin'!" Sammi exclaimed happily. "I would love that! In fact, I will even make lunch for us. Your aunt is not the only one in the neighborhood who can cook. My kitchen skills are not too shabby."

"Sounds great," Jake agreed, trying to stay cool even though his heart was pounding. "I thought that since the leaves are starting to turn, maybe we could drive up to Pilot Knob and have our picnic there."

Her eyes lit up at the idea. "Jake, I can't wait! That is gonna be such a fun day. There are walkin' trails on that mountain so we should definitely plan to stay the whole afternoon."

Jake was both relieved and excited by her response. He had already thought out every detail of that day. First, they would enjoy a nice, relaxing lunch on a soft picnic blanket.

After eating, he would invite her to take a walk to one of the lookout points. Finally, when they stood looking out at the beautiful mountain landscape, he would once and for all reveal the secret that he had been storing in his heart for months. He would express his love for her, then he'd take her in his arms and kiss the lips that he had for so long denied himself. Nervous excitement coursed through his veins every time he rehearsed the plan in his mind.

Interrupting his fantasy, Sammi cried out, "Oh Jake, I am so excited! I wish it wasn't two whole weeks away!"

It was a usual Friday night at the grocery store. The shift went by quickly because of the steady flow of customers. Jake spent the evening daydreaming about the upcoming trip to the Knob and didn't even give his mother a second thought. In fact, it wasn't until he and Sammi were headed home after work that he even remembered that Jo would be there waiting for him. As they approached the trailer park, Jake's heart began to race and he could feel sweat moistening his palms, but he resisted the temptation to let his anxiety overcome him.

Upon entering the trailer, he saw his mother perched nervously on the edge of the couch and Aunt Hazel relaxing in her recliner. Because Jo had not seen or spoken to her son in over three weeks, she was unable to contain her excitement. Bouncing off the couch, she ran to him, threw her arms around his neck, and kissed him repeatedly on the cheeks and forehead.

"Mom! Mom! Enough! That's enough," Jake protested.

"I'm just so glad to see you, Baby Boy!" she cried. "You have no idea how bad I've missed you."

As Jake looked into his mother's face, he could see that her eyes were bright and clear. She also exuded a level of energy that he hadn't seen in a long time. He longed to believe and embrace the person who stood before him, but past experiences kept a tight rein on his hopes.

"You look good," he said, in an attempt to encourage her. "You look healthy."

"I *am* healthy," she declared. "I'm healthy in mind, body, and soul. I know I've told you that before, but somethin' feels different this time, Son. I just know I'm gonna make it this time."

Not wanting to discourage her, Jake nodded his head and gave Jo a hug. But he was not yet willing to commit his heart to her or to her claims. For the next couple of hours, the three of them sat together in the living room as she told them all that she had learned about herself, about her addiction, and about how she planned to stay clean.

There was an undeniable tone of hope in her voice as she spoke. She sounded like a giddy teenager chattering about her experiences at summer camp. As Jo continued, Jake noticed that his aunt seemed to be buying into every word his mother said, but he needed proof, the kind of proof displayed through longevity. *How long could she do it?* he wondered. How long before she grew weak and gave into temptation once more?

Unfortunately, the answers to his questions came fairly soon. As is so often the case with addicts, Jo was strong when surrounded by counselors, doctors, and other recovering addicts. But once she was on her own, it wasn't long at all before she began showing signs of weakness. This time, it took only one week before Jake began to see evidence of wavering. For the first two days after her return, she seemed strong and hopeful and even talked about going back to school and starting a new career.

By Monday though, she was beginning to come down a little. She became nervous and somewhat withdrawn. By Tuesday, she was cranky and easily agitated. On Wednesday, she didn't even come out of her room. Aunt Hazel had to serve her meals in bed. By the next Thursday and Friday, Jo complained of a headache and stomach pains. When Jake and Aunt Hazel woke up on Saturday morning, Jo had already left the house. When she returned that evening, she seemed dazed and very subdued. Rather than eat dinner or talk with Jake and Aunt Hazel, she went straight to bed.

"I've never seen her fall this fast," Jake admitted, as he sat down to have breakfast the next morning. "In the past when she has gotten clean, she has been able to last at least a month."

"I still stand by what I told her before," Aunt Hazel said with conviction. "If she goes down this path again, she's gonna have to leave, but you don't have to go with her this time."

"That means more than you know," Jake said gratefully. "Principal Taylor says I can probably pick any college I want so I plan to stay focused and not let anything or anyone get in my way, especially her."

Jo stayed in bed all day Saturday and Sunday, emerging only a few times in search of food and the bathroom. Jake and Aunt Hazel decided not to engage her until she was a bit more clear-minded. But when Monday morning came, his attention drifted from his mother and turned back to his school activities and to Sammi. With each passing day, he grew more excited about their trip to the Knob.

A nervous knot developed in the pit of his stomach every time he thought about what he was planning to say to Sammi. His gut told him that she would be receptive to an exclusive relationship with him, but there was still a whispering voice of doubt in his mind. But Jake didn't have much time to sit around listening to that or to any other negative voice. As the Fall Festival drew near, they both were swamped with afternoon team meetings to make all the final preparations.

They were so busy, in fact, that they didn't even notice what was going on with Jo. By the time Jake got home from work each night, she was already in bed so he didn't see her much. Emotionally, mentally, and physically he was doing all he could to distance himself from her, but he would not be able to ignore her much longer. Just three days before the Fall Festival, Jake came home after work to find that a small representation of the neighbors had gathered at his home. Entering the house, he saw Mayor, Fanny, Mr. Jones, and a few others sitting around the living room. As usual, Aunt Hazel was serving coffee and cake, but something was different about this meeting. A very solemn tone filled the room.

"Where's Mom?" Jake asked Aunt Hazel.

"We really aren't sure," she replied. "Have a seat, Jake. We've been waitin' for you. There are some things we need to talk to you about...concernin' your mom."

A wave of apprehension came over Jake and his heart felt like it was going to beat out of his chest. He knew that this was not going to be a positive meeting. Silently taking a seat on the couch next to Mr. Jones, he looked into the distressed faces of his neighbors and prepared himself for the worst.

Mayor, being the eloquent man he was, began the uncomfortable conversation, "Son, some things have come to our attention that are causin' a measure of alarm among the neighbors."

"I'll say!" Fanny angrily interrupted. Aunt Hazel gave her a stern look that quickly silenced Fanny's protest.

Mayor continued. "Over the past several days, while you and your aunt have been away at work and school, your mother has been entertainin' a sordid array of male guests. They come for half an hour or so and then they leave. It's not usually too long before the next one arrives. We know that your mother has had a difficult past—and we are very sympathetic to that—but here at Hope Park we have always made every effort to maintain an environment that is safe and conducive to family life. We want our children to be able to play outside freely without their parents worryin' about an element of danger that may suddenly appear. I know that Miss Hazel took her to a rehabilitation center, but apparently her time there was not successful. You know her better than any of us, Jake. So, is there something more that we can do to help your mom?

Jake sensed that old familiar anger knocking at the door of his heart. He was embarrassed that his mother's sins were now so public. Lowering his eyes to the floor, he shook his head and said, "No sir, Mayor. I'm all out of ideas where she's concerned."

"I'm sorry to hear that, Son," Mayor replied with compassion in his voice. "And I am greatly saddened to say that we are going to have to ask her to leave. Miss Hazel and I will be havin' that conversation with her at the beginning of next week, and of course we will help her make the transition as best we can. We will give her time to find another place to live."

A question suddenly came crashing into Jake's mind, but he was afraid to ask. *Do they want me to leave too?* he wondered to himself. The anger he had felt moments earlier turned to anxiety at the thought of having to leave Hope Park.

It was almost as if Mayor could sense what Jake was thinking. Placing a comforting hand on Jake's shoulder, he said, "But now, you are a different story. We know that your mother's life choices are not your fault. We also know that you are working hard and doing well in school. That being said, we hope you will stay with us for as long as you like."

A wave of relief washed over Jake, setting him immediately at ease. Throwing his arms around Mayor's shoulders, he exclaimed, "Thank you so much, Sir!"

"You are welcome, Son," Mayor said, patting Jake on the back. "We will take care of things with Jo. But goin' forward, I want you to focus on the bright future you have. I'm friends with your principal, Dr. Taylor, and she has told me many good things about you."

Turning to the others in the room, Mayor motioned for them to follow him as he made his way toward the door. Everyone walked out without saying a word, but each of them smiled at Jake with sympathy as they departed.

As the door closed behind the last visitor, Aunt Hazel turned to Jake, "Now Son, I want you to let me and Mayor handle this. Don't say a word to Jo. Do you understand?"

"Yes, ma'am," he replied.

As Jake got ready for bed that night, the conversation he had just had with Mayor replayed in his mind, and he wondered how his mother would react to the realization that she had, once again, destroyed an opportunity to have a good life, a normal life. He also wondered how she would take the news that he would not be going with her this time, but would be staying with Aunt Hazel.

As he pondered the path his mother's life was taking again, darkness began to invade his soul. To stop the onslaught of negativity that was attacking his mind, he turned his thoughts to Sammi. It would be only four more days before their trip to the Knob, only four more days before he would finally tell her how he truly felt.

With Jake's busy schedule, it was not too hard to avoid contact with Jo. He didn't see her at all on Thursday and, since she was now in the habit of sleeping in, he was long gone before she got up on Friday. By the time she stumbled out of her room, the house was quiet and empty, which was perfect because it gave her a chance to shoot up before starting her day. After sleeping it off, she got up again, made herself some toast, and took a quick shower in preparation for the clients she was expecting throughout the afternoon.

The first two came and went rather quickly. But when the third one pulled up, he seemed hesitant to get out of his car. It was Garrett, the dog-walker she had met when she first pulled into town. Looking out the window, Jo could see him walking slowly toward the trailer, glancing over his shoulder.

"What's wrong, Sweetie?" Jo asked flirtatiously, popping her head out of the screen door. "Don't you wanna get in here and spend some time with me? You're usually eager to come in."

Garrett looked nervously at Jo, then looked back toward the gate entrance. "Uh, Baby," he said anxiously, "I think I'll just call and set up somethin' later."

"Why?" she asked, puzzled. "What in the world is wrong with you?"

Garrett pointed toward the front gate "Darlin' there are two Kernersville police cars sittin' across the road at the Tavern and they are looking this way. I'm not sure what they're up to. Might be nothin', but I'll see you later."

As Garrett sped out of the park, Jo began to panic. The first thought that came to her mind was that somebody must have called the police. The second thought nearly paralyzed her with fear. Inside the little hole in her mattress was enough cocaine to last a week. If they found it, she would certainly go to jail. She quickly threw on a ragged T-shirt and a pair of jeans and stepped outside to see if they were still there.

To her horror, a third police car had joined the other two and all three were pulling up to Hazel's trailer with their blue lights flashing. Gripped by hysteria, Jo ran back inside and removed the cocaine and paraphernalia from her mattress, but, before she had time to hide it in a less obvious place, the police were already knocking loudly at the door.

"Jo Ledger!" shouted the officer. "This is the Kernersville Police! We have a warrant to search the premises! Open the door now, Ma'am!"

This was not a new experience for Jo, and she knew she only had seconds before they would break the door down and enter by force, especially if they expected to find drugs. The smart thing to do would be to flush the cocaine, but she selfishly dismissed that idea. She could not bring herself to part with her treasure.

"MS. LEDGER!" the officer yelled; his voice slightly muffled by the door. "You have ten seconds to open this door voluntarily or we will break it down!"

Jo knew he meant business and that she had to act quickly. In that moment of panic and fear, Jo had a lapse in judgment that would have dire consequences for her son. Dashing into Jake's room, she stuffed the drugs under his mattress, telling herself that the police were only after her and that they wouldn't search Jake's room.

Stepping into the hallway, she yelled, "I'm comin', Officer! Don't break down my door!"

When she opened the door, four police officers—three males and one female— were waiting impatiently on the other side. The lead officer presented Jo with the warrant and then asked her to step back.

Pointing to the kitchen table, the officer growled abrasively, "Ma'am, I'm going to need you to sit right there and do not get up while we conduct our search."

"What are you searchin' for?" Jo asked innocently.

"We have reason to believe there are drugs on the premises," he answered sternly.

His no-nonsense demeanor intimidated Jo and she decided it would be best not to ask any more questions. The female officer stood watch over Jo while the three male officers conducted a very thorough search, turning over every piece of furniture, every cushion, every scrap of paper. In fact, there was nothing they left unturned in the kitchen and living room. As they began making their way down the hallway, Jo became very nervous.

"They don't need to check my son's room," Jo said to the female officer, trying to sound nonchalant. "He's never been in trouble a day in his life. He makes good grades and he works real hard. I can tell you there's no drugs in his room."

"Which room is his?" the female officer asked.

"First one on the right," Jo replied, sure that she had just averted disaster.

Jo's desire to keep them out of Jake's room only fueled the officer's suspicion. "Better check the room on the right," she called to the others. "It's her son's room."

When she heard them enter Jake's room, Jo's face turned pale and she began to tremble. To make matters worse, Jake and Sammi were just getting home from school and had walked into the trailer at that exact time.

"Mom! What in the world is going on?" Jake demanded. As he approached the table where his mother was sitting, the female officer raised her hand to stop him.

"Mom, what did you do? Why are the police here?" Jake asked with desperation in his voice.

Jo could barely speak above a whisper. Dropping her face into her hands, all she could say was, "I'm so sorry, Jake. I'm so sorry."

She had hardly gotten the words out of her mouth when the lead officer came out of Jake's bedroom and saw him standing in the kitchen. "Son, is this your room?" he asked.

Jake looked at his mother with confusion, then looked at the officer. "Yes sir," he answered respectfully.

"Step in here a minute, young man," the officer instructed gruffly.

While Jake went into his room with the police officers, Sammi stood before Jo in shock. "Jo?" she said, on the verge of tears. "Can you tell me what's goin' on?"

Jo didn't answer, but just kept looking down at the place mat on the table. Sammi could see that she was crying. After a few minutes, Jake emerged from his room, his face as white as a sheet. He looked like he was going to be sick.

"What's wrong, Jake?" Sammi asked fearfully. "Why are you tremblin' so?"

Jake walked over and sat down at the table across from his mother. He didn't speak a word, but only glared at Jo who still had not looked up from the place mat. Sammi stepped up behind Jake and put her arms around him. The moment she touched him; tears began to trickle down his cheek.

"Mom, look at me, please," Jake pleaded with a trembling voice. His words fell on deaf ears.

"Mom, you need to say something to these officers," he said, trying to get her attention a second time. Still, there was no response from Jo.

After the officers had thoroughly searched the rest of the trailer, the lead officer walked up to Jake who was still seated at the table staring at his mother through eyes that were now red and wet.

"Son," the officer said to Jake, "stand up and put your hands behind your back."

Jake slowly rose from the table, never taking his eyes off of his mother.

As the officer cuffed his hands, he spoke the words that Jake never dreamed he would hear.

"Jake Ledger, you are under arrest for possession of narcotics. You have the right to remain silent..."

17

"NO!" Sammi screamed, no longer able to hold back the tears. "Please don't arrest him! He hasn't done anything wrong!" she sobbed. In her panic, she unwittingly grabbed the officer's arm in an attempt to stop him.

"Young Lady," the officer retorted, "remove your hand from me right now or I'll arrest you too."

Realizing the foolishness of her actions, Sammi quickly pulled her hand away and stepped back a few feet.

Once more, Jake tried to get his mother's attention. "Mom...Mom...you need to look at me. Don't you have something you need to say?"

Jo remained almost catatonic, seemingly unaware of anyone else's presence in the room.

"Let's go, Son," the officer said firmly, propelling Jake towards the door.

"I'll call Aunt Hazel right now, Jake," Sammi said, her voice quivering with fear. "We will figure somethin' out, I promise."

"Call Principal Taylor too," he said, trying to stay strong. "She'll know what to do."

"I will do all of that right now," Sammi said, following Jake and the officers out the door. Suddenly, she was overwhelmed with uncontrollable crying fueled by both shock and anger.

"Sammi, look at me," Jake said as he was pushed toward the police cars. "I need you to stay calm. They are going to search my car, but when they are finished, you take my keys and you can use the car until this thing is settled. You still have the festival you have to go to tomorrow night."

"I am not goin' to the festival without you," she asserted.

"You need to go," Jake insisted. "They're counting on at least one of us being there. Call Principal Taylor and Aunt Hazel. They'll know what to do. But you need to be at the festival."

Sammi nodded her head in reluctant consent. As the officer held Jake's head down so he wouldn't hit it getting into the backseat of the patrol car with his hands cuffed, Sammi leaned over the door and whispered frantically, "What is goin' on here? I don't understand why they're arrestin' you."

As the officer closed the door, Jake's eyes locked with hers. For the first time since they had met, she saw fear in his eyes. "She hid *her* drugs under *my* mattress," he answered in bewilderment.

Sammi stepped back in shock. She couldn't believe what she had just heard. She could not imagine the kind of person who could betray her own son and put him at such risk. As she watched them drive Jake away, Sammi began to seethe with anger. By nature, she was quick to forgive and slow to confront, but she knew she could not keep quiet about the indescribable act of selfishness and betrayal she had just witnessed.

186

Storming back inside the trailer, Sammi found Jo still sitting in a stupor at the table. In an uncharacteristic move, she grabbed the back of the chair that Jo was sitting in and jerked it away from the table, creating enough room for her to place herself directly in front of Jo.

"You have to fix this, Jo!" she cried. "You cannot let them put him in jail! He's a good person! He doesn't deserve this!"

"Yes, yes," Jo said, still in a state of shock. "He *is* a good boy. They'll figure that out and when they do, they'll let him go. Right? It'll all be just fine."

"NO, IT WON'T BE FINE!" Sammi screamed. "They found drugs, YOUR drugs, in his room! I can assure you; they WILL put him in jail and his future will be ruined!"

"They won't put my baby in jail," Jo slurred, barely able to keep her eyes open. "He's a good boy. My Jake is a good boy."

Realizing she was getting nowhere, Sammi called Aunt Hazel at the bank and told her what had just happened. It seemed like only minutes before she was home, but by that time Jo had locked herself in her room and refused to come out regardless of the threats Aunt Hazel repeatedly fired at her through the door.

Finally giving up, Hazel and Sammi headed to the police station to see if they could post bail and get Jake home, but they had little success. A very kind officer explained that, because of his age and due to the amount of drugs found in his room, Jake would likely be held over the weekend at the juvenile detention center in Winston-Salem and be brought before a judge on Monday morning. Hearing those words from the officer unsettled the ladies even further.

"I met the young man when they brought him in," the officer said with compassion. "He didn't strike me as the kind to use drugs."

"He's not!" Aunt Hazel and Sammi exclaimed simultaneously.

"I've been here a long time," the officer continued. "Seen lots of teen drug addicts and he just doesn't fit the profile. He seemed clear-minded and spoke with respect to everyone who addressed him."

"What can we do for him?" Aunt Hazel pleaded. Sammi had never seen her neighbor so frazzled.

"I would certainly be present on Monday when he goes before the judge," the officer stated. "And it wouldn't hurt if you know someone with a solid reputation who would be willing to speak on his behalf."

As soon as those words left the officer's mouth, Aunt Hazel and Sammi looked at each other. They both knew exactly who to ask: Mayor and Principal Taylor. In the eyes of the community, Mayor was a successful, honest, businessman and property owner. His family had lived in Kernersville for over a century. Principal Taylor was also highly respected by many. If the two of them couldn't help Jake, then no one could.

There were two pay phones in the lobby of the police station. Aunt Hazel handed some loose change to Sammi and instructed her to call the school and get hold of Principal Taylor. She got on the other pay phone and started trying to track down Mayor. Neither had any luck. The school secretary told Sammi that Principal Taylor had just left for an out-of-town conference and wouldn't be back until Monday afternoon. Mayor was in Charlotte for the weekend visiting his son and daughter-in-law and would not be back until Sunday night. Frustrated by their failed efforts, the ladies once again approached the officer who had been so helpful to them and explained that the two most influential people they knew were away for the weekend.

The officer assured them that Jake would be safe and well cared for until he was brought before the judge on Monday. Until then, there was nothing they could do. The ride back home was silent with the exception of a few times when some very choice words were spoken of Jo. Neither Aunt Hazel nor Sammi could understand why she would let her own son go to jail for something she had done. This sealed the deal for Aunt Hazel: Jo would be out of her house by Monday morning.

When Saturday morning came, Sammi was beside herself. There was much to do at the school in preparation for the festival that night, but her heart was not in it. However, to honor Jake's request, she set her mind to it. She was not surprised by his desire for her to be at the school to help. In the few months that she had known him, she had discovered that Jake was always putting the needs of others first. Even while being cuffed and shoved into the back of a police car, he was concerned about letting the other members of the committee down. It was a quality about him that Sammi greatly admired and respected. It was a quality that made him rare and valuable in her eyes.

Around 4:00 o'clock that afternoon, Sammi drove Jake's car to the school and began setting up the gym for the games she and Jake had prepared for the students. The other students on the committee noticed Jake's absence and also picked up on the fact that Sammi was distracted. She was determined not to tell them what had happened and made up an excuse about a family emergency that had come up, keeping Jake from being able to attend the festival.

Thankfully, they seemed satisfied with her story and turned their attention back to their individual responsibilities.

Around 6:30 that evening the students began showing up in droves. By 7:30, there were several hundred teenagers dancing to the booming music, playing games, and eating an abundance of hotdogs, hamburgers, and chips. It was a truly festive occasion and everyone was having a blast except one—Sammi. She wore a fake smile that fooled everyone, but her mind was tormented as she played the events of the previous afternoon over and over again in her head. Jake had told her to remain calm, but when she pondered the possible repercussions of Jo's betrayal, she couldn't help but be overcome with worry.

This arrest could affect Jake's entire future, beginning with college. There were several universities that were already showing interest in Jake, but if they thought he had been arrested for drug possession, it would all end in a second. Sammi also could not stop thinking about the plans they had made for Sunday to drive up to Pilot Knob for a picnic. She had been so excited about that and now even that was gone. All through the evening, she kept watching the big clock on the wall of the gym. The festival was scheduled to end at 10:30 and then she would have to stay to help clean up. It would likely be midnight before she would be able to head home.

The crowd finally began to dwindle as the festival drew to a close. It was after 11:30 when Sammi and the other committee members were able to part ways and head home. Her mind was still focused on Jake as she made the long trek across the dimly lit campus to where she had parked his car. She was exhausted. All she wanted to do was go home, take a bath, and crawl in bed.

After getting into the car, she couldn't help but notice how nice and quiet it was. No one else seemed to be around so she decided to sit for a moment to sort out her thoughts. The parking lot was empty and the night sky was filled with beautiful twinkling stars. Sitting there in the silence, she thought about all the nights that she and Jake had sat up on her roof: star-gazing, eating, talking, and listening to music. She remembered the night they danced and how her heart pounded rapidly as he'd held her in his arms.

Though they had never spoken the words, she knew that she was in love with him and that there would never be another man who would ever hold a candle to Jake Ledger. She had been waiting for him to make the first move and secretly had hoped that the trip to Pilot Knob might be the moment when things would change between them. From the time he'd told her about the trip, she had dreamed of what he might say to her and what she might say in response. Maybe he would finally get up the nerve to kiss her and then their relationship would move beyond friendship to something more intimate, more permanent.

Sammi smiled as she thought about how Jake made her feel, but the smile quickly dimmed when she remembered the horrible mess that he was in. She wondered how he was doing. Was he thinking about her? Was he frightened? Would Mayor and Principal Taylor be able to fix all of this when they returned to Kernersville? As she thought about all these things, she could feel the anxiety rising in her. Leaning back against the headrest, she closed her eyes and began to pray. *"God, please keep Jake safe and help him not to worry. I ask that you make his mom do the right thing and confess her sin. Please let the judge be wise enough to see what's really going on and bring Jake back to me real soon."* After praying, she felt herself becoming calm again and decided to head home.

She placed the key in the ignition, but when she turned the key, the engine did not start. *Oh no*, she thought to herself. *What more could go wrong?* She turned the key again, but the engine still did not start. She sat there for a moment trying to figure out what to do. She knew her grandparents would be asleep by now and it was too far to walk home, especially in the dark. The other committee members were probably already gone. Just as panic was about to set in, a figure appeared out of nowhere and tapped twice on the driver side window. Her first thought was that it might be the school custodian, a man she had known for years, and relief flooded her. She could trust him to get her home safely.

Sammi turned her head to see who this Good Samaritan might be, but it was not the custodian. As she fixed her eyes on the man who stood next to the disabled car, she became paralyzed with fear. Her first impulse was to lay down on the horn and scream, but she was unable to move her hands from the steering wheel. Her blood ran cold as she found herself staring into the face of a demon.

The man standing next to the car was not the custodian, it was not the assistant principal, and it was not one of her friends. Any of those faces would have been a welcomed sight. But this was not the face of a friend. The tall, dark figure looming over her was Scott Robertson and he was holding something in his hand, a wire of some sort. She did not know what it was, but she knew it was the reason the car wouldn't start.

"Car trouble, ma'am?" Scott asked, grinning like a cat that had just cornered a mouse. "I don't think it's gonna start without this," he smirked, dangling the coil wire in front of the window. In that instant, Sammi knew that she was in grave danger and that he had likely been planning this for a while, but there seemed to be no way of escape for her this time. The last time she had run into Scott in a parking lot, Jake had been with her and together they were able to fight their way out. But this time she was on her own. Utter and absolute fear seized her heart as she thought about what might happen next.

Scott's demeanor changed as the evil grin on his face turned into a leering, lustful gaze. "Time for you to pay what you owe Little Lady. And this time, as luck would have it, there's nobody here to help you."

18

As Scott reached to open the car door, Sammi gathered her senses quickly enough to lock it. But she was so focused on Scott that she didn't notice Eric creeping up along the passenger side of the car. Before she even knew he was there, he had opened the car door, reached in, grabbed her by the hair, and pulled her out onto the pavement. She kicked and screamed with all her might in hopes that someone would hear, but there was no one around. As Eric jerked her to her feet, she came up swinging and caught him on the bridge of the nose, hitting him hard enough to draw blood, but he didn't back off.

By now, Scott had come around the side of the car and he roughly grabbed her arms, immobilizing her so she couldn't hit Eric again. Eric looked toward the woods that were adjacent to the parking lot and motioned with his hand. At that moment, Jonathan drove the Ford truck out from behind the trees where the three of them had been hiding and waiting. She knew then that this whole thing had been planned in the evil mind of Scott Robertson. After pulling out into the parking lot, Jonathan jumped out to help the other two. But when he saw the fear on Sammi's face, he began to have doubts about the plan.

"Maybe we should forget this and just let her go," Jonathan said. "I'm startin' to think this ain't such a good idea."

Scott released his hold on Sammi and Eric quickly grabbed her so she couldn't run. Grabbing Jonathan by the shirt, Scott slammed him against the side of the truck and snarled, "Boy, don't go gettin' weak on me now. She's had this comin' for months."

"But look at her," Jonathan argued. "She's scared to death."

Angered by Jonathan's change of heart, Scott slapped him hard across the mouth. "Shut up and get back behind the wheel of the truck! We've gone too far to stop now. This is gonna happen whether you want it to or not...and by the way, you've been a part of this since the beginnin', so you'd best be gettin' on board with the plan."

Jonathan nodded his head and reluctantly obeyed, wiping a trickle of blood from his lip. As he climbed back into the truck, Sammi began to plead with her captors.

"Scott, please, I'm beggin' you, don't do this to me," she pleaded, tears dripping down her cheeks. But Scott's mind was firmly fixed, and he had no intention of letting her go. As he and Eric tried to move her to the bed of the truck, she resisted with everything she had and was able to free one of her hands from Eric's grip. She managed to punch Scott hard in the throat before Eric grabbed her hand again.

Enraged by Sammi's resistance, Scott hit her in the stomach. The force of his fist sent shock waves throughout her entire body, causing her to drop to the ground in a fetal position with a heart-rending scream. Still driven by anger, Scott lifted her off the pavement and slammed her petite body into the bed of the truck like a sack of potatoes, throwing her down so hard that she was knocked unconscious.

Witnessing the violence from inside the cab, Jonathan knew he had to do something to stop it. He stepped out of the truck and attempted to confront Scott one more time.

"Scott, this thing's goin' too far," he implored. "It's not too late to stop. She seems to be a forgivin' person. Maybe she won't say anything if we let her go."

Scott had heard all he wanted to hear from Jonathan and struck his jaw with a hard right punch, knocking him to the ground. Then, grabbing him by the back of the collar, Scott lifted Jonathan off the ground, shoved him into the passenger side of the truck, and slammed the door.

"Eric, you're drivin'!" Scott ordered. "I'll ride in the back with Sammi to make sure she don't jump out. We're takin' her to the Johnson farm. There's an old white barn on the backside of the property. There's a private gravel road that'll take us right to it. There won't be anybody around to hear her if she starts screamin' again. Do what I say and I'll let you have a turn with her when I'm done."

Eric knew better than to resist Scott's orders and, like the spineless minion he was, put the truck in gear and headed out to the country. After a few minutes, Jonathan came to from his dazed condition caused by Scott's sharp blow to his jaw and realized where they were.

"Eric, you need to listen to what I'm about to say," Jonathan pleaded. "Scott is out of control. What we are doin' could put all of us in prison. You need to help me stop him."

"Stop who? HIM?" Eric replied. "You would have a better chance at stoppin' a train. No sir, we been puttin' this thing together for months and so far, it's workin' out just like we planned. Besides, he told me he would give me a turn with her. He might do the same for you if you just go along with it."

"I don't want a turn," Jonathan said, disgusted at the thought. "Look man, she's never done anything to any of us. We need to help her before he kills her."

"He is NOT gonna kill her," Eric said with a laugh. "You and I both know what he wants, and after he gets it, he'll be satisfied and move on."

"Yeah," Jonathan answered. "And all three of us will end up behind bars."

Eric shook his head. "You know better than that. His daddy will never let him go to jail, or us for that matter. As long as all three of us cover for each other, it'll be the word of a trailer trash girl against the richest boy in town. You know the law can't touch a man with money."

Eric's smug attitude was sickening. Jonathan had always been up for a little vandalism or even a good fight every now and then, but this was different. This was truly a cruel act, a criminal act. Sammi was innocent and at the moment she was quite helpless. Realizing he was fighting a losing battle with Eric, Jonathan remained quiet and tried to think of a way to rescue Sammi once they got to the Johnson farm.

The drive seemed to take forever, but finally they pulled up to the old white barn. Jonathan had hoped that there might be someone close by, but as he looked around, he saw nothing but the black night. The only light came from a small yellow bulb that hung just over the barn door. As Eric brought the truck to a stop, Scott jumped out of the back.

"Help me get her out onto the ground!" Scott ordered.

Eric hopped out of the truck in eager anticipation, but Jonathan was slow to emerge, his mind still searching for a way to save Sammi. He was willing to do whatever it took to rescue her. Eric opened the gate of the truck bed and grabbed the still unconscious Sammi's feet, pulling her towards the tailgate, and lifting her out. "Lay her down in that grassy spot over there," Scott instructed. "There's enough light from the barn to see, but she'll still be in the shadows...no chance of anyone seein' what's going on."

Jonathan realized that it was now or never. Whatever his move was going to be, it needed to happen now. Glancing into the back of the truck, he noticed a metal pipe about three feet in length. A plan began to come together in his mind. If he could get behind Scott unnoticed, he could take him out with the pipe. Eric would be no problem after Scott was down as he didn't seem to have a mind of his own. Just as Jonathan started to reach for the pipe, Scott called to him.

"Jonathan," Scott smirked, "you get the honor of takin' her clothes off."

"I won't do it, Scott," Jonathan replied with determination. "I'm done with this. You do what you have to do, but I'm out."

"Suit yourself," Scott replied. Looking at Eric, he said, "help me get her out of her clothes. I've been waitin' to lay my eyes on this ever since I first saw her."

Eric wasted no time, but as he began to loosen her jeans, Sammi came to and immediately started frantically screaming and fighting. Scott jumped in to try to help Eric restrain her and Jonathan saw his opportunity. Grabbing the pipe out of the back of the truck, he crept up to them from behind, but he made the mistake of stepping between Scott and the light from the barn.

When Jonathan raised the pipe over his head, Scott saw his shadow and quickly rolled out of the way. As he jumped to his feet, Jonathan took a swing at his head, but Scott ducked and then charged toward Jonathan, knocking him to the ground. Eric held Sammi down with his hand over her mouth while the other two wrestled for several minutes, each one trying to gain control of the pipe. Scott, being the larger of the two, eventually overpowered Jonathan and beat him nearly to the point of unconsciousness.

Watching the fight from the shadows, Sammi realized that Jonathan had, at some point, become her ally. But her would-be hero was down and unable to defend her now. Scott tossed the pipe in the bed of the truck, brushed the dust off of his clothes, and walked over to his victim who was still being restrained by Eric.

"Time for me and you to dance, Sweetheart," Scott sneered, still out of breath from the fight.

At that moment, Sammi decided she would rather die fighting than to give in and let Scott violate her. As soon as he touched her, she bit Eric's hand. He yelped and released his grip on her. As soon as he pulled his hands away, Sammi began swinging and kicking, all the while screaming at the top of her lungs in hopes that someone would hear. But Scott swiftly overcame her, battering her mercilessly with his fists. Some blows landed on her face while others struck her in the stomach and ribs. Her desperate pleas for help were futile and after several minutes of battling for her life, Sammi was nearly unconscious and simply had no more strength to resist.

With the fight gone out of her, Eric began to remove her jeans while Scott violently ripped open her blouse. He was about to tear off her bra when he noticed a shiny object lying flat against her chest. It was the butterfly necklace Jake had given her on the Fourth of July which she had worn every day since then. Snatching the necklace from around her neck, Scott stuffed it into his pocket as if it were a souvenir to commemorate this horrific event.

For the next hour, both Scott and Eric took turns using Sammi's body to gratify their sadistic urges. There seemed to be no limit to the lewd and unspeakable acts they inflicted upon their defenseless victim. Jonathan was in and out of consciousness during the attack, but the atrocities he witnessed when he was awake were so brutal in nature that they made him vomit. He lay there in complete shock as his two life-long companions descended into depths of pure evil that he had never before witnessed in them.

Until now, their usual antics could be described as mischievous, often even bordering on illegal, but tonight a line was crossed, a line that could not be erased or ignored. The acts perpetrated in the dim light that shone from above the barn door were acts that would forever change the lives of all four of them. There was no going back.

Struggling to pull himself up, Jonathan dragged himself over to the truck and leaned against the back tire, the effort sending pain shooting through his body. Though he was still unable to stand, he could see her lying about twenty feet from him in the grass. Sweet, gentle Sammi, the most beautiful girl in town, the love of Jake Ledger's life, now lay naked and covered in her own blood. He couldn't tell if she was breathing or not and he wondered if she was even alive. Her eyes were bruised and swollen shut, and her once angelic face was unrecognizable from the beating she had received from Scott.

The sight was painfully unbearable to Jonathan and his stomach heaved. But what he heard next enraged him even more. Scott and Eric were actually laughing and congratulating one another as if they had just won a championship game. There seemed to be no remorse at all for the horrible things they had just done to this innocent young girl. The anger he felt inside gave him the strength to pull himself to his feet but, before he was able to stand straight, Scott grabbed him by the back of the neck and pulled him over to where Sammi was lying, still unconscious.

Forcing Jonathan to his knees, Scott shoved him to within inches of Sammi's face. "Take a good look at her, you sorry traitor," he sneered. "Get a good look at her face because if you even think about sayin' a word to anybody, you will look a lot worse than she does right now. You're as much a part of this as we are and if this goes to the police, I will make sure they know that it was you who planned the whole thing. I will make sure they know it was you who raped her, not me and Eric. Do you understand what I'm sayin' to you?"

Jonathan nodded his head, fighting back the bile rising in his throat.

"Let's toss her in the barn," Scott ordered. "They won't find her for days."

"I'll do it," Jonathan quickly volunteered.

"That's more like it," Scott said with a heinous smile. "We're a team. We work together."

As Jonathan summoned the strength to lift Sammi off the ground, she let out a soft moan. It was a sweet sound to his ears because it meant she was alive. While Jonathan carried her into the barn, the other two made sure no evidence was lying around outside. Just inside the barn door was a pile of hay where Jonathan carefully placed Sammi's limp body and then covered her with his jacket.

"Sammi, can you hear me?" Jonathan whispered. She moaned again which made him hope she could.

"Listen to me," he continued. "I'm so sorry for my part in all of this. I didn't think they would really go this far. But don't leave this barn. I'll be back for you in a little bit and get you to the hospital, I promise."

"What's takin' you so long in there?" Scott hollered.

"I'm comin'!" Jonathan yelled back.

The ride back into town was long and painful for Jonathan. All he could think about was getting back to Sammi, and he hoped that she would still be alive when he got there. After Scott and Eric dropped him off at his house, he stumbled inside and waited a few minutes to make sure they were out of sight. As soon as it was clear, he jumped in his car, ignoring the pain coursing through his body from the beating he'd received, and raced back to the Johnson farm as fast as he could, dust billowing up behind him on the gravel road.

Skidding to a stop in front of the barn, he dashed inside and found Sammi in the same position he had left her. But now her body was cold, she was unresponsive, and her breathing was very shallow. He knew he had very little time to get her to the hospital, which was a good thirty minutes away, so he wasted no time carrying her to the back seat of his car.

As he pulled up to the entrance of the emergency room, Jonathan laid on the horn to get someone's attention. By the time he had the back door of his car open, two hospital attendants were already outside with a gurney.

"Her name is Sammi," Jonathan told the two attendants, his voice cracking from the fear and guilt he felt. "She's been raped and beaten. You've got to help her. I'm afraid she's dyin'."

Noticing the cuts and bruises on Jonathan's face, one of the attendants looked at him with an air of suspicion, "You need to let us look at you too." he said.

"No! Just take care of her!" Jonathan breathlessly demanded.

"You can't leave," the other attendant stated firmly. "The police will need to talk to you."

Suddenly Jonathan began to panic. The gravity of his circumstances was becoming clear to him. If he waited for the police, they would likely become suspicious and arrest him. At that point, he would either have to tell them the truth or take the blame for the rape. Telling the truth would get Scott and Eric involved and, even though he no longer felt any loyalty to them, he remembered Scott's threats. As the attendants wheeled Sammi down the hall, Jonathan began to edge toward the door. Looking back and realizing that he was about to run, one of the attendants called back to him, "Son, I wouldn't do that if I were you. They'll find you and it will be worse if you run."

They don't know my name, Jonathan thought to himself, *and I don't think they saw my license plate.* Keeping one eye on the attendants who were now focusing their attention on Sammi, he bolted for the door, hopped back in his car, and was gone in seconds.

Back inside the emergency room, Sammi was now surrounded by several nurses and doctors. The team worked frantically to stabilize her. Her injuries were so severe that one nurse thought she had been in a horrific car accident. Her face was bruised and bloody. She had bled so much, in fact, that her hair looked red instead of its usual strawberry blonde.

Both of her eyes were swollen shut and there was evidence on her neck that she had been choked and possibly even punched in the throat. The skin on her stomach had turned purple and blue with bruising and her knuckles were bleeding from where she had fought her attackers. Both of her legs were covered with scratch marks and when they lifted Jonathan's coat off of her, there was clear evidence that she had been sexually assaulted.

"Do we know what her name is?" the doctor asked.

"I believe it's Sammi," a nurse answered.

Leaning over her, the doctor called to her loudly, "Sammi? Can you hear me, Sweetheart? We are going to help you, but I need you to try and communicate with me if you can. I know you can't open your eyes right now and I know you can't speak, but if you can hear me, squeeze my finger."

The doctor put his finger in Sammi's palm and closed her hand around it. "Squeeze if you can hear me, Dear."

Much to the doctor's satisfaction, Sammi was able to weakly squeeze his finger. "That's good, Sammi," the doctor said. "While the nurses are working on you, I need to ask you some very important questions. I want you to squeeze once for yes and twice for no. Do you understand?"

Sammi squeezed once.

"You're doing good, Sammi," the doctor said gently. "I only have a few questions for you and then I'll let you rest. Were you raped tonight?"

She squeezed once.

"Do you know who raped you?" he asked.

She squeezed once.

204

"Okay, Sammi, last question, I promise. Can you tell me who did this to you?"

Sammi squeezed once, but she was unable to speak because her throat was so swollen, so she made a writing motion with her hand. The doctor pulled a pad of paper out of his pocket, placed a pen in her hand, and held the pad for her. Though she struggled, Sammi was able to scratch out a name.

The doctor looked at the name on the piece of paper. He again placed his finger in the palm of her hand and asked, "So, just to be sure I understand, the name you wrote down is Scott Robertson. Is this the name of the person who raped you?"

Sammi squeezed once. Tears were now beginning to stream from her swollen eyes. The doctor stared with disgust at the name on the paper. It was familiar to him. Though this was the first time Scott's name had ever been associated with a rape, Sammi was not the only person to end up in the emergency room because of him. Scott Robertson had left quite a trail of victims over the last couple of years.

"You're going to be okay, Sammi," the doctor assured her. "We are going to contact your family, but in the meantime, we are going to give you the best care we can."

Stepping out of the room, the doctor called one of the nurses to his side. "This is the worst rape case I've ever personally witnessed," he said. "It's a miracle that she is still breathing. We need to call the sheriff and get him here as soon as possible."

"I'll call him now," the nurse said.

The doctor turned back toward Sammi and looked at her sympathetically. "That poor girl has a long road ahead of her," he said.

19

"You've got visitors," the guard announced. It was early Monday morning, and Jake was still lying atop the shoddy mattress that the detention center tried to pass off as a bed. Laden with lumps and springs, any hopes of sleep were beyond reach; and it smelled horrible, a combination of body odor and dried urine. Needless to say, Jake's weekend was the worst he had ever had. He was exhausted and hungry. Since Friday afternoon, he had experienced a whole gamut of emotions from shock to fear to anger and then finally hatred. Hate was the strongest of all of them and, at the moment, was in full control.

"Who's here?" Jake asked.

"Do you want to see 'em or not?" the guard growled. "I don't care either way."

"Yes, I want to see them," Jake answered. "Let me get my shoes on."

The guard led Jake down a dimly lit corridor and stopped in front of a huge wooden door.

"They're right in here," he said to Jake as he threw open the heavy door.

When Jake stepped into the room and saw who had come to visit him, he could barely contain his excitement. Standing to their feet to greet him were Mayor, Principal Taylor, Mrs. Rossman, and of course, Aunt Hazel. The four of them were joined by a distinguished looking gentleman holding a briefcase. After lots of hugs, Mayor introduced him as Roger Dobson, an attorney.

"Let's all have a seat," Mayor said. "Jake, Counselor Dobson has some good news to share with you this mornin'."

"I think Dr. Taylor would be the better choice to start this conversation," Counselor Dobson said. "Dr. Taylor, tell Jake what you and Mrs. Rossman have been up to this weekend."

Dr. Taylor leaned forward, giving her star student an assuring smile. "Jake, I didn't hear about what happened to you until Saturday afternoon, but as soon as word got to me, I made arrangements to leave the conference early so we could get this thing settled as soon as possible. No one sitting in this room believes for a second that the drugs they found in your room were yours. We know exactly who they belonged to, and we were shocked to learn what your mother had done when the police showed up on Friday. I can't begin to express how grieved I was for you and how angry I was at her. So Mrs. Rossman and I made a surprise visit to your house early Sunday morning and we confronted your mother. To be honest, we confronted her so loudly that the neighbors probably heard us on the other end of the street. The long and short of it is, we drove your mother to the police station yesterday and she confessed what she had done. She told them that the drugs were hers and that you didn't even know they were in the house. Of course, they arrested her on the spot and it will be her, not you, going before the judge later this morning."

A tremendous sense of relief washed over Jake. "So, what's going to happen to me?" he asked nervously.

"Well," Mrs. Rossman said with a smile. "The news gets even better. Dr. Taylor contacted some very influential friends of hers. To say she has friends in high places is an understatement. She explained the situation to them and they, in turn, made some calls. The good news is we've come to take you home. This whole matter will be completely wiped away. No one will ever know what happened."

Jake could not contain himself. Jumping to his feet, he grabbed each one in the room and hugged them. He even hugged the lawyer, making him drop his briefcase.

"I don't know what to say!" Jake exclaimed. "I just can't find words to express how thankful I am for everything you all have done for me."

"That's okay," Mayor interrupted. "We're just glad it all worked out. By the way, we brought Counselor Dobson because he will be takin' your mother's case and we thought you might want to know what's gonna be happenin' with her . . ."

"I don't care what happens to her!" Jake snapped. "I don't want to hear her voice; I don't want to see her face; I don't even want to be in the same room with her." The room fell silent at Jake's outburst, but no one was surprised by his words and no one attempted to change his mind.

"So, when do I get to leave?" Jake asked with anticipation.

The room was suddenly filled with an anxious silence as all eyes turned to Mayor.

"Well, Son," Mayor said softly. "There's somethin' else we need to talk about."

"I'm going to step out for this, if you don't mind," Counselor Dobson said. Reaching out to Jake, he shook his hand and handed him a business card, "It was a pleasure meeting you, young man. If there is anything I can do for you, don't hesitate to call or come by my office."

As the counselor closed the door behind him, Mayor instructed everyone to sit back down. Jake sensed that something was wrong, but nothing could have prepared him for what he was about to hear.

Taking a deep breath, Mayor looked at everyone around the room and then he turned to Jake. "Son, there's something we have to tell you, and it's gonna be very hard for you to hear."

Jake gripped the arms of his chair. His muscles tensed as he prepared himself for the obviously bad news that Mayor was struggling to get out. "I'm ready. What is it?"

Before Mayor could answer, Aunt Hazel stood up, walked over to Jake, and sat down on the arm of the chair where he was sitting. When she put her hand on his shoulder, he knew something horrible had happened and suddenly, he realized who was not in the room.

"We all know that you and Sammi have become very close in the few months that you've known each other," Mayor said. "Everyone can see how much you mean to each other and so that makes what I have to say even harder, but the only way I know how to do this is just to say it right out. So here it goes. Before I tell you what has happened, I want you to know that Sammi is alive and currently being well cared for, but Saturday night after the school festival, she was abducted from the parkin' lot, taken to a remote location, and there she was beaten and raped."

Mayor's words hit Jake's ears like burning coals of fire. His head began to spin as he tried to process what he had just heard. His bloodshot eyes filled with tears and his entire body began to tremble with rage. A barrage of thoughts pelted his mind as he realized the extreme fear and pain Sammi must have experienced. He wanted to race to her side, but he also wanted to find and kill the one who had done this to her. Everyone in the room remained silent for a few moments to give Jake time to respond.

"I already know who raped her," Jake gritted his teeth, "but I want you to say his name. I need to hear you say his name."

"According to Sammi, it was Scott Robertson and his friend Eric Miller," Mayor said.

"And the third one?" Jake asked.

"I think you're referrin' to Jonathan Clark," Mayor answered. "Sammi said that he was there and that he tried to stop the other two, but took a beatin' from Scott for it. We think he was the one who took Sammi to the hospital. She doesn't actually remember how she got to the emergency room."

Jake gripped the arm of the chair tighter and closed his eyes. "Please, tell me they are in jail."

Mayor was hesitant to respond, but knew that Jake needed to know everything. "The sheriff interviewed Sammi at the hospital and naturally, he picked Scott and Eric up for questioning. No one has seen Jonathan since Saturday night. Unfortunately, they each gave the other an alibi. They said they were at Calhoun's Pool Hall at the time of the rape and when the sheriff visited Calhoun's, there were several others who corroborated their story."

"Sammi wouldn't lie!" Jake declared.

"We know that," Dr. Taylor affirmed. "But there is a process that the police have to follow. They are looking for Jonathan. We think that if he turned on the other two to try and help Sammi, he may be willing to testify to what he witnessed."

"Don't count on it!" Jake argued. "He and Eric are cowards. They're afraid of Scott."

"We are not gonna give up and neither are the police," Hazel interjected.

"I want to see her!" Jake cried. "Where is she?"

"Sadly, that's not possible right now," Mrs. Rossman said with sympathy. "To begin with, we don't know where she is. You have to understand, Jake, that she has experienced trauma on many levels. The physical assault was very violent and she sustained numerous bodily injuries. She has also suffered great damage mentally and emotionally. In order to adequately treat her on all those levels, the doctor has sent her to a facility designed to help her with not only the physical healing, but the emotional and mental recovery as well."

"She can't have visitors?" Jake asked.

Aunt Hazel answered, "The reason we don't know her whereabouts is because she told the doctor she doesn't want to see anyone right now other than her grandmother. Betty is with her now, but even Gerald doesn't know where she is."

"I don't understand that at all," Jake said. "We've been together just about every day since we met. Why would she not want to see me?"

"None of us can even begin to imagine or understand what she is going through right now," Dr. Taylor said. "The best we can do for her at the moment is to respect her wishes. I have no doubt that when she is ready, you will be one of the first people she wants to see. But for the moment, much patience is required."

"And prayer," Aunt Hazel added.

"Amen to that," Mayor acknowledged.

The ride home was quiet and contemplative for Jake. Aunt Hazel couldn't get him to say two words. While he was relieved that he would not have to appear in court, he could not get his mind off of Sammi and wanted nothing more than to be with her to help her through this nightmare. His thoughts darted back and forth between Sammi and Scott, and whenever the latter came to mind, all he wanted was revenge for what he had done to Sammi. As soon as they got home, Jake went to his room, closed the door, and stayed there the rest of the day.

Aunt Hazel coaxed him out at supper time, but he only poked at the food on his plate. When supper was over, he volunteered to do the dishes, and while standing in front of the sink, he happened to notice the silhouette of a solitary figure out in the gazebo. The figure was leaning against the rail staring off into the woods behind the trailer park. Though the sun had dropped below the tree line and it was beginning to get dark, he was able to discern that the lonely individual was Gerald, Sammi's grandfather. Leaving the rest of the dishes in the sink, Jake quickly dried his hands on a kitchen towel and made his way out to the gazebo.

"Mind if I join you?" he asked as he approached the gazebo steps.

Startled by the sudden presence of another person, Gerald quickly turned to see who had called to him. Relieved that it was Jake, he waved him up, "Yeah, come on in."

Jake could see that Gerald had been crying, but chose not to acknowledge it. "Have you heard anything from Sammi?" Jake inquired.

"Betty called about an hour ago," he answered. "She said that Sammi is havin' a real hard time. She wakes up screamin', and they have to give her medicine to calm her down."

Gerald paused, choked by emotion as he thought about his granddaughter. "We didn't even know what had happened until about 3:00 in the mornin' when a deputy came to take us to the hospital. I figured she was already in bed by that time. She's always been a good girl, Jake; came home when she was supposed to; never argued with us about anything. She didn't deserve any of this."

"I know," Jake said, placing his hand on Gerald's back.

Gerald dropped his head and began to weep. Jake was surprised by the tearful display. He had never heard the man speak a complete sentence, much less show any emotion.

"I ain't been there for her," Gerald said, pulling a wrinkled handkerchief from the pocket of his overalls.

"What do you mean?" Jake asked, trying to console him. "You've provided for her all these years, kept a roof over her head, made sure she had clothes and food."

"Yeah," Gerald answered. "But a girl needs more than that. She needed a daddy to protect her, but I was so mad at her mama for leavin' her with us that I always took it out on Sammi. Her mama was a hard one to raise. Growin' up, Blythe gave me and Betty a lot of trouble and kept me worried all the time. I decided I wasn't gonna let that happen to me again...so from the time Sammi was little, I kept her at a distance. I never let myself get too close; never held her when she was a baby; never played with her. Betty always did those things. I never let her in my heart, Jake. When we got to the hospital that night, Sammi said she only wanted her grandmother with her. It was then that I realized how much I've let her down."

"Don't be too hard on yourself, Gerald." Jake said. "She loves you. I know she does. Sammi loves everybody."

"I don't know if I can ever forgive myself," Gerald said pitifully, wiping his nose with the handkerchief. "But I will tell you one thing for sure. When she gets home, I'm gonna be different. I'm gonna be what she needs and deserves. A girl like Sammi deserves to be protected and defended."

Gerald's last statement resonated with Jake: a girl like Sammi deserves to be protected and defended. The words rang loudly in Jake's ears. *He's right*, he thought to himself. *She DOES deserve to be defended…and I need to be the one to defend her.*

"I'll see you later, Gerald," Jake said. "There's something I have to do."

Jake hurried back to the trailer. "Aunt Hazel, since my car hasn't been returned to us yet, can I borrow yours for a few minutes?" he asked. "I need to go see Mr. Newlin at the grocery store."

This was the first time Jake had ever lied to his aunt and so she didn't suspect that he wasn't telling the truth. "Sure," she gladly obliged. "Keys are on the dresser next to my purse."

Jake thanked her, grabbed the keys, and darted out the door. As he was about to get in the car, he stopped dead in his tracks and looked back toward the trailer as if he suddenly remembered something. *I wonder if it's still there?* he thought to himself. Sprinting back to the porch, he knelt down beside the steps and pulled a section of the lattice work off of the bottom. Then he crawled under the porch and felt around in the dark until he found it.

It was the baseball bat he had tossed under there the day they moved in, the one his mother used to hit him with when he was smaller. It was now a bit weather-worn and splintered from its time in the damp, musty area, but still solid. With weapon now in hand, Jake jumped in the car and headed toward Calhoun's where he hoped to find Scott Robertson.

20

THERE IT WAS, JUST AS HE'D EXPECTED.
Scott's red truck was sitting right in front of Calhoun's. Jake
pulled in and cautiously circled the parking lot to make
sure Scott wasn't outside somewhere. He wanted to catch
him off guard. There was no sign of Scott, so Jake knew he
must be inside, probably boasting to his friends about his
weekend's exploits.

Am I really going to do this? Jake asked himself. *Yes, I
am...for Sammi.*

Before getting out of the car, he played over in his
mind all the horrible things Scott must have done to her.
He imagined the terror she must have felt. He visualized
her tears and imagined her pleas for him to stop, pleas that
Scott ignored for the sake of his own pleasure. Jake imagined the pain she endured when he struck her with his huge,
powerful hands.

And finally, Jake pictured Sammi lying helplessly on the
ground, naked and bleeding at the feet of the monster who
had dared to lay his violent hands on one so innocent. All
of these thoughts converged in Jake's mind bringing him

to a point of frenzied rage. He was now ready to confront his adversary. Grasping the bat tightly in his hands, he stepped out of the car and marched with fierce determination toward the entrance of Calhoun's.

Once inside, it didn't take long for him to spot his target. Scott's height and muscular physique made him easy to find in a room full of beer-bellied rednecks. In the middle of the room, with his back to the door, Scott was leaning over a pool table about to make his shot. With laser focus, Jake swiftly and stealthily moved toward Sammi's rapist.

Eric, who was on the other side of the billiard table, saw Jake coming and shouted a warning to his friend. Scott wheeled around to see that his attacker was only feet away. Grabbing an empty beer bottle from the edge of the pool table, Scott stepped toward Jake and took a violent swing at his head but Jake ducked in time to avoid impact. Then, raising the bat high above his head, he brought it down with substantial force on Scott's right shoulder. Jake struck him so hard that everyone standing within six feet could hear Scott's bones breaking when the bat made contact.

With a scream, Scott grabbed his shoulder and slumped back against the pool table, unable to retaliate. But Jake was nowhere near being finished. Stepping back, he raised his bat again and this time, swung low, shattering the bones in Scott's left ankle, dropping him to the floor. By this time, Eric was rounding the corner of the table to come to his friend's defense, but Jake saw him out of the corner of his eye just in time. With the precision of a professional baseball player, Jake landed the bat squarely on Eric's face, shattering his jawbone. The force of the blow knocked him out cold and landed him about five feet away on top of another table.

Turning back to Scott, Jake was unable to restrain his fury. Again and again, he raised the bat high above his head, blow after blow battering Scott's body. Jake pummeled Scott's legs, his arms, his rib cage, and his hands. Each time he made contact with the bat; he could hear the snap of another bone. But no matter how many times he hit Scott, Jake's anger refused to be satisfied. Instead, his rage only grew. In an attempt to escape his attacker, Scott writhed in pain on the floor, unsuccessfully trying to avoid the bat. But Jake was unstoppable and intended to inflict upon Scott as much pain as he had dished out to Sammi. Jake did not plan to stop until he heard the coward crying and pleading for his life.

Finally, Scott rolled over on his back and raised his hands in surrender, but when he did, Jake spotted something that sent him into a wild fury: hanging around Scott's neck was the butterfly necklace Jake had bought for Sammi before the fourth of July festival, which Scott had been wearing like a trophy since the rape. Jake would later tell people that he became so blind with rage that he did not remember what happened next, but there were plenty of witnesses to tell the story. When Jake saw the necklace, he threw down the bat, straddled Scott's chest, and began to rain blows on the face and head.

Some said the brutal beating went on for at least five minutes and, after Jake was finished, Scott's nose was broken, several teeth were missing, and he had lost so much blood that his face, his hair, and his shirt were soaked. Jake also suffered several broken knuckles but he didn't seem to be aware of his own injuries. Those standing close by were hesitant to intervene for fear that they too, would become targets of Jake's wrath.

Once Scott was unconscious, Jake reclaimed the necklace and stood victoriously over the one who had so brutally violated Sammi. With the necklace in hand, Jake picked up the bat and headed for the door, but as he passed by the men's room, Jonathan stepped out completely unaware of what had just happened. The moment Jake saw him, he lunged toward him with the bat once again raised high in the air.

Dropping to his knees, Jonathan began to plead, "Jake, stop! Please, don't hit me. Please don't! I tried to stop him, but he wouldn't listen to me. I...I...I'm the one who came back and took her to the hospital, Jake. PLEASE, you have to believe me. I did all I could!"

Jake lowered the bat slightly. "Why didn't you go to the police?" he demanded. "Why have you been hiding, you coward?"

Still on his knees, Jonathan explained, "Because he threatened me, Jake. I didn't know what he might do to me. I saw a side of him that night that I'd never seen before. I...I was afraid he might kill me."

Jake was in no mood for excuses. Still holding the bat with one hand, he grabbed Jonathan's collar with the other and pulled him up off the floor. Pinning him against the wall, Jake placed the tip of the bat under Jonathan's nose. "Can you see Scott right now?" he asked.

Jonathan cut his eyes over Jake's shoulder and saw the carnage. "Yeah," he stammered, his voice quivering with fear.

Jake leaned in so close that Jonathan could feel his breath on his face. "You are going to go to the police tonight and tell them everything he and Eric did to her. If you don't, I will come after you with everything I have. You won't even know I'm in the room until I'm on you. Do you understand what I'm saying to you?" As Jake asked the question, he pressed the bat harder against Jonathan's nose causing a small trickle of blood to flow.

Jonathan realized in that moment that he feared Jake more than he had ever feared Scott. "Yeah, Jake," he agreed. "I...I'll tell them everything. I promise."

Satisfied that he had accomplished his purpose, Jake slowly released his grip on Jonathan and walked out the door only to see a parade of blue lights entering Calhoun's parking lot.

"Lay your weapon on the ground, NOW!" an officer shouted. His firearm was pointed right at Jake, who immediately dropped the bat and raised his hands in the air. The officer holding the gun instructed another officer to cuff Jake and put him in the back of one of the police cars. Jake felt no remorse for what he had just done. Sammi's honor needed to be defended, and he knew in his heart he'd done what had to be done. Jake knew he would probably go back to jail, but his sacrifice would be worth it. At that moment, he didn't know if Scott was dead or alive and he didn't care. In Jake's mind, any person evil enough to do what Scott had done to Sammi no longer deserved to be on the earth.

As he sat in silence, another officer drove up and parked right next to the car in which Jake had been placed. It was Sheriff Blake. He recognized Jake right away. The two made eye contact, but no words were spoken. Instead, the sheriff gave a faint, but assuring smile to Jake which gave him a measure of comfort. Just then, a deputy came out of the pool hall.

"Sheriff," the deputy called. "There's a young man in here who says he needs to talk to you...says he has a confession to make."

Jake knew the deputy was referring to Jonathan. *Maybe he will actually man up and do the right thing,* he thought to himself.

Nearly an hour passed before the Sheriff returned. During that time, Jake saw Scott and Eric, both apparently still breathing but alive, being wheeled out on gurneys and loaded into two waiting ambulances. When Sheriff Blake finally emerged from Calhoun's, he had a deputy with him and they were headed in Jake's direction.

"Let him go," the sheriff ordered.

"But sir," the deputy replied, "did you see what he..."

"Are you questioning me?" the Sheriff asked angrily. "Yes, I saw what he did, but we also now have an eye witness account of the rape that occurred Saturday night, an account that will put at least two of them in prison for a while. And at least a half dozen witnesses said that Scott took the first swing tonight, so Jake's actions were self-defense. As far as I'm concerned, Jake here is a hero who aided the police in the apprehension of two very dangerous criminals. So, I'm telling you one last time...LET...HIM...GO!"

"Yes, sir," the deputy replied.

As the cuffs were removed, the sheriff noted Jake's bleeding, broken knuckles. "You okay, Son?" he asked.

"Yes, sir," he replied, finally realizing the condition of his hands.

"That was a brave thing you did tonight," the sheriff said, "a little foolish, but brave. It could just as easily have gone the other way, and you would have been the one riding out of here in an ambulance."

"I know," Jake said, "but I had to take the chance... for Sammi."

Sheriff Blake smiled, "When you graduate, how about you come see me? We can discuss a career in law enforcement."

Jake smiled, "Thank you, sir, but I have a slightly different career path in mind."

"I'm sure you do," the sheriff responded. "And I have no doubt you will do well. In the meantime, I'm going to have one of my deputies take you to the emergency room. I think you may have some fractures in your hand. He'll stay with you until the doctor releases you and then he'll bring you back to get your car."

As Jake was getting into the police car to go to the ER, he noticed Jonathan being escorted out of Calhoun's by another officer. He was in cuffs.

"Sheriff," Jake called out. "You're arresting him too?"

"Oh, yes," the sheriff answered, "all three will be charged tonight. The other two will go away for a long time, but I suspect that Jonathan will get some time as well because of his part in planning the attack. However, I'm sure the judge will take into consideration his attempt to stop the rape, his efforts to get Sammi to the hospital for help, and the fact that he is now an eye witness will also work in his favor. But he will get much more than just a slap on the wrist."

Jake smiled and nodded appreciatively to the sheriff.

"Have a good night, Son," Sheriff Blake said. "And when you talk to Sammi, tell her I'm very sorry for all she's been through."

Jake smiled and gave Sheriff Blake another nod. As he and his police escort pulled away from the pool hall, a great sense of satisfaction fell over Jake as he realized that justice was going to be served: Scott and Eric would finally get what was coming to them. But as his thoughts turned to

Sammi, Jake was overwhelmed with grief and sadness. He had no idea how she was coping, how long she would be away, or when he would see her again.

As he and the deputy made their way toward the hospital, it suddenly dawned on Jake that everything that had happened over the past three days— his arrest, Sammi's attack—all of it was the fault of one person. One individual carried the primary blame, especially for what happened to Sammi. Had Jake not been in jail over the weekend, the attack probably wouldn't have happened because he would have been there to protect Sammi. One person and one person alone was at fault.

There would need to be one more confrontation, and from an emotional standpoint, it would be even more brutal than what had just happened at Calhoun's. His mother, Jo Ledger, was the one common denominator in all of the chaos that had unfolded over the weekend and Jake could not—he *would* not—allow her to go unpunished. It was now Jo's turn to face the harsh reality of all the pain she had caused.

21

As much as Jake hated the thought of going back to school, he knew he had to do it. He also needed to go back to work at the grocery store, which was not going to be easy because Sammi had become such an integral part of his life. They rode to and from school together every day. They worked the same hours at the store. They were together almost constantly. He couldn't imagine what it was going to be like to go through even one day without her, but he knew he had to find the strength to keep going until Sammi came home to him. There *were* some positive things to focus on.

The judge sentenced Jo to time in the county jail until the end of May or early June the next year. The sentence included getting her some much-needed help—she would have to attend classes three days a week and at least two religious services each week during her sentence, all of which were held right there in the county jail. Because of the brutal nature of their crimes, Scott, Eric, and Jonathan would be held in the county jail without bond until their trial, which was set for late December.

But none of that really comforted Jake. He desperately missed Sammi. All he could think about was how badly he wanted to talk to her, to see her, to hold her, and to tell her how much he loved her. He couldn't sleep at night for thinking about her. He now regretted waiting so long to express his feelings for her.

Word of what Jake had done to Scott and Eric quickly circulated throughout the high school's campus and, when he returned to school, he found he was being looked upon by the student body as some kind of superhero. While he appreciated the new level of respect, it was all meaningless to him without Sammi.

Getting through that first week without her was hard, but he made it. He spent all day Saturday at work, which had some challenges of its own since his right hand was now in a cast. Nonetheless, he persevered. Sunday was the day he had been anxiously anticipating. Visiting hours at the county jail were Sunday afternoons from 2:00 to 4:00 PM.

All week long, Jake had thought about the words he wanted to say to his mother, the woman he now hated. For many years he had overlooked the pain and frustration she had caused him, but now her actions had brought pain to someone he loved with all his heart. Sammi would never be the same after the rape, and he knew that. He also knew that it was his mother's fault. No one would ever be able to convince him otherwise.

Rather than go to church with Aunt Hazel that Sunday, he stayed home to rehearse the speech he'd planned to give to his mother and, by the time he got to the jail, his temper was hot and his anxiety level was high. The guard led him into a room that looked like a cafeteria with tables and chairs placed at intervals around the room. The walls were a drab light brown and the floor was nothing but cold, gray concrete.

The place had the stale, sweaty odor of a gym, and there was not a single window in the entire room. There were already several other inmates scattered throughout the room meeting with their families. Everyone there seemed to be happy to see their loved ones, but Jake knew that his meeting with Jo would not be a happy one. He nervously began to tap the table with his fingers while waiting for the guards to bring her in; he just wanted to get this over with.

Finally, Jo appeared in the doorway wearing a gray, prison-issued jumpsuit. She was accompanied by a guard, who brought her all the way to the table where Jake was sitting. When she got to the table, Jake did not stand to greet her despite seeing the tears that were already running down his mother's cheeks. He was determined to show his mother no mercy, and he could barely bring himself to look her in the eye. For several awkward moments the two sat in complete silence, neither one looking at the other.

Jo, hating the silence, decided to start the conversation. "Baby Boy," she said with tears, "I am so sorry..."

"Stop, talking!" Jake bitterly interrupted. "You don't get to talk right now, and you don't get to call me your Baby Boy. I've thought long and hard about what I'm going to say to you, and you are not going to interrupt. I will let you know when you can speak, if I let you speak at all. Do you understand?"

Jo nodded her head. She had never seen her son so angry, and her heart began to fill with dread at what he was about to say.

Jake took a moment to muster up the strength and boldness required for the bitter diatribe he was about to launch in Jo's direction. With a clenched jaw, he looked her sternly in the eye and cleared his throat before speaking, "When I was in junior high school, an English teacher once told the class to take out some paper and write a short essay on one of the fondest memories we had from our childhood. She'd said that, after we finished writing, everyone was going to have a turn to read their essay out loud. While the other students started writing immediately, I sat there for the longest time, with a huge knot in my stomach, searching my mind for a memory that I wasn't ashamed to share, a memory that actually brought me joy. I couldn't find one."

Jake paused in an effort to control the rage that was rising up within him. After a few seconds, he continued, "My memories would have given the other kids nightmares. I couldn't tell them about all the times I found you passed out on the floor with a needle stuck in your arm; I couldn't tell them about all the filthy men that marched in and out of the sleazy motel rooms we've lived in, men that paid you for sex just so you could go and buy more drugs; I couldn't tell them about the scars and bruises I've received from your hands when you were high; I couldn't tell them about the number of times when all we could afford for dinner was a pack of crackers or a bag of chips; and I couldn't tell them about how you dragged me from town to town, from one school to another, just so no one would get suspicious of you and hold you accountable for the horrible life you'd forced me to live."

Becoming very uncomfortable, Jo attempted to interrupt, "Jake, I can't..."

"I told you not to talk," he reminded her firmly. "For my entire life, I have had to live each day with the fear and worry that you might be dead by the end of that day. Your foolish choices robbed me of a normal childhood. Instead of being a kid, I had to be a parent. Your main priority in life has always been you. You're the most selfish and reckless person I've ever met. You care about no one but yourself. When you hid your drugs under my bed just to keep yourself out of trouble, it proved to me that you care about no one other than yourself. You could not possibly love me if you were so willing to destroy my life. I begged you to come clean with the police that day, but you ignored my pleas, and you let them put cuffs on me and arrest me. As they walked me out to the police car, I kept waiting for you to come to your senses and run out the door and confess what you had done, but as always, you weren't there for me. You have no right to be anyone's mother, especially mine!"

Jake paused; his face now flushed deep red from the anger surging through him. Hot tears streamed down his cheeks. With his tense jaw jutting slightly forward, he glared directly into Jo's dispirited face. Unmoved by her fragile emotional state, with his teeth clenched, he continued, "Up until recently your careless lifestyle has only hurt me, so over the years I learned to just endure it. But now your actions have hurt someone I love and care about very much."

Jo looked up at Jake, uncertain of what he meant. She hadn't heard about what happened to Sammi. "What are you talkin' about?" she asked, her voice trembling.

Jake clenched his fists and took a second to gather himself before answering her question, "On the night of the Fall Festival at school, while I was in jail for your crime, Sammi was raped and severely beaten by Scott and Eric."

Jo gasped, covering her mouth with both hands. "NO, JAKE! Tell me you're just makin' that up to make me feel bad..."

Jake raised his voice, "I told you, YOU DON'T GET TO TALK right now! If I had been there to protect her, Sammi wouldn't have been hurt! But because of your actions, I was *not* there! She was raped and beaten, and I am holding you responsible! I will never forgive you for this! From this moment on, you are no longer my mother and I am no longer your son!"

Jo began to cry profusely, "Jake, Baby, don't say that. You know I have a problem..."

Jake jumped to his feet. "STOP MAKING EXCUSES!" he screamed at the top of his lungs. "STOP...MAKING... EXCUSES!" he yelled again, pounding the table with each word that erupted from his mouth.

At this point, the entire room became silent as everyone's eyes were riveted to the drama being played out before them. Ashamed and embarrassed, Jo whispered, "Jake, please sit down. Everyone's lookin' at us now."

"WELL, MAYBE IT'S TIME EVERYONE KNOWS WHAT YOU REALLY ARE!" he bellowed.

"Oh, please don't say anymore," Jo pleaded, as she buried her face in her hands. "Please...just stop talkin'."

Jake took a step back from the table and looked down upon Jo with disdain. "There's just one more thing I need to say, but I need you to look at me when I say it."

Jo removed her hands from her face and slowly raised her eyes, but the scornful expression on her son's face was too painful for her to bear. She looked away in shame.

"It wasn't too long ago that you looked me in the eye and told me you hated me," Jake reminded her. "So I want you to know that I am sincere when I say that I hate you, too. Truth be told, I hate you with a passion and I don't care if I never see or hear from you again. In fact, it won't sadden me one bit if you die in this prison."

With those words, he turned and walked away. As soon as he'd disappeared behind the large metal doors, Jo melted into a heap at the table and wept uncontrollably. She knew that she had lost her son forever.

22

BACK AT HOPE PARK, JAKE'S DAYS TURNED into weeks and the weeks turned into a month with no sign of Sammi's return. Her grandmother, Betty, stayed with her every weekend and always brought back reports that were positive; though Jake sensed Betty wasn't telling him everything. "Sammi is improving, albeit slowly," she would always say. Jake sent letters to Sammi with Betty every week, but he never got any in return.

"She'll write you when she's ready," Sammi's grandmother assured him.

Jake missed her as he had never missed anyone in his whole life. What had only been a month seemed like a year. Several nights a week, he visited with Gerald and Betty, talking about Sammi and looking at pictures of her in their old family photo albums. It seemed to help. Being in her house made him feel closer to her. He and Gerald even began to develop a bond having many conversations about Sammi and about how much they missed her. Thanksgiving came and went, but Jake didn't feel much like giving thanks. Understanding his grief, Aunt Hazel didn't press the holiday on him, but instead prepared a modest Thanksgiving meal that the two of them shared alone.

On the Saturday afternoon following Thanksgiving, the neighbors gathered around the gazebo with boxes and bags full of Christmas decorations. Several of the men went into the woods and emerged an hour later with a beautiful pine tree. Once it was set up in the gazebo, the folks gathered around and began to hang ornaments and string lights on its branches. Aunt Hazel insisted that Jake participate, informing him that Christmas was Sammi's favorite time of year and that she would have been the first one at the gazebo if she were here. He reluctantly agreed to help but soon found himself enjoying the festivities.

As the neighbors labored together to transform the gazebo into a Christmas Wonderland, they sang Christmas carols, consumed an obscene amount of Christmas cookies, and drank a ton of steaming hot cider. Jake caught himself laughing out loud when the image of a children's Christmas classic came to mind. *I'm trapped in Whoville,* he mused to himself, although surprisingly, the thought didn't seem to bother him.

Sleep eluded Jake that night, so around 2:00 AM he got up, grabbed a thick blanket from his bed, and went next-door to climb up on Sammi's roof. It was a cold, clear night, and the stars were out in full force. The celestial lights had some competition tonight though. From the rooftop, Jake had a clear view of the gazebo in all its yuletide glory. All the rails and poles were wrapped in garland and interlaced with bright white lights. Huge red bows were fastened to the greenery exactly three feet apart along each of the horizontal rails. On the very top of the roof, the Star of Bethlehem shone brightly, a reminder of the divine birth.

Flowing from the star atop the gazebo were streams of multi-colored lights, placed about an inch apart, running from the pinnacle of the gazebo down to the roof's edge. Under the roof, the tree was the star of the show. Like a king robed in radiant jewels, the freshly cut pine stood tall and proud, dazzling the eye with red, green, and white lights, silver tinsel, red ribbons with bows and a plethora of home-made ornaments. Cotton batting, stretched out and stashed between the branches, added the illusion of freshly fallen snow. And, if that weren't enough, an abundance of red and white striped candy canes dangled from the tree's still vibrant branches. At the base of the tree, the neighbors had assembled a miniature manger scene complete with Mary, Joseph, three wise men, a handful of shepherds, a few barn-yard animals and, of course, the baby Jesus.

Tightening the blanket around his neck and shoul-ders, Jake gazed into the night sky. As he lay there, his mind became filled with memories of all the times he and Sammi had spent on this roof together. He remembered the first night they'd fallen asleep across from one another on the blanket. He remembered the late-night snacks. He remembered how Sammi laughed at him when he'd tried to impress her with his knowledge of astronomy. He thought about the music they'd listened to far into the night, and he replayed in his mind some of their rooftop conversa-tions almost word for word. His heart grew warm when he thought about the night they'd danced under the stars. Sammi had been so gentle and caring, and he remembered how badly he'd wanted to kiss her in that moment. He now wished he had.

For the next three weeks, Jake continued to go through the motions: school, work, home...school, work, home. Without her, all his busy activity seemed pointless. Somewhere along the way, Sammi had become the one who gave him purpose and a sense of direction. She had become his compass. With each passing day, his desire to see her increased, and he began to wonder if she was ever going to return. Christmas was just around the corner, and he desperately hoped she would be home by then.

Finally, on the Sunday before Christmas Day, Betty returned to Hope Park with some good news: Sammi would be coming home on Friday, just in time for Christmas. Jake was elated, but he was also nervous. He had not talked to her or received any correspondence from her since the attack. He wondered if she blamed him for what had happened, since he was the one who had insisted she go to the festival without him. If she did, in fact, hold him responsible, he worried whether there would there still be a chance that they could be together or whether what they'd shared would be over before it had even started? These and many other questions raced through his mind as the days passed, which kept him in a state of emotional turmoil for the rest of the week. He couldn't focus on anything other than Sammi and how she would respond to him upon her return. By the time Friday arrived, his stomach was one big knot.

Mr. Newlin had asked Jake to work all day Friday at the grocery store since school was now closed for the holidays. Though he wanted to be there when Sammi got home, he realized that it might be best if he wasn't. He knew himself well enough to know that his first impulse would be to rush right over the minute she arrived, and the last thing he wanted to do was make her feel crowded or overwhelmed. It was 9:00 o'clock before he arrived home. Betty's car was parked in the driveway, so he knew Sammi was there.

Jake's heart was pounding loudly in his chest at the thought of seeing her for the first time in so long. Gerald and Betty's house looked dark with the exception of a dim light beaming from the living room. He knew it was the floor lamp that sat next to Gerald's chair, so he decided to take a chance and knock. He could hear someone moving inside the house, and he stood anxiously at the door in hopeful anticipation that Sammi would be the one to open the door.

"Well, hey there, Son. Come on in."

To Jake's disappointment, Gerald, not Sammi, stood in the open door, and from the looks of things, he was the only one still up. He could see the disappointment on Jake's face knowing he had come to see her. "She was exhausted when she got home," he gently explained. "She could barely keep her eyes open, but she wanted me to tell you that she is excited about seein' you and she wants to know what you're doin' tomorrow."

Gerald's words were like honey. Jake was relieved to know that Sammi was not only thinking about him, but actually wanted to see him. "So, she's not...angry...with me?" he asked.

"Angry? Why would she be angry with you?" Gerald asked, puzzled. "You were the first person she asked about when she got home."

"I don't know," Jake muttered. "She's never responded to any of my letters, so I thought she might be upset with me for some reason. She didn't want to go to the festival without me that night, but I made her go, so I was afraid she might blame me for what happened."

"No, Son," Gerald replied, putting his hand on Jake's shoulder. "I wouldn't even bring that up to her. She knows who's responsible for what's happened and it's not you. So put that out of your mind right now. She'll be glad to see you. Will you be able to visit her tomorrow?"

Jake paused before answering. An idea was forming in his mind, a beautiful, sweet, romantic idea. "Actually," he answered with a smile, "I have to work all day tomorrow, but when she wakes up in the morning, tell her I've missed her and I definitely do want to see her, but not until midnight tomorrow night. Tell her to meet me at the gazebo right at twelve, when it'll officially be Christmas." Gerald smiled and agreed to pass the word along. Jake was so excited about seeing Sammi that he barely slept at all that night. The gazebo with all the beautiful lights and Christmas decorations would be the perfect place to finally tell her how he felt, and the stroke of midnight on Christmas day would be the perfect time. This was it; the moment he had been waiting for so long was finally at hand. Sammi's response would set the course for the rest of his life.

23

At 11:55 PM, on Christmas Eve—Jake had been watching the clock in the kitchen for the last hour— he had rehearsed what he was going to say a million times, or so it seemed. He clearly understood that the conversation he was about to have with Sammi would be the most important conversation of his entire life. In the time they had been apart, his love for her had only grown. Not being able to see her for the last two months confirmed for him just how much he needed her in his life. He had never truly felt alive until he met her. She had brought so much good into his chaotic world; she gave him a sense of purpose and direction; she gave him a sense of peace.

At 11:58 PM, zipping his coat, Jake wrapped a woolen scarf around his neck and stepped out of the door to meet Sammi. It was a gorgeous winter's night and the air was cold and crisp. A little snow had fallen earlier that evening, leaving the ground covered by a soft blanket of white that sparkled under the shimmering lights from the gazebo. Standing in front of the Christmas tree, Jake turned his gaze toward her house and, with bated breath, he waited in silence for her to appear.

Just seconds past midnight, Christmas Day, Sammi appeared—she was right on time, not a minute too soon and not a minute too late. As she stepped outside, everything seemed to move in slow motion for Jake: the opening and closing of her front door, the sound of the snow crunching underneath her feet as she stepped off the porch onto the frosty ground, the poetic movement of her hair as it was slightly tossed about by a gentle breeze.

In the soft glow of the Christmas lights, Sammi was as radiant as an angel. Jake was even more enamored by her beauty than he had been the first time he ever saw her. The closer she drew to him, the more rapidly his heart throbbed, and when she crossed the threshold of the gazebo, the very power of her presence took his breath away. Now, standing before him, she didn't speak a word. In the stillness of the night, they stood inches apart gazing deeply into one another's eyes. As a few tears began to trickle down her cheeks, Jake placed both hands on her face and wiped the tears away with his thumbs.

Placing her hands over the top of his, she whispered, "I've missed you so much."

"I've missed you," he whispered back, "more than you'll ever know."

Sammi leaned into Jake, laid her head on his chest and began to cry in earnest. In response, he wrapped his arms around her and held her as tight as he could.

"I was savin' myself," she said softly. "I was savin' myself for the man I'm gonna marry someday and now that part of me is gone."

Jake wasn't sure what he needed to say, but he knew he wanted to comfort her and he wanted her to know that what had happened to her didn't change how he saw her or how he felt about her in any way. Composing himself, he said, "I have something to say to you, and I want you to look me in the eyes when I say it."

Sammi lifted her head from his chest and, with her beautiful blue eyes wet with tears, she met Jake's gaze

"You are as pure today as you ever were," he assured her. "What happened was not caused by anything you did or said. None of it was your fault and, even though I can't begin to understand what you experienced or what you're going through now, I need you to know that it doesn't change the way I see you or the way I feel about you."

His soothing words were exactly what she needed to hear, alleviating her fears that somehow Jake might feel differently toward her after the rape. Sammi had been blaming herself for what happened and was afraid that he might also have blamed her. But it was the last statement he made that had her intrigued, and she wanted a little more clarification.

"How *do* you feel about me, Jake? Who are we to each other?" she asked.

The moment had arrived. He knew he was standing at a crossroads and that the next words out of his mouth would forever alter the direction of his life; so he wanted to make sure to choose the right words. He wanted them to be simple and clear, and he wanted them to be words she would never forget.

Placing his hands on her face again, he gently caressed her soft cheeks, "Sammi, there have been a lot of uncertainties in my life, lots of confusion. But there is one thing that has become crystal clear to me, one thing that I will never be confused about. I have been in love with you since the day we met. I know some folks don't believe it's possible to fall in love at first sight, but I know it's true. I fell in love with you then, I love you now, and I know that I am going to love you forever. Sammi, there is no one else I want other than you, because there is no one in this world who compares to you. You are the strongest, most amazing, most beautiful woman I've ever known. No one knows me like you do, and I can't imagine my life without you beside me."

Gazing deeply into his eyes, Sammi smiled, "I love you too, Jake. I started fallin' in love with you the night you opened up to me about your life, that night you told me about the scars on your back. We danced for the first time that night and, as you were holdin' me in your arms, I knew then and there that I never wanted to dance with anyone else. I feel safe when I'm with you, Jake, and I've never felt that way with anybody before."

He could hardly believe what he was hearing. Sammi's words were wonderfully overwhelming, surreal even. He never imagined that someone so amazing, so exquisitely beautiful, would fall in love with him. Pulling her body tight against his, he pressed his cheek against her cheek and whispered into her ear, "I will always take care of you."

"I know you will," she whispered back, "you're my hero. But I have a question."

Jake pulled back to look at her. "Ask me anything," he said.

Sammi placed her hand softly on his face. Then, gently stroking his cheek with her thumb, she asked, "In this story, does the boy ever kiss the girl?"

Jake didn't say a word but looked longingly into Sammi's sparkling blue eyes. He had envisioned this moment often since the first day he'd seen her. Placing both of his hands on the small of her back, he firmly drew her body close so that it was pressed tightly against his. She didn't resist his lead but responded by putting both her arms around him, resting the palms of her hands on his upper back. As he nervously leaned forward, Sammi closed her eyes and slightly tilted her head back; both of their hearts raced with anticipation.

The moment his lips touched hers, Jake immediately realized they were softer and sweeter than he had ever imagined they'd be, and he knew these would be the only lips that would satisfy him for the rest of his life. It was Christmas day, and Sammi was the greatest gift he had ever received.

After a few tender moments, Sammi pulled back, "Jake, there's somethin' I need to tell you, and I'm afraid it's gonna upset you. The butterfly necklace you gave me...I wore it every day from the time you gave it to me, but somehow, it's gotten lost. I intended to wear that to my grave. I'm so sorry."

Jake smiled, "I was going to save this until the morning, but I have a surprise for you." Reaching into his coat pocket, he pulled out a small gift-wrapped box and handed it to her. "Merry Christmas," he said.

Sammi took the box and eagerly ripped off the wrapping. When she opened the box, she gasped, "You found another one just like the one I lost?"

"No," he answered. "It *is* the one you lost. I got it back for you."

Sammi's eyes glistened with tears, "But, how did you..."

"It's not important how...it's only important that you have it back," he said. "Turn around and I'll put it on for you." Sammi turned around and lifted her hair off her neck. As Jake fastened the necklace, he softly kissed the back of her neck as he had wanted to do the first time he'd put it on her. At the touch of his lips against her skin, Sammi shivered. Once the necklace was secure, she turned back to him, threw her arms around his neck, and kissed him again. "I'm cold," she said. "Let's go inside."

It was nice and warm in her living room. The only light was from a small candle sitting on the coffee table in front of the couch, which she'd had apparently lit before coming out to meet him. After hanging their coats on the coat rack by the door, she led him over to the couch and instructed him to lie down. He wasn't sure what she had in mind, but he quickly complied. "Slide over," she said. "I want you to hold me."

Jake slid over and Sammi snuggled up beside him with her head on his chest. He put his arm around her and pulled her as close to him as he possibly could.

"Merry Christmas, Jake," she sighed. "I love you."

"Merry Christmas," he softly replied. "I love you too."

After kissing him once more, Sammi snuggled tight against him, closed her eyes, and drifted off to sleep. Jake held her close to him through the whole night. Her breath against his neck was warm and comforting, and he knew this was the way he wanted it to be for the rest of his life.

24

THE HOLIDAYS WENT BY QUICKLY, BUT JOY-
ously. With Sammi home, everything in Jake's world seemed
to be coming into perfect alignment. The four individuals
who were his greatest source of grief were safely tucked
away behind bars: his mother, Scott Robertson, Eric, and
Jonathan. Jake hadn't seen or talked to his mother since the
day he'd told her off at the county jail. She had written him
numerous letters, but all of them had gone right into the
trash unopened. Jake hadn't heard much about Scott and
his cronies and he was confident that they would be locked
up for years to come.

Trials for all three of them had begun just after the first
of the year, but the sessions were not open to reporters, so
very few people really knew how it was going. Sammi had
been asked to write a full account of what had happened to
her and, with her story being corroborated by Jonathan, she
was not expected to have to appear in court. The judge felt
that she had been through enough. A lawyer, Mr. Morris,
was appointed on her behalf. He had met with Sammi several times during her recovery period to go over the events

of the night she was attacked and he went before the judge and jury on her behalf. Jake was glad she didn't have to see her perpetrators again. All that mattered to him now was Sammi and the future they were planning to forge together. He was ready to put all the pain behind them.

Everyone in the neighborhood was glad to see Sammi back, and news had traveled quickly through the little community that she and Jake were now an official item. Of course, they had all seen it coming and were delighted that he had finally found the nerve to *seal the deal*, so to speak. Things finally seemed to be looking up for the two young lovers, but it was about to get even better.

It was Tuesday, January 10, and the spring semester had just begun the day before. When the two arrived home from school that afternoon they were surprised to see a dark Cadillac Seville sitting in Sammi's driveway.

"I wonder whose fancy car that is," Jake asked.

"I don't know," she replied, "but you're coming in with me to find out." Both exited his car eagerly and wasted no time getting inside to see who had come to visit. As they entered the trailer, they saw a distinguished, gray-haired gentleman sitting at the kitchen table with Betty and Gerald. He was wearing an expensive navy blue suit and had a shiny leather briefcase open on the table in front of him. A sweet, musky scent of expensive cologne hovered around the table where he sat poring over a pile of official-looking papers through a pair of outdated horn-rimmed glasses. As soon as he saw the young couple, the visitor stood to his feet and greeted them both with a smile.

"Sammi, it's so good to see you again," he said, shaking her hand enthusiastically. "You look healthy and strong."

"I'm much better," she announced. "I've had a lot of support." She glanced at Jake and smiled.

"And, you must be Jake Ledger," Mr. Morris said, extending his hand. "I've heard a lot about you."

Jake was a bit bewildered.

"This is Mr. Morris," Betty explained to Jake. "He's Sammi's lawyer and has been handlin' her case in court. Y'all sit down. He says he has some good news for us, but he didn't want to say anything until you were home."

After they were all seated around the kitchen table, Mr. Morris drew attention to the papers laid out in front of him.

"I wanted to come by today," he explained, "to let you know that the trial for the three boys ended today at noon, and I wanted you to hear the outcome from me rather than reading it in the newspaper tomorrow. Sammi, your written testimony along with Jonathan's testimony was very convincing to the jury. The fact that those troubled young men have a very bad reputation in the community made the jury's job very easy. After hearing the evidence, both Scott and Eric were found guilty of rape and the judge gave them each fifteen years in the state prison. They will serve their time in two separate facilities, so they won't even see each other for the duration of their sentences. Within the next two weeks, both of them will be transferred from the county jail to the state prison system, which will be their home for the next good while."

Relieved and exhilarated by the good news, Sammi, her grandparents, and Jake jumped up from the table with shouts of joy. As they were celebrating, Sammi interjected, "Wait a minute. What about Jonathan?"

Well, Jonathan's case was a little different," Mr. Morris explained. "His lawyer was able to convince the jury that he didn't fully know what Scott and Eric were planning that night. Because he put himself at risk trying to stop the assault, because he came back and took you to the hospital, *and*, because he testified against the other two, his sentence was not as stiff. Jonathan will serve four years behind bars followed by another two years of probation."

Jake's countenance quickly changed. "That's NOT acceptable!" he shouted. "I don't believe for a second that he was unaware of what they were planning. He had to have known."

"Jake," Sammi interrupted, "I know you don't like the sentence he got, but I have to be honest. As soon as Scott hit me that night, Jonathan did his best to stop him. He took a pretty good beatin' himself because he defended me. He truly seemed scared that night and he deserves some credit for gettin' me to the hospital as soon as he did—Jake, I would probably be dead otherwise—and he's put himself in further danger by testifyin' against the other two. I say we let this go and trust that the judge did the right thing. We can't let this thing have any part in our future."

Jake didn't like the fact that Jonathan would be out in four years, but Sammi's words calmed him and he decided to support her view. Besides, if she was right about Jonathan saving her life, then maybe he did deserve a lesser sentence than the others.

"There's one more thing," Mr. Morris said, "and you're probably going to want to sit back down for this. Because of the severe cruelty of the crimes committed against you, Sammi, and because of the extensive emotional damage you've endured, the judge awarded you a financial settlement, which will be paid directly to you by the Robertson family on your eighteenth birthday, which is May 26 of this year, I believe. In addition to the financial settlement, the Robertson family has been ordered to pay, in full, all tuition costs for any college or university you may choose to attend."

Betty and Gerald gasped, Jake's mouth dropped open, and Sammi sat stunned at what she had just heard. All four stared at one another in amazement. No one knew quite what to say.

After a few moments of awkward silence, Gerald spoke up, "I don't want to sound over anxious, but I don't think you mentioned the amount of the financial settlement."

"I was hoping someone would ask me that question," Mr. Morris said with a smile. "Sammi, on Friday morning, May 26 of this year, at 9:00 in the morning, a check will be deposited in your account in the amount of one hundred thousand dollars. Now, I know that all the money in the world won't take away the pain and suffering you've endured at the hands of those two boys, but the judge firmly believes that you deserve this money so that you can have a chance to get your life off to a solid start."

The room was silent as everyone took a moment to ponder this news. It was bittersweet: sweet in the sense that the money and the college tuition would be helpful, but bitter in what it had cost Sammi to get it. One thing they all agreed on was that Sammi deserved something for what she had endured on that awful night.

Over the next couple of weeks, Jake and Sammi tried to resume a normal life and not allow the events of the past few months to loom over them like a dark cloud. He was amazed at her ability to forgive and he tried to follow her example, but it was not easy. He still harbored a great deal of anger toward his mother and toward those devils who had hurt the girl he loved so dearly. Sammi was different, however, and he knew he could learn from her. He had never met anyone with such a positive outlook on life.

Every day, they drove to school together, went to work together, ate together, took walks together and, on some nights, Sammi would invite Jake to come over after Betty and Gerald were asleep so that they could snuggle on the couch. He was always a gentleman, though, and never pressed Sammi for more than she wanted to give. He was quite content holding her in his arms through the night, knowing that if he continued to be patient, an amazing life awaited them. He was also patient about mentioning the word *marriage*, but he knew there was no one else he wanted to spend the rest of his life with. With each passing day, Jake became more convinced that they were meant to be together.

Things could not have been going better for them until one Friday night when Aunt Hazel's phone rang about 8:00 o'clock. When Jake answered the phone, he was surprised to hear Sheriff Blake on the other end of the line.

"Jake," Sheriff Blake said, his voice laced with urgency and alarm, "I hate to be making this call, but there's something you need to know. About two hours ago, they were transporting Scott Robertson to the state prison. I'm not sure yet how it happened, but in the process of the transfer, Scott managed to escape and we've not been able to find him just yet. I've got some deputies on the way out to Hope Park in case he's stupid enough to come there. Where's Sammi?"

"She's at home," Jake answered, as the severity of the situation started to sink in.

"You might want to take her and her family to Mayor's house," the sheriff instructed. "My boys will be there in a matter of minutes and, in the event he shows up, they'll know what to do."

The Sheriff's words had barely landed in Jake's ears, when suddenly, a blood-curdling scream coming from Sammi's house pierced the night air. "Get here now, Sheriff!" Jake yelled. "He's already here."

Dropping the phone to the floor, Jake bolted out the screen door, nearly ripping it in the process. Adrenaline shot through his entire body as he tore across the yard as fast as he could toward Sammi's trailer, preparing himself for the worst. As he approached the front door, he saw that it had been kicked in and was dangling off its hinges. Entering the house, he was horrified by the sight before him. Betty was slumped over on the couch with a gash across her forehead; Gerald was lying on the floor in the hallway, dazed and bleeding from the nose.

But it was what he saw on the living room floor that sent Jake into a maddening rage. Lying on her back with a cut over her right eye, Sammi trembled beneath the shadow of Scott Robertson, who loomed menacingly over her shivering body. Jake lunged toward Scott, who quickly jumped to his feet and stepped over Sammi to confront his challenger. The two collided like a couple of warring titans and began trading violent blows. Though Jake was landing some solid punches, Scott's strength seemed almost demonic, and it wasn't long before Scott began to get the upper hand, landing two to three heavy blows to each one of Jake's.

Realizing that Sammi's life depended upon him, Jake gave all he had, but it didn't seem to be enough. He kept telling himself that if he could hold on for just a few more minutes, the deputies would be there to bring this nightmare to an end. But Scott kept charging like an angry bear, vengefully unleashing his fury on Jake, who withstood his foe like a valiant warrior but could clearly see that he was losing ground.

Finally tiring of toying with his opponent, Scott let out a bone-chilling, demonic shriek and, in a display of near superhuman strength, positioned his forearm against Jake's neck and thrust him hard against the wall. As his back made impact with the wall, Jake suddenly felt a sharp, burning pain followed by what felt like warm water running down his stomach, waist, and legs.

Dropping his eyes to determine the source of this unfamiliar pain, Jake was horrified by what he saw. At some point in the struggle, Scott had pulled a knife which was now deeply embedded in Jake's abdomen. Before Jake had even had a chance to process what had just happened, Scott withdrew the knife and plunged it into him again. This time it was like a lightning bolt penetrating his body, producing an intense heat he had never experienced before. But Scott's thirst for revenge was not yet quenched and, with no mercy, he pulled the knife out and viciously stabbed Jake a third and fourth time.

By this point, Sammi had become alert enough to be aware of what was going and screamed in shock as she saw blood gushing from the wounds Scott had inflicted upon the man she so adored. Within seconds, the extreme pain that Jake felt turned to numbness as all of his strength ebbed from his body. As he slumped toward the floor, Scott threw him down on his back and straddled his chest. Jake was still conscious, but his concern was not for himself.

Turning toward Sammi, who was still lying on the floor, Jake fixed his gaze on her and whispered, "I'm sorry. I love you."

Sammi looked on with horror and was so terrified that she could not speak. She desperately wanted to throw herself over Jake to prevent Scott from hurting him further, but Scott had hit her so hard that she still could not stand. They locked eyes with one another and in that moment a thousand wordless thoughts passed between them, each one an expression of the love they had for one another. Suddenly, the intimate moment was interrupted by the sound of laughter. But it wasn't the kind of laughter one might hear at a joyful celebration.

No. It was evil; it was wicked; it was coming from Scott who was still sitting on top of Jake. When Jake turned his head to look, it seemed as if Scott's face was contorted into the very image of the devil himself. His lips were curled up on each end, his brows were furrowed, and his eyes were filled with pure, unfiltered hatred. Slowly leaning forward, Scott positioned his face as close as he could to Jake's and snarled, "I told you that if you ever laid your hands on me again, my smilin' face would be the last thing you ever saw on this earth, and now you're gonna know that I meant every word I said."

As the words spewed from his mouth, Scott raised the knife high above his head and prepared to thrust it into Jake's heart.

25

JUST AS SCOTT WAS ABOUT TO STRIKE THE death blow to Jake, he was interrupted by an unexpected sound: the sound of someone racking a round into a shotgun. Scott knew it wasn't the police, because he was facing the front door and the sound had come from behind him. Lowering his knife, Scott slowly turned his head to determine the source and, when he saw who it was, a contemptuous smile crept across his face.

"STAND UP!" a trembling voice demanded. "STAND UP NOW, SCOTT ROBERTSON, AND TURN SO I CAN SEE YOUR FACE! I AIN'T KIDDIN'!"

Scott appeared to be amused, but he slowly stood up and turned around as he had been told. Standing no less than eight feet from him with a shotgun aimed right at his head was none other than Gerald. Blood was still dripping from his nose and his hands trembled a bit, but his feet were planted firmly and the butt of the shotgun was pulled tight against his shoulder.

"Old Man," Scott sneered, "you run and hide every time I pull into this trailer dump. I don't believe for a second that you've got the nerve to pull that trigger. And, even if you did, you'd miss. Look at your hands. They're not too steady."

Gerald scoffed, "It's a shotgun, ya dang fool. I don't have to have steady hands—just have to point in your direction."

Angered by Gerald's mockery, Scott snarled, "Okay, Old Man, I've had enough of your mouth. Put the shotgun down or you'll get what he just got." Scott gestured toward Jake who lay bleeding profusely on the floor. Gerald did not back down but only tightened his grip on the gun.

"I'm gonna to count to three," Scott threatened, "and when I get to three, if that gun ain't layin' on the floor—you will be. ONE...TWO...THREE..."

The old man stood firm even though he knew this devil meant business. Gerald's unwillingness to comply with his demands infuriated Scott even further.

"I gave you fair warnin', Old Man," Scott growled as he stepped over Jake's bloody body and lunged at Gerald with ominous intent. Realizing that he was in imminent danger, Gerald took a breath, set his jaw, and fired the gun.

The shotgun's blast hit Scott squarely in the face, neck, and chest driving him back several feet. Tripping over Jake's body, he fell to the floor, landing hard on his back. Racking the shotgun again, Gerald cautiously walked over to Scott to assess the damage. The buckshot had ripped through the flesh on Scott's face and upper body, leaving him an unrecognizable bloody mess. Aiming the shotgun once more toward Scott's ruined head, Gerald leaned over to get a closer look. As Sammi's grandpa watched, Scott's chest heaved up and down three times, and then he stopped breathing. Scott Robertson, the devil of Kernersville, was dead.

"He's gone," Gerald noted with a sigh of relief as he lowered the shotgun. Looking at Sammi, he said, "He ain't gonna bother you no more, Honey."

"JAKE!" Sammi screamed, mustering up the strength to crawl to his side on her hands and knees. She wasn't even aware that she was kneeling in a pool of his blood. "JAKE!" she screamed again; her voice marked with anguish. But there was no response. Jake had lost consciousness due to the loss of blood, and Sammi knew that if help didn't arrive soon, Jake would die. She tried to stop the bleeding by placing her hands over the knife wounds, but her efforts were futile as the blood continued to flow freely, each drop carrying more and more of his life away.

Sammi leaned over him and kissed him on the lips, saying "Jake, I love you. Please, don't die," and she wept. With one hand still on his wounds, she took her other hand and tenderly caressed the dark brown locks of his hair which were now stained with his blood. Placing her quivering lips gently next to his ear, she whispered to him. "I promise I won't leave you," she sobbed. "I'll stay right by your side. That's the only place I feel safe. I'll take care of you, just like you always take care of me, always my hero, my knight in shining armor. Help is comin', so hang on, Jake. You always fight for me; I need you to fight for yourself now. Don't give up. There is still so much that we have to do together." As she spoke, her tears fell on his cheek. "Stay with me, Jake," she pleaded.

As she lay there with him, the room lit up with flashing blue and red lights, and the sweet sound of police sirens filled the air. In just a few moments, Sammi's house was crawling with police and EMS workers. Because of the severity of his injuries, Jake quickly became their first priority. Due to her persistence, Sammi was allowed to ride in the ambulance with Jake but, as soon as they arrived at the emergency room, she was separated from him to have her own injuries examined.

Within minutes after she and Jake arrived, Gerald and Betty were brought in as well, but thankfully, their injuries were superficial. Jake's, however, had the doctors concerned enough that they rushed him into surgery right away. After being bandaged up and given a change of clothes, Sammi and her grandparents were ushered into a large room where they would wait for news of Jake's progress. Sammi began to weep when she saw that the room was filling with people she knew.

Every single resident of Hope Park was there. Pastor James was there with all of the deacons as well as several other members of the church. Numerous police officers were present, including Sheriff Blake, and in the center of them all was Aunt Hazel, who ran to Sammi and wept on her shoulder as soon as she saw her. Pastor James then called everyone to bow their heads and he prayed a prayer that Sammi would later describe as the deepest, most heartfelt prayer she'd ever heard. As the next hour passed, the room became solemn and filled with quiet anticipation. Another hour passed, but surprisingly, no one left. Everyone was anxious to hear a good report from the doctor.

Finally, after three excruciatingly long hours, the door swung open and the surgeon stepped in to give his report. The expression on his face was one of shock when he saw the number of people who had lingered so late into the night in support of Jake. As he cleared his throat to speak, every eye in the room was fastened on the doctor. Some who had dozed off were now wide awake and on the edge of their seats.

"Wow!" the surgeon exclaimed, "I didn't expect such a crowd! This must be a very special young man, greatly loved."

Just about everyone in the room either nodded or gave verbal approval to the doctor's assessment of Jake.

He continued, "I won't keep you in suspense. There was quite a bit of internal damage, but the surgery went well and he's going to be fine. He will have to stay with us for several days, but I expect him to be back to normal within four to six weeks."

The room erupted with cheers as everyone jumped to their feet, hugging and patting one another on the back. Both Sammi and Aunt Hazel were swamped with hugs and kisses as the weary crowd slowly made their way out. When the last one had left, Sammi informed her grandparents and Aunt Hazel that she would not be going home, but planned to stay with Jake until he woke up. They knew better than to argue with her and, after exchanging several affectionate embraces, they parted for the night.

A nurse escorted Sammi to the room where Jake, still under the effects of the medication, was sleeping peacefully. The room was dark with the exception of a soft, yellow glow emanating from a nightlight in the bathroom. Standing next to Jake's bed, Sammi looked admiringly upon her valiant guardian, thinking to herself how blessed she was to have him in her life. Her eyes filled with tears as she thought about how he had risked his own life to save hers—and he'd done it without hesitation.

Sammi had not known him for even one year yet but, somehow, he had become the most important person in her life. She could barely remember what life was like before he came along, and she certainly couldn't imagine her future without him. After peering down at his face for several minutes, she leaned over the bedrail and gave him a lingering kiss on the lips.

"Will you be staying all night?" the nurse interrupted.

"Yes, if that's okay," Sammi replied.

"Of course," the nurse said, "I'll bring a cot with some blankets and a pillow."

"Thank you," Sammi replied gratefully.

The nurse did all she could to make sure Sammi was comfortable, but after an hour of lying on the cot, she was still unable to drift off. She knew that she would not be able to rest unless she was close enough to Jake to feel his heart beating; so, without concern for hospital rules, she slipped quietly next to him on the bed and, in a matter of moments, was sound asleep with her head on his chest.

26

EARLY THE NEXT MORNING, SAMMI WAS awakened from her sleep as she felt lips pressing softly against her forehead. When she opened her eyes and saw Jake looking down at her tenderly, a wide smile came across her face, but for the next several moments no words were spoken by either of them.

"Are you okay?" he asked, finally breaking the silence. "Did he hurt you?"

"Just this cut above my eye," she answered. "You showed up before he could do anything worse."

"And your grandparents?" he enquired.

"They're okay too. You saved all of us, Jake," she said. "We weren't ready for him. We were watchin' television when he came through the door—caught us off guard. Then you came chargin' in like the Marines."

Jake paused for a few seconds. "I don't remember much after he stabbed me the second time, but it seems like I remember hearing a gunshot. Is Scott de..."

"Yes," Sammi stopped him mid-sentence. "Yes, he is."

"And was it Gerald shot him?" Jake asked.

Sammi nodded her head in silence, not wanting to relive the awful nightmare from the night before. She was just happy that all of the people she loved the most were alive.

The doctors kept Jake in the hospital for the next three days and Sammi never left his side. A few weeks later, both of them were back to a normal routine, doing their best every day to put the past behind them. Letters from Jake's mother continued to arrive week after week, but each one went into the trash still sealed. Despite all that he had been through, Jake was able to maintain the highest GPA in the entire school and was officially named the valedictorian of his graduating class. By mid-spring he learned that he had been offered full academic scholarships by three separate universities.

Sammi also bounced back with full force. Her grades soared and, because her tuition would now be paid in full, she too, had bright collegiate hopes. They were both in agreement that they would attend the same university; because, after all they had been through, there were two things they had learned for sure: they were better together and they were stronger together. Everyone else knew that too. On the high school campus, you never heard one name without the other and you seldom saw one apart from the other.

The fires Jake and Sammi had faced had melted them together into one. As each day came and went, they moved farther from their shared painful past and closer to a hopeful shared future. The subject of marriage came up from time to time, but they both agreed that they should graduate college first. Jake had decided to study law at Chapel Hill and Sammi discovered a love for business administration. They dreamed together of someday owning their own law firm—he would handle the legal side and she would oversee the business side. They often joked about which one of them would actually be the boss.

Their dreams became so deeply entrenched in them that nothing could discourage them. In fact, Jake was so focused on his future that he was undaunted by the news that Jo would be returning to Kernersville exactly one week before his graduation. He remained determined not to let his mother derail him again. He told Sammi and Aunt Hazel that he would be respectful, but distant, where Jo was concerned.

Hazel assured Jake that when his mother came home, she would not be there long. She explained that, in one of her prison visits to Jo, she'd told her in no uncertain terms that she would be allowed to stay in the trailer for six weeks—long enough to find a job and another place to stay—but after six weeks, Jo would have to leave. She'd received Aunt Hazel's decision without argument and was in full agreement.

It was a warm Friday morning when Aunt Hazel drove to the prison to bring Jo home. For the entire ride back to Kernersville, Jo seemed quiet, but peaceful. She didn't talk much about her experiences in prison and didn't make any boastful promises like she had done before when she returned from rehab. The conversation was pleasant and very normal. Hazel couldn't help but note that she seemed like the old Jo, the one she knew before the life of drugs and prostitution. As they approached the town limits, Jo made an unexpected request of her aunt.

"Could you drop me off at the church?" she asked. "I made arrangements about a week ago to meet with Pastor

James and his wife as soon as I got home. I may be a while, so I'm sure his wife or the church secretary will bring me home."

"Sure," Aunt Hazel replied, pleasantly surprised by Jo's request. Several questions popped into her head but, not wanting to pry, Hazel refrained from asking them. When they pulled up to the front doors of the church, Jo opened the door, but paused before getting out of the car.

After several seconds of silence, she turned toward her aunt and, with a tone of sincere conviction that Hazel had never before observed in her, she said, "Aunt Hazel, you have always been so good to me and Jake. You took us into your home, you gave us a roof over our heads, gave us warm beds to sleep in, you put food on the table for us, and you did all of that knowin' the kind of life I'd been livin'. You didn't hold anything back from us. You made us feel like your home was our home. But I didn't appreciate it like I should have. I took advantage of your kindness: I lied to you, I hid things from you, and I put you and my baby boy at risk."

Tears began streaming from Jo's eyes and she had to pause for a moment to bring her emotions under control before she could continue. Hazel remained silent, but the sincerity in Jo's voice brought tears to her eyes as well. Something seemed different this time. There was a humility and vulnerability in her niece that hadn't been there before.

Hazel reached in the glove compartment and pulled out some tissues for both of them. After Jo had wiped her eyes and blew her nose, she looked Hazel directly in the eyes and said, "There's only one thing I want from you and Jake, but I know I don't deserve it and if you can't give me this one thing, I won't blame you at all." Jo had to pause again as all of her emotions welled up in her throat.

"All I want from you, Aunt Hazel, all I need from you and Jake…is your forgiveness." As soon as those words fell from Jo's lips, she began to weep. As Hazel looked at her broken niece, she suddenly saw for the first time in years, the little girl who was once so innocent, so bright, and so full of hope. She saw the little girl who used to come and sleep over at her house for entire weekends when they would play games, watch movies, and indulge in sinful amounts of popcorn, ice cream, and cookies; she remembered watching little Jo and Charlie walk off toward the river with fishing poles over their shoulders when she was so small that the top of her head barely reached Charlie's waist; Hazel remembered how Jo would ride Charlie's back pretending that he was a horse, a ritual that Jo always insisted on before she would consent to go to bed. Charlie would ride her on his back down the hall to her bedroom and then buck her off onto her bed, just like a wild horse would throw off a cowboy. Jo would scream with delight every time. Then, Hazel remembered the night she'd walked into Jo's room at home and saw what her father was doing to her.

At that point, Hazel could no longer contain her tears, nor could she hold on to the anger and resentment that she had been harboring toward Jo. Compassion filled Hazel's heart and she grabbed her niece and pulled her close. Wrapping her arms around her, Aunt Hazel squeezed Her niece as tight as she could.

"I forgive you, Doodlebug," Hazel choked out as they sobbed on one another's shoulders.

Through her tears, Jo laughed and said, "You've haven't called me that since I was a little girl. Uncle Charlie used to call me that too."

For the next several minutes, the two held on to each other without speaking a word.

"I guess I need to go inside," Jo finally said, as she pulled back from her aunt. "Don't wanna keep the preacher waitin.'"

Hazel placed both her hands on Jo's cheeks, and gently wiped her tears away. "Before you go, there's a verse in the Bible I want you to remember. It's Jeremiah 29:11. It says, 'For I know the plans I have for you,' declares the Lord, 'plans to prosper you and not to harm you, plans to give you hope and a future.'"

"That's nice, Aunt Hazel," Jo said. "I heard that verse a lot when I was in prison. I'll remember it always."

As Jo got out of the car, Aunt Hazel called after her, "There's always hope, Jo. As long as you're breathin', there is always hope."

Jo smiled at her aunt, then turned to go into the church where Pastor James was already at the door waiting for her. Hazel drove out of the parking lot and wept all the way home. Later that evening, Jo and Aunt Hazel enjoyed a dinner alone because Jake and Sammi had to go straight to work after school. Jo was brought up to speed on all the good things and the not so good things that had happened to the kids over the past several months. She was told about her son's scholarship to UNC and about his interest in becoming a lawyer. Jo was so proud that her son had been named the class valedictorian and hoped that he would not mind her coming to the graduation to hear him give his speech.

Jake and Sammi decided to take in a late movie after work, which meant that his mother was already in bed by the time Jake got home. Sammi suspected that his desire to go to the movies was an attempt to avoid Jo, because he was always too tired after work on Fridays to do anything. The fact that he fell asleep during the movie confirmed her suspicions. His avoidance would be short-lived though, because Aunt Hazel had planned a family breakfast the next morning to welcome Jo home. Sammi came over bright and early to help prepare the food and was put on biscuit detail. As she was standing in the kitchen mixing the ingredients together, her attention was drawn to an unusual sound coming from Jo's room.

"Is she playin' a radio," Sammi asked.

"Nope," Hazel replied, a smile on her face. "She's singin.'"

"Wow!" Sammi exclaimed. "Never heard that before. She's not bad."

Hazel replied, "She went to bed singin' last night. I haven't spoken to Jake since she got home, but somethin' is different. I know she has made lots of promises in the past that she ended up breakin', but she and I had a conversation yesterday that left us both in tears. And you'll never guess where she wanted to go first when we got back to town."

"Where?" Sammi asked.

"She wanted to go see the pastor," Hazel answered. "I couldn't believe it. She told me she had made an appointment to meet with him before she'd even left the prison. His wife brought her home about two hours after I dropped her off. Jake won't believe it, I'm afraid, but I'm tellin' you, she's a different woman. I feel it in my heart."

"I sure hope that's true," Sammi said hopefully. "But you're right about Jake. I don't know if he will ever trust her again. He won't even let me bring her up in conversation. He changes the subject every time I mention her. I see him broodin' sometimes, and I just know he's relivin' some bad episode from his past with her. I'm afraid that what used to be anger is pure hate now."

The kitchen conversation was suddenly interrupted by the sound of both Jake and Jo's bedroom doors opening at the same time, leading to an awkwardly silent encounter in the hallway. Both of them had been headed to the bathroom, but when Jake realized his mother was standing in front of him, he dropped his eyes to the floor, refusing to look her in the eye. Jo took a step back and gestured for him to go ahead of her, an offer he quickly accepted, slamming the bathroom door behind him. Jo started to go back to her room when she noticed who was standing in the kitchen covered in flour.

"Sammi!" Jo exclaimed as she bounded into the kitchen. Throwing her arms around her, Jo wept as she kissed her cheeks over and over again. The intensity of her emotions and the sincerity of her repeated apologies greatly encouraged Sammi. After what seemed like half a dozen hugs and kisses, Jo asked her out to the front porch for a private conversation. Aunt Hazel suspected that it would be a conversation similar to the one she had had with Jo the day before. About fifteen minutes passed before the two ladies came back in. After one more hug, Jo returned to her bedroom, and Sammi, whose face was red and wet from crying, resumed her duties in the kitchen.

"You were right," Sammi said to Aunt Hazel, sniffling a little. "She's not the same woman—somethin' is definitely different."

During breakfast, Jo was polite and expressed genuine interest in everyone around the table, asking lots of questions. Even Jake had to admit to himself that this was a new thing. Usually, his mother only wanted to talk about herself.

True to his word, though, he remained respectful, but distant, only giving his mother short answers to her questions, all the while avoiding eye contact.

Normally after a meal, Jake would stay to help clean up, but as soon as he'd downed the last bite on his plate, he looked at Sammi and said, "We better get going or we're going to be late for work."

Sammi knew they had plenty of time before they had to be at Newlin's, but she went along with his request, knowing that he just wanted to get out of the house and away from his mom. As they were walking out the door, Jo called out to him.

"Son," she said. Hearing her refer to him as her son made Jake cringe. He stopped and slightly turned his head to acknowledge her, but he still would not look her in the eye.

She continued, "I just wanted to say that I really hope you and Sammi will be at church tomorrow. Pastor James and I have a big surprise for all of you."

Jake nodded his head but didn't say a word, not even a goodbye, as he and Sammi walked out the door.

Once they were in the car, Jake asked Sammi, "What kind of surprise would she and the pastor possibly have?"

"I don't know," she replied, "but we both need to be there. Whatever it is, it seems to be really important to her."

27

THE NEXT MORNING THE CHURCH WAS SO packed that the only available seats were in the front row. As Mr. Wade ushered them down the aisle Jake and Sammi looked around to see if they could spot Jo, but she seemed to be nowhere in sight. When the choir began to sing, Jake noticed that Pastor James was also missing from his usual place on the platform. The choir anthem, chosen and led by Aunt Hazel, was well received by the congregation as evidenced by a round of *Amens* when it was finished. A hush fell over the church when Pastor James suddenly appeared in the baptistery behind the choir. He was dressed in the fancy white robe that he always wore whenever he performed a baptism. As was his habit, he cleared his throat in preparation to speak.

"We have a very special surprise for everyone this morning," Pastor James beamed. "I had the pleasure this past Friday of meeting for nearly two hours with Jo Ledger. As you know, she had to be away from us for several months and many, if not all of you, have been praying for her. It is my joy this morning to inform you that your prayers for her have been answered. While she was away, God did a miraculous work in her life and, as we talked together on Friday, it became clear to me that Jo is not the same person she was when she left us. She shared with me all that God has done in her heart and, before she left my office, she asked if I would baptize her today."

An uncomfortable knot quickly formed in the pit of Jake's stomach. *This has to be some kind of show on her part,* he thought to himself. He didn't believe for one minute that her had truly changed and he was very skeptical as she stepped from behind the wall and down into the water with Pastor James. The knot in Jake's stomach grew tighter when the pastor turned to Jo and asked her a question,

"Would you like to say anything to the congregation before I baptize you?" he asked.

Don't say anything, Mom, Jake silently pleaded. His heart sank when his mother turned toward the microphone that dangled above the baptistery.

Looking out at the congregation, Jo smiled, "I'm sure that most of you know about the horrible life I used to live. Some of you in here today have even heard me make promises to change my ways, promises that I've never kept. But, while I was in prison, I realized that the reason I could never keep those promises is because I tried to make those changes alone. I thought I could do it by myself, in my own strength. I'd never really learned to lean on other people and I've never learned to lean on God. Because of that, I've hurt a lot of you; but the one I hurt the most was my son, the one person in this world who I love more than anyone else." As Jo spoke those words, she'd turned to face Jake, looked him in the eye, and said, "Baby Boy, I love you and all I want is for you to forgive me. I know it will take time, but I promise

I'll keep waitin' and I'll keep hopin' that, someday, you will let me be your Mama again."

Jo's words struck Jake like a sledge hammer, cracking open the hardened exterior that had formed around his heart. Looking into his mother's eyes for the first time since she had returned, he was on the verge of tears and, for a brief second, he thought about rushing up on the platform to hug his mother and forgive her in front of everyone. He glanced over at Sammi who was an absolute puddle of emotion. Jake could hear others in the congregation sniffling behind him; his aunt, still seated on the platform in front of the choir, wept unapologetically; and, to make the situation even more uncomfortable, Pastor James was looking down at him from the baptistery as if he was expecting Jake to respond to Jo's plea for forgiveness.

For just a second, Jake felt compassion for his mother; for just a second, he felt a longing in his heart to forgive her. He could feel his body leaning forward, but just as he was about to stand to his feet, his mind was flooded with memories of all of her lies from the past, of all the broken promises, of all of the abuse he'd had endured at her hands. These painful memories were like cement pouring over his heart, sealing the newly-formed cracks that threatened to release the pain and hate that had taken root deep inside of him. Overcoming the onslaught of emotional impulses, Jake just leaned back against the pew and cast his eyes to the floor.

Sensing the moment pass and the need to move forward, Pastor James looked at Jo and asked, "Jo Ledger, do you confess Jesus Christ as your Lord and Savior?"

With a wide smile on her face, Jo boldly responded, "I do!"

"Then, it is my joy," he exclaimed, "to baptize you in the name of the Father, and of the Son, and of the Holy

Ghost." Pastor James plunged Jo into the water and ,when he brought her up, both of her hands were raised high in the air as if she were about to take flight. With the exception of Jake, everyone stood to their feet with rapturous applause and joined in as the choir began to soulfully and joyously sing one of their favorite celebration hymns, "Oh, Happy Day." There was such a joyful spirit in the place that, when they finished that song, they jumped right into another song and then another.

They were still singing when Jo and Pastor James returned to the sanctuary and, as soon as the congregation saw her, many of them moved spontaneously toward her, surrounding her and covering her in hugs and kisses. Still seated on the front pew, Jake observed the scene with skepticism, unwilling to believe that his mother's conversion was genuine. The remainder of the service was a blur to Jake.

Jake impatiently anticipated the pastor's final *Amen,* and when it came, he grabbed Sammi by the hand and bolted through a side door that led directly into the parking lot. He was in no mood to speak to anyone or hear even one person brag on his mother. The ride home was quiet as he brooded over the events of the morning, and Sammi knew him well enough to know that when he was in a mood such as this, it was best to leave him alone while he sorted out his thoughts.

Aunt Hazel had a very special lunch planned. The table was filled with all of Jo's favorite dishes in honor of her homecoming. Two folding card tables had been added to each end of the kitchen table to make room for several special guests which included the pastor and his wife, Mayor and his wife, and of course, Betty and Gerald. As they sat down to eat, Jake happened to be seated right across from

Jo with Sammi by his side as always. The food was amazing, but the conversation was difficult for Jake to swallow. His mother was the center of attention, and she was being bombarded with questions as well as words of praise. To the ears of her dubious son, Jo's talk of God and religion was the epitome of hypocrisy. *How can they all be buying into this,* he thought to himself. *She's such a liar. She has them all fooled.*

As Jo continued to converse with the pastor and the others around the table, anger was boiling up inside of Jake like hot lava and, just as hot lava eventually forces its way up the throat of the volcano, he suddenly could not hold back his rage any longer. With absolutely no thought of consequence, he angrily yelled out, "SO, *YOU* FOUND JESUS!"

The loud, angry tone of sarcasm in Jake's voice brought an immediate hush to the table talk. Sammi squeezed Jake's leg hoping to calm him, but he didn't even notice. All eyes were on him as he glared at his mother across the table.

"What did you say, Honey?" Jo asked, somewhat shocked by the outburst.

Still fuming, Jake shook his head in disgust, "SO, *YOU* FOUND JESUS! AND BECAUSE OF THAT WE ARE ALL JUST SUPPOSED TO FORGET ABOUT EVERYTHING? I ENDED UP IN JAIL BECAUSE OF YOU! SAMMI GOT HURT BECAUSE OF YOU! NOT TO MENTION THE LITERAL HELL YOU'VE PUT ME THROUGH MY ENTIRE LIFE! AND WE ARE JUST SUPPOSED TO LET ALL OF THAT GO...AS IF IT NEVER HAPPENED?!?"

Jake had expected to shame his mother with his sharp words as he had often been able to do in the past. He knew that Jo lived with a sense of guilt because of her lifestyle, and he had learned over the years how to quickly silence her with shame. But it didn't work this time. Jo locked eyes with her son, and, with words that were soft and gentle, she spoke to him as if the two of them were the only ones at the table.

"No, Baby," she said with compassion. "I don't expect you to just forget all that has happened. I was a horrible person and what I put you through was selfish and unfair, and I know it's gonna take you a long time to work through all of that, but I promise you I will be here to work through it with you. I aim to do all I can to help you forgive me. But there is one thing I want to make clear to you: I didn't find Jesus, Son. He found me. He came crashin' through those prison walls and met me right where I was. If I live to be a hundred years old, I will never forget how He came to me that night. It happened the same day you came to see me. The things you said to me were painful and they were hard to hear, but I knew they were true. After you left, I felt so horrible; all I wanted to do was die. I even gave serious thought to killin' myself. I laid in my cell all day, cryin' and hatin' myself for what I had done to you. I felt completely worthless. I felt dirty. But that night, a church group came to the prison to lead a worship service. I didn't want to go but I had no choice. Some women from the church sang several songs, but I didn't hear a one of them. It wasn't until the preacher started preachin' that somethin' began to stir inside of me. He preached out of the Book of John about the woman caught in the act of adultery. He said she was probably a prostitute and that her sinful actions were worthy of death. He told about the evil men who brought her to Jesus and threw her down as His feet. He said they had rocks in their hands and were ready to stone her. She was certain that she would die that day. She knew she had come to the end of the road and there was just no way out. All of her bad choices had led her to this moment and now she was gonna have to pay the price for her sin. Son, I could see myself in that woman. Just like her, I was a prostitute, but even worse, I was an addict. My bad choices had brought me to the point where I'd lost you and I'd lost my freedom. I was at the end of the road and there seemed to be no hope at all. Death seemed to be all that was left for that woman in the Bible, and death seemed to be all that was left for me. But then the preacher said that Jesus ran off all those evil men. After they were gone He looked her in the eye and He asked her where all her accusers were. When she saw that her accusers had left, Jesus told her that He didn't condemn her either and that she should go and leave her life of sin. After he told the story, the preacher said that no matter what you've done, no matter how bad you've messed up your life, there is always hope, even when you think you've reached the end of the road. He said that God's forgiveness is available for the takin'. Jake, as soon as he said those words I just crumbled to the floor in a heap of tears and I started beggin' Jesus to forgive me. And then something happened that I don't expect you to believe. It's even hard for me to believe sometimes, but I know it happened. After I asked Jesus to forgive me, I raised up my head and, when I opened my eyes, I was surrounded by the brightest light I've ever seen. It seemed brighter than the sun. It was so bright, in fact, that I couldn't see anything or anyone else in the room. And then somethin' even more amazin' happened. Out of that light, a voice called out to me. It was a man's voice and it was the sweetest, kindest, and most compassionate soundin' voice I've ever heard. He called me by name like he knew me. He spoke only two sentences to me, but those two sentences changed my life and they gave me a freedom I've never known before. He said, 'I forgive you. You are clean.' As soon as He said that to me, it was like every ounce of guilt, shame, and evil was washed out of me. But as all the bad was being washed out of me, it seemed as if somethin' else was being poured into me—somethin' warm, beautiful, and powerful. It seemed as if chains were fallin' off of me. I felt clean and I felt free. Then, just as suddenly as it had appeared, the light vanished and I saw that I was surrounded by some of the women from the church. They were prayin' hard over me and when I sat up one of them told me she knew I had just met Jesus because she heard me singin'. I didn't even realize it. You may not believe me yet, Baby Boy, but I promise you that the old Jo is dead. I left her on the floor that night and when I stood to my feet, I was a new woman. God is real, Son. *This* is real."

Jake could see the sincerity in his mother and he desperately wanted to believe everything she had just said. He wanted to be able to forgive her, but there were so many wounds in his soul, wounds that she had inflicted, that he simply was not ready to let go of the bitterness. He wasn't even sure he knew how. When the love of his life had been hurt so badly because of his mother's actions, he had vowed he would never forgive her.

For the next several days, Jake spent most of his free time in his room preparing his valedictorian speech. Aunt Hazel's trailer was small, so it was impossible to avoid his mother. However, his encounters with her were pleasant and by the end of the week he had consented to allow her to come to his graduation. While he liked the version of Jo that he was seeing, he wasn't ready to accept it as genuine, and he continued to keep a respectful distance.

The graduation ceremony was set for Saturday morning at 11:00 AM and was to be held on the school's football field. Jake slept very little the night before due to excitement, but when morning came, he was alert, energetic, and ready to go. Sammi came over for breakfast and he could barely keep his eyes off of her while they ate. She had risen early that morning to make certain her hair and makeup were perfect. She was gorgeous without all of that stuff, but when she fixed herself up like that, it was more than Jake could stand. He still could not believe that he had won the heart of such a beautiful woman. He wanted to arrive early to the graduation, so as soon as they finished eating, he began nudging Sammi toward the door. Just as they were about to walk out, he felt a hand on his arm. It was his mother.

As he turned to face her, she placed both of her hands on his cheeks. With a huge smile on her face, she said, "I'm so proud of you, Baby Boy. But I guess I can't call you that anymore after today. You're a man now, and what an amazin' man you've become! I know you're gonna do some great things and I can't wait to hear your speech. I promise I'll be there cheerin' you on. You can count on it." Tears filled her eyes as she gazed intently into the face of her son.

Then, without asking his permission, she threw her arms around him and pulled him close to her. As she held on to him, Jake realized that he couldn't remember the last time she had shown him this kind of affection. He didn't pull away, but he didn't return the hug either.

As Jake and Sammi headed toward the car, Jo stepped out on the porch and called out, "Oh, Jake! I forgot to tell you that Aunt Hazel has some errands to run this mornin', so I'm gonna borrow Fanny's car and meet y'all at the school." Jake acknowledged her comment by giving her a thumb up, but he didn't turn around.

"I love you, Son," he heard her say.

He would have just kept on walking, but Sammi stopped him and gently urged Jake to return the sentiment. When he turned around to face his mother, she was standing just on the outside of the screen door with her hands shoved into the pockets of her bathrobe. He could see the hopeful anticipation on her face as she waited for his response. With no emotion, he replied, "Love you." Those two simple words seemed to be all she needed and with a smile of satisfaction, Jo turned and walked back inside the trailer.

"See," Sammi said. "That didn't hurt so bad, did it?"

"It was excruciating," Jake replied sarcastically. "We may need to stop by the emergency room on the way to the school."

"Ha, ha," Sammi said. "You're so funny."

Secretly, Jake felt a sense of pride in the fact that his mother was going to be present at his graduation and would be able to hear his speech, but he was not about to let anyone know how he was feeling, not even Sammi. As soon as they pulled onto the campus, his mind turned quickly to the events of the day. The parking lot was already filling up. Much excitement was in the air as parents, students, teachers, and administrators scurried about trying to find their places in preparation for the ceremony.

The graduates had been instructed to meet in the gym where they would be lined up alphabetically before marching out onto the field, which meant that Jake and Sammi would have to sit separately during the ceremony.

But, before they parted ways, she kissed him and wished him luck on his speech. As they marched out onto the field, Jake was overwhelmed with a sense of achievement. He reflected briefly on all the challenges he had faced throughout the past year. He thought of how fortunate he was to have Sammi and how he couldn't wait to start a new life with her. This was a day filled with hope, a day that marked a new beginning.

So many people were sitting in the stands that Jake had no idea where Aunt Hazel and Jo might be, but he felt their presence and support. His mother's presence seemed especially strong and knowing that she was out in the crowd somewhere strangely gave him a great measure of satisfaction. When it came time to give his speech, he held the audience captive with words that were wise beyond his years. He even had the crowd laughing at times. Sammi sat among her peers, beaming with pride as Jake challenged his classmates to look to the stars as they forged their future, never allowing anything or anyone to stand in their way.

When he was finished, the entire graduating class gave him a standing ovation. When the ceremony was over, the crowd was so thick that finding little Aunt Hazel and Jo seemed to be an impossible task. Holding tightly to one another's hands, Jake and Sammi trudged across the field trying to spot a familiar face. The effort was made even more difficult by strangers who kept stopping them to congratulate Jake on such a good speech. "Humble, but brilliant," commented one spectator.

As they continued making their way through the crowd, Jake suddenly felt a strong hand grab his shoulder from behind. "You made me proud today, Son!"

Jake turned around to see who had just spoken to him. It was Mayor. "Thank you very much, Sir," Jake respectfully replied.

"I rode here with your aunt," Mayor explained. "She spotted you from the bleachers and sent me out here to get you. We're to meet her at the gym."

Because of the noisy crowd, there was little conversation as the three made their way across campus. When they got to the gym, Aunt Hazel was pacing nervously back and forth in front of a pay phone. The look on her face was unsettling.

"What's wrong?" Jake asked.

Sammi quickly panned the lobby and then asked, "Where's Jo? Is she in the bathroom?"

"No," Hazel answered, struggling to remain calm. "She never showed up. After your speech, Jake, I came in here and called the house, but I got no answer. So, I called Fanny and she said that Jo never came to pick up the car. She said she would go check on her, but now I can't get an answer at my house or at Fanny's—and she's had time to get back. We need to get home as soon as we can."

"I think we all know what we'll find when we get there," Jake said disapprovingly.

"We don't know anything for sure, Jake," Sammi assured him. "Somethin' could be wrong."

"Well," Mayor interjected, "we won't know anything until we get there, so let's go."

Jake's mood was dark on the way home. "You know she's relapsed," he scoffed. "We will walk in the door and find her passed out with a needle either on the floor or still in her arm."

"You know I love you," Sammi affirmed, "and I am always on your side, but this time I think you might be wrong. You should have heard the things she said to me on the front porch the first mornin' she was back. I think she's really changed this time and, to be honest, I'm worried about her."

Jake shook his head in disgust. "No! This is what she does. It's what she's always done. She convinces everybody that she's gonna change, and she may actually mean it at the time, but it's not usually very long before she's back doing the same old crap. I've seen it my whole life and I'm tired of it. You'll see that I'm right. Unfortunately, I'm always right when it comes to her. She always puts herself before everybody else. She couldn't stay clean long enough to even make it to my graduation."

Deciding not to press the issue, Sammi remained silent the rest of the way home, but she could see that Jake's anger was increasing with each passing mile. As they approached the entrance to the trailer park, she leaned forward and gasped. "There's an ambulance and a police car in front of your house!" she screamed. "Speed up, Jake, please!"

As they turned in, they could see Aunt Hazel running from the car toward the front door with Mayor on her heels. Jake's heart pounded within his chest as he contemplated the worst. The police car was bad enough, but an ambulance meant something even more ominous. A dozen possible scenarios ran through Jake's stricken mind, but it wasn't until he pulled up to the front of the house that the reality of the situation hit him in the face. He hadn't seen it when they first pulled in, but there on the other side of the ambulance was a car that Jake recognized. Sammi spotted it at the same time as he did.

With a tone of apprehension in her voice, she turned to Jake and asked, "Why is Pastor James here?" They both jumped from the car and ran toward the house but before they reached the door, the pastor stepped out to stop them on the sidewalk.

"What's happened?" Sammi demanded. "Is it Jo?"

Pastor James looked first at Sammi, then he turned to Jake. The look on his face betrayed the fact that he had bad news to share. "Son," he said, "there is no easy way to tell you this, but, uh...your mama is gone."

Jake was stunned, "Wha...what do you mean, she's gone? Did she pack up and leave, or..."

"No, Son." Pastor James paused and then shaking his head despondently he said, "She's died."

As soon as she heard those words, Sammi buried her head in Jake's chest and began to weep inconsolably. Attempting to comfort her, Jake put both arms around her and pressed her tight against his body, but it only made her cry harder. A couple of minutes passed before she was able to compose herself. Pulling back from Jake, she looked at the pastor and said, "I wanna see her. She's still in there, right? Can I see her?"

"Yes," Pastor James answered. "She's still on the couch where Fanny found her. By the time the ambulance arrived it was apparent that she had been gone for a few hours, so they didn't even try to revive her. Hazel's with her now."

After Sammi went inside, Jake looked at Pastor James and dispassionately asked, "Did she relapse? Did they find the needle?"

"No, Son," the pastor replied. "There were no needles, no drugs...not a sign of anything like that in the whole house. The officers looked around some but didn't find a thing."

"Then, what happened?" Jake asked. "How did she…"

The pastor looked him in the eyes with compassion, "They aren't sure just yet, Son, but they think it might have been a heart attack."

"Heart attack?" Jake asked in disbelief. "She wasn't even thirty-five years old yet. How could she have had a heart attack?"

"Years of drug abuse can weaken the heart," Pastor James explained. "They believe it just gave out on her. But I want you to take comfort in the fact that she did not relapse. I believe she was very serious about starting a new life. Had she lived, I have no doubt we would have seen her take a new path."

Jake gave no response but just stood silent for what seemed like minutes, trying to comprehend the situation.

Finally, Pastor James reached out to put his hand on Jake's shoulder and asked, "Do you want to see her before they take her away?"

Jake gave no verbal response, but nodded his head and slowly walked toward the door. Pastor James followed close behind. As he entered the house, Jake saw his mother lying lifeless on her back on the couch. She was still in her bathrobe, which indicated she had probably died shortly after he and Sammi had left for the graduation. Aunt Hazel, sobbing painfully, was on her knees beside Jo with her head on Jo's chest. Sammi, with tears still streaming down her cheeks, sat beside Jo on the couch holding and rubbing her hand. Mayor stood at the end of the couch with his head bowed.

Noticing Jake's presence in the room, Sammi turned to him, "Come, say somethin' to her."

Jake stood back several feet from the couch. "I don't have anything to say," he replied stoically.

"At least, come say goodbye," Sammi pleaded.

"I told you, I don't have anything to say to her," Jake reiterated sharply. Both Hazel and Sammi turned and looked at him. His cool reaction to the untimely death was concerning to all in the room. The awkward silence that ensued made Jake so uncomfortable that he quietly dismissed himself, walked out of the house, and retreated to the gazebo. He half expected Sammi to follow, but she didn't. It was a half hour before Jo's body was brought out on a stretcher and carefully loaded into the ambulance. Another thirty minutes had passed before Sammi finally emerged from the trailer to join Jake on the gazebo. Sitting down beside him, Sammi took Jake's hand in hers and laid her head on his shoulder.

"I love you, Jake," she said tenderly.

"I love you too," he whispered. As they sat together in silence, Jake began to contemplate how important Sammi had become to him. He now knew with certainty that, as long as she was by his side, he could endure anything, conquer anything. She was like a bright light that led him out of the dense fog that had enshrouded him his entire life. She was now his anchor, his strength, and his hope. After they had sat there in silence for a few minutes, Sammi told Jake that Pastor James wanted to see him, because he had something to give to him. When they went back inside, the pastor was leaning against the kitchen counter downing a cold glass of sweet iced tea that Aunt Hazel had no doubt served him.

Setting the glass on the counter, Pastor James motioned for Jake to come to him as if he had a private matter to discuss. Reaching into his shirt pocket, he pulled out a small piece of paper with something scribbled on it. "Fanny found this in your mother's hand when she came to check on her earlier. She must have sensed that something bad was about to happen when she penned this. You can tell by the handwriting that she was struggling as she wrote it. It's obviously for you."

Jake took the piece of paper and stared in silence at the note his mother had written. Though the writing looked like chicken scratches, he was able to make out the following words: "Baby Boy, I love you with my whole heart. Please forgive me."

"Do you think you can grant her request?" the pastor asked softly.

Jake didn't answer, but as he continued staring down at the note, he honestly was not sure if he could ever completely forgive his mother for all the things she had done. Rather than sadness or remorse, Jake seemed to feel nothing but anger and bitterness towards his mother. After all, her very last act on earth was to break yet another promise she had made to him, *"I promise, I'll be there cheerin' you on; you can count it,"* she had said. But, once again, she had failed to stay true to her word. Jake held on to the note for a few minutes, but as soon as the pastor left, he crumpled the paper and threw it into the trash.

The funeral was spectacular. It seemed as if the entire town had turned out. Everyone had heard of Jo's miraculous transformation in prison and wanted to come and pay last respects to her and her family. There were about as many people standing as there were sitting. Some even had to stand outside the door of the church. The choir sang and the pastor preached a wonderful sermon about hope and the power of God to change one's life. The funeral was both sad and joyful, but Jake remained indifferent throughout the entire service, never shedding one tear.

After the graveside service, all the residents of Hope Park gathered around the gazebo for a covered-dish meal. Just about all the members of the church came as well, each bearing a delicious plate of something homemade. Sammi was about to prepare a plate for Jake when she realized he was not in the crowd. As she was about to go into the house to look for him, she happened to glance toward the woods just in time to see him disappearing into the trees.

28

Normally, Sammi would have left him alone for a bit, but something in her heart told her to follow him; so, putting down the still-empty plate, she followed him into the woods. She knew right where he would be, so it didn't take her long to find him sitting cross-legged on the ground in front of the fallen tree by the river. Instinctively, she sat down right in front of him, crossing her legs as well and bumping her knees up against his. This was the position they had agreed they would take whenever one had something important to say to the other: knee to knee, eye to eye.

When she sat down, Jake smiled at her, something she hadn't seen him do since their graduation. Before she could say a word, he took her face in his hands, pulled her forward, and pressed her lips tightly against his. It was the most passionate kiss she had ever received from him, so passionate in fact, that it caused chills to sweep over her body.

"Whew!" she exclaimed, fanning her face with her hands as he finally released her. "What was that all about?"

Jake laughed, taking both her hands in his. Then the expression on his face became pensive. "There's something very important I want to talk to you about and it can't wait," he said, breathlessly.

"What is it?" she asked, apprehension coloring her voice.

"I want you to hear me out before you react," he said.

Sammi shifted her position anxiously. Whatever it was that he was about to say was obviously important to him.

"I cannot stay in this trailer park or even in this town another week." Jake continued. "I've decided that in the next few days, I'm moving to Chapel Hill. I was going to be moving there anyway in the fall for school, but I can't wait that long. There's too much pain here; too many bad memories; too much death. If I don't get out of here right away, I'll go crazy."

Sammi swallowed hard. She had also been accepted at Chapel Hill and would be moving there in the fall, but the thought of going all summer without being close to Jake was unbearable. They still enjoyed frequent late-night dates on her roof. Several times a week, they slept cuddled up together on her couch after falling asleep watching television. They literally did everything together. They had become inseparable. Sammi's heart began to pound with trepidation at the thought of not having him right next door, even if it was only for a few months.

"But there is just one thing," he said, interrupting her troubled thoughts. "I can't live one day without you in my life. Sammi, I love you more than I've ever loved another human being. You are the one part of my life—the only part of my life—that is consistent. My heart belongs only to you. I know that even if I took the next twenty years and searched through the whole world, I would never find a woman who I could love like I love you. You were made for me, Sammi; and this might sound corny and cliché, but I'm at peace when I'm with you. You have filled in all the pieces that were missing in me and I do not want to wonder, for even a minute, what my world would be like without you. So I have a question for you."

Jake reached in his shirt pocket, pulling something out that he was careful not to let her see right away. "Sammi," he continued, "I want to leave here before the end of the week and I want you to go with me, but I don't want you to go with me just as my girlfriend. I want you to go as my wife. I want to marry you...tomorrow. Sammi, will you marry me tomorrow?"

As he asked the question, Jake opened his hand to reveal a ring. He had been saving his money for a while in preparation for his move to Chapel Hill in the fall, but on the very day of his mother's death, as he and Sammi were sitting together on the gazebo, he knew there was no other woman for him other than her and he'd decided right then to ask her to marry him. So as soon as the bank opened on the following Monday, he withdrew $250 and bought a small, but beautiful diamond ring.

Sammi gazed at the ring for a few seconds in disbelief. There was no doubt in her mind that she loved Jake as much as he loved her, so she didn't need to consider her answer to his question. "I'd marry you today, Jake Ledger, if that's what you wanted," she cried enthusiastically.

Jake slipped the ring on her finger, kissed his new fiancé, and then the two ran back to the crowd at the gazebo to announce their engagement. Everyone was overjoyed at the news, but no one was surprised. The only surprise came later when they told Aunt Hazel that they planned to marry immediately and then move to Chapel Hill to start their life together. While the news was difficult to hear, she understood why Jake felt the need to get away. Pastor James helped them get the license and then married them the next afternoon at the church in front of twenty or so witnesses from Hope Park.

Their honeymoon plans were as simple as their wedding. They would stay the night at a hotel in Chapel Hill and then spend the next day searching for an apartment near the campus. They promised Aunt Hazel that they would find a two-bedroom apartment so she could come and stay with them anytime she wanted. Sammi had recently received the payment from the Robertson family so they now had the money they needed to get started in their new life as husband and wife.

That night, the newlyweds treated themselves to a special honeymoon dinner at a fine restaurant in town. As they entered the establishment, they were greeted by the hostess who turned them over to the maître d' dressed in a finely tailored black suit. He escorted them through the dimly lit dining area to a table that was draped with an elegant white table cloth and pulled the chair out for Sammi to be seated. Uncertain of the rules of etiquette for fine dining, Jake remained standing, expecting to have his chair pulled out for him as well. The sophisticated gentleman smiled and graciously motioned for Jake to seat himself. Sammi could not contain her delight at her husband's awkwardness. "You're so cute," she giggled.

After Jake was seated, they were both handed a menu and assured that a waiter would be there to serve them shortly. It seemed like only seconds before the waiter appeared dressed in black pants, a white shirt, a white coat, and a black tie. He was very respectful and seemed eager to serve them. Jake ordered a steak, medium rare, with a baked potato and asparagus. Sammi ordered chicken cordon bleu with glazed carrots and a salad. A small candle, burning in the center of the table, cast a soft glow on their faces, adding yet another romantic element to the experience. As they waited for their food, they talked about their plans for the next day while nibbling on soft rolls that were covered in butter with a honey glaze. One thing they did not talk about, however, was the nervous anticipation they both felt regarding what was to happen in the hotel room after dinner.

There had been many nights when they had fallen asleep in each other's arms on Sammi's grandparents' couch, but Jake had always respected her wish to wait until they were married, and he never pushed for anything beyond cuddling. Now that the wait was over, both of them were a bundle of nerves on the inside, neither of them wanting to disappoint the other. She wanted to fully reward him for his patience, and he wanted to demonstrate his intense passion for her without seeming overbearing or out of control. He couldn't help but think back to what she'd gone through last October and he longed to show her what making love was supposed to feel like. He wanted her to feel the difference. He wanted her to feel safe.

When they got to the room, she pulled two candles and a book of matches out of her handbag and gave them to Jake. "You know what to do with these," she said with a sensuous smile that he had never before seen on her face. As he began lighting the candles, she disappeared with her overnight bag into the bathroom. As soon as the door closed behind her, he rushed over to the bed and pulled back the sheets. Turning off all the lights in the room, he removed his shirt, shoes, and socks and sat on the foot of the bed, tapping his knees nervously with his fingertips.

He had imagined this night in his head a thousand times, but all of a sudden, he wasn't feeling so confident. Jake's eyes were fixed on the bathroom door; he stared at it for what seemed like an eternity. Finally, after about fifteen minutes the door began to open very slowly and his heart leapt with anticipation. When Sammi emerged, she looked so beautiful that he momentarily forgot how to breathe. With her soft, strawberry blond hair descending down upon her bare shoulders, Sammi's whole body trembled as she stood before him.

Without speaking a word, she took her husband by the hands, gently pulling him to his feet. Then, placing both hands on his face, she moved them slowly down his neck onto his strong shoulders and biceps, admiring his body as if she were seeing it for the first time. Her touch caused his heart to beat wildly within his chest. He was like clay in her hands, wanting nothing more than to yield completely to the passionate thoughts that were coursing through his mind. Then, she did something he didn't expect. Moving behind him, she began kissing his back. But after a few seconds, he realized that it wasn't just his back she was kissing—it was his scars. She kissed every inch of each scar on his back, then came around and kissed each scar on his stomach: the ones he had received the night he risked his life to save hers.

When finished, she pressed her face against his and whispered in his ear, "I never want you to hurt again."

As she spoke those tender words, Jake could feel tears from her eyes running down between his cheeks and hers. Tightening his hold upon her, he placed his lips against her ear and said softly, "I love you, Sammi Ledger."

"I love you, Jake Ledger," she replied.

No longer able to contain the fire that burned for her in his heart, Jake swept his bride off her feet and placed her gently on the bed beneath him where they made impassioned love throughout the night. The euphoric emotions and pleasures they found in one another were far beyond anything that either of them had dreamed possible. As the hours passed, they talked, they laughed, and they dreamed about their future; and every time they made love, the intensity of their unbridled passion and desire for each other caused them both to tremble.

It wasn't until a couple hours before dawn that they finally fell asleep in one another's arms. Jake was the first to wake up the next morning and, as he lay next to his sleeping wife, he realized that she was the answer to the prayers he had prayed as a child. God had heard his prayers after all, and he knew what a treasured gift she was. If he never achieved another thing in the world, Jake would still have all he needed, as long as he had her. She was his everything.

After checking out of the hotel the next morning, they began their search for an apartment and it didn't take them very long. As soon as they produced an official copy of Sammi's bank statement, apartment managers were all too happy to offer them a place to live. They ended up in a beautiful two-bedroom, less than a mile from the college campus. There was just one last thing to do, but Jake was dreading it. They had to return to Hope Park for the rest of their belongings.

When the newlyweds drove into the trailer park, they were greeted warmly by all the neighbors, but it was an emotional time for Gerald, Betty, and Aunt Hazel. After sharing one last meal together with their families, the two newlyweds loaded up their car and prepared to leave.

"We'll come see y'all at least twice a month on weekends," Gerald said, as he gripped Sammi in a bear hug.

"You better," she said, returning the hug.

Hazel embraced both of them and, trying hard not to cry, said, "You're always welcome here, but I understand why you need to go and why it would be hard to come back. Just don't forget us, okay?"

"We could never forget you, Aunt Hazel," Jake assured her. "After all, we rented a two-bedroom apartment and one of those rooms is yours."

Hazel smiled, "I'll be there probably more than you want me to." Pausing for a moment, her tone turned serious as she looked directly at her great-nephew. "Jake, I know you still have anger and resentment toward your mama, but I think she would want me to tell you how proud she was of you. She loved Sammi, and I know she's in heaven right now braggin' to Saint Peter about her son and daughter-in-law. I really hope that someday you can forgive her."

Jake smiled, but remained silent, not wanting to make any promises he couldn't keep.

As Jake and Sammi got in the car to leave, Aunt Hazel had one last thing to say. "I know big things are in store for both of you. After everything you've overcome together, I can't imagine that there is anything you will ever face that you can't handle so long as you face it together. The two of you are better together; you're stronger together. Don't forget that."

"We won't," Sammi promised.

Jake backed the car out of Aunt Hazel's driveway and quickly headed down the road, leaving a cloud of dust behind him. They stopped briefly at the entrance to Hope Park and looked back to see Aunt Hazel, Gerald, and Betty standing side-by-side watching them leave. Jake put his hand out the window and waved goodbye.

Then, as he pulled out of the trailer park for the last time, Jake turned to Sammi, extended his hand toward her and said, "Stronger together!"

Placing her hand firmly in his, Sammi smiled and affirmed, "Stronger together!"

29

"AFTER WE LEFT THAT DAY, WE NEVER LOOKED back," Jake said to CJ, whose full attention was still riveted on him as he finished sharing his life story. "I never gave this place another thought. We both graduated from college. I earned my law degree and she earned a degree in business administration. And then— we lived happily ever after, as the fairytale goes. After graduation, I was offered a position with a law firm in New York City and several years later, with the addition of three beautiful little children we branched out and started our own firm, Ledger Law. About that same time, Aunt Hazel found out that she had terminal cancer so we brought her to live with us until she died. A few months after Aunt Hazel moved in with us, we learned that Mayor had died of a heart attack leaving the trailer park to his kids. It's a shame they let it go to ruin like that. Aunt Hazel was the last one to ever live in her trailer."

Jake suddenly became silent, as he stared through the window at the rundown park across the gravel road. "We were happy," he said wistfully. "She was everything to me."

"Was?" CJ asked.

The question burned Jake's heart with the intense pain of a thousand yellow-jacket stings. Once again, the tears began to pour from his eyes without restraint. Looking down at the now empty pie plate, Jake took a breath and tried to rein in his emotions. "Yes," he said, his voice trembling, "was."

"What happened?" CJ asked, concerned.

Jake's mouth was so dry he could hardly answer. Swallowing another gulp of sweet tea, he wiped his eyes with a napkin and answered CJ's question. "It was two months ago. I had been in court all day and Sammi had been handling business at the office. She didn't always accompany me when I was in court. I was so exhausted, all I wanted to do was go home, but we had agreed to meet at our favorite restaurant for dinner. She was always early wherever she went, so when I arrived, I expected her to be there waiting for me, but she wasn't. I assumed she got tied up at the office, so I got us a table, ordered drinks for both of us, and waited. A half hour later, I was still waiting. I called her cell phone, but got no answer; called the office, but got no answer; called the house, but still no answer. I called each one of our kids, who also work with us at the firm, and they all said that she had left the office over an hour ago to meet me. My heart sank. This was not like her at all. I knew something was very wrong. I rushed out to the car and headed home as fast as I could, hoping that maybe, for some reason, she might have decided to go home before meeting me. I hadn't gotten two miles from the restaurant when my cell phone rang. I didn't recognize the number, but for some reason I just had a sickening feeling that it had something to do with Sammi. When I answered, a lady on the other end of the line identified herself as a nurse from the trauma center. She asked me to come to the hospital right away because my wife had been involved in an automobile accident. I can't even describe the effect those words had on me. I called the kids and we all got there about the same time. They took us into a room where we had to wait for an interminable amount of time for a doctor to come and explain what had happened. I was inconsolable. I couldn't even stay seated. The doctor finally showed up, but when he walked into the room, he was accompanied by a chaplain. At that moment, I knew the news was not going to be good. I knew something horrible had happened to my Sammi. They explained that she had been involved in a head-on collision with a drunk driver. He was moving very fast and crossed over into her lane. She had no time to get out of his way. Ever since that day, I've had to go home to our big, empty house alone; I've had to drive to work alone; I've had to walk past her empty office on the way to mine every single day. I always knew that she was my anchor, but until the accident I didn't realize how utterly dependent on her I had become. She made me forget the pain of my past. The sound of her voice alone could soothe and calm me down on the worst of days. Now, every night before I turn the lights out, I listen to voice messages from her that I still have on my phone. It's the only way I can get to sleep. CJ, she truly was everything to me and without her, I'm lost—plain and simple. I'm just completely lost."

CJ looked upon her new friend with empathy and compassion. She could not only see the pain on his face, but she could hear it in his voice. "I'm so sorry, Mr. Jake," she said softly. "Not many people find love like that in this world and I'm so sorry for what you're goin' through. You're such a sweet man and, if I could, I would take your sufferin' on myself, but I know you're gonna find your way through this and I know you're gonna be okay."

Jake shook his head, "I don't know, CJ. This is the hardest thing I've ever had to face. We always took on the giants together, and some of those giants were quite fierce. I could tell you lots of stories. We were strong together. This is the first time since the day she and I met that I've had to fight all alone."

CJ paused for a moment, then she asked, "Mr. Jake, I have a question. If this place was so painful for you, if it's a place you've tried to put out of your mind all these years, then why are you here? Why come back and relive everything?"

Smiling back at her through wet eyes, he answered, "You are going to think I've completely lost my mind when I tell you this, but a voice brought me back here."

"A *voice*?" she asked, surprised. "What kind of voice? Whose voice?"

"I'm not really sure whose voice it is," he answered. "I only know that it's a female voice. I started hearing the voice in my dreams exactly one month after Sammi's accident. At first, I thought maybe it was her voice, but it wasn't."

"What did the voice say?" CJ asked, leaning forward with eager anticipation.

"Just two words," Jake replied. "'*Come home*.' That's all she said. The first night I heard it, I jumped out of bed because I thought someone was in the room. Each time I heard those words, I immediately thought of this place. It would never let up so I knew that, for some reason, I was supposed to come back here."

"Maybe you have some unfinished business here," CJ suggested.

"None that I can think of," he mused.

"Can I ask you another question?" CJ cautiously ventured. "It might be hard for you to answer, though."

"I'll do my best to answer it," he promised.

"Did you ever forgive your mama for all the pain she caused you?"

Jake hesitated. The question made him uncomfortable, and to his surprise, he felt angered by it. The anger was not toward his hostess, however. The anger was directed at his mother, a person he had tried hard to put out of his mind over the years. "Of all the questions you could've asked me, why that one?" he queried.

"Now, just hear me out," CJ pleaded, noting that at the mere mention of his mother, Jake became visibly agitated. "While you were tellin' your story, I noticed that every time you talked about her, your tones became harsh—even your facial expression changed—your jaw tightened up and you clenched your fists. That tells me that you haven't forgiven her."

"It's not that. I'm just indifferent towards her," Jake protested.

Pressing further, CJ said, "I know that the words *indifferent* and *unforgivin'* mean two different things in the dictionary, but when it comes to relationships, they're the same. If somebody hurts me and I say I'm now indifferent towards that person, it's just another way of sayin' I ain't gonna forgive 'em. The end results are the same 'cause in both cases, the relationship is still busted up. You said that when you left here all those years ago with your wife, you went off and lived the fairy-tale life. You said you were happy. It just seems interestin' to me that after the accident, you suddenly start hearin' this voice that tells you to come home. And I can see on your face, Mr. Jake, that you ain't so happy no more. I'm just wonderin' if, over these past years, your sweet wife became like a cushion between you and all the pain your mama had caused you. Your wife was such a strong and beautiful woman. Could it could be that your love for your wife covered over the fact that you still got some hate and anger toward your mama and it's buried down so deep that you forgot it was there? Now that your wife is not a presence in your life no more, all that hate and anger is comin' back to the surface. I once heard an old farmer say that if you don't kill the roots, the weeds will just grow back. I know that you're grievin', Sweetie, and I get it. Grief is a part of life, but we're not supposed to grieve forever. We are supposed to be happy. I believe God wants us to be happy. Maybe that's why the voice in your dreams called you back here. The hate and bitterness you have in your heart toward your mama is blockin' you from movin' forward. You've been tryin' to punish her all this time by refusin' to forgive her for what she did to you, but it's not your mama you're keepin' in prison; it's you. You're the one who's not free. Maybe, just maybe, if you can truly forgive your mama, you can start healin' from what happened to your wife— and then you can find joy again."

Jake sat speechless before this simple, small-town wait-ress who had just become his counselor. As she spoke, his heart burned inside of him. He knew she was right. Her words peeled back the layers of his heart like an onion and revealed the awful truth that a mountain of hate and bit-terness still resided deep within him, ruling over his mind and his emotions, robbing him of peace and happiness.

Suddenly he could see Jo standing in the baptistery of the church asking him to forgive her in front of the entire congregation, asking him to let her be his mama again. But the battle to forgive and let go of the past was not an easy one to win. Not only could he see Jo asking his forgiveness, but he could also see her coming after him with a bat and with a knife when he was a child. He could see her sitting in silence at the kitchen table that fateful day when it all fell apart, letting the police carry him away for something she had done. He could envision Sammi, bleeding and crying, while she lay in that cold barn near death that night when she was raped—something that would not have happened if not for his mother's failure to own up to her choices and actions.

"Even if I wanted to forgive her," Jake said, "I'm not sure I know how."

"You can't do it by yourself, Mr. Jake," CJ said earnestly. "You need God's help. You need help from other sources too, like a counselor or somethin'. They even have support groups now to help people with this kind of thing. But there might be a way I can help get it started. Maybe it would help if you could see things from your mama's point of view."

"What do you mean?" Jake asked.

"Your mama and me are not far different from each other," she explained. "Now just hear me out. When I was young, I also had a very close family member abuse me in the worst way you could imagine, so I know what happens to a girl when she's hurt like that. She feels dirty; she feels violated; she feels guilt and shame, like it was somehow her fault; she feels alone and afraid; she wants to tell someone, but she doesn't know how; she loses trust in everybody, especially men. The adults in our lives are supposed to protect us, but when a man you trust hurts you like that, you lose all sense of security. It's like bein' thrown onto an emotional rollercoaster: one day you're depressed to the point of wantin' to die and the next day you're so ragin' mad that you want to kill somebody. You can never just walk away from the effects of abuse. It's always with you, and some people deal with it by gettin' drunk or high. When your granddaddy did what he did to your mama, it made her forget who she was and who she was intended to be. She got lost, Mr. Jake."

"She went to rehab centers numerous times," Jake retorted, "but she always went right back to the drugs."

CJ reached across the table placing her hand gently on his, "That might be because the rehab center focused more on the drug use, but not on the reasons she was usin' the drugs. Remember what I said about the root? If they didn't help her with the root, which was the abuse she suffered at the hands of her daddy, then it was just a matter of time before the weed grew back. But there's somethin' else you need to realize, Mr. Jake: you're an abuse victim too. You may not have been abused sexually, but you were abused in other ways: mentally, physically, and emotionally. And you did the same thing your mama did."

Jake pulled his hand away, offended by CJ's statement. "I'm *nothing* like my mother," he declared. "What do you mean by that?"

CJ explained, "She never dealt with the root. Instead she buried her pain in drug abuse. Just like her, you never dealt with the root of your pain. Instead, you buried it in a successful career, in your marriage, and in your family. Success and family are good things, but they can also become hidin' places. You and your mama are alike in the fact that you both avoided the very thing that was causin' you the most pain. You've been runnin' all these years, Mr.

Jake; but no matter how hard and fast you run, you've ended up circlin' back to the very place where you were hurt the most. I think there's a reason for that. I think God is tryin' to help you face the root of your pain so you can be set free once and for all. Don't you wanna be free, Mr. Jake?"

Jake's hands began to tremble uncontrollably. Soon his whole body was shaking. The wisdom of this waitress was beyond her years and her words penetrated him to the very core. For decades he had pushed back against all of his rage, like holding water behind a dam, but he could feel the dam weakening as CJ's counsel began to chip away at its foundation.

Who is this woman, he thought to himself, *and where did she get all this insight?* No longer able to restrain his emotions, Jake covered his face with his hands and began to weep, heartbroken. CJ remained silent, allowing him time to process all that she had just said.

After a few minutes had passed, CJ spoke again. "There's another similarity between me and your mama, Mr. Jake."

Wiping his tears away with his hands, Jake asked, "What's that?"

"I have a son too," she said. "I understand a mama's heart, and I think I know what your mama would say to you if she were here right now. Give me your hands."

Locking eyes with CJ, Jake reached across the table and placed his hands in hers. They were soft and warm and, in some strange way, holding them seemed to bring him a great measure of comfort.

"Close your eyes," she said, "and imagine that the words you're hearin' are comin' from your mama."

Jake followed her instructions without protest.

"If she were here right now," she said softly, "this is what I believe she would say to you:

'Jake, I never truly knew what it meant to love another person with my whole heart until I held you in my arms on the day you were born. From the second I looked into your eyes, I knew that you were a gift to me from God. You were so tiny, so helpless, and so sweet. All I wanted to do was be a good mama to you. But I failed at bein' the mother you deserved. I failed at makin' you feel safe and secure. I failed at puttin' your needs above my own. I never fought hard enough for you or for the life we could have had together. I allowed my many demons to control me and because of that, I had to leave you long before I wanted to. But there is one thing that I desperately want you to know, Son. I want you to know that I always loved you fully and completely, even though I didn't know how to show it. I am so proud of the amazin' man you've become in spite of my many failures. So I ask you to please forgive me for all the pain and hurt I caused you. I am askin' you once more, to open your heart to me.'"

When she finished, Jake kept his eyes closed for a few moments, pondering everything she had said. It would have been nice to actually hear those words from his mother, but the reality was that she was dead and had wasted all of her opportunities to make peace with him. When he opened his eyes, he gave CJ's hands a squeeze, "Thank you, CJ. You've caused me to do a lot of thinking."

"So, do you think you can forgive her?" she asked hopefully.

Jake nodded his head, "It's not going to be easy and it will take a while, but you have my promise that I am going to give careful consideration to your words."

"You should find a good counselor," she suggested.

"I'm pretty sure I just found one," he laughed. "I think you missed your calling."

Smiling, she said, "I'll be prayin' for you, Mr. Jake."

"Thank you," he replied as he looked at his watch. "Oh my," he exclaimed apologetically. "I've kept you for three hours. I'm so sorry."

"No need to apologize. I've really enjoyed our talk."

"Well, I need to be going," he said, "and I'm sure you would like to get home. What do I owe you for all the great food?"

"Not a dime," CJ said. "It's on the house."

"Nonsense," he replied. "You fed me and listened to me go on and on for hours about my life. A counselor back home would charge me a thousand dollars for the time I've taken with you."

Reaching into his wallet, Jake drew out three crisp one-hundred-dollar bills and put them in her hand. "Please, take this," he pleaded, "you've earned it."

"I'll take it on one condition," she bargained. "You give serious thought about gettin' some help."

"It's a deal," he said, shaking her hand as if they had just completed a business transaction.

"Let me get you a receipt," she said, as she walked behind the counter to the register.

Jake walked to the door and looked out the window toward the trailer park. The anxiety he felt when he first arrived was gone. For the first time in months, he felt a sense of peace and he knew that CJ had everything to do with that. Just having someone to tell his story to was like medicine to his soul. *This was why I was supposed to come back home,* he thought to himself. *I was supposed to meet her.* His heart was full of gratitude toward CJ because of the things she'd had the boldness to say to him: things his family, friends and colleagues had not had the nerve to say. He vowed to honor his promise to her. He did not want to let her down.

"Here's your receipt, Mr. Jake. It's been a pleasure talkin' to you."

Taking the receipt, Jake folded it without a glance, stuffed it in his pocket and said, "I hope I see you again before too long. It feels like I've known you for years. I'd like my kids to meet you sometime."

"I have no doubt we'll be seein' each other again," she said with a smile.

Jake returned the smile and headed across the parking lot towards his vehicle. Just as he was about to open the door, CJ called to him from the doorway of the tavern.

"Mr. Jake!" she yelled, "Your mama was right! There's always hope! And remember, I'll be right here cheerin' you on."

Jake smiled, climbed into his Navigator and started down the road, but not before getting one last glimpse of the trailer park. As he slowly pulled away, his heart felt strangely warm, which was something he had not expected to experience while revisiting his arduous past.

Looking down at the gas gauge, he saw that the tank was almost on empty. He remembered seeing a convenience store when he first turned onto the gravel road, so he stopped there to fill up. As he started to remove the nozzle from the gas tank, he noticed a sign on the pump that read: Pay Inside. Locking his car doors, Jake walked into the store, approached the counter, and laid down a hundred-dollar bill in front of the cashier. "I'm at pump number two," he said. "Let me have $50 worth."

The cashier took the bill and began ringing him up, "If you're hungry, there's some hotdogs in the warmer at the back."

"Oh, no thank you," Jake said with a chuckle. "I couldn't put another bite in my mouth. I just had a nice big meal down at the tavern. Met the sweetest waitress."

The cashier stopped what he was doing and stared quizzically at Jake. "Uh, I'm sorry, Sir, but I don't think I heard you right," he stammered. "Where did you say you just ate?"

"At the tavern," Jake answered casually. "Right down the road. The lady who served me was CJ. I'm sure you know her. About five feet, five inches tall? Pretty brunette, maybe thirty years old? Makes an amazing hamburger?" Jake could see that the more he talked the more uncomfortable the cashier was becoming. "Is something wrong?" he finally asked.

"Well, Sir," the cashier answered nervously, "nothin's wrong really. It's just that you're talkin' about a place that ain't there no more."

"What?" Jake asked in disbelief. "Of course it's there. I just spent the last three hours talking to an employee there by the name of CJ. We had hamburgers, fries, apple pie, and sweet tea...lots of tea." Jake knew his tone of voice had now become intense. If this was a joke, it wasn't funny at all. He could feel himself becoming angry.

A look of alarm came over the cashier's face. Struggling for words, he finally said, "Sir, I know just about everyone 'round here and I ain't never met nobody named CJ. And the tavern you're talkin' about—it burned to the ground some fifteen years ago. They never rebuilt it. It's not there.

The only thing left is an old parkin' lot. Are you feelin' okay, Sir? Do I need to call somebody for you?"

Jake took a step back from the counter. His entire body became so hot that he broke into a sweat. His mind began to race, *I'm not crazy! It was there; I was there; she was there.* Forgetting that he hadn't received his change for the gas yet, Jake rushed out the door, jumped in the Navigator and sped away from the gas station in the direction of the tavern. The old rundown trailer park was there, just as he had seen a short time before. But as he pulled into the tavern parking lot, he was overcome with horror. The cashier had been telling the truth. The tavern was not there. All that lay before him now was a sea of broken pavement with clumps of grass and weeds growing through the cracks.

30

FEARING THAT HE WAS HAVING SOME KIND of delusional episode, Jake jumped from the vehicle and ran to the very spot where the tavern had been just moments earlier. Standing in the middle of the empty lot, he tried desperately to make sense of what was happening to him. It all seemed so real: CJ, the food, the conversation, the soft touch of her hands, the receipt she handed him as he left. *The receipt! She handed me a receipt!* he thought to himself.

Desperate to prove that he was not insane, Jake plunged his hand into his pocket to see if it was still there. If it wasn't there, then surely, he was on the precipice of a mental breakdown. But if it was there? What would that mean? These kinds of things only happen in books and movies. How would he ever make sense of the last three hours of his life? The contents in his pocket were always the same: a handful of loose change, a small pocket knife, a tube of chapstick, and his keys. Fumbling through all those items, his fingers fell upon a small piece of folded paper. The discovery made his spine tingle; the hair on the back of his neck stood straight up as his heart began pumping faster and faster.

He knew that there had been no paper in his pocket before the encounter with CJ. This tiny slip of paper in his pocket was about to change his entire view of reality. He had spent his whole career dealing with facts, things that could be proven by evidence. This small thing that was now pinched between his thumb and forefinger represented a dimension that he had never before encountered; a dimension he did not even believe existed. Was this a paranormal event? Was it a God thing? Whatever it was, Jake sensed that his whole understanding of how the universe worked was about to be challenged. How could something so small, so seemingly insignificant as a piece of paper in his pocket have such an enormous, life-altering impact?

Jake closed his eyes, took in a deep breath, and held it for several seconds. Then, releasing the air from his lungs, he slowly withdrew his hand from his pocket, unfolded the paper, and opened his eyes. "This can't be!" he gasped. "It... it's not possible!" He stared in shocked disbelief at what he held in his hand. It was not a receipt that CJ had given him, but a note, the contents of which caused his entire body to tremble uncontrollably.

The words on the small piece of paper were painfully familiar: *"Baby Boy, I love you with my whole heart. Please forgive me."* The words were penned in the same chicken-scratch handwriting that his mother had written to him moments before she died, forty-two years ago. This wasn't just a copy of her note; it was the exact same note. But how could that be? He remembered throwing that note in the trash. But how...how did it end up in CJ's possession? And, exactly who was CJ anyway? Where did she come from? The question had barely entered his mind when he suddenly remembered something he had long forgotten: his mother's first name...Crystal...Crystal Jo...*CJ*.

As the reality of what had just happened to him began to sink in, Jake could feel all of his strength ebbing away. Falling to his knees, he began to weep unreservedly. He now understood why he'd felt so at ease with her; why he was able to unveil his very soul to her so freely; why her words were able to penetrate the stone wall that had held back a sea of hatred and bitterness for all these years, keeping him captive for so long. He heard once more the words she spoke to him as she had held his hands at the table.

At that moment, Jake realized that it had been her voice he heard in his dreams calling him to come home. He remembered how his heart burned within him when, once again, she asked for his forgiveness. Suddenly, the heart that had been so embittered toward his mother began to soften; the dam that had been cracked by the force of CJ's words now started to give way, causing a wave of emotion to sweep over him, weakening the anger and hate that he had harbored all these years against Jo. As an unfamiliar sense of love and compassion toward his mother began to swell within his heart, Jake closed his eyes and whispered the words, "I want to forgive you. I just don't know how. God, show me how to do this. I need your help."

The words were barely out of his mouth when Jake opened his eyes to find himself surrounded by a light so bright that he could not see anything else. Though the light was far brighter than any light he had ever seen before, he was somehow able to look directly into it without any harm to his eyes. As he narrowed his focus, two images, one directly in front of the other, began to take shape and appeared to be walking towards him.

The image in front was small and feminine in form while the other image was much taller and more masculine. The brilliant, white light seemed to move inexplicably in correspondence with the movements of the masculine figure, almost as if he were wearing the light as a garment. It soon became apparent that the light was actually emanating from within the taller figure who remained behind, but protectively close, to the other. As the two mysterious figures drew closer, fear gripped Jake to the very core causing him to shake, yet he was unable to take his eyes off of them.

With each step they took, the two figures came more clearly into Jake's view, eventually revealing the one in front to be a beautiful young woman. Overwhelmed by her stunning appearance, it wasn't until she knelt down in front of him that he discovered her identity. He didn't understand *what* was happening or *how* it was happening. All he knew for certain was that he was gazing directly into the radiant face of his mother. Her dazzling appearance took his breath away and her warm smile flooded him with a deep sense of peace.

Tears gushed from Jake's eyes as he could no longer restrain the intense emotion that had been building up in his heart. In typical motherly fashion, Jo placed both her hands on his cheeks and wiped the tears away. As she held tightly to his face, she noticed that his eyes kept glancing back and forth from her to the figure who stood behind her.

"Beautiful, isn't He!" Jo declared adoringly. "That's my Jesus! I haven't been able to take my eyes off of Him since the day He came to take me to my new home."

Jake looked intently into the face of the magnificent figure that still stood directly behind his mother. The light pouring forth from Him was so bright that it was difficult to discern the details of His appearance. But what Jake *was* able to see caused all the fear he had felt earlier to dissipate. The Visitor's penetrating eyes exuded compassion while the smile on His face was soft and reassuring. Jake sensed that he was in a safe place and his soul took ease in the presence of One he now understood to be Divine. Jo, still holding her son's face in her hands, pulled him towards her and gently kissed his cheek. Then slowly rising to her feet, she stepped to the side so that her son had a direct view of Jesus, whose appearance was so glorious that Jake was unable to look away.

"He loves you, Baby Boy," Jo said tenderly. "He wants you to know He never left you. He's been with you since the day you were born. He heard every prayer you prayed and He saw every tear that fell from your eyes. He's good Jake. He's *so* good. He even allowed me to keep the last promise I made to you before I left. Do you remember the last promise I made to you?"

Jake's eyes remained riveted on Jesus, but he nodded his head to acknowledge that he remembered her last promise to him. Jo continued, "I promised you I would be at your graduation. You didn't know it, but when you were givin' the valedictorian speech, I was standin' right in front of you listenin' to every word. You made me so proud that day."

Jake turned toward Jo, fastening his eyes on her. Once again tears streamed down his cheeks. He remembered how hopeful he had been about her promise to attend the graduation and how hurt he was that she'd died without ever having heard his speech. "You were there?" he sobbed.

"Yes," she replied, looking at Jesus with a smile. "We both were."

Jake lowered his head and began to weep. Jo stepped closer and placed her hand on his shoulder. "He has somethin' very important that He wants you to do for Him, Jake. He has a work for you to do that will help countless numbers of people who are lost and in pain. They feel like they are alone. They've given up hope, but He wants to use you to remind them that hope is a gift from God and it's theirs if they want it, even when they feel that they've reached the end of the road and there's nowhere else to turn. Life is filled with pain, Baby Boy, but the pain means somethin'. It has purpose, even though we don't see it. He wants to use you to help other people see that. He wants you to help them find hope." Once again, Jo knelt in front of her son and looked into his eyes. "But He can't use you for this great work, Baby Boy, until you let go of the bitterness and the hate. You've got to forgive, Son, so that His love can move through you and into the hearts of others."

After she spoke, Jo once again stood to her feet and stepped to the side. As Jake lifted his eyes, he noticed that Jesus was extending a hand toward him. "Can you forgive me?" Jake asked, looking into the compassionate eyes of the One clothed in light. "Will you forgive me?" he asked again as he reached out to take the hand of Jesus.

The One clothed in light didn't speak a word, yet the smile on His face spoke volumes and Jake knew in his heart that he had been forgiven. Jake extended his hand, taking the hand of Jesus, and the moment they touched, he was overcome by a brilliant flash of light that took his breath away, momentarily blinded him, and knocked him flat on his back.

31

GASPING FOR BREATH, JAKE OPENED HIS EYES and was surprised to find himself sitting in the Navigator, which was still parked in front of the gate to the trailer park. His seatbelt was fastened tight, as if he had never gotten out of the vehicle.

"That could not have been just a dream," he said out loud. Looking at himself in the rearview mirror, he could see that his face was stained with tears. His heart felt light and free. He didn't know if what he had just experienced was a dream or not, but it had certainly seemed real; and something else that was very real was the love and compassion he now felt toward his mother. The anger and bitterness he had lived with for so many years were miraculously gone. The clock on the dashboard read 6:00 PM, so he figured he had a couple hours of daylight left. With a sense of renewed enthusiasm, he nudged the gate open with the bumper of the Navigator and drove down the grass-covered lane to lot number nine.

His aunt's old trailer was not the beautiful, well-kept mobile home it had once been. The primary color was now a faded, rusty brown; the doors were hanging off the hinges; the windows had been broken out; what used to be luscious green grass was now weeds; and, upon entering his former abode, Jake had to knock down a jungle of spider webs. A twinge of sadness surged through his heart as he thought about how quaint and serene this little community used to be.

Stepping into the living room, Jake fixed his eyes on the spot where the couch used to sit. He remembered seeing his mother lying there when he returned home from his graduation and suddenly, he felt something deep inside for her that he had never truly felt before: empathy. Tears filled his eyes again as he pondered the pain she must have endured her entire life. This new found empathy was a sure sign, he thought, that he had finally forgiven her.

As he walked into his old bedroom, his eyes were immediately drawn to the window which looked out onto the trailer where Sammi used to live. He reminisced about their many late-night encounters on the rooftop. It was up there, sitting next to her under the starry sky where he'd realized that he had discovered the one and only person he would ever fall in love with. The memories made him realize afresh how badly he missed talking with her. Methodically, Jake passed through each room in the trailer until he finally came to Aunt Hazel's room. As the sun was just about to disappear behind the trees, a ray of light shot through the bedroom window casting a beam of golden light directly into her closet. Lying on the floor in the very back of the closet Jake noticed a small metal box.

The movers he had hired to bring Aunt Hazel to New York must have missed it, he realized. He couldn't believe it had just been sitting there undisturbed all these years.

He picked it up, placed it next to his ear, and shook it. It sounded as if it was full of papers. There was a lock on it, but no sign of a key. He carried the box outside, placed it on the hood of his Navigator, and began picking at the lock with his pocket knife.

After tinkering with it for several minutes, Jake managed to get the box open. Inside the box was something Jake did not expect to find. Stacked neatly and wrapped with twine was every letter Jo had written to him while she was in prison. Aunt Hazel had apparently retrieved them all from the trash and stored them away, still sealed. But it was what was sitting on the very top of the stack of letters that took his breath away: it was the note to him from his mother that she had been holding in her hands the day she died. Very carefully, Jake untied the twine, retrieved the small piece of paper, and read it out loud. *"Baby Boy, I love you with my whole heart. Please forgive me."*

"I love you too, Mom," he whispered, "and I forgive you. I really do forgive you."

Grabbing a flashlight from the Navigator, Jake took the letters to the gazebo, which was still in surprisingly good condition. He cleaned off a place to sit down on one of the worn benches, and for the next several hours, he read every word of every letter his mother had written to him. Aunt Hazel had numbered the envelopes in the order they'd arrived, so he was able to follow the progress Jo had made after the night she said Jesus found her and transformed her. She poured her heart out to Jake in each letter, even telling him about the night she was raped behind the tavern by Scott Robertson.

As he read each letter, he could see that she had truly changed. Like the water Jesus had turned into wine, his mother had indeed become something new, something better. Jake couldn't help but think of the conversation he had had long ago with Sammi about the caterpillars and how they were transformed into beautiful butterflies, no longer bound, no longer forced to live life in the dirt; casting off their old shells, they were now free to fly. His mother had certainly become something beautiful, something free. Each letter drew him deeper into her heart and gave him greater understanding of her. It was like getting to know her all over again.

By the time he'd finished the last letter, it was 10:00 PM, and Jake was exhausted. *I'll stay at a hotel tonight and head back to New York tomorrow,* he thought to himself; but, as he was about to drive out of the trailer park, he happened to glance at his phone, still sitting on the passenger seat where he had left it. He noticed that over the last several hours, his daughter had called him numerous times. Panicked and thinking that something must be wrong, he wasted no time calling her back. She answered on the first ring.

"Maddie, what's going on?" he asked. "I just saw all the missed calls!"

"Dad, where in the world have you been?!?" she demanded. "I've been trying to reach you for hours. You've had all of us worried to death!"

The tone of excitement in her voice was alarming to Jake. "I'm sorry, Honey, I'll tell you all about it later," he explained. "But you're worrying me. Has something happened? What's wrong?"

"Dad, you're not going to believe it," she said, starting to cry. "It's Mom! She's awake, Dad! She came out of the coma about five hours ago. The doctor said he's never seen anything like it. She opened her eyes and just started talking!

They've already run several tests and the doctor says there is no reason not to expect a full recovery. He can't explain it, but she's wide awake and she's asking for you. Your name was the first word out her mouth. How quick can you get back?"

Jake was so overjoyed at the news that he couldn't find words to respond to his daughter's wonderful and unexpected announcement.

"Dad, are you there?" she asked. "Did you hear me? She's awake! She's going to recover!"

Jake finally found the strength to speak. "I heard you, Honey," he said, his trembling voice filled with emotion. "Are you with her now? Can I speak with her?"

"No," Maddie answered. "I'm home now. Besides, she's probably resting. But I know she's going to want to see you first thing when she wakes up."

"I'll head home right now," he promised. "I should be there by 8:00 o'clock tomorrow morning."

"Okay, Dad, but please, drive carefully," she pleaded. "We don't want anything bad happening to you now."

"I'll be fine, Sweetheart," he assured her. "I love you."

"Love you too, Daddy," she answered. "See you in the morning."

Emotionally, Jake felt like he was on a rollercoaster, swaying back and forth between tearful weeping and outbursts of laughter. His sweet Sammi had come back to him, even though several doctors had told them that she would not recover due to the extensive damage her body had suffered in the accident. For nearly two months, she had not shown one sign of hope and now, without medical explanation, she was not only awake, but was talking and asking for him. Jake had never been one to believe in miracles, but he was a believer now.

318

The good news from Maddie had driven all the exhaustion from his body. He was now wide awake and speeding up the interstate in excess of 80 miles per hour toward New York, hoping he would not be deterred by any vigilant state troopers along the way. While driving, he tried to make sense of everything he had experienced back at the trailer park. Was his encounter with CJ real? Was it a dream? Was it a vision?

Whatever it was, it had had a profound impact on him, one that would change his life forever. The thought of his mother appearing to him in a dream in the form of a young waitress was overwhelming. There had to be more to it than meets the eye, he thought. There had to be a greater purpose behind it all. And what did his mother mean when she said he was going to help people find hope in their pain? As he pondered what that could be, an idea suddenly began to formulate in his mind; it was a grand idea, one he knew he could not bring to fruition alone. He would have to have help, lots of help in order to turn his idea into a reality. He couldn't wait to tell Sammi.

It seemed like no time at all before Jake pulled into the parking lot of the trauma center. As he quickly made his way to Sammi's room, he was stopped by her doctor who took him into a small office to explain everything that would be happening with her over the next several weeks, possibly months. Sammi had not walked or exercised any of her limbs for two months, which meant she would have to undergo lots of physical therapy before she could be released to go home. Jake was fine with all of that so long as she made a full recovery, which the doctor seemed confident would happen. As soon as the consultation was over, Jake wasted no time getting to his wife.

As he entered the room, the morning sun was just breaking through the window, casting a soft glow on Sammi's face. Her eyes were closed, so he stepped softly across the room to her bedside. As he gazed upon her adoringly, something caught his eye that brought a smile as well as tears. Resting gently upon her chest was the butterfly necklace he had given her more than forty years ago. True to her word, she wore it every day.

Seeing the silver butterfly gave Jake hope that better days were ahead. Sammi looked so beautiful Jake could not resist leaning over to kiss her soft lips as he had done so many times over the past two months, even though he'd never gotten a response from her. But this time was different. The very moment their lips met, she placed her hand on the back of his head and returned his kiss intense passion.

"You came back to me," he said softly, gazing longingly into her eyes.

Wiping his tears away with her hand, she whispered, "I love you." Over the course of their marriage, she had spoken those words to him countless times every single day. But today those three simple words brought life and hope into his soul as never before. He had wondered if he would ever hear her voice again much less hear those three amazing, wonderful words.

"I love you so much!" he cried fervidly, as he kissed her again and again. "I was so afraid I had lost you."

"I'm right here, my love," she assured him. As he continued to gaze into her face with wonder, she pulled the sheet back, inviting him into the bed beside her. "I'm afraid I'll hurt you," he protested.

"Get in here," she said with a smile. "I'll be fine. I need your arms around me."

Jake climbed carefully into the bed and gently positioned her head on his chest with his arm around her shoulders. "Where have you been the last couple of days?" she asked. "The kids told me you took a road trip."

For the next hour, he explained everything to her beginning with the voice that kept calling him back home in his dreams. He recounted all the events of the previous day: the encounter he had had with CJ; the revelation that she was actually his mother who had come to him in some kind of dream or vision; the letters he found in Aunt Hazel's old trailer, including the final note Jo had scribbled to him the day she died.

Jake told Sammi how he had come to fully forgive his mother, and that he now had peace about her like he had never before experienced. He also told her that, as he was driving home, he had an idea, but that he didn't want to tell her about it just yet. Instead, he wanted to wait until she was strong enough to travel back to Kernersville so he could explain it to her there. Although she was eager to hear about his idea, she agreed with his plan.

Though Sammi grew stronger each day, it took several months before she was back to herself. It was late November before she was ready to travel and, as soon as her recovery was complete, Jake booked two plane tickets to Greensboro, North Carolina, where he rented a car for the drive to the trailer park in Kernersville. It was dusk before they pulled up to the park's entrance, but he stopped short of driving past the gate.

Putting the car in park, Jake turned to his wife to reveal the big idea that had come to him months earlier. During her recovery time, he had arranged to have all the old dilapidated trailers removed from the property. The only structures still standing were Mayor's old house at the entrance to the park and the gazebo at the far end of the gravel drive. All the weeds had been cleared away as well. Sammi's eyes were wide with anticipation as he began to unfold his big idea.

Taking his wife's hand, Jake began, "When we drove out of here in 1978, I vowed we would never come back because of all the pain that was associated with this place and, until your accident, I kept that vow. But it seems that God had a different plan, a big plan, a plan I never expected. As I drove back to New York on the night that you came out of the coma, I began thinking about my mom. I thought about all the times she went to a rehab facility to get clean. I remembered how hopeful she always was afterwards. I remembered all the promises she'd made about staying clean and starting a new life. But it was never too long before she was back on the drugs. I think I now understand why she was never able to stay clean. When she went to those places to get help, they only dealt with the addiction, but not the root cause of the addiction. In my vision, CJ—my mom—told me that if you don't get the root, the weeds will always grow back. I have not been able to get her words out of my mind. The rehab places mom went to only helped rid the drugs from her system, but they never dealt with the root of her issue, which was the sexual abuse she'd endured at the hands of her father. That's why the weeds—the drug addiction—kept coming back. It was the only way she knew how to deal with the pain he had caused her. She wasn't being selfish like I assumed all those years; she was running from the pain. So as I was driving back to New York that night, a thought came to mind. What if we buy this property, a place with so many memories of pain and death, and turn it into a place that gives life and hope to those struggling with addictions? Sammi, the idea I had that night was to build a residential counseling center, a place that not only deals with the biological issues of addiction, but also the psychological, the social, and the spiritual issues, all of which are associated with addictive behavior. And, I don't think there is a better place to build it than right here in the very place where my mother died because of her addiction. But there is one more thing: I want to name it Jo's House of Hope. What do you think?"

Sammi was elated by her husband's idea. "Jake," she bubbled. "I think I might cry! Sweetheart, that is a beautiful sentiment and a wonderful way to honor your mother." Sammi looked out over the property in front of them. "Oh my, Jake, I can see it already! So many people are going to be helped through this. So many lives and families will be restored."

"That's my hope," Jake replied, brimming with excitement. "We probably should have done this sooner, but because of my own bitterness and unwillingness to forgive my mom, I was never able to see it. By coming back here, I was forced to confront my anger, and once that was dealt with, I was able to see a much bigger and a much better picture."

"I am so excited about this, "Sammi beamed. "So, what's the next step?"

"Well," he answered, "while you were in recovery, I did some preliminary work. I tracked down Mayor's children, because they still owned the property. Mayor's oldest son looks just like his dad as I remember him. He also has his dad's heart, because when I told him what I wanted to do with this land, he contacted his family and they all agreed to donate it. I've got quite a few investors involved and we have enough money pledged to get it started. I've just been waiting for one thing."

"Oh, really?" she asked. "What's that?"

"I want you to oversee the entire venture," he said, taking her hand in his. "I want your fingerprints all over this thing."

Sammi was overwhelmed. After a few seconds, she nodded her head and smiled at her husband "I'll do it," she said, determinedly. "I can't wait to get started. But I would like to get the kids involved as well."

"Absolutely," Jake affirmed. "But I have just one request—one thing I would like to include in the center." Reaching over to Sammi, he took hold of the butterfly necklace. "Do you remember what you told me on your rooftop that night when I asked you why you liked butterflies?"

"Yes," she replied. "I remember every word."

"I've been thinking about that a lot lately," he said. "I can see my mom in the butterfly. Because of the abuse she endured and the addiction that followed, she spent most of her life limited by her circumstances, like a caterpillar. Her time in prison was like being in a cocoon. She went in a caterpillar, but when she came home, she was a butterfly, a new creation. I was just too angry to see it. So, here's my request: inside of this new counseling center, I want a butterfly room with real butterflies—a place where the residents can go to find peace and solitude, a place where they can think and pray."

"I love it, Sweetheart," Sammi agreed. "I think this will probably be the most important thing you and I have ever done together. I am so proud of you. You're a new man, Jake. I can't remember seeing you so happy, so at peace. And, your enthusiasm about this counseling center is contagious.

I don't think you were even this excited when we started our own law firm."

"This is different," he explained. "I'm different. For all these years I've had a career, but now I feel like I have a mission, a purpose."

"As soon as we get home, I'll get started on it," Sammi promised. "So, are we staying in Kernersville tonight or flying back home?"

"Oh, I have one more surprise," he said, smiling. Jake flashed his car lights down the gravel road toward the gazebo. When he did, a man stepped out of a small pickup truck which Sammi hadn't noticed as it was partially hidden behind the gazebo. While Jake was having the trailers removed, he had arranged for power to be piped in to the old gazebo. The man walked over to the gazebo and flipped a switch. Suddenly the entire structure was lit up with Christmas lights. There was even a decorated tree in the center of it.

"Jake Ledger," Sammi gasped. "I can't believe you did this! You are just the most amazing..." Without taking the time to complete the sentence, she leaned over and kissed him. The look of delight on her face made all of his efforts worthwhile. As he pulled toward the gazebo, the man who had flipped the switch got back in his truck and left, giving the two of them some privacy. As Jake and Sammi stepped into the gazebo, he walked over to the bench where a small record player, just like the one Sammi used to have, was plugged in and ready to go, complete with some 45s of the same songs they used to listen to on the roof of her trailer.

Taking Sammi's hands in his, Jake drew her close to him, "I've been waiting for this."

"Waiting for what?' she asked, fixing her gaze on him.

"When I got the call that night from Maddie telling me that you were awake and that you were going to be alright, I was sitting right in front of this gazebo. The first thought that came to my mind was that as soon as you were ready, I was going to bring you back to this place, hold you tight in my arms, and dance with you all night. You're my whole life, Sammi. When I thought I had lost you, I lost my way. You're my anchor, and if it's possible, I love you now more than I ever have. My whole life changed the day I met you, and I don't know how I would get through the rest of it if you weren't here. We're stronger together, remember?"

Deeply moved by her husband's words, Sammi laid her head on his chest as they began to sway back and forth to the soft music that flowed from the old record player.

After a couple songs had played, Jake interrupted the moment and said, "By the way, when you get hungry, dinner is over there in that box under the tree."

"Wow. I'm impressed! You thought of everything," she exclaimed. "What are we having?"

A mischievous smile came across Jake's face. "One of your favorite meals: cold fried chicken and cherry pie."

They both laughed at his idea of a romantic dinner, but they also both remembered the significance of that meal. It was the meal they had shared on the rooftop the night she first realized that she loved him.

After another song had finished, Sammi raised her head from Jake's chest and, looking passionately into his eyes, said "I just have one question for you, Jake Ledger."

"And what would that question be, Sammi Ledger?"

"In this story," she asked, "does the boy ever kiss the girl?"

"Always," he said. And then, standing in the very place where he had kissed her for the first time so long ago, Jake placed both hands on the small of her back, pressing her body firmly against his. Over the years, they had never allowed the embers of their love for one another to grow cold, so, as he leaned forward to kiss her, both of their hearts raced with passionate anticipation. As the sun settled behind the forest, they held tightly to one another, dancing in the light of the Christmas tree. After forty-two years together, he was still her hero, and she was still his everything.

CONCLUSION

BECAUSE OF AN ABUNDANCE OF AVAILABLE resources provided by many willing investors, the holistic residential counseling center that Jake and Sammi had envisioned was completed in a short time. Within two years of operation, it became one of the top ten counseling centers in the nation. It became so successful, in fact, that Jake and Sammi moved back to Kernersville and took up residence in Mayor's renovated old house so that they could oversee the center. All three of their children soon followed, deciding to raise their families in the same town where their mother had grown up.

The old gazebo, located in the center of the property, was beautifully decorated each year at Christmas, just like it had been when Hope Park had been full of families. On Christmas Eve, Jake and Sammi would gather the current residents at the gazebo and serve hot cider and homemade cookies, always going the extra mile to make everyone feel as though they were part of a family.

Each year, a countless parade of broken people came in and out of Jo's House, always finding help and hope from staff and counselors who truly cared. From the moment the residents arrived, they were greeted with love, acceptance, and hospitality. Regardless of age, race, or financial status, every troubled soul who walked in the door was treated with dignity and respect. There were many features of Jo's House that were intriguing to new arrivals: the butterfly room, a gym, nice clean bedrooms, and a dining room surrounded with wide open windows overlooking the wooded area where walking trails led down to the river.

But, of all the beautiful aspects of Jo's House, there was one that Jake treasured the most: the very first thing new residents saw when they entered the lobby was a large painting of Jo hanging over the door that led into the living quarters. Above the painting were the words of Jeremiah 29:11: *"For I know the plans I have for you," declares the Lord, 'plans to prosper you and not to harm you, plans to give you a hope and a future."'* Underneath the painting was a beautiful porcelain plaque that every new arrival was encouraged to stop and read. The words were simple but powerful, and they embodied the message of the woman in the portrait:

There's Always Hope: Even When You Think You've Reached the End of the Road.

CPSIA information can be obtained
at www.ICGtesting.com
Printed in the USA
LVHW081745140222
711109LV00014B/551